Canopic Jars: Tales of Mummies and Mummification

Edited by Gregory L. Norris

GREAT OLD ONES PUBLISHING
NEW HAMPSHIRE
U.S.A.

Published by Great Old Ones Publishing
New Hampshire, U.S.A.
http://www.greatoldonespublishing.com

Editing by Gregory L. Norris http://gregorylnorris.blogspot.com

"Chamber of the Gods" first appeared at *Fangoria.com* (June 2002).

"Under the Pyramids" first appeared as *Imprisoned with the Pharaohs* in *Weird Tales*, May-June-July 1924 edition. The story is sometimes noted as co-written with Harry Houdini. A third title the story is known as is *Entombed with the Pharaohs.*

Readers: Douglas B. Poirier, Philip C. Perron, Gregory L. Norris

Cover artwork by M. J. Preston http://www.mjpreston.net

Manuscript to book by Philip C. Perron http://www.darkdiscussions.com

First Edition

ISBN: 0615912028
ISBN-13: 978-0615912028

CANOPIC JARS

TALES OF MUMMIES AND MUMMIFICATION

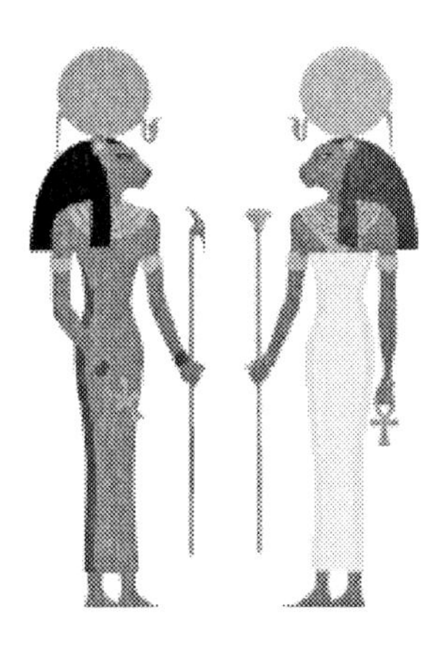

☥

DEDICATION

This book is dedicated to those who support the small press.

Canopic Jars: Tales of Mummies and Mummification

Edited by Gregory L. Norris

GREAT OLD ONES PUBLISHING
NEW HAMPSHIRE
U.S.A.

CONTENTS

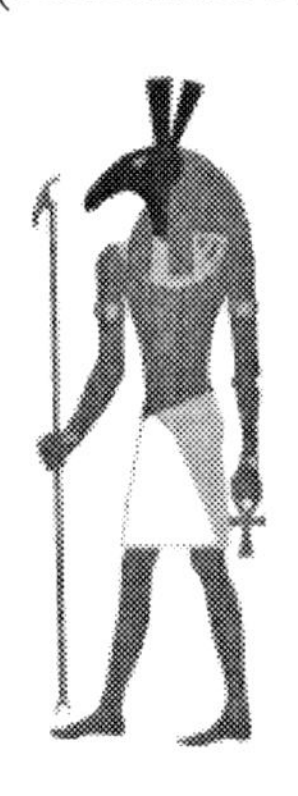

"... he was conscious of being involved in an affair not altogether reputable, and for many years afterwards he clung to the commonplace ..."

—Arthur Machen, "The Great God Pan"

ACKNOWLEDGMENTS

The publishers and editor would like to thank all those who submitted stories to this wonderful anthology. There were so many fantastic tales and yet only so few could be included within.

We would also like to thank the genre fans and speculative fiction readers. Without you, this book would not exist.

Moreover, the Nashua Writer's Group has played a great part in this publication. Their ability to inspire and motivate cannot be overlooked.

Lastly, M.J. Preston, author and artist, created the wonderful cover art you see here. His artwork is superb and all accolades are well earned.

Foreword

PATRICK REA

Horror for me has always been something of an escape from reality. Growing up in the Midwest, I found myself always gravitating toward the macabre, whether it was films, television or written stories. A great deal of it had to do with the fact that horror was the forbidden fruit, especially in a small town in Nebraska. I often think back to what sparked that interest in horror. Was it the excitement of being scared, or was it more about watching or reading something I wasn't supposed to? Whatever the reason, I was very young when my love of the genre began. I would find myself every weekend renting horror movies from the local mom and pop video stores, despite not being legally old enough to rent them. Regardless of what my initial inspiration was, I know that currently my love for horror has grown into something much deeper. It has become cathartic. It has become a way to quench my primal need to be scared.

It all started for me my sixth grade year in 1991. I wrote my first short story, which I then turned into a play for my entire class to perform. The play was a hilariously awkward combination of *Friday the 13th* and Stephen King's *Cycle of the Werewolf*. It involved a camp being ferociously attacked by a lycanthrope. At the tender age of eleven, I thought the concept was brilliant. God bless my teachers and my parents for playing along and encouraging my 'creativity'. I asked one of my close friends to be the head counselor, who to everyone's shock, was actually the blood-thirsty werewolf. We rehearsed for an hour every day leading up to the performance that would be in front of all of the other sixth grade classes and some unsuspecting parents. They had no idea that I was preparing a bunch of 'extras' to play the mutilated corpses of counselors and campers. The plan was to have them laying in a dog-pile on stage covered in stage blood. I also had no inclination that my lead actor was going to go home sick the day of the performance. To this day, I suspect that his 'illness' was just a case of stage fright. I have always pointed to this moment as my first and definitely not my last experience in real 'Director Anxiety" or what I like to refer to as 'Director Dread'. Despite my actor flaking, I did what any other director would have done when the going gets tough. I played the character myself. The play, while disturbing in retrospect, went off without a hitch. And luckily the problem of an actor being replaced by myself has never reared its ugly head since.

A great deal of my career so far has been spent making short films, which tell a three-act story in an abbreviated duration. There is no question that my love for the short film medium was invigorated by the stories of the supernatural and other spooky campfire tales we would tell while sleeping under the stars. I embraced any story that could get in and out in a short period, all while creating compelling images in the reader's mind. I also truly believe that some stories aren't meant to be longer than their central idea allows and to stretch them past the intended length can destroy their power. The real beauty of storytelling and the ultimate challenge for the storyteller is to keep the audience compelled for the entire duration.

In the summer of 2006, I began creating a series of short films financed by a local television company in Lawrence, Kansas. Each film was inspired by the short stories I read in my youth and anthology television series like *Tales From The Crypt*, *Monsters,* and *The Twilight Zone*. It was through making short films that I truly felt like I found my voice. Each story had to be unique and tell a beginning, middle and end in a limited amount of time and still leave the audience satisfied. Some of these short films had humor, others were more serious, and some were just plain strange. By 2012, my production team and I have made over thirty short films that have played worldwide at film festivals and have garnered several regional Emmy awards. While making these films, I always went back to those short stories I read as a kid. I remembered my mantra to get in and get out and keep the audience engaged in that short span of time.

Despite my recent journey, a long journey I may add, into feature film making with *Nailbiter*, I fully intend to keep telling 'short' stories between the full-length projects that sometimes eat up several years at a time. For me, short films keep me creatively juiced. I feel alive while making them and even more alive while writing them. I have stacks of short film scripts that have yet to be made, that someday I hope to complete or publish in a short story anthology. I can see why many authors continued to compose beautifully written short stories while still producing novels. The short story format is and will always be very satisfying to the artist. From a filmmaking point of you, technology has opened itself up to giving the storyteller new and affordable tools to tell their stories, many of which are best told in truncated form.

With the prevalence of short form entertainment growing to accommodate a faster moving world, the anthology continues to thrive, whether it is in film or books. The collection of stories you are about to read, *Canopic Jars: Tales of Mummies and Mummification*, is a strong example of the power of the anthology. Many of the stories deal with mummification, and the inability to let go. These fantastic authors take the reader on a unique journey, while creating mood and tension and incorporating the supernatural. What is the appeal of mummies or mummification to the masses? Why do these stories continue to reign in our world? I believe the answer is much deeper than just the visceral thrill of seeing a decaying human wrapped in cloth. Mummies are a symbol of retaining something past death. They represent a way to deal with our mortality. We all dream of cheating death, or reaching out to someone who has passed on, or preserving our beauty. That is why these tales will continue to thrive among readers.

Beyond the mass appeal of mummy tales, I can honestly say that from a filmmaker's perspective, these stories are truly cinematic, with compelling plots and well-drawn characters. While reading them, I saw images in my mind; I put faces to the characters and I even heard a musical score to accompany them. It's anthologies like these that will inspire a new generation of storytellers and keep the current ones working overtime to move and entertain. Who knows, there may even be a mummy film in my future.

DEATH IN A HIGH PLACE

ESTHER M. LEIPER-ESTABROOKS

The Incas of the Andes possessed no written language, thus
This mummified and sacrificial girl has no name we can know.

Step by ever steepening upward step
Through wind and desiccate frozen ice,
I held knowledge of my own death with me.

Myself—now idly nicknamed Juanita—
Became fast-frozen, static, into place
Atop the dormant fire-mount, Amputo.

What could I do save obey priests? The gods
Deserve the best, they said. I acquiesced
But at the summit they bashed in my skull.

My last meal, thus my last taste of Earth
Was vegetables to chew as I ascended
Twenty thousand feet high; air too thin.

I was drugged then ritually sacrificed.
—Now, waking—millennia have hurtled by.
I did my part; the land stays safe below,

But time fleets onward and a Sister Mountain
By spouting fire melted Amputo's ice
Which turned to liquid, giving me release.

DEATH IN A HIGH PLACE

I did not fall far, thus explorers found
My small and toppled form still tight-gripped
By core of cold. "An ice maiden," they cried.

Although I could not speak, yet in my heart
A strong store of resolve kept spirit firm
Plus hatred of a belief that dealt me death.

I've half-forgotten life, but now, new wakened,
My frozen spirit hears the whine of wind,
And foreign speech from those who lower me.

They bring me homeward, briefly back to lowlands
As I pray oncomers prosper and keep safe,
But none recall my name—nor can I tell.

Inca ancestors, from birth you doomed me;
—Too beautiful to not reserve for death,
Thus I passed on before I barely lived.

Do you call removal ***rescue,*** white men;
White as the snow embracing me long years?
Now mere body proves a useless weight

Spirit flies in and out from, like a window
Perpetually open to keen wind and cold,
—I wished for children. What I bear are thoughts

Of rigid, frigid emptiness, no babes
Have suckled at my breast or gazed on me,
Babbling gladly as only small ones can.

—The fact is, I am but an empty pod
Doomed in limbo; no part of earth or sky,
Plus slain too young. Gods, let me summon fire

To utterly consume these scant remains
Into shreds of ash too small to see,
Till dissipated, at long last, by wind!

—Or can you do this for me? But you won't.
I've named my wish. In time all wears away
By fire, ice, hate or atrophy; flesh fails.

So: Let my smashed head and slender form
Remain as warning: eternity has no need
Of anything that holds mere human hope.

MUM

MICHAEL BAILEY

Fire eats her face, her shoulders, arms, hands, torso, and thighs. Fire eats all of her with an inhalation of hungry breath until her bedroom is void of air and the exhalation caused by an opened door draws the fire's attention elsewhere to feed. Away from Mum as she sleeps.

We have an important decision to make. Some call it pulling the plug, but it's not really pulling the plug; it's simply a button to push or a switch to switch and the connected device hums hums hums and then clicks to deathly silence as a risen chest falls one last time.

There's no power cord to yank from the wall. There is, but that won't kill her. These machines have battery backups to keep the machines living when they should otherwise be dead, which keep the living alive when they should otherwise be dead. These machines, when we push the button or switch the switch, the lights go out, or burn out, perhaps, like a no-longer-hungry fire. The jumping jagged lines revealing life in digital form flatten, tired perhaps and ready to move on, like the fire, or they fall flat one last time, like the chest.

We look to each other before looking to the machine keeping her alive.

The last thing you said to Mum before the fire was to stay out of your life, to stop asking about Emma. It doesn't matter why Emma left you. Mum knows that. She wanted to help you through the bad because she went through the bad with Dad, when he started seeing someone, when they were still together. Does it make you happy now? You told Mum to go away, to 'literally burn in hell,' you'd put it. Here she is, burned all to hell. Do you wonder if you did this to her? Where were you? Were you with Emma?

I watch her breathe and it helps me breathe: a slow rise, a slow fall; a click before every long exhale. The rhythm is stable and hypnotic and nearly puts me to sleep until the machine beeps, or starts to hiss as blood pressure is automatically taken, or when the nurse comes in to change her bandages. Eighty-seven percent. That's how much of Mum is covered in bandage. The nurse, she tells me I'm going to need to learn how to change them.

Her skin, once black, is raw underneath the layers of gauze. Doctors, or surgeons, or whoever works on burn patients, peel away the burnt parts of Mum. Skin will not grow on dead skin, the nurse tells her, though she cannot hear any of these words.

Mum, she no longer has ears.

Hers skin smells of lotion or ointment or whatever is put on burn patients. Some kind of minty emollient or gel/jelly substance she cannot smell.

Mum, she no longer has a nose.

The softest parts of the body burn first, the nurse tells her.

Even though we're told it might be best to leave, we stay through the changing.

The doctor, or surgeon, or whatever he is, the man with the white mask covering his face so he won't smell the horrible smells, he removes a red blotch and unwinds a once-white wrap, which coils to the stainless steel tray like a carefully placed snake. He doesn't want us to see the mess, but it's there: the yellow/red/brown mountain of skin-fused bandages. Coagulation.

"You should come back in an hour," he says. "This will take about an hour."

The machine silently blinks blinks blinks with a pulse. Blood pressure automatically takes as a plastic lung rises, stronger than the chest for which it breathes. After a slow exhalation hiss, a double-digit number over smaller double-digit number displays on the screen and neither of us understands the meaning.

We stay.

A flame's only hungry if there's something new to burn. The smoking fireman in the front yard told you this an hour after you'd told Mum you'd be there. Once burnt, things no longer like to burn. A flame looks for something wet and moist, something new. A flame would rather devour a living tree and flourish than starve on a charcoaled husk of a tree and die. Fire would rather move one trunk to the next, spreading through limbs, branches, and leaves: a viral fire. A damn social network of destruction.

Trunks: torsos. Limbs: arms. Branches: hands. Leaves: fingers.

It could have been both of you.

With Mum blackened and dry, the fire was done with her husk. The fire had moved on to dryer things, like the kitchen, the bathroom, the front half of the house. Black seeped through exterior walls by the time the giant white snakes doused what was left of the roof. Smoke wafted from the soggy ashes the way it wafted from Mum when they wheeled her out.

You bummed a cigarette from the fireman, something new, let him light it from the ember of the one dangling from his mouth, then moved it to your lips. This something new, you carried the torch. Did you think about Mum, then, as you inhaled the smoke?

The handheld breathing device covering her face as they wheeled her out then, the paramedic at her side squeezing regulated air into and out of her lungs…

The machine at her side now, plugged into the battery-backed power, it pumps the air into and out of her lungs instead of a man, breathing for her, keeping her alive because she can't do it on her own…

Do you think about assisted breathing when you leave her side every hour on the hour to find 'fresh air' outside the patient waiting room as you spread fire and billow smoke, or do you wonder about the house and what the insurance will cover?

I rode with her to the hospital. Mum's red and charred-raw hand, it stuck to me as I held onto what was left of a fading grip that barely held back. I'd squeeze, and she'd squeeze. I'm here for you Mum, I'd say. When paramedics rolled her away, her skin stuck, adding another layer to my own, as frail as black tissue paper.

I rode with her to the hospital…

Her body is human jerky: dried in the heat, shrunken, brownish red.

There are degrees and she's mostly third. The third-degree is what peels away like weathered paint. The third degree involves all layers of the skin, or epidermis, as the pamphlet says. The charred areas that used to be her epidermis, and the dry white areas, some of this clings to her burned clothes to form a new layer of skin. A special blend of cotton polyester epidermis.

She should have the burnt parts elevated above her heart, the pamphlet says, but there's no proper way to raise eighty-seven percent of her body above her heart.

Her other thirteen percent, this part of Mum is a mix of second- and first-degree burns, according to the pamphlet. The blisters and the intensely red and the splotchy parts: second. The lighter red and swelling: first. The little yellow book also says burns are susceptible to tetanus, but Mum hasn't been to the hospital since she last gave birth.

She's still alive. For a reason, she must want to live. There must be something she wants to get off her chest besides the skin, something left to say.

We remove the expired gauze as the nurse instructs. We do this when the white goes away, when the red seeps seeps seeps through to the surface, but only when the blood starts to dry and brown. Like the fire, the bandages look for something wet and moist, something new, while the blood they soak searches for the opposite. Blood would rather move one bandage to the next, spreading through gauze after gauze after gauze: a viral bleeding. A damn social network of red blood cells escaping the body while white blood cells stick around to help.

The old gauze, we coil it on the stainless steel tray. The new gauze, we make it moist with some kind of minty emollient or gel/jelly substance, the same stuff we spatula onto Mum's open wounds. This makes them look worse.

White blood cells are leukocytes, the nurse tells us, as if that means anything at all. After we both offer a 'don't-understand' expression, she tells us that leukocytes are part of the immune system. Blood pools to a wound so it can help fight infection. The little white warriors are there to help. The snot that runs down our nose, that's mostly white blood cells. When we pick our nose, we're mostly picking dried white blood cells. When our children eat what they find up there, they're learning to become albino vampires.

Mum's nurse thinks she has a sense of humor.

We silently watch as she demonstrates the things we need to learn.

The endless white bandages, they go round round round her arms and legs as we lift, winding up her thighs to the place that brought us into this world, around her ankles and wrists; the bandages climb her neck. After dabbing ointment on the red half-moons under her eyes where there used to be bags, we cover the wounds on her face.

"She's in a coma," the nurse says, "though some believe she can hear your words."

We give Mum silence and sit her upright.

"This requires two," the nurse says.

One of us holds her upright while the other unwinds the old bandages from her chest and winds on the new. The more we layer, the less seeps through.

You bring Emma to see Mum like she's part of the family. You bring her in and the two of you sit across from the bed, watching; not helping, but watching, wanting to say goodbye. You stroke the back of Emma's hand like she's some kind of pet, a purring cat. You watch your sister take Mum's hand, cautious of the wound.

I read an article once that cats will eat the soft parts of the face first if left alone long enough with the dead. Domesticated cats starve because they cannot feed themselves. They rely on the dead to feed them, and they resort to eating faces. This article, the words make me think of the hungry fire that ate Mum's ears and nose, the droopy bags that once hung below her eyes, as well as her lips and the soft skin outlining what used to be her smile.

I read an article once that domesticated cats were worshiped by ancient Egyptians and seen as symbols of poise and grace. These poised and graceful face-eating cats, they sometimes received the same mummification as their owners. The cat goddess, Bast or Bastet or something like that, she was the deity of things like motherhood, protection and fertility.

The bandages, they cover a majority of Mum's body.

I read an article once…

White wrappings preserve her while she sleeps the long sleep. The blood does its work underneath: white cells fighting for her life while the red watch her die. One of her daughters is like the red; the other is like the white. One of her daughters wants to leave the figurative plug plugged into the wall for as long as it takes; the other wants to pull.

She resembles a cocoon. Mum underneath, ready for metamorphosis, she is ready to pass from this life to the next.

We argue until we're no longer sisters.

You don't want her alive. You want her plugged in, but that's not really living; that's a CPR dummy mocking life when someone else does the breathing.

"Goodbye, Mum," you say, followed by a kiss on her bandaged brow.

Emma, she pulls your hand to let you know it's time to go.

I want her to live, so I pull the plug.

At four in the morning, the hospital sleeps. All is quiet, but for the gentle hum of the machine doing the breathing. All is dark, but for a few florescent lights, the soft green glow of EXIT signs spotting the hall, and the jumping jagged lines revealing life in digital form.

"Goodbye, Mum" I say, followed by a kiss on her bandaged brow.

I squeeze her hand to let her know it's time to go.

It's not really pulling the plug, but pushing a button and the connected device hums hums hums and then clicks to deathly silence.

A risen chest falls one last time.

The machine, when I push the button, the lights go out, and I'm reminded of the no-longer-hungry fire I had set. The machine, it's done with Mum. The jumping jagged lines revealing life in digital form flatten, tired, ready to move on; they fall flat one last time.

"Hello, Mum," I say, and change her bandages.

Her body sits upright.

THE MONASTERY

KYLE RADER

They took the village by surprise. Heathens from the Northlands seeking to claim the riches; their arrival masked by heavy fogs stagnating over the choppy sea.

The battle, if one could even consider the sacking in such terms, was over before the thought of resisting entered the frightened minds of the people. None could stand against the Northmen. Most were simple fishermen or farmers more at home with their hands in the dirt than wielding a sword. By midday, the overcast sky was thick with black smoke as the heathens set the village to the torch.

But not all were to die. Marched away from the only home they'd ever known by a rogue group of the invaders were two boys, Declan and Thomas, brothers who, up until that morning, had maintained their innocence in a world that hungered for it. Their abductors, six in total, shadowed their footsteps, prodding them with sharp axes and spears coated in the blood of their parents as they stumbled along the narrow path that led to their destination: a bog so expansive it appeared to have swallowed the horizon.

The skies swelled with thick clouds of black and grey as the Northmen piled into a waiting ferry, which was little more than rotting planks of wood lashed together with cracked leather. The brothers were set before oars and made to row their captors into the swampy unknown.

"Hey, boy!" a heathen named Gunnar called. The man's eyes, black as coal, glinted as they processed the terror in their faces. "Row faster! I've been far too long without the sound of gold in my pocket."

"Please don't kill us, sire!" Thomas, a fair-haired boy of only nine, said. "W-we've done all you have asked of us!"

"Quiet your mouth, Thomas, you fool!" Declan whispered to no avail. Gasped hysterical breaths billowed out of his brother in loud bleats, much to the amusement of the heathens aboard.

"Oh, stop all this carrying on! The women I fucked in that shit-pile of a village of yours didn't cry half as much!" Gunnar grabbed Thomas by his hair and draped the whimpering boy over his round shield and produced a knife. "What say you, men? He can surely row without his tongue!"

Cruel laughter and jeers of encouragement filled the air as his fellow murderers agreed with this course of action.

"Declan! Help me!"

Declan's breath caught in his chest. He dropped his oar and clutched at the crucifix his mother made for him and prayed. *Oh, Lord Jesus above, please don't let them take my brother. He's all I've left now.*

In the end, it was not the son of Mary, but the leader of the Northmen that provided salvation for the boy. "Let loose of the boy, Gunnar." his voice was reserved, barely audible over the sounds of battle that were carried on the winds from the village behind them.

Gunnar's smile dropped into a befuddled smirk. "Come on, Alrek! I'm just having some fun with the lad is all!"

Declan felt the weight of Alrek's meaty hand clamping down on his shoulder. "Your 'fun' is preventing us from moving towards true riches, *brother.* Unless you find the odor of this place to be agreeable then by all means continue. I don't believe the boy has pissed himself yet, maybe you can achieve that."

"Aw, the hell with it all!" Gunnar shoved Thomas off his shield and onto the deck of the ferry. "I'll have his weight in gold and silver and not an ounce less, Alrek! This place best be worth my while."

The brothers continued rowing on in silence. The bog was ancient; filled with the decayed remains of the great forest that once flourished there. The mist that served to be the precursor to the deaths, or worse, of everyone they knew in this life had settled over the valley around them, limiting their vision to mere yards.

"Boy," Alrek spoke to Declan after a time. "When your brother was about to be cut apart, did you really expect your God to save him?"

Declan's cheeks burned hot. He buried his chin into his chest and directed his anger towards the oar, which had become entangled on a fossilized tree stump. "Yes. I believed it with all my heart."

Alrek smiled. The tales that preceded the arrival of the

Northmen—vile men who did not bathe and had with insects in their hair—did not seem to apply to the man. His long blond hair was neatly combed and the only scent that clung to the man that Declan could smell was that of the sea air.

And the metallic stench of his father's blood, which coated the front of the man's tunic.

"You Christians amuse me," he continued in his hushed tone. "How do you expect your White Christ to defeat our gods? He is one and they are many, and his only weapon is that of two sticks tied together. Why, our god Thor carries a hammer that can strike down the mightiest of creatures. It was his will that brought us here and continues to bring us fortune, while your little Carpenter-God abandons you."

Declan touched his crucifix for reassurance. At that moment, it truly felt like nothing more than the two twigs bound with leather that comprised it. "I'm just a boy, sire. I cannot even read the pages in the Bible that the monks teach us from. My father knew more on the subject than either Thomas or I. You could have asked him this question, if you hadn't killed him."

Thomas broke down into a fresh round of sobbing at the mere mention of his deceased parents. "Declan, don't make them angry!" he whined, eyeing Gunnar and the remaining grim faces in the ferry.

Alrek laughed. "That was your father I killed, then? He seemed a bit too young to have sired one so old. My eyes aren't what they used to be."

A portly heathen named Rolf chimed in from the front of the boat. "That must mean that the woman was these pups' mother! I cut the bitch's throat myself! After I *fucked her!*"

The barbarous laughter of the Northmen cut the young brothers far deeper than anything their blades could have managed. Thomas swooned, and would have simply laid down on the ground if not for Declan's hand holding him in place. "Easy now, Thomas," he whispered to his brother, "It will be over soon."

"O-okay, Declan. Okay."

Declan managed a weak smile. For all his stoicism, he was on the precipice of breaking. The attack on his village took place mere hours ago, yet he felt as though he hadn't slept in days. The dying pleas of his mother haunted him, serving both as a source of inspiration and torment. The scene replayed in his head over and over again. Hearing her voice felt like a physical slap that made his body recoil.

"Spare my sons, I beg of you! They are merely boys! They cannot possibly harm any of you!" She clung to the breeches of Rolf, preventing him from pulling them up.

"Get the fuck off me!" A snarl and a blur of flesh split her lips wide open. Droplets of blood arched through the room as she fell. "Shall I kill her now or does anyone else want a turn?"

"P-please! Kill me if you like, but if you spare my sons, I will take you to where the true wealth is hidden. As much as you desi—"

The remnants of the woman's last words entered the world by way of arterial spray. Rolf's knife opened her neck, creating an eye-shaped window through her flesh. She reached not for her fleeing blood, but for her sons, cowering in the corner with hungry blades placed against their own throats. She managed a half-smile and then followed her husband into the next life.

A blurred object dangled before Declan's weary eyes, snapping him from a past Hell into his present one. "Tell me, boy, what does this *truly* unlock?" Alrek said.

Declan laid the oar against his knees for a moment so he could rub his vision clear; his palms fit perfectly in the dark hollows under his eyes. The bow of the key was sculpted into a pair of curved wings; angelic-looking, yet the cold metal gave them an aura of something far from divinity. "As I told you before we set out, it is the key to the monastery just outside of our village. Where the treasure is."

Alrek clenched his fist around the key, enveloping the wings in his hard calluses. "Why would your monks give control over their wealth? It seems nonsensical and foolish."

Declan shrugged and resumed rowing. "It has always been as so. A family is chosen to guard the key and to act as steward of the riches and provide the brothers with food, fresh water and whatever else they require for their studies of God."

"How far is this damned shack anyway?" Gunnar yelled.

"My father always told us it takes a half-day's journey through the Maw of the Ogre. The monastery rests right in the middle," Declan said.

"Why would this place be named after such a horror?" a slender heathen called Toki spat overboard into the dark waters; his spittle barely causing a single ripple.

Declan shrugged. "This place has a habit of swallowing men whole. Father used to tell us it had a particular taste for those of mean dispositions, trying to scare us."

"Superstitious nonsense!" said Ulf, a gray-bearded man with only one ear.

"The sacrifices we made to Odin will protect us from this filthy hole!" Gunnar added.

"That's right! The priests told us it would be so!" Frodi, a man with hair as red as fire, agreed.

The spiritual debate continued with Alrek's warriors reassuring one another with great vigor until all stood and shouted at each other, and to the skies, of the might of the *Aesir.*

"*Enough!*"

Alrek unsheathed his sword and rose to his feet. A silence fell over the boat until all but the sounds of the bog were rendered mute. The tip of Alrek's blade hovered over them until all were rendered docile. He remained standing long after each had taken their seats, when the call of a loon broke the tension. The bog obscured the creature's position; the echo bounced off itself, amplifying the noise until it felt as if the swamp itself were laughing at them all.

The ferry swayed. A hollow thud reverberated through the damp, moss-encrusted wood, causing each beam to protest against the sudden rough treatment. The shuddering of the rotting craft drove the Northmen, each an experienced seaman, into a near-panic.

"What was that?" Rolf said, lifting his axe.

"Quiet, you fucking idiot! You'll awaken the ogre that dwells at the bottom of this bog!" Frodi said.

A burning sensation erupted in the small of Declan's back, followed by a trickle of hot liquid spilling out of him. His blood, he knew.

"That better have just been another dead tree we hit, boy." Alrek twisted the tip of his knife into the tiny wound he'd created, carving a half-moon into the boy's skin.

Declan bit his tongue hard to keep from crying out, an act born more out of love for his brother than defiance. *Mustn't let Thomas see me afraid or he will be lost.* He looked over the side as much as the leader of the heathens would allow for. "We are close now," he said, taking up his oar with a large sigh of relief. "We will be there within the hour."

"A tiny bump of the boat and you suddenly know our position?"

He felt the knife retract from his back slightly. Alrek rested the edge against his spine and held it there.

"I find this to be suspect."

"Look over the side and tell me what you see," Declan said.

Alrek scoffed. Who was this mere boy to give him orders? He was Alrek Leifsson, *skeppare* of his own vessel. He'd half a mind to drive his dagger into the boy's throat and let the final words he heard be promises to sell his brother to the worst kind of perverts he'd had the displeasure of dealing with.

Yet, the eyes of his men—filled with superstitious fear conjured from the unfamiliar place—were watching him; pleading him to show the bravery that earned his family their position and Alrek the right to wear a sword.

"Very well," he said, sliding his knife back into his tunic. "If this is just some kind of game, then you *will* regret it ver—"

"What is it, Alrek?" Rolf asked.

"Yes, what is it you see?" Ulf pleaded.

Alrek slumped back in his seat. A smile appeared, followed by an icy laughter that chilled Declan and Thomas to the marrow. "See for yourselves, you cowards! See what the great and horrible ogre has in store for you!"

The dead man floated a foot below the surface. A rope wrapped around his shoulder kept him tethered to the sunken boat that he once piloted. His neck had been broken in the wreck resulting in his dead eyes being forever fixed upwards. The brackish bog water kept him well-preserved; his skin had just begun to swell and wrinkle. The motion of the bog caused him to sway from right to left, making the corpse appear to be inviting them to come down and visit him in his dank, dark grave.

"His name was Martin," Declan said as the Northmen looked overboard. "We came across him about a week ago, Father and I. There was a storm that rolled in from the ocean and he must have gotten stranded and crashed. It took Father less than an hour to row us to the monastery after we found him, and neither has moved since."

The other heathens soon forgot their superstitious fear and joined in their captain's merriment. Soon, all notions of evil and monsters dwelling underneath them in the abyss or in the fog were forgotten in favor of things more pressing; gold, for instance, and the promise of lots of it.

Declan nodded to his brother and they took up the task once more. The ferry protested, but eventually had no choice but to surrender to momentum. The oar brushed against the face of the corpse as they rowed on, shredding off a strip of its flesh, now the consistence of jelly. It floated to the surface, clinging to the moss and fauna before a loon, the same one who'd been watching them, swooped down and spirited it away.

The monastery sat at the top of a craggy hill on what was little more than a slab of volcanic rock too stubborn to sink into the bog. The fog, suffocating and all-encompassing, did not touch the building; the wisps curled halfway up the slope before rolling back into its collective.

"Go on, boy. Open the door."

Alrek nudged Declan towards the ancient metal door. The iron was discolored a sickly brown from exposure to the sea air. No hinges were visible, as if the mighty door had always been sitting there and the monks built the stone walls of their church around it.

"Hurry it up, boy. You don't want to see what happens when Rolf and Gunnar grow impatient. Limbs tend to get *lost* when they do." Alrek shoved Thomas into the waiting arms of his grinning warriors. They poked and prodded the boy until big, fat tears spilled down his cheeks.

Declan took a deep breath. He gripped the key with both hands, thrust it into the keyhole, and turned. The door swung open almost instantly, as if the building had been anticipating their arrival. Air belched forth from the interior, kicking up the dirt and dead plants at their feet into a dust cloud. Dim light shone from the end of a narrow hall with a slanted roof that lead down into the island itself.

"What in Lõke's name are you waiting for? An invitation?" Alrek drew his sword and pointed into the bowels of the monastery. His warriors, filled with avarice, ran forward into the black hole, knocking their axes and spears against their round shields as they descended inside.

Alrek ushered the young brothers together until they stood shoulder to shoulder before him. "If this proves to be nothing more than an empty slimy hole, it will be the last place your screams are heard."

The heathens found themselves wandering through a maze of tunnels that moved them ever deeper into the island. The network had been in disuse for quite some time. Spiders claimed dominion over the cramped space; thick cobwebs hung like curtains from ceiling to the earthen floor. This did little to stifle the battle cries of the Northmen. The warriors ran through the webbing, which formed ghostly beards upon their own.

After a period of stepping over fossilized roots and broken pieces of ceramics, they noticed the faintest hint of natural light, nothing more than a thin sliver of the gloomy day they had left behind outside. The floor took on an upwards slant as they approached, ending at a door of rotting wood that hung from two hinges barely tamped into the frame.

Alrek patted the back of Rolf's neck and the burly man turned the door into splinters with a single kick. Light poured into the tunnel as the invaders swarmed into the chamber.

The chapel was modest by the standards of Christendom. There were three rows of pews—two of which were almost gnawed away entirely by vermin—and a small altar. Books by the hundreds lay scattered upon the floor, each riddled with dust and mold.

"What in the name of Hel is this?" Gunnar asked, spinning his axe in his palm.

"There's no fucking gold here!" Frodi screamed.

"Aye. Naught but fucking nothing!" Toki kicked a stack of books over; the pages flew free from the disintegrated binding and were caught on a breeze brought on by the centerpiece of the room, a large circular window that had long since been shattered.

Alrek stared out of the rose window and beheld Declan and Thomas's village through the swirling mists. The fires they had helped to set raged on. "See that boy?" he said to Declan. "From way up here, the flames appear to be devouring the entire countryside."

Declan regarded the demonic burning below and said nothing. He pulled Thomas close and hid his face from the sight.

"What the fuck, Alrek? You told us this place contained wealth beyond anything we'd find in the village," said Rolf.

Alrek turned from the window, a peculiar smile affixed upon his face. "Why, Rolf, whatever are you implying? That I have knowingly led you astray?"

Rolf stiffened as Alrek approached him. He didn't like the wild look that danced behind the man's eyes and he most assuredly did not care for the way his sword was raised at him. "Where is the treasure then?" Rolf gripped the hilt of his axe tighter. "No one, not even a stupid worshipper of the White Christ, has dwelled in this place for years. These two little liars were just trying to buy time for more of their kind to escape and you were stupid enough to fall for it!"

The slaying occurred with such swiftness that none of the Northmen realized it had happened until Rolf lay dead upon the dirt-encrusted floorboards. In a single seamless motion, Alrek stepped towards his subordinate, plunged his blade deep into his guts, twisted it, and pulled it back out. Viscera and chunks of pinkish meat that were once Rolf's organs spattered against the pews as Alrek swung his blade in the air, cleansing it of the stain.

"Now then! Is there anyone else here who wishes to question my decision to come to this place?" Alrek pointed his bloodied blade at the remaining heathens. "No? Shall we continue on with the search of this stinking place or shall I cut you all down until there is no one left to share in the spoils?"

Gunnar stepped forth and spat green phlegm onto the forehead of Rolf's corpse. "We never really liked him anyway," he said with a laugh.

Thomas tugged at his brother's tunic as the Northmen continued on with their disparaging of the dead. "D-Declan? Where are the monks? Won't they help us?"

A lie perched on Declan's tongue. *I could tell him the monks are simply waiting for the right time to unleash the fury of Jesus himself.* He debated the merits of speaking this falsity to his brother versus the truth with all its horror, as his father spoke it to him upon his first visit to the monastery.

"*Door! Door!*" Frodi screamed.

A small door behind the altar swung open. Three men cloaked in dark purple hooded robes walked into the chapel. The heathens were upon them before they had walked five paces. Ulf smashed into the lead man with his round shield, knocking him to the ground. Frodi and Toki fell upon the next their axes, hewing at his body long after the monk stopped moving.

The last was left for Gunnar. He impaled the man with his spear and lifted him off the ground. The man's hood fell away from his head, revealing not a face but a hideous mask. The leather was cracked and worn, with two small glass-covered slits for eyes and a long, curved nose shaped like a bird's beak.

"What the fuck are these men supposed to be?" Gunnar said, dropping both spear and masked man to the ground.

"Bring the one that still breathes to me," Alrek commanded. "And the boy."

Declan and the sole surviving masked man were thrown to their knees before Alrek. The boy tried to see the man's eyes behind his mask, but the glass was too dark for him to glean anything but his own reflection.

Alrek lifted the man's hood back with the tip of his sword. The mask was more extravagant than those of his fellow monks. The leather was well-polished; intricate etchings of two men ran down either side of the beak; each man held a large open jar, from which, wisps of gold spewed forth.

"I certainly hope that you have not taken a vow of poverty, monk, for your sake and for the sake of these two boys. You see, the pathetic walking bags of flesh that brought them screaming into this world told us *such* tales of your home. *Wondrous* treasures barely comparable to our imaginations. Yet, I look around and what do I see?" Alrek picked a strand of gossamer web from his mustache and flicked it into the air. "Dust and memories. It appears that we have both been made the fool, monk. You, from a God that demands servitude, and I by the forked tongues of those who you have allowed into your service. While I can bring you no relief from your choice, I can rectify my problem here and now. Toki, bring me the young one."

Toki lifted Thomas off his feet and dropped him at Alrek's. The boy's eyes reflected an entire lifetime's worth of pain and suffering. He looked to his brother with an expression one that young should not have known.

His quivering mouth opened to form the syllables that made up

Declan's name but were forever silenced as Alrek drove his sword through the base of his neck.

"*Thomas!*"

A torrent of emotions surged within Declan, causing him to lose his senses and strike against Alrek. This attempt was halted almost at once by something hard and blunt colliding with the small of his back. The image of his dead brother tripled in his vision as he was pulled to his knees.

"T-Thomas…Oh Jesus, save him." Declan muttered the Lord's Prayer and kissed his mother's crucifix. *Take his soul from this place before they claim it!*

"I *did* warn you what would happen, boy," Alrek smirked, kneeling down and using Thomas's tunic to wipe his blade clean. "And yet, you still place your faith in your White Christ. You see that, monk? True dedication to his God. He would make for a good candidate for this place, don't you think? Or, rather *would have*, as I have the sudden urge to see it in ashes."

The masked man turned from Alrek and regarded Declan's crucifix. The boy's reflection spun over itself as the monk tilted his head from side to side. The beak of his mask brushed against the symbol of the boy's faith. A loud snort emanated from somewhere within the man's body, killing any semblance of benevolence.

Though he had no earthly way of proving it, Declan could swear the man was laughing at him.

"The treasure exists, Odin-Son," the monk finally spoke, his voice strained, as if the beak of his mask was filled with loam. "As extravagant and plentiful as you were lead to believe. You warriors from the north are welcome to as much as your hearts desire."

"The treasure is near?" asked Alrek.

"Very."

"I'd press you to gaze upon the bodies of your fellow worshippers, and that of the boy that this one here weeps for, lest you claim ignorance to the *lengths* that I am willing to go to claim what is mine."

The monk looked at the corpses and nodded. "Indeed, Odin-Son, indeed."

The masked monk led the Northmen through a long hallway with a high ceiling. Ghosts of glorious tapestries hung haphazardly from the walls, all but having been devoured by moths. Intricate paintings once adorned the ribbed vault ceiling but they, too, had long fallen into tatters. "Yes, this place was once as grand as your great *Vahall*," the monk said. He leaned on Declan, using him as a human walking stick as they shuffled along. "But that was long ago, when your grandfather's fathers were only possibilities."

Gunnar showed his interest in the storied history of the monastery by tearing a tapestry from the wall and rubbing it against his crotch. Declan felt the monk tense slightly at the insult; his grip tightened on his shoulder but relaxed as they came to a great arched door.

"Here it lies, Northman. Everything you prize and desire lies behind this very door."

"Well, then what the hell are we waiting for? Boy, unlock the door!"

A raspy, strained laughter chased the cheery echoes of heathen laughter down the hall. "Odin-son, the door is not locked. It is *never* locked! The treasure is yours and always *has* been."

Wealth beyond that of the richest of kings filled the room. There was no discernable order to the fortune; it spread from one end of the oval-shaped room to the other. Gold coins were piled as high as a man's waist and precious gems lay scattered on the ground.

Declan looked at the variety of currencies, each in varying shapes and design, and despised it all. *My family was slaughtered for this? Precious gems and stones?*

The Northmen ransacked the room of treasure with the unbridled enthusiasm of children at play. All save for Alrek, who lingered at the threshold, studying his conquest. "Monk, what lies beyond that door there?" he asked while peering through an emerald the size of a walnut.

The door was plain and unremarkable save for one glaring characteristic: the same markings that ran the length of the monk's beak were carved into it.

"That door leads to our inner-most place of worship. Where we go to pray to our God. There is nothing there of any interest to you, I can assure you."

Alrek smiled. "Do not presume to tell me what I find of interest, monk. Did you not proclaim that this treasure was mine? As such, I lay claim to whatever is in that room. Gunnar! Break it down."

The big man lifted his axe and prepared to hew the mighty door when something stayed his hand. A loud creaking sound filled the air as the door slowly swung open on its own accord.

Alrek shoved the befuddled Gunnar aside and strode inside the chamber. A large altar of polished marble took up the majority of the space, leaving barely enough room for Alrek to move. The altar served as a stark contrast to the rest of the monastery. There was no sign of neglect in this place, no state of decay. Instead, vibrant paintings depicted scenes of men holding large jars over their heads while other men cowered at their feet. Bright gold and greens spilled out of the open tops of the containers and swirled around the standing men, all of whom had looks of defiant bliss painted on their faces. The smoothness of the granite made the colors pop, as though they were alive.

As breathtaking as the artwork was, it paled in comparison to the jar that rested in a hollow at the center of the altar. Painted black with golden runes etched across its body, its beauty instantly captivated the heathen leader.

The Northmen paused in their pillage and encircled Alrek as he walked the jar out of the chamber. Their collective mouths salivated at the idea of what riches it held within as their leader slowly unscrewed the lid.

A hiss of air escaped as Alrek broke the seal. The lid clattered to the floor, landing atop a pile of gold jewelry. Alrek peered into the dark interior of the jar and then plunged his hand inside.

"What's inside?" Toki asked.

Alrek cried out in excruciating pain. He stumbled away from the jar, pulling back an arm coated in dark liquid. "*Get it off me! Get it off!*" he screamed as the liquid bubbled, filling the room with the stench of scorched flesh.

Ulf and Frodi held their leader down as Gunnar attempted to wipe the substance free. The ichor sprang from Alrek and coated the big man's hands. He screamed as it forced itself into his body through the cuticles of his fingertips. Dark crimson leaked from his nose and ears as large swells of his own blood pushed through his tough skin.

"*Odin save us!*" Toki screamed.

He turned from his friends and ran past Declan and the monk, leaving a trail of untold riches behind him, and was stopped at the door by the very monks they had murdered not more than an hour ago.

"*Draugr! They are the undead!*"

The first monk's body was missing his right from below the elbow and his neck clung to his shoulders by a few sinews of veiny blue flesh. His bird mask hung in pieces, revealing a hideous pair of maroon lips. Despite his decayed state, the monk possessed a strength that overshadowed anything the heathen could muster. He clamped his remaining hand on Toki's shoulder and squeezed. The heathen's collarbone shattered as he was lifted off the ground and thrown back into the room.

"*Madness! This is madness!*" Ulf frantically stripped out of his tunic as Gunnar coughed tainted blood on him.

"Madness? No, my dear Northman. What you are witnessing is a *miracle!*" the masked monk said. "Our God has deemed you to be worthy offerings and has granted us with favor for loyal service."

Ulf's hands clawed at his face as the foulness of the jar worked deeper. He made swift work of the flesh of his cheeks and by the time he collapsed into a semiconscious state, his left eyeball dangled from his fingers.

The monks stood in a circle around the dying heathens. They removed their bird masks, revealing the true scope of their decay. To Declan, all but forgotten in the whirlwind of greed and death, their heads had the same consistency of rotten apples that had been left out in the sun, stench and all.

"And now, my brothers, we shall honor our great God, whom we have worshipped since the time of the Exodus. Where once were ten, only one remains, but it is the mightiest of the ten that were visited upon the Pharaoh, and remains so even now."

Alrek crawled through the blood and bile of his dying men towards Declan. "*You! Boy!* I will see you suffer the same fate as I for leading us to his demon's den!"

The lead monk placed his foot gently on Alrek's back, halting his advance. The heathen struggled for air as his tormentor ground his heel into his ribs. "The boy is hardly to blame in all this. His fate in this life was determined long before his birth. One bloodline to provide the brothers of this monastery with fresh sacrifices to our God until the sun goes dark. We would gladly seek them out ourselves, as tradition dictates, but alas, we are forever bound to this place by the will of our God. Didn't you think to question why the doors swing outwards? And are *locked from the outside?*"

"What kind of God is your White Christ to demand sacrifices and to command demons?"

The monk's maroon, worm-like lips squirmed into a crude mockery of a smile. "Who said that we worshipped the Carpenter? Our God is the one that courses through your veins this very moment. The one that sickens you and devours all the life in its wake. Our God is *Plague!*"

Declan watched as the monk descended upon the heathens, now too far gone with sickness to resist. They hovered around each man, sticking their corpse-blue fingers into the soft points of their flesh. A wet, sucking sound followed as the heathens lives were slowly drained from them, continuing on until each was little more than a dried-out husk. The act itself he had witnessed once before when his father brought him along so he could learn the family trade.

It failed to frighten him then. Now, it brought tears born of joy to his eyes.

A shadow moved beside him. He did not need to look over to know who it was. "I'm sorry that you died, Thomas."

The living corpse that was once his brother reached out and grasped Declan's hand. "All is how it is supposed to be, brother."

"They saved the one who killed you for last. For you."

Potato-sized boils had swollen up over Alrek's eyes, yet a tiny opening remained for him to see the newly-born *Draugr* child walking towards him with tiny blue fingers outstretched, hungry to drink his life. His tongue, now too large for his mouth to contain, lolled out and prevented him from screaming as he felt the ten digits enter him like daggers.

The sucking sounds of Alrek's life being drained from him followed Declan as he left his brother to his new life; his thoughts turned towards the rebuilding of his own.

And to that of the next offering.

JARRED EXPECTATIONS

ERIN THORNE

The jars stood on the top shelf behind the cash register. They were not overly ornate; carved from plain gray stone, with no gilt figures or detailed embellishment, they bore only simple lines of etched hieroglyphics. The squat containers were each scarcely larger than a man's fist, and not visually captivating by any standard. However, they were prohibitively priced for some indiscernible reason.

Dexter Shaw approached the cashier at Timeless Treasures with the intent to negotiate with her over the ridiculously high cost of the collectibles. He'd been a patron of this consignment shop for the past fifteen years, and had never seen an item marked above two hundred dollars, yet here was a set of 'genuine Egyptian funerary jars' which overshot that sum by well over a thousand.

To the casual observer, the shop had the appearance of a yard sale that had been moved indoors. Porcelain salt and pepper shakers, collectible dolls in dusty cardboard boxes, and a random assortment of candleholders in all shapes crafted from copper and brass, met the eye when one entered. There was a pewter lamp missing its finial, several mismatched pieces of furniture, and a massive, heavily scratched sideboard that looked as though it had been forced through several front doors in its lifetime. Scattered rings and pendants lay under glass around the register, most of tarnished silver, but with a few small pieces in gold. Amethysts and carnelians glowed dimly in the afternoon light that filtered through the front window, as they waited patiently for requests to be examined.

Dexter had seen many of these items sitting unmoved for nearly a decade; they greeted him like old friends when he crossed the threshold, and highlighted the store's new acquisitions by their own stubborn refusal to be sold. However, nothing like those odd little receptacles had ever been found in this establishment on the outskirts of rural Woodstock, Connecticut.

The man sauntered up to the jewelry cases, leaned over, and tapped on one with his index finger to gain the attention of Jill Lash, the proprietress. She slowly raised her large blue eyes from the book in which she'd been absorbed, and surveyed her most loyal customer with an air of nonchalance. Mr. Shaw was well known for his parsimony, and his appearance caused no hope of a large expenditure to spring forth in Jill's breast. She did not rise from her antique wooden seat, but merely addressed him in a tired tone.

"Hello, Dexter."

"Greetings, Ms. Lash. I wish to inquire about the curious objects above your head, just there." He pointed to the shelf.

"The description's on the sign," Jill sighed.

"Well, yes, I saw that. I also noticed that the placard gives the price at two thousand dollars, and wondered why."

"We've been over this before, Dexter. I set my prices according to my clients' requests. If they don't specify how much they want their stuff to go for, I pick a number. If they do, then I have to respect that. The lady who brought those in said they'd been in her family for years, and she wouldn't take a penny less for them."

Dexter furrowed his brow. His prospects for a good haggle were waning before his eyes. "They're actual canopic jars, are they?"

"I suppose so."

"Must they be sold as a set, or could I purchase only one?"

"I was told they need to stay together."

"Ah. Suppose I offered eight hundred dollars in cash, to be paid today."

"I would tell you that you were still twelve hundred short."

Shaw bit his lip. "Nine hundred?"

"No."

"Surely, you'd take a thousand?"

"Dexter, my hands are tied. If you want to barter, you'd better do it with Mrs. Widdermeyer."

He bowed his head. Clearly, he would make no progress on this with Jill Lash. The man was sorely intrigued as to the justification of the asking price. He'd seen these things at auctions before, but they were far more prettily carved and half the cost. They'd belonged to Egypt's later dynasties; perhaps these were much earlier. He decided to take her advice.

Shaw climbed into his brown Buick, itself an antique, and rattled across town to the stately gingerbread Victorian painted in three shades of purple. He parked in the driveway, right behind the golden Mercedes that belonged to the octogenarian he sought. Boldly, without any inkling of intrusion, he strode up to the door and rang the bell. Shuffling steps approached, and soon a tiny, wrinkled face peeked out at him from behind the aged lace curtain.

The widow recognized her visitor, and opened the door a few inches. "What do you want?" she asked in a thin, reedy voice.

"Hello, Mrs. Widdermeyer. I was hoping to have a word with you about the lovely Egyptian jars you're selling in Timeless Treasures. You see, although they may be quite rare, I thought that the two thousand dollar price tag was a bit extravagant. While I'm perfectly willing to pay for quality, I don't think I could spend so much without knowing something about the items in question." He hoped, by a mixture of flattery and fairness, to convince the venerable dame to accept an offer of eight hundred. While it would be his largest purchase of the last decade, it would also represent a victory in the realm of bargaining. Such a testament to his power of persuasion was a desired feather for his cap, one which he could wave at Jill Lash the next time he stopped by her shop.

The woman's beady brown eyes glinted at Dexter. She didn't speak for several seconds; finally, she stood aside.

"Come in."

He walked past her birdlike frame which was tastefully clad in a neck-to-ankle muslin dress, and paused to admire her vintage décor as she locked the door.

"We'll go into the parlor. I cannot, in good conscience, allow you to proceed further without telling you about their origin."

Dexter was curious; he sat on the red velvet sofa with its beautifully carved wooden legs, and his hostess sat on its twin directly across from him. She folded her bony hands on her lap and fixed him with a sharp look. After a few moments of tense silence, she spoke.

"The objects you desire belonged to my father, William Carter, who brought them home from his final trip to Egypt."

"William Carter? Not the one who pioneered the excavation of the Valley of the Kings?"

"The same. He was brilliant, yet it must be confessed that he was guilty of taking souvenirs from some of the tombs he discovered.

Granted, the items were of minor significance, and most of them wouldn't have been missed. The burial chamber that yielded those canopic jars abounded in gold and lapis, and those little pots had been set into a corner. One would never know that they were considered sacred to the priests that placed them there.

"He loved to tell me and my sister the story of how the superstitious native workers had no qualms about lugging the shining treasures out of the pit and packing them snugly for their trip to the British Museum, but shrank from touching the quaint jars. They knew what was inside, as did he, and they were convinced that the gods and goddesses charged with protecting the desiccated organs would wreak their vengeance upon anyone who touched them.

"My father set no store by these tales; he scoffed at those of his colleagues who lent them any credence, and in his later years, cited his advanced age as proof against their veracity. However, this same level-headed old man also told us in a hushed whisper of a strange encounter concerning them. He said that, as he prepared to leave Egypt for the last time, he was approached by an elderly, hooded man. This fellow told him that he was wise to choose those particular treasures for his private collection, for they held the key to an extended lifespan.

"This was in total contradiction to what the skittish servants had claimed, and my father asked him to elaborate. The mystic said that, though the tale had been twisted to fool the gullible, the original story had been carefully guarded by the firstborn males of his bloodline. One of his remote ancestors was a high priest in charge of the mummification rites, well-versed in the occult lore of the period. He'd discovered a secret property of the preserved organs, a latent byproduct of the spells that were carefully chanted over each one. Supposedly, if a man unwrapped and ate one of the dried body parts, he would live well beyond his appointed time of death. Of course, there was a caveat. If the man became greedy and ate more than one, in the hope of gaining immortality, the gods would strike him dead on the spot for his hubris.

"My father was dubious, as any sane man would be. His visitor read the doubt on his face, and said that he himself was over one hundred and fifty years old. He was as lively as ever, and insisted that he possessed the same energy he had in his youth. He'd eaten a stomach at the age of thirty; since then, he'd been fit as a fiddle. His family had maintained their longevity by raiding the tombs for organs. They took what they were after, and replaced what they'd stolen with linen-wrapped rocks. He offered to examine the jars my father had, to determine whether their contents were intact.

"He humored the old man, who pronounced them untouched with a gleam in his eyes. The Egyptian said he'd given him a valuable gift by imparting his family's secret, and wished for one of the organs in return. His son was aging, and unspoiled canopic jars were becoming more difficult to find. My father obliged him, thankful for the evening's entertainment, and the man took the deceased king's royal intestines away into the night.

"Father brought the rest home, and the stone pots sat behind glass in his curio cabinet for several years. Not long after he returned, he began to suffer from stomach pains. He dismissed it at first; as the months passed, he bore the discomfort with increased difficulty. During one of his more severe bouts, his physician was called in. I hovered by the bedroom door as he lectured my father for not consulting him sooner. He said his official diagnosis was one of a rare and life-threatening hernia, which would require a risky surgery. He was given no more than a month to live, should he refuse the procedure.

"The doctor left, and my father did not mention his professional opinion to the family. Two weeks passed; as I lay awake one night, haunted by the image of my father's pain-distorted face, I resolved to tell my mother the next day. I couldn't stand the thought of her remaining in the dark about her husband's condition, and thought it unfair that she'd have no time to prepare for his impending death.

"However, at breakfast, my resolution was shattered. My father ate more in one sitting than he had in the last three days, and his hollow-eyed pallor had been replaced with ruddy cheeks and a bright smile. I was overjoyed at his recovery, yet I feared it was his body's last hurrah before it gave up the ghost.

"My apprehension dimmed as the months marched on, and he was as hale and hearty as ever. My mother, a devout Catholic, ascribed his miraculous recovery to her abundant prayers to Saint Jude. I had my own suspicions, far from the realm of the Holy Church. To test them, I feigned sleep one evening, and waited until the house was quiet.

"I crept downstairs and into my father's study. My sister and I were forbidden from venturing in there without him, and his cabinet was unlocked on the strength of his prohibition. I tiptoed across the thick Turkish rug to the glass door that beckoned me. It opened with the tiniest creak, but did not betray my curiosity. I took down the jars one by one; two contained small, bandaged bundles, and the other two were empty."

Dexter was enthralled. He wasn't given to flights of fancy, but he'd enjoyed Mrs. Widdermeyer's narrative. He hastened to bring it to its arcane conclusion.

"Had your father consumed one of the organs, then?"

"I never asked, and he never told us. If the old Egyptian man's story was true, it would certainly account for his sudden recuperation. He died at the age of one hundred and fifteen; not a supernatural lifespan, but longer than average."

"That's remarkable! He must have been a happy man, to have had such a long life with his family."

"He was, for the most part," said Mrs. Widdermeyer. "I wish I could say his passing was an easy one. During his last few years, he suffered from severe dementia. He was convinced that he was being followed by threatening beings, shadowy humanoid creatures with the heads of animals. We were convinced he'd harm himself, so we made the heartbreaking decision to send him to a hospice. He'd always been so strong and self-sufficient; not long after he took up residence at Golden Acres, he passed away. The official cause of death was apoplexy. I have never seen a stroke leave such odd marks, though, as the ones I saw on his neck. They were dark purple, ranged in orderly lines."

"That is rather strange," remarked Dexter.

"Indeed, it is. I could not help likening them to hieroglyphics, as outlandish as that may sound. I suppose I'd lent too much worth to the old myths and fantastic tales from the country about which my father was so passionate. Perhaps I'm more superstitious than I would comfortably admit to anyone, even to myself. In my advancing age, I've been tempted by the foul notion of eating one of those innards, which was one of the main reasons I put them up for sale at Timeless Treasures."

"I see. If I may be permitted to return to my original line of questioning, what made you choose two thousand dollars as the cost of the set?"

"I desired to elevate them above the price range of the average customer. To be honest, I had hoped they'd be purchased by a museum."

"They are, doubtless, of sufficient quality to justify your hope. Well, Mrs. Widdermeyer, I'm afraid the hour is growing late. I really must be going now. I apologize for disturbing you, and I thank you for taking the time to speak with me."

They both rose, and as Dexter grasped the doorknob, the widow laid a hand on his arm.

"I'd like to tell you one more thing, although I'm sure you'll think me terribly silly once you've listened to what I have to say. The evening before I brought the jars to Ms. Lash's shop, I was enjoying a solitary dinner in my lonely old house. The cleaning lady had left hours before, and there was no one here except myself. In the stillness, I thought I heard someone in the parlor. I entered the dark room, armed only with a steak knife, and turned on the lamp.

"No one was there, yet it looked as though someone had been. One of the pots had fallen on the floor, and its bundle rested beside it. The shelf on which I'd kept it was behind glass, so I wasn't sure how it ended up that way. I replaced the contents, and put it back. When I turned to leave, I saw a woman in my way.

"It nearly stopped my heart. She was there for no more than an instant before she vanished, but I'll never forget her. She was beautiful, with bronzed skin and long, braided black hair. Her layered necklaces shone in the lamplight, and she wore a regal golden headdress crafted in the shape of a giant scorpion. I looked at her, and she looked back with intense anger in her heavily lined black eyes. Before I could speak, she was gone. The next day, I rid myself of the jars. I've neither seen nor heard anything strange since then.

"I've told you this because it's clear you're still interested in the items. I can't stop you from buying them; all I can do is implore you to be careful."

Dexter gently placed his hand over hers. "Rest assured, madam, I will not do anything foolish. I also promise not to breathe a word to anyone regarding what you've told me today."

Mrs. Widdermeyer sighed. "Very well. Take care, Dexter."

She watched him get into his car and drive away, toward the east side of town. The old lady knew where he was headed. She shook her head, and retreated into her home.

It was lucky for Dexter that he passed no cruisers as he sped back to Timeless Treasures. All thoughts of haggling had disappeared; he would gladly pay two grand to own a group of artifacts that had come from the collection of William Carter himself. The Buick's tires crunched onto the gravel in the shop's parking lot, and the car jolted to a stop. The anxious customer charged through the door and quickly walked over to a startled Jill Lash.

"They're still there, excellent! Ms. Lash, I believe you accept credit cards."

The wide-eyed, disbelieving shopkeeper rang up the purchase, and stared after Dexter as he gleefully carried his spoils back to the car. The old brown behemoth was piloted slowly along to its owner's residence, an apartment complex on Main Street.

Dexter gingerly carried the white plastic bag into the building, up the stairs, and into his second-floor living quarters. He locked the door behind him then withdrew his thickly wrapped treasures one by one and set them on the coffee table. The gray stone jars were carefully wiped free of dust and lovingly gazed at by their proud new owner. He had no plans to sell them, at least not yet.

When he was ready to retire for the evening, Dexter set his relics on the highest shelf of his bookcase, where his cat, Mitzi, would be unable to reach them. He went to bed and dreamed of ancient Egypt, with its god-kings and bizarre sacerdotal rites. The figures of his fantasy were hazy as they drifted through his consciousness; he awoke with the feeling that he'd traveled far and rested little.

He rubbed the sleep from his eyes as he stumbled to the bathroom. After he'd splashed his face with an invigorating amount of cold water, he wiped it dry and stepped over to the toilet. Dexter saw Mitzi huddled behind it; she must have been spooked by something, and had made herself as small as possible in order to fit between the bowl and the wall.

"Tut-tut, Mitzi; you shouldn't hide back there! You'll get all dirty." He knelt to remove her. "I know, Daddy needs to clean more often…" She held her ground; the cat had wedged herself firmly into position, and barely budged. Her frustrated owner attempted to get a better grip on her stiff hind legs. He didn't want to hurt her, but she needed to be taken out of there. On the third firm tug, she was freed.

Dexter took a good look at his pet for the first time. She was rigid and unmoving; at some point during the night, she had passed away.

He curiously touched her face, which had frozen in a hideous snarl. This baffled him. Mitzi had always been a quiet, gentle creature. Although she did occasionally climb the curtains or scale the bookshelves, she'd never hissed at anyone or exhibited aggression.

The loyal feline was wrapped in an old pillowcase and driven to a cemetery just outside of town that had fallen into disuse at the end of the nineteenth century. There, Dexter tearfully dug a small grave with a garden trowel in the corner of the grounds and then laid his beloved pet to rest. He stood over the grave and, though he didn't speak, he allowed himself to dwell on fond memories: the day he'd brought her home in a shoebox, the many nights she'd sat on his lap while he read, how she had danced around his feet when it was time for her to be fed. He'd be alone now in his one-bedroom bachelor pad. As he walked back to the car, he pondered getting a kitten in a few months, once the mourning period had expired.

He spent the rest of the day tidying up. Mitzi's bed was washed and placed on the highest shelf in the bedroom closet, and her emptied litter box found a new home under the kitchen sink. Dexter's steps dragged across the living room floor as he made his way to the silent scratching post. He lifted it in his arms and turned away from his little girl's favorite window, the one that looked out onto the overgrown backyard. As he bore his burden toward the doorway, he nearly tripped over something in front of the bookshelf.

It was a canopic jar, which sat upright on the floor. The man frowned as he picked it up and placed it next to its three comrades. He hadn't seen it on his way to the window, nor had he heard it fall. He didn't pause to give it much thought; grief superseded all other impulses and emotions, including curiosity.

That evening, once Dexter had drained multiple glasses of merlot in honor of his deceased companion, he reeled into bed. He passed out at once; when he came to, it was still dark. He squinted at the bleary red numbers on his alarm clock. It was three in the morning, and his bladder was screaming for relief. Nature's call was heeded in the gloom, without benefit of artificial light. He was about to slide back under the covers when he saw the shadow across from him, an inky, hominid smudge that hovered between the four-poster and the wall beyond.

Dexter jumped back, and his feet were barely able to refrain from becoming entangled with one another. He halted in the doorway for a moment. As he stared at the phantom, it solidified into a substantial form, yet unlike any human the frightened man had ever seen. Elongated, scoop-like ears rose from the sides of the being's head, erect and tapered at the ends. A long, pointed nose—the snout of a scavenger—jutted forth from its face, and two onyx eyes flashed briefly in the glare from the streetlight outside.

Without warning, the entity disappeared in a cloud of swirling smoke. Before Dexter could regain any measure of equilibrium, the stillness was shattered by the phone's strident ringing. He walked to the kitchen in a daze, and unconsciously avoided the tiny table that shared a wall with the telephone. Dexter lifted the wireless from its cradle.

"Hello?"

At first, no one replied. Then a choked sob was heard, followed by the tremulous voice of Dexter's sister, Doris.

"Dad's gone."

Dexter sighed; this call came as no surprise. Their father had been in a nursing home for the last six months, having outlasted the doctor's prognosis by several weeks. His chronic liver disease had morphed into full-blown cirrhosis, and he'd clung to life by the most slender of threads for four days. While it was sad news, at least the old man was no longer in any pain.

"I'll come over later on today to help with the arrangements."

"Thank you, Dex."

He could hear her crying. Doris had always been closer to their dad, and he knew she was taking the loss poorly.

"Okay, I'm going to go wake up a bit. I'll be there around eight-thirty, if that's all right."

"Sure. Love you."

"Love you, too." He hung up, and turned on the overhead light. Coffee was needed at once; it was going to be a long, trying day, not at all compatible with a hangover.

As expected, Doris fell apart at intervals throughout the ordeal. Her tears spilled when they talked about what sort of coffin Dad would have liked, whom should get up and talk first at the wake, and how he'd be reunited with Mom both in the hereafter and side by side in the graveyard. Dexter was exhausted by the time he returned home in the evening.

He experienced a brief pang, as he almost called for Mitzi upon his entrance. Once he'd changed into his most comfortable pair of blue pinstriped pajamas, he found the rarely-used bottle of sleeping pills in his medicine cabinet. He shook one tablet out, and on second thought, increased the dosage to two. Rest was needed tonight; if anyone called, they'd simply have to leave a message.

Sleep came quickly, attended by a strange dream of sun and sand. Once he'd left the mundane world behind, Dexter found himself wandering in the desert. He trudged barefoot through the sand toward a distant river, and tested the cool water with his toes when he arrived at it. The moment his feet were immersed, a mass of bubbles churned in the river's center. A crocodile rose to the surface, followed by three more. Dexter withdrew onto the shore, his eyes on the beasts as they circled. Suddenly, in their midst, a woman appeared, seemingly consolidated from the water itself.

She floated effortlessly in his direction, and the reptiles made way before her. Her caramel skin glistened in the noonday sun; her soft brown eyes gazed into the man's own with a serenity that bespoke utter wisdom. She carried a bow in her right hand and an arrow in her left, yet there was no hint of a threat in her aspect. The vision of beauty passed her human admirer with a smile. He watched her as she sat on a rug spread under a cluster of palms at the beach's edge. She beckoned to him and patted a spot next to her voluptuously reclining body.

Dexter needed no second invitation. He was there in an instant, lying down next to the smiling maiden. She smoothed his hair back and stroked his forehead then lightly trailed her fingers down his cheek. He thrilled at her touch; though part of him knew he was dreaming, he had never felt so alive. She slowly ran one fingertip around his lips' perimeter. He groaned, and sent forth liquid heat from his eyes.

The woman laughed, a tinkling sound like water trickling over tiny golden bells. She withdrew a small bundle from the depths of her robe and unwrapped it. Inside was a resinous brown nugget, shriveled and aromatic of exotic spices. She passed it under his nose; the scents of cedar and cinnamon wafted into his nostrils, a not unpleasant combination. Before he could object, she thrust the object into his mouth. He chewed the leathery morsel, and his companion gave him water from a golden cup to wash it down.

The transformation was instantaneous. Dexter stood on the

intricately woven carpet and raised his hands to the sun, as a burst of energy shot through his veins. He felt like a conqueror, a hero, and he turned to thank the lady for this mighty gift. As he opened his mouth, a rapping sound was emitted. Horrified, he snapped it shut. Shortly, the noise was repeated, and his desert paradise began to melt away into mist. He reached for the woman's hand, determined to take her with him, but she shook her head and vanished into a spray of water that swirled in midair before it dissipated.

The horrid knock sounded once more, louder than ever. There was a rush of disorientation, followed by brightness. Dexter blinked; with a start, he realized he was standing in his living room. The sun had risen hours before, and someone was hammering on his front door. He walked across the room, and as he raised his hand to the doorknob, he was aware for the first time that he was clutching something round and hard. It was one of his prized jars, empty and lidless.

He swallowed hard in an attempt to rid his mouth of a sudden metallic taste.

"Just a minute," he called as he put the jar back. He trotted back to the door and threw it open. It was his landlady, Mrs. Pierce.

"Shaw, what the hell went on up here last night?"

"What?" The question caught Dexter off his guard; he'd certainly gone to bed without any hubbub. Of course, he'd also had his first experience with somnambulism, but it had been quiet enough. Hadn't it?

"The Porters downstairs claim that you were up half the night, stomping around. They could hear splashing, too. Lucky for you, their ceiling doesn't appear to have any water damage."

He tried to disguise his confusion. "I'm not sure what it was that they heard, since I—"

"I heard you myself, not fifteen minutes ago! I was inspecting the Porters' place, and it sounded like a herd of rhinos was charging back and forth over my head!"

"But I—"

"Never mind, I can see I won't get a straight answer out of you. I'll cut you a break this time, since I know you've just lost your father. I ran into your brother-in-law at the supermarket yesterday, who told me what happened. Poor Doris; she's always been so sensitive." Her tone had grown lachrymose, yet quickly regained its sharp edge as she glared at her tenant. "I'm warning you, though. If it happens one more time, just once, you'll be out on the street. I won't tolerate noise and disruption in my building. Understand?"

He didn't, but nodded anyway.

"Good. I'll be back next Thursday for the rent. Sorry for your loss." The last sentence was tossed over her shoulder like an afterthought as she stalked away.

Dexter eased the door shut. He had no idea that he'd been either noisy or disruptive, and no clue how to prevent a similar incident from occurring in the future.

The funeral was on Sunday. A light drizzle coated the varnished casket with miniscule drops, and placed evanescent diamonds in the carefully coiffed hairstyles of the female mourners. Dexter shed a few tears during the service, but could not compete with Doris. She soaked her husband's shoulder as she sobbed then drenched her little brother's jacket when Craig handed her off to him so he could smoke at a respectable distance. She hadn't shown such grief when their mother had died; then again, they'd had Dad to keep them steady.

A month marched wetly past. Dexter hadn't caused any further trouble for his neighbors; however, he was moody and depressed. His dreams had become darkly disturbing. Mitzi had featured in one which he'd endured numerous times over the last week, and while her presence should have brought comfort, the scenario rendered it terrifying. She'd been walking side by side with her owner down a dark suburban street on a warm summer night. They were weaving in and out between the streetlights, with no one around to ridicule or bother them. As they circled around the final lamp, it went out, followed by the rest.

Dexter quivered with fear. He felt hunted in the gloom that surrounded them. Alarmed, he knelt to gather his cat, when a massive black head lunged out of the darkness. It seized Mitzi with its sharp teeth; she screamed in the raw pitch that only a dying animal can produce, and the enormous jackal's snout slipped out of sight. The distraught man yelled for her again and again, to no avail. He awoke in a cold sweat, overcome with helpless dread. He never screamed out loud when he jerked himself out of this nightmare, but each time, he trembled for several minutes.

He'd had one of these dreams last night. With shaken nerves, he made a cup of chamomile tea and retreated to the living room to relax. In a rare moment of indulgence in mindless activity, he switched on the TV. There was a game show on; a large, overjoyed woman was jumping up and down and yelling with delight. The host led her to her prize—a brand new car! She was just endeavoring to get into the cheap compact when the power died.

Dexter sat in silence for a moment. He heard the cars go by on Main Street, soft automotive whispers that rose in volume then fell again. It would drive him mad if he didn't find something to do soon. A trip to the liquor store seemed like just the thing to lift his spirits, so he rose and fetched the keys from their rack by the door. He opened it, and was greeted by a brisk draft that blew up the stairs. One of the Porter kids must have left the front door wide open again.

He turned to grab a jacket from the row of hooks. As he lifted the garment, he felt eyes upon him. Nervously, he glanced around, only to receive a nasty shock when he saw what looked back.

Not five feet away, a man stood and surveyed him. Dexter had the awful sense that he'd lost his mind as he stared. The brawny, scantily clad fellow in his home had the head of a baboon, and fiercely bared his teeth. The creature's breath reeked of decay; hallucinations could be olfactory as well as visual, or the Abnormal Psychology textbook that Dexter kept from his college days was mistaken.

The man-beast took a step forward. Terrified, its intended victim slammed the door and fled down the steps. When he had reached the safety of the street, he looked back; to his vast relief, he hadn't been pursued. He decided to prolong his journey as much as possible, and walked across town for his wine.

He was trying to choose between an Australian shiraz and a domestic malbec, when he spied Craig by the beer cooler. Shiraz in hand, he walked over to ask after Doris. Craig didn't see him; Dexter moved closer and called his name. He turned, sucked in his breath, and looked embarrassed.

"Oh, hey Dexter. Just getting some beer." He grabbed a case without further deliberation, and pushed past his brother-in-law in the direction of the registers. Dexter placed a hand on his shoulder.

"Please wait. I haven't seen you since the funeral; how have you been? How's Doris?"

Craig picked at a hole in the cardboard carton.

"Craig? What's wrong? Is my sister okay?" Dexter felt the first tendrils of panic climb up his spine.

"I told her I wouldn't say anything, and I won't break my promise. You should come to the house and let her tell you herself."

He found his tongue after a dry-mouthed moment. "May I ride with you? I didn't take my car." Craig nodded; the men made their purchases, walked to the parking lot, and rode to the one-story ranch in silence.

Dexter entered his sister's house with trepidation, unsure if he wished to know her secret. Doris was in a recliner in the parlor, wrapped in an afghan their mother had crocheted. Her face was drawn and sallow; she looked up at her brother with sad surprise. He sat on the sofa nearby, and took in her sunken eyes and emaciated chest.

"Doris," he said weakly.

"Oh Dex, I didn't want to worry you." She reached out a skeletal hand crisscrossed with blue veins, and he took it carefully. There was no need for her to speak; Mrs. Shaw had looked just the same in her last month of life, and Dexter knew the verdict.

"How long do you have?"

"Maybe two months, if I don't overdo it." Her lip trembled slightly, and the smallest drop leaked from the corner of her right eye. Dexter's head swam; she couldn't die, not yet. There were no cousins in Connecticut, no other family, no real friends. He'd be left all alone.

"Are you sure? Perhaps there's something you haven't tried, some new treatment or a drug they're willing to let you test."

"It's too late. It has spread too far; surgery would almost certainly kill me at this point."

Dexter chewed his lip. Then he raised his head, his eyes aglow with excitement. "I know a way! Doris, I think I can save you!" It might give her bad dreams for the rest of her life, but at least that life would be prolonged. She appeared doubtful; his enthusiasm was contagious, however, and hope soon illuminated her expression. "I'll be right back."

He dashed out the door and jogged back to Main Street. His breath was short by the time he reached his building, and he was dizzy from the unwonted effort. He flew inside, full of anticipation for his new role as the family's official savior, taking the stairs two at a time in adolescent fashion.

His front door opened at his touch. With a chill, he considered the confrontation that had forced him to flee. He hadn't stopped to lock his door, but no matter. He had bravery in spades, now that his sister's life was at stake. No intruder, human or otherwise, would deter him from his mission.

He fearlessly walked into the living room, right up to the bookcase, and reached toward the top shelf. He snatched all four jars and set them on the coffee table then pushed aside the one whose lid was still missing. Dexter lifted one stone cap after another; he expected to find two of the jars empty, if old Mrs. Widdermeyer's story was true. Something bumped inside the third one when he shook it.

He emptied its hidden prize onto his sweaty palm. It may not have looked like much to anyone else, but it meant the world to Dexter.

The bundle was brought downstairs with the greatest care; on the short drive to Doris's home, it remained tightly clutched in her brother's hand. He burst into the house and fell to his knees before her. With a reverential air, he presented the artifact, and gingerly handed it to the withered woman.

"Open it," he said breathlessly.

The thin fingers picked at the bandages until they found an end then slowly pulled the linen apart. It cracked dryly as the carefully woven pattern was undone. When the last bit of cloth fell to the floor, Doris held up what it had concealed for so many years.

It was gray and shapeless, lumpy and hard, and of the same substance as the jar that had held it.

THAT'S A WRAP

DAVID C. HAYES

"Fuck Karloff," he said. It was out there, right in the middle of the room, and he could never take it back.

The *room* was The Actor's Studio in New York and the year was 1964.

The *he* was Lance Polland, an up and coming thespian, who was contemplating changing his name to Lance Rivers because it sounded powerful.

Lance scanned the room, the shocked faces of his fellow Actor's Studio classmates staring back at him, and swallowed hard. It had taken him a long time to get here, not everyone auditioned their way into that exclusive training ground. Making a quick decision, Lance double-downed on his earlier sentiment. Feeling particularly courageous (since he had just been cast in a new picture), he put on his best Brando and sneered.

"As a matter of fact, fuck Chaney, too…and that limey, Lee!" Lance smirked. Usually, that was enough to disarm anyone. His now-official movie star good looks had carried him through school and social events with ease. He was charming, square-jawed and blond. Just a hair over six feet tall with a body that harkened back twenty years to a savage Johnny Weismuller, Lance was used to getting away with saying just about anything.

Not in here, not in the Studio. To make matters worse, he just shit on Hollywood royalty…and the British guy. The room was aghast.

Nicholson stepped forward, fists balled. He had just finished a picture for Corman with the ailing Boris Karloff and respected the man immensely, even if the rest of the country had forgotten about him. Newman and the skinny kid, Pacino, each grabbed an arm before Nicholson's patented temper vested itself in Lance.

"How the fuck can you say that," Nicholson growled. "You ain't half the actor that Karloff is…and Chaney? He's a fucking *legacy*, you mother…"

No one thought to restrain Fonda. She marched up to Lance, tears streaming from her eyes, and slapped him across the face, hard.

Shocked, Lance recoiled and turned toward her. His eyes blazed. He may have been in the Big Apple just then, but he was Mississippi born and bred and that doesn't get workshopped out like a drawl does. He stepped forward ready to put a woman in her place.

To her credit, and probably due to genetics, she held her ground. Pacino and Newman were ready to unleash Nicholson on Lance, the other members of the Studio stood unified. It looked grim. Lance's only saving grace was that Keitel wasn't there that day.

Strasberg stepped forward. He had been watching from the corner of the room, seeing just how this scene was going to play out. First and foremost, even above an actor, Strasberg was a behavioralist. Understanding how and why people behaved in the manners they did was absolutely essential to understand the cause and effect of the human condition. That understanding was needed to replicate the human condition honestly on stage, screen, etc. He had studied the acting techniques of Constantin Stanislavski, the Russian genius, and had taken over the artistic directorship of the Actor's Studio in 1951 based on what he called The Method.

Studying under Strasberg was akin to learning strategy from Sun Tzu. The Method required the actor to dispel the memory, context and emotions of their normal, every day life. It forced the actor to adopt, physically, mentally and emotionally, the role that he or she was playing as reality. It was a painful process. One of his students, who couldn't handle the process, incidentally, had said that with Strasberg, one gets an idea of just how painful birth is. Strasberg chuckled when he heard that and quipped, "Birth is painful, rebirth is excruciating." There were people in the room, so all of his subsequent denials fell on deaf ears. Strasberg was right, though, The Method exacted a great price from its practitioners.

In that vein, the master of the The Method commanded a healthy dose of respect, so when he stepped between Fonda and Lance, both of them shook off their anger and backed up. Pacino and Newman let go of a suddenly-calm Nicholson and Burstyn put down the telephone in the studio where she was trying to get through to Keitel's answering service.

Lee Strasberg was a quiet man, normally, and this was no exception. He was a master, he didn't need tricks and gimmicks to convey any emotion; he simply embodied it. Strasberg turned that intensity onto Lance.

"What did you say, Lance?" Strasberg asked.

Lance stuttered and sputtered. "It was just a joke, Lee. I mean, I wasn't seri..."

"What did you say?"

Lance took a deep breath and then, as quickly as he could, said, "I said fuck Karloff and Chaney and Lee…not you! The British guy, from that Hammer outfit."

The rest of the room hid smiles as effectively as they could. Lance shifted from one foot to another, nervous. Strasberg had that effect when he wanted to.

"Fuck Karloff…hmmm," Lee said. "Intriguing proposition, but I don't think the old chap would much enjoy that."

The room exploded in laughter. The tension was diffused and Lance, quite noticeably, relaxed.

Strasberg turned to the other students, exhorting them to resume their exercises, and took Lance by the arm. He led the young actor back to the office, sat Lance down in a desk chair, and then took a spot on the edge of the cluttered desk. The teacher folded his arms and looked at Lance, assessing the young man.

Lance withered under that gaze and Strasberg held it for quite some time before speaking.

"I understand you booked a job today, Lance," Lee began.

"Yes sir."

"And, based on the vitriol in the studio and your chosen targets, I assume you are to be performing in some sort of horror film?"

Lance nodded. "Yes, sir. A mummy movie."

"Of course. Tell me about it."

Lance brightened there. This was familiar subject matter…himself. "I am going to play Seti the Fourth, raised from the dead after two thousand years to claim his lost love!"

Strasberg nodded. "And, so, you effectively shit on legendary performers, although we'll have to wait and see about that British guy, because you were really, really excited about playing a mummy. And you did that in front of the class."

Lance's excitement plummeted. He shrank in the chair and had problems making eye contact. "Uh. Yeah…" he said.

"You did the one thing I ask everyone not to do here. I need all of you, every time you walk in, to leave that Hollywood bullshit at the door, right?"

Lance nodded.

"So what did you do? You not only brought that Hollywood bullshit in here, you flaunted it around like some goddamn Vaudeville act." Strasberg didn't raise his voice, he never had to.

"I'm so sorry, Lee," Lance managed to squeak out as he started at his shoes.

Strasberg took a deep breath. He looked at the cluttered desk and pushed some papers away to uncover a Rolodex. He flipped through it, eventually landing on the name he was looking for. Snatching the card out, Strasberg handed it to Lance.

"Ramses Egyptian Catering," Lance read aloud.

"I want you to do well, Lance, I really do, so you'll need to do some homework. What's the name of the picture?"

"*Curse of the Mummy's Shroud.* That makes me the title character, right?"

Lee cringed at the title but recovered in time to nod. "Yep, sure does. For this particular role, Lance, I don't think we can help you very much here, at the Studio."

"Why not?"

"This is The Method, son. Becoming the role. That name and address I gave you is for just that. Ramses runs an Egyptian Catering service, true, but he is also well-versed in what that crazy Russian brought over here and realizes what we need for The Method and is a certified expert on Ancient Egypt. I want you to see him."

Lance looked down at the card and then back at the Rolodex. "What else do you have in there?"

"Everything, Lance. The whole world. That's my job."

Lance nodded and slipped the card in his pocket. "Should I get back out with the others?"

"Not this time, Lance," Strasberg said. He helped the young man to his feet, pushing him toward the back entrance. "You need to get your head straight with this mummy picture, so look up Ramses today. Head out the back way, you know how Nicholson gets."

"I sure do." Lance whistled his way out of the Actor's Studio into the muggy New York air.

Lance looked around, cautiously. It was nearing dusk and he had taken two trains, with two bus transfers, to get to the ass end of Queens. He walked down a lonely sidewalk with a summer breeze like dog breath blasting him in the face. Lance stopped and fished the paper out of his pocket again and read it. It hadn't changed: 45367 Pyramid Drive.

Lance lifted his head and looked up and down the sidewalk. There were tenement buildings, three story walk ups, basement apartments, but nothing that could be confused for a catering company. He looked at the building numbers. 45361, 45353, 45365…and there it was.

Lance swore he had looked up and down this street a thousand times since the last bus transfer but now, just as the sun dipped below the urban skyline, he found a little storefront. The sign read: *Ramses Egyptian Ca ring*. The 't' and 'e' must have fallen off at some point. The window was cloudy, but Lance could definitely see a light on inside. He reached for the handle and pushed.

The door opened, tinkling a small bell as Lance entered. He was hit immediately with the coolness of the room. It was dry, too. He looked around the area and, contrary to his previous trepidations, it looked like a small, ethnic grocery and catering shop, apparently.

Lance craned his neck to see a counter at the rear of the store.

"Hello?" he called out.

"Enter," a deep, thickly-accented voice returned.

Smiling, in part due to the new climate—air conditioning was incredibly rare in this particular borough—and the successful navigation of the tough, New York streets. If the boys back in Missoula could see him now!

Lance wended his way through the store. The shelves were filled with bottles, carafes and odd, slender jars. There was funny writing on all of them and pictures like he saw in National Geographic on others. Nothing was labeled in English and Lance figured, rightly so, that anyone that couldn't speak Egyptian, or whatever this was, wouldn't have a need for it anyway.

Passing the rows of bottled leaves, spices, homeopathic remedies and odd foods, Lance finally made it to the rear of the store where Ramses waited for him. As Lance approached, the small, dark man looked up.

He was approximately five feet tall and all of, maybe, 110 pounds. He was dark-skinned with a large, hooked nose that nestled itself over a bushy, black mustache with salty flecks of white throughout. He smiled at Lance, baring two rows of brown, stained teeth. His gums nearly matched the color of his suit jacket which reminded Lance of fried okra.

Lance extended his hand. "Hello, sir. My name is Lance…uhh…Rivers and Lee Strasberg sent me over."

Ramses stared at Lance's hand until the actor pulled it away, awkwardly. "I am Ramses. You have come to learn, I know."

Lance nodded. He thought he knew what was happening here. "Yes, sir! I am playing Seti the Fourth in *Curse of the Mummy's Shroud*, shooting right here in New York!"

Ramses shuddered at the mention of the title, hiding it less effectively than Strasberg did.

"And I'm real eager to learn as much as I can," Lance continued. "This could be my big break."

Ramses nodded. "Big break, certainly. There are many people that desecrate the values of others to shock or scare an audience. What did you say the name of your mummy was?"

"Seti. The fourth."

"The fourth," Ramses said to himself. He turned then and shuffled toward the rear of the store. "I thought Imhotep was bad enough."

Lance just watched the strange little man go until Ramses turned to look at him.

"Well, you are coming?" Ramses asked.

Lance jumped and scooted behind the counter. "On my way. Do you want me to shut the door or lock it or something?"

Without turning back, Ramses parted a beaded curtain and entered the rear of the store. "Taken care of," he said.

Lance stole a glance up the aisle and he'd be damned! The door was closed and locked from the inside.

"Hey! How did you lock the door?" Lance asked.

Ramses called out from the dark beyond the bearded curtain. "Come!"

Biting his lower lip, Lance entered the gloom.

He could see that the room was lit with candles, but the stark difference between the overhead lights of the store and this back area had his pupils growing, trying to compensate. As he adjusted, Ramses voice floated from the ether.

"How long before the shooting of your film?"

"About three months."

Ramses chuckled. "Good."

Lance's vision had just acclimated to the dimly lit room when he noticed a large stone slab, like some kind of weird bed, in the middle of the small area. Three large jars, with the heads of birds for lids, stood along one wall and two sconces, each containing a flickering candle, illuminated the room. Ramses was nowhere in sight.

"Wow, this is groovy, Ramses! I should tell the producer about this place. I bet they could shoot here and you'd get a location fee or someth…"

Ramses brought the truncheon down across the back of Lance's head silently and swiftly. The small but deadly club smacked into Lance's head with a crack and the good-looking oaf crumpled to the floor.

Ramses stood over the young man and chuckled. "End scene."

Lance blinked his eyes. His head ached and, when he squinted, he thought he could see a cheap, water-stained drop ceiling. This wasn't his apartment. He turned his head, but even a simple motion caused lights to explode in his eyes and pain to shoot down and back up his spine, nestling right behind his ears and burning.

"What the hell?" he managed to groan out.

"Good, you are awake," Ramses said.

Fighting the pain, Lance turned his head to see Ramses, dressed in some kind of costume, approach him. It took Lance a moment to realize that he was in the back room and on the concrete slab. He tried to raise his arm or sit up but also realized that he was tied down.

"Uh, Ramses, man. What's going on?"

"You are training for your big film. You are of The Method, no?"

Lance tried his arms again, but they were bound at the wrist, to the table, with leather thongs. "Yeah…yeah, but what is this horse shit? Y'all playing some kind of joke on me?"

Ramses chuckled and reached under his tunic. He pulled a vial of salt from some hidden pouch, and sprinkled pinches of it across the length of Lance's body. "Funny, you see? When you lose concentration, lose the moment of the character, your old voice slips in."

Lance struggled against his binds, the leather rubbing into his wrists and ankles. "I don't know what in tarnation you're talkin' about, old man, but if you don't untie me there is a Sphinx-sized ass whoopin' in your future!"

"Listen to the voice coming out of you. The moment is gone. All the work of learning a new way to talk has been lost." Ramses finished salting Lance's body. He stood stock still and mumbled something under his breath.

Lance struggled underneath the mumbling/chanting/incantation. He lifted his head and, seeing that he was naked, could only think of what was going to be rammed up his ass in the next few minutes. He had experienced the casting couch before, but the casting slab was something completely different.

Ramses stopped chanting and smiled. He looked down at Lance.

"Who is the producing of the film?"

"What? Let me go, man! I won't say anything!"

"Who is the producing of the film?"

"You want a part, right? This is some weird audition thing so I can tell Friedman about it. I get it, man. Look, let me go and I will talk you up to those boys like yer the goddamn god of acting. Cool?"

Ramses laughed, long and hard. His greasy black mustache bent around the yellow-toothed smile, making the entire visage look like some cautionary tale hieroglyphic in the gloom. "I will call Mr. Freidman when we finish. Ready for the close up, you will be!"

Ramses laughed again and pulled a long, metal rod from under the tunic. It was at least twenty-four inches long and had a wave near the end before turning at 120 degrees and forming a hook. It was polished, possibly stainless steel, and glimmered in the firelight.

Lance's eyes opened wide in terror. "Oh, sweet Jesus, Ramses! Please don't shove that thing in my ass!"

Ramses shot Lance a look of utter disgust, his lip curling back over diseased gums. "I am not some kind of the sex pervert!"

Lance relaxed a bit, "Thank God, man. What the hell are you going to do, then?"

"The Method! You will be a fine actor of the screen. The finest to ever be a sacred mummy!"

"That metal thing will do it?"

"No, this is for removing the brain before the process of mummification can begin. You will be legend!"

Lance's mouth dropped open as Ramses bent over him. The little Egyptian man nestled the business end of the hook in Lance's left nostril.

"Very simple. The brain is removed with this. Then organs are removed and cleaned. Each of those jars will hold the dried lungs, intestines, stomach and liver so you may claim them again. Exciting, no?" Ramses took a deep breath, preparing to ram the hook into Lance's skull and extract his brain, bit by bit, though his nostrils.

"Wait! Just wait a minute! Seriously, Ramses, the joke is over, all right? Did Nicholson put you up to this?"

Ramses shook his head. "This is your training, Lance. Your body will be rinsed out with the finest wines and your heart…your heart will be placed back inside so you may perform! The finest linens will fill your chest after forty days. These will give shape to the role, letting you show the audience the pain of Seti, but knowing that his heart belongs to his princess as it rests on down. A metaphor!"

Lance whimpered. "I didn't want this."

"Of course you did. After seventy days I will wrap you in the finest muslin. You will then be ready. You will be a star!"

Lance sobbed and stopped fighting. He accepted the inevitability. "Is this gonna hurt?"

"Only a little," Ramses said and then rammed the hook into Lance's nose.

Lance squealed for a moment, a high-pitched cry that, under other circumstances, may have been called nasally. He convulsed, his body flopping against the concrete, as Ramses worked the hook in and out of Lance's brain pan.

After the first few thrusts Lance had undergone an impromptu frontal lobotomy resulting in fewer convulsions and less overall motor activity. He was dead, officially, before Ramses could even get a third of the brain out.

This was the process that Ramses hated the most. It took so long. Such a useless organ, too. Always getting people in such trouble.

Ramses looked at Lance's vacant eyes, staring up at the ceiling. "Fuck Karloff, indeed. Hmmph. Karloff played at monster…you will become one!"

The little man returned to his work.

Fred Freidman, schlock producer, walked into the temporary production office of Shroud Pictures shaking his head.

Leon Kassinger, the director of *Curse of the Mummy's Shroud*, looked up at the producer's entrance, taking a welcome break from going over script rewrites on this, his latest opus. "What's up, Freddy?"

"I don't believe this shit."

Leon's shoulders slumped. "We lost the funding, didn't we?"

Freddy smiled and shook his head. "No. For once, things are looking our way!"

"How so?"

"You know that hillbilly we cast as Seti? The tall guy that walked real stiff in the audition?"

"Yeah," Leon said. "Lance something or other."

"Lance Boil, whatever his name is. His new agent just called and said that since the kid is into this acting bullshit, he will be, at no cost to us, providing his own craft service, transportation and special effects tech in order to stay in character. You believe that shit?"

"Wow. He's making SAG minimum on this picture! That dumb kid is going to lose money!"

Freddy smiled and pulled a half-smoked cigar from his jacket pocket, lighting it with flourish. "That's fine with me, just as long as this picture doesn't lose any money."

Leon and Freddy laughed and laughed. What these kids wouldn't do to make it in the movies.

CRACK IN THE SARCOPHAGUS

JOE KNETTER

The house on Jackson Street had been empty for years. If asked no one in the neighborhood would have been able to recall a time when someone lived there. Most big cities had these types of homes scattered throughout the communities. The massive front yard was basically a barren landscape. It was so convoluted with rocks and harsh soil that weeds didn't even seem to want to take up residence amongst it. The paint had all but peeled off the outside of the two story home, leaving a gray and weathered wood underneath. Somehow termites had never moved in, eating away the wood and doing the city a favor and demolishing the house. People did their best to simply pretend that it wasn't there. Kids, on dares would run up to the front door on occasion. Halloween was the big night for this. Throughout the night dozens would find themselves on the front porch…stretching their candy covered hands towards the doorknob. Some even had the guts to touch it. No kid ever tried to open it. If they did they would have probably been surprised to find that it was unlocked. Some deep feeling of dread and fear always stopped them from taking that step. Maybe it wasn't even fear. Maybe it was just common sense and good judgment. So the house sat for years while the world changed around it. Its secrets remained hidden, right in plain view only a few blocks from a multitude of restaurants, businesses and commuters more interested in their five dollar cups of coffee than an old abandoned house. A twelve-year-old boy named Davey was the first person to enter it for almost twenty years. The previous one was a homeless crackhead named Roland.

Roland closed the door behind him and looked around. He knew the house was abandoned the moment he saw it. He didn't expect it to be empty though. He knew from experience that his fellow crackheads were like rats. Scurrying around wherever they could. A big house like this would be perfect shelter for those strung out and homeless. As he looked around he was shocked to see that there were none of the telltale signs of it being occupied. Nothing was broken or dirty. There was a layer of dust on everything but not the down and dirty grime he expected. It didn't smell like a combination of shit and decay as most self-appointed homeless shelters were. There was even a faint smell of spice. He inhaled deeply, reminiscing about the cinnamon rolls his mother used to make him when he was young. He remembered them fondly which was a surprise since most thoughts of his childhood involved beatings. He never really blamed his mother though. She did her best to earn money to give them a place to live and food to eat. Her face and hair was usually sticky with dried come when she came home late in the night but that was part of her job. He was too young to understand what it was back then, that came later. Sometimes she even worked from home. He overheard his mom talk to a guest one time about, "Being paid an extra five spot to take it on the face." Eventually she married one of those guys and luckily for Roland the only thing he took to the face was a fist.

Roland walked over to a dusty red couch sitting in the middle of the room. He looked at the wood trim around it and wondered how old it was. It certainly had to be an antique. Roland wondered why it was left there. He took off his gloves and patted the seat hard, spraying dust in the air. He waved his hands trying to get it to dissipate and sat down.

He had been really lucky to find this place. The temperature outside was below zero. He had been sleeping soundly on the train when he was awoken. Awoken was a nice way of putting it. Getting pulled out and violently thrown down a hill was better. Still he couldn't be too mad. He knew the risk he took being a hobo, especially a cracked-up one. Roland had no idea where he currently was; just that it was a big city. He was thankful for that. Finding crack had been easy. He had six rocks in his pocket very quickly. He just needed a place to smoke them. He wandered the streets for an hour before the wind picked up. The cold began to bite and even under the multiple layers of clothes he began to shiver and go numb. He knew from experience that this was the kind of cold that could kill. He thought about going to a legitimate homeless shelter but knew that wouldn't work for him. Roland could easily sneak his drugs in but knew temptation would be too great and at some point he would end up smoking crack in the building. He couldn't risk getting arrested as he was quite sure there warrants out for him; nothing major, but enough to put him away for a bit. Roland couldn't deal with that. He was very claustrophobic and the few times he had been locked up he came close to going completely mental. Of course detoxing from the drugs didn't help as he'd feel things crawling all over him. He was ready to give up and toss the rocks when he saw this house.

Roland dug the rocks out of his pocket. He looked at them in his hand and grinned. He was surprised to find that he was perspiring. Now that he was indoors the three pairs of underwear, four pairs of socks, two pants, three shorts, four shirts and two jackets he had on were not required. Nor the multitude of scarves that wrapped around him. It's how he traveled though. Bags of clothes could be stolen. He learned that lesson quickly. If he wore everything he kept everything. During the winter months it was easy. It's probably what kept him from freezing to death before finding the house he was currently occupying. The house was insulated well and Roland knew that he'd have to strip down a bit at some point. He smirked wondering if anyone had gone from hypothermia to heat stroke in so short a time. First things first though. He needed a hit. It was imperative.

He pulled out his glass pipe and put a rock in. He lit it and inhaled deeply, letting the poison fill his lungs. He immediately felt a wave rush over him. Sitting in that house, smoking a rock was as close to Heaven as Roland dreamed he could be. He leaned back and basked in the euphoria. Outside the wind howled and the snow fell. He was inhaling his third hit when he heard a noise from somewhere in the house.

"Hello", he called out, feeling that his luck had been too good to be true. Surely there were plenty of other folks trying to get out of the cold, some of whom were in there with him. They probably scattered when they heard him come in. He just hoped they weren't territorial. He waited for an answer and heard no response. He quickly put the pipe away, not in fear of being arrested. He had no intention of sharing what crack he had. Roland stood up and listened for the sound. After almost half a minute he chuckled to himself. It was simply paranoia. He was alone after all. He took the pipe out and took another hit. He blew the smoke out and sighed.

The cinnamon smell still lingered and it caused his belly to rumble. He rubbed it through the layers of clothes like a mother caressing her young. It had been a day since he had eaten anything. He knew full well food should have been the first priority over drugs but that's the price you paid as an addict. You know what you are doing is horrible and wrong, still, you can't help it. You go headfirst towards your own destruction willingly. Roland harbored no delusions of grandeur. While he was an addict and it was technically a disease it was still a choice at least it was at some point. There wasn't a choice for him now; time had taken care of that. There was in the beginning but those days, like youth, were long gone. Now it was endless cycles of getting high and falling down. Still he needed food to stay alive in order to get high so he followed the smell out of the room he was in and walked down a long hallway wondering what he'd find.

Paintings lined the walls on both sides of the hallway. They reminded him of his time in Vegas. Roland had spent a winter there panhandling on the strip. On one joyous night a man with a smile equaled in size only by his belly came out of a casino and gave him a thousand dollars. Roland was dumbfounded. The man had just hit a jackpot and a thousand dollars was mere pittance to him now but to Roland it meant so much more. Roland had a moment of clarity and knew he'd blow it all on rocks so he thought he treat himself to a night's stay in the hotel the man came out of. It was shaped like a pyramid with a light shooting out the top that seemed to shine to the heavens. It was his favorite in all of Vegas. He would sit and look at it at night. Dreaming of the good life. He could think of no better place to get high. Management threw him out before he could even get to the reservation desk. Having money wasn't enough. You had to have a certain look…or more to the point not look a certain way. While they were escorting him out he looked around at all the Egyptian stuff and marveled at it. It felt like another world.

The paintings on the wall fit that motif. Roland wasn't exactly surprised to find a sarcophagus at the end of the hallway. Whoever previously owned this house was obviously a collector. It was puzzling though why it was still here and hadn't been stolen or been victim to kids and their youthful aggressions. It was beautiful and shiny and he intended to look inside. He opened up the lock on the side and was saddened to see that it was empty. While there wasn't much room, a person would have to squeeze to fit in, he still expected something to be in there. He gave it one last look, rounded the corner and continued towards the smell of spice. It grew in intensity as he entered the room at the end of the hall. He expected it to be a kitchen but it wasn't. The room was small, no bigger than a closet, but there were shelves of spices held in glass canning jars. There were covers on most of the jars. Sitting in the center was the one that brought him down there. It was definitely cinnamon. There was no denying it. The lid was sitting next to it. Roland picked up the jar and smiled. He reached his finger in expecting it to be hardened with age but instead it was like fine grains of sand. Roland twirled his finger around and then brought it to his mouth, tasting the spice. It was hot and made his mouth water. He stuck his finger in again, making sure to coat it with saliva and brought another taste to his mouth. He licked his lips and again thought of his mother. If only she came home covered in spice rather than semen, maybe his life would have turned out differently. He had never been to her grave but he decided right then and there to change that. Maybe he'd even get some cinnamon rolls to eat there. He dipped his finger in for a third taste when he saw a beetle crawl out of the cinnamon. It wasn't large, just a hair bigger than a quarter. In this case size didn't matter. Roland dropped the jar and stepped back, revolted by the sight. The glass jar landed hard on the wooden floor and shattered, throwing cinnamon in the air like a dust storm. Roland was rubbing it out of his eyes when he looked down. The small piles of cinnamon pulsated as though alive. Hundreds of tiny baby beetles began crawling out of the wreckage, skittering across the floor. Roland threw the door shut, fought the urge to throw up as his hands shook and did the only thing he could think of to calm down: he took another hit of crack.

As his head swam in the cloud of smoke Roland did his best to regain his composure. Bugs are a common thing to the homeless. You just sort of get used to them. They are everywhere. On the streets, in the garbage bins where you dig for edible slop. He even knew a couple of crazy fuckers that kept them as pets. He couldn't help cringing though. He hated bugs with a passion. Gross little bastards. He'd stomp them all out if he could.

Roland walked away from the spice closet and headed back to the main room. He had begun to sweat quite a bit underneath all the layers of clothing and intended on removing some and having a seat on the couch. As hungry as he was he knew a couple more hits of crack would put him into a nice restful slumber. He'd worry about food in the morning. Plus thinking of the beetles made his skin crawl. He could almost feel them on him right now. He shivered and continued on.

The room looked exactly as he left it but it certainly didn't smell like it. The faint cinnamon smell was gone and had been replaced by an earthy odor. It reminded him of the red, clay filled dirt from the south. Most people didn't notice the difference in smell of various parts of the country's dirt. That was something you developed as a bum. Your surroundings became your home and within that context you explored all the sights and smells. You learned what was best. The red dirt had astonished him at first. It was pretty cool and was good to lie on. But the clay made it sticky as hell and it adhered to all your clothes and your clothes were your life. Even if they were tattered and torn they still kept you alive and made you human. It was a given that they'd be dirty, but still you wanted to do what you could to look civilized.

Roland stood next to the couch and reached up to strip off the outer layers of clothes. He guessed that there wouldn't be running water in the house but if there was, even in the back of the toilet, he thought it might be a good idea to wash them. It had been a while. If all else failed he'd bring in some snow. He'd need water to drink anyway. As long as it wasn't yellow. That joke you heard when you were a kid was certainly true. Yellow snow, although not always piss, was to be avoided at all costs.

He sensed movement in the room even before he saw it. In his peripheral vision, all around him the room began to vibrate. Not a full on earthquake-style rumble, lord knows he had been through a few of those in his time. It was more subdued shake. He reached his hand out to grab the couch, wanting to steady himself. Rather than feel the soft fabric he felt something hard. It moved underneath his touch. He looked down at the couch which was now covered in large black beetles. He stepped back instinctively and heard a crunch underneath his feet. Glancing down, he noticed more beetles on the floor. As he watched them move to and fro he was astonished to see an impossibly large one scurry by carrying one of the gloves he had left on the couch. It was carrying it like a trophy. Roland's first instinct was to grab it. He even reached his hand out but then out of the corner of his eyes he felt the vibration of the house again and quickly looked around. He cried out at the sight. The house itself wasn't vibrating; it was the beetles crawling all over the walls and floor.

Roland saw the beetles piling in from every opening in the room; endless seas of black rippling death. They rushed at him in waves, one on top of the other. He backed away from the horror, the sound of crunching echoing in his ears as he stepped on them. They began to fall from the ceiling on top of him. He swatted them away, not wanting to feel them on him at all. In desperation wrapped a scarf around his head, leaving only a small slit to see out of. What he was seeing was completely unbelievable and revolting. He knew if he felt them crawling on his skin madness would overcome him. He backed into the hallway. He heard the sound of the beetles from all around him. They began to crawl out of all the doorways that lined the hallway. It was just a matter of time before he was engulfed and slowly eaten alive. He turned around, looking for a sign of salvation. The sarcophagus at the end of the hallway remained open. So far there were no bugs down there. Seeing no other choice Roland ran towards it. Roland could almost hear the bugs cry out in surprise and anguish at the thought of losing him. He stepped into the sarcophagus and closed the lid. The sarcophagus was meant for decoration, not holding a live human. The multi layers of clothes he was wearing didn't help. Roland was scrunched in, unable to move more than a few inches. He could hear the beetles outside crawling over the sarcophagus, looking for dinner. The sound was loud and echoing. Roland didn't understand why it wasn't heard for miles. He hoped that they wouldn't find a way in. He thought he could wait it out. Eventually they'd either get tired or forget and they'd crawl back into whatever hell they came out of. When that happened he would burst out and run for the door. Shit he'd even risk jumping through a window. Cuts were a hell of a lot better than bug bites. Until then he'd just have to deal with it and wait. It was even hotter in there and since there was no airflow he felt the sweat soak through his clothes. Roland wished that he wouldn't have pulled the scarves up over his face since that wasn't helping things. He was hot, hungry and tired. And he really wanted another hit of crack. It was right there in his pocket. So close, yet so far away. Maybe he could smoke them out. He had heard something about bugs hating smoke. Yeah, he thought, maybe that would work. He had just enough room to maneuver the pipe and crack out of his pockets. He could bring them no further though. Roland would just have to open the lid a bit to light it. He could be fast. He tried pushing the lid open but he couldn't get any leverage. All he could do was lean on it and try to rock forward. So that's what he did.

The sarcophagus tipped forward and Roland realized his mistake too late. It fell forward and landed with a loud thud. Roland knew there was no hope for him. His mouth was all but gagged with the scarves and being facedown meant his breathing ability was not going to last long. He just hoped it would be quick and was thankful that there wouldn't be any more bugs although the sound outside was maddening. He couldn't have gone out that way, being eaten alive. His stomach rumbled again, this time more fiercely. Roland couldn't reach down to rub it. The rumbling in his belly changed. He began to feel something moving around inside him. He shrieked as loud as he could as he felt the baby beetles he had swallowed with the cinnamon begin crawling up his esophagus. They entered the back of his throat and crawled across his tongue. Roland wasn't surprised that they had a slightly cinnamon taste. Roland began throwing up baby beetles and bile. With the scarves over his mouth they had nowhere to go but back down. He gasped for breath and choked on the vile mix. Roland again thought of his mom and all of the disgusting things she had to choke down in her life. He had made a promise to visit her grave and forgive her…now, God willing, maybe he would get a chance to tell her himself.

Davey walked up to the front door and opened it. There was no fear in his eyes. It was simply a house, no different than any other. The stories about it were meant to frighten people away but they had never planned on a boy like Davey coming along. He loved monster movies and prided himself on never closing his eyes in fear. He walked in and looked around. Nope, nothing out of the ordinary. Dusty and dirty for sure but otherwise a pretty decent place. He looked around and began to envision all the things he could break in the house. It was open for him to use and abuse it. No one else had the guts to go inside. He had intended to brag about it, him being the first to go in and all. But now he just wanted it all for himself; his own private chill pad. He walked down a hallway and saw an Egypt thing on the floor. He couldn't remember what it was called but knew what it was. It had tipped over and was the only thing out of place in the house. Davey was a big boy for his age and had no trouble rolling it over. He stood over it, anticipating some sort of treasure. He found the latch, unlocked it and swung it open. His eyes grew wide and he found that he wasn't quite as immune to fear as he thought. There was no doubt in his mind what he was looking at. It was a mummy. The body was wrapped in layers of clothing and scarves covered the head and face. A glass pipe and a bag of what appeared to be small stones lay next to him. It was customary to bury the deceased with their favorite items, their treasures. Davey learned that from watching T.V. Yes, he knew exactly what he was looking at. A god damn mummy right in the middle of the city.

DESERT OF DEATH

ROXANNE DENT

The Tarim Basin is part of the Taklamakan desert in northwest China. It borders Kazakhstan to the north, Tibet and India to the south, the Gobi desert to the east and Pakistan and Tajikistan to the west.

Part of the Silk Road, the area was once home to a large lake formed by the runoff from the Tien Shan and Kunlan Shan mountain ranges that tower over the desert. They also provided rivers that fed vegetation and thriving oasis towns.

But as the region became more and more arid, fierce dust storms arose, burying villages, farms and outposts and creating giant, shifting sand dunes. The rainfall and melted snow runoff from the mountains was reduced to a trickle. The lake and rivers dried up until now only scrub brush and sand dominate the landscape. It was here the mummies were found.

In the evening, when the night sky fills with stars and lights twinkle in the distance from camps where men drill for gas and oil reserves, it is said evil ghosts roam the desert and bleak ruins. Tourists occasionally disappear. Locals say the ghosts call to them. The barren desert is known as Takla Makan, where, "You go in and you never come out."

When it was discovered the Small River mummies were Caucasian with traces of Tibetan—not Chinese—DNA, the news created a stir all around the world. Speculation abounded as to who they were, where they'd come from and how they'd arrived in China.

Eli Skofield, a junior archaeologist at the History Museum in New York City was intrigued. When he was told he had to take some of his vacation or lose it, he decided to visit the Bowers Museum in Santa Anna, California where the mummies were currently being exhibited.

At twenty-eight, Eli, tall and thin with black glasses and short, dark hair, was the original poster boy for geeks. He didn't see himself as another Indiana Jones. He loved cataloging artifacts on his computer at work, giving talks on pottery and basket weaving to visitors, and arguing with colleagues over the date man first appeared on Earth.

Standing on line in the museum along with other tourists, Eli viewed the tall mummies' desiccated remains. He read how the two hundred bodies were discovered in the Taklamakan desert under upside down boats, thirteen foot wooden poles sticking up in the sand to indicate the burial site. With the unusually tall bodies were beaded skirts, woolen and fur cloaks, and skillfully carved bronze masks. Demon masks

The exhibit cast a spell over Eli, who returned every day for a week to stare at the mummies. Not one to remember his dreams, once he returned to New York Eli began dreaming every night.

The dreams always started out the same. He was by a lake. He heard the pure, sweet sound of a flute. A voice called out to him. He looked up to see a tall woman with long, reddish blonde hair walk gracefully toward him. Her only clothing was strings of beads that hung from her slender waist down to her knees. Her prominent cheekbones and sensual features were tattooed in red and black swirls and triangles. Her slanted, blue eyes beckoned him to join her.

Eli awoke groaning, bathed in sweat with an erection. After two weeks, he knew he had to go to China to see the place where the mummies were first unearthed or he would go mad.

A former colleague was working on a site a couple of hours from the Small River Cemetery. Eli contacted Pete in Xinjiang who replied by telegram.

"Don't come. Too dangerous."

Eli sent back his reply, "Be there in a month." He finished projects, put in for all his accrued vacation, packed frugally, made sure his papers and shots were in order, bought the tickets and flew to Peking.

It was a long journey, with several stay over's, but he was so anxious to get there he didn't even visit the Imperial Palace or the Great Wall of China.

Arriving in the city of Minfang during a wind storm, Eli spotted his colleague as he got out of a beat up, black jeep. Tall, tan and muscular, Pete's fair hair was streaked from the sun, worn long and pulled back into a pony tail with a rubber band. His face was covered in a day's growth of stubble. Pete had a reputation as a maverick. He took chances, was ruthlessly ambitious and a magnet for women, everything Eli wasn't. Working beside Pete had never done much for Eli's ego.

"You shouldn't have come," Pete yelled above the roar of the wind as he dumped Eli's case and a sleeping bag in the back of the covered jeep.

Eli struggled to keep upright as he walked around to the passenger side, trying not to swallow sand. The grains were stinging his exposed flesh like a lash and clinging to his scalp. He climbed in and shut the door with relief. Pete started the motor and they took off.

"It's a bad time," Pete grumbled. The Han and the Uighurs are at each other's throats. There've been bombings, riots and raids."

"Nothing to do with us," Eli muttered, shaking off sand and cleaning his glasses.

"All Westerners are foreign devils."

"You're here."

"I am."

Eli waited but Pete didn't explain and, judging by the closed look on his face, didn't intend to. *Screw him*, Eli thought.

As they rode through the city in silence, a shrouded figure in a doorway shouted something and threw a rock at the car, which slammed into the passenger side, causing Eli to jump.

"I see what you mean about the hostility. How does Professor Eng feel about my coming?"

Pete shot him an uneasy glance. "Look, you have to promise to obey the rules. Weird things happen at base camp."

"Like what?"

"A Russian scientist and an English intern walked out in the middle of the night. It was thirty degrees. The temperature dips as soon as it gets dark. We searched for them for days. The sands swallowed Dave up. We found Anton. He was still in his pajamas and barefoot, half buried in a sand dune."

"Why did they go off like that?"

Pete stared straight ahead. "The wind called to them."

"The wind?"

"It only happens at night when we're asleep. It gets into your blood like the call of a Siren. We wear earplugs."

Eli smiled. "Okay, good one."

"I'm not kidding," Pete said grimly, gunning the motor and throwing Eli back against the seat.

Eli was pissed. He was sure Pete was pulling his chain, trying to spook him. He let a few seconds of silence grow between them. "Will we reach camp tonight?"

"If we don't get shot," Pete said, peering out the window at the blowing sand.

"How long?"

"A few hours."

"Are you driving like a maniac to avoid an attack?" Eli asked, clutching onto the seat to keep from being thrown.

"I want to reach camp before dark," Pete said but slowed a little.

The heat, constant motion of the car, and the inability to see much combined with all his traveling, wore Eli out. He dozed off.

When he woke up it was late afternoon. The sandstorm was over.

They passed wattle and daub hamlets, and men dressed in embroidered caps, Middle Eastern robes, and turbans sitting on camels. The Chinese were in modern dress and drove cars. Eli waved but even the children didn't wave back.

"We're almost there," Pete said.

Rubbing his gritty eyes, Eli couldn't wait to wash off the sand. "How do the locals feel about the discovery of the Small River mummies?"

"Since their DNA establishes they're not Chinese it's a powder keg."

"Do we know yet where they came from?"

"The general consensus indicates they're Tocharians, a European race. The Uighur are Muslim and insist they're related to them, which means they were here before the Han. They want to break away from China and Turkey supports that."

"Sticky," Eli agreed.

"On the other hand, they're both suspicious of what we're doing. They want us to stop."

"What are you doing?"

"Interesting stuff," Pete said flatly.

It wasn't like Pete to be mysterious. He was the first to brag about his work but if he didn't want to talk about it that was fine with Eli. He wasn't there to horn in on Pete's dig.

By the time the tents came into view, Eli breathed a sigh of relief. As soon as Pete turned off the engine and they got out of the jeep, Eli heard what sounded like a car backfiring. Pete shouted, "Get down."

Eli fell to the ground as shots rang out followed by a bomb exploding not far away. The explosion caused Eli to temporarily lose his hearing. He cautiously looked up to see eight armed Uighurs on camels on top of a sand dune ride off.

As Eli stood up, a short Chinese man in his fifties with thinning hair in western clothes and holding a pistol came running toward them. Three armed guards with the latest in long range weapons shot at the men on the ridge and missed. Two Europeans, also fully armed, emerged from a tent but seeing the assault was over, ducked back inside. The older Chinese spoke to Eli.

At first Eli couldn't hear what he was saying. He felt like he was under water. His hearing returned in a rush.

"Are you all right," the man asked. "Can you hear me?"

Eli nodded. He was shaken.

Relief washed over the older man's face. He held out his hand. "I'm Professor Eng. I'm in charge of the dig here. You must be Eli Skofield, Pete's friend." They shook hands. "Pete tells me you're interested in our mummies?"

"I saw them at the Bowers Museum."

"And you wish to visit the original site."

"Yes."

Professor Eng looked skeptical. "It's desert. What do you hope to see?"

Eli was prepared. "I thought I'd do a paper on the region at the time the mummies first arrived."

"You're not here to spy on us by any chance," Professor Eng laughed.

"Spy?"

"I'm joking of course." He was suddenly all smiles. "You've come so far. I can tell you are an enthusiast. The mummies are beautiful and so intriguing, are they not?"

"They are," Eli agreed.

"Come on," Pete said, "You're bunking with me."

Eli noted a tent with three guards around it.

"What's in there?"

"Artifacts," Pete said shortly.

The inside of their tent was a little cooler and somewhat spartan, containing a duffle bag with clothes tumbling out, a table with an oil lamp, a thick, black notebook, one chair, and an unmade bed roll. Eli wiped the sweat off his forehead with his sleeve.

Pete possessively snatched the notebook up. "I hope you brought warm pajamas. As hot as it is now, the nights are freezing. I'll show you around later." He left.

A servant in a turban came in with a metal basin and a large jug of water. Setting a bar of soap and a towel on the desk, he bowed and left.

Eli stripped down to his boxers. The lukewarm water felt orgasmic on his hot flesh and he even scrubbed his hair, trying to get rid of the sand and grit.

After changing into shorts, Eli went to the entrance and pulled aside the flap. A guard, six foot two Eli guessed, stood with a rifle and ammunition wrapped around his broad chest. When Eli tried to go past, the guard stepped in front of him, blocking his way. The guard then glared at him and pointed to the tent. Eli tried the few words in Arabic and Chinese he knew but they had no effect. Frustrated, he was about to go back inside when he heard shouting.

A teenage boy rushed out of the artifacts tent. A guard tried to stop him. The boy jumped him. Despite his size, he overpowered the guard, knocking him down and tearing chunks out of his neck with his teeth. The man gushed blood and screamed. The other guards were also screaming in their native tongues, slamming the boy with their rifle butts, but he wouldn't let go.

Professor Eng, Pete, and the two other Europeans ran out of the tent. The Professor held an old fashioned .45 and shot the boy in the head three times. He fell back and one of the guards, using a scimitar, cut off his head.

Eli stood frozen, shocked at the violence. The guard shoved him back inside the tent. He heard a second shot.

A few minutes later Professor Eng entered.

"I apologize for the unpleasantness you witnessed."

"Unpleasantness! A boy was killed and beheaded."

"Poor Ali was one of our assistants. A dog bit him and he

contracted rabies. We didn't realize the dog was rabid until it was too late. He was lost to reason. If he lived, he would have infected all of us."

"Was it necessary to remove his head?"

"Superstition. The guards believed the boy had a demon inside. I don't condone it but without the guards, we would be vulnerable to attacks."

Eli glanced at the guard outside. "Am I a prisoner?"

"Of course not. What an idea," Professor Eng chuckled. "Unfortunately, because of the attacks, it's necessary to have either myself or Pete escort you around camp." Looking at his watch he added, "It's almost time for supper." Withdrawing from his pocket a pair of brand new earplugs still in plastic he offered them to Eli. "Wear these when you sleep. Make sure they fit in the ear properly. It's essential if you wish to get a good night's rest."

"Pete told me about the wind. I thought it was a joke."

"It's no joke, Mr. Skofield. If you do not promise to follow the rules I cannot be responsible for your life."

"Fine," Eli said shortly. He refrained from saying there was nothing supernatural about wind.

"Excellent." Professor Eng beamed, leading him to the dining tent.

Supper consisted of platefuls of rice pilaf with a healthy helping of mutton dripping with fat, a traditional Uighur dish washed down with tepid beers. For desert, they ate giegao, a nougat made from nuts, candied fruits, flour and corn syrup

Eli was introduced to the other members of the team. The stocky, red-faced German geneticist named Dieter put away a half dozen beers with little effect and laughed loudly at his own bad jokes. Next to Eli sat Dr. Hunt, a middle aged man whose eyes were puffy with dark circles and who didn't say much.

Pete drank almost as much beer as Dieter and told amusing stories about previous digs. No one mentioned the boy, the wounded man, or their work. Professor Eng was unfailingly polite to everyone and promised to show Eli some Roman coins he'd uncovered.

The wind picked up and an unearthly moan reverberated around camp. All conversation ceased.

Professor Eng stood up. "It's late," he announced. Everyone rose and went to their tents like robots. The servants cleaned up and vanished.

When Eli stepped out, the sky was purple and it was twilight. The temperature had dropped considerably and he shivered. Professor Eng accompanied Eli and Pete part of the way.

"Tomorrow whenever you get up, a camel will take you to the Small River Cemetery," he informed Eli. "Cars can't make it."

"How's the guy who was attacked?"

"His wounds were severe. I'm afraid he didn't make it. Goodnight, Mr. Skofield."

Eli felt a chill that had nothing to do with the drop in temperature. He glanced at the artifacts tent as they passed, recalling the second shot.

In their tent, Eli faced Pete. "Cutting that boy's head off was pretty extreme."

Pete shrugged. "Rabies isn't fully understood out here."

"Won't his grisly death bring the authorities down on you?"

Pete shrugged. "We brought Ali with us. He has no close family ties."

Repulsed by Pete's callus attitude, Eli added, "The guard the boy attacked didn't have to die. There are treatments for early stages of rabies."

"His artery was severed. He was dead before he reached the medical tent."

"Jesus!" Eli shuddered at the image of the boy driven mad by rabies severing a man's artery with his teeth.

Pete grabbed his notebook. He was angry. "It was a hell of a setback."

"A setback! Nice. Very compassionate."

"Our work is at a critical stage." Pete looked like he wanted to say more but stuffed his earplugs in and stared at Eli. When Eli didn't do likewise, he shouted, "Put the God damn things in."

"Relax, man." Eli obeyed but vowed to leave as soon as he'd been to the Small River site.

Eli overslept, only having time for some warm naan bread dipped in milk before he was led to a camel and hoisted up into the saddle.

Two armed guides accompanied him.

There were no more attacks but by the time they arrived at their destination, Eli was eager to get off the smelly camel. He wasn't paying attention and the beast swatted him across the face with its tufted tail. It stung and he nearly lost his balance. The guides laughed and the camel smirked as if to say, "*Take that foreign devil.*"

Eli took a long swig of water. He blinked against a relentless, blazing sun. Walking over to the dried up riverbed, he looked over miles of broiling sand dunes, recalling the erotic dream that lured him all the way to China.

The guards squatted by the camels. They were looking at him and laughing. They probably thought he was nuts. Maybe he was.

Sitting down, Eli closed his eyes and tried to imagine what it must have been like when the rivers and lake were full of fish and there were forests of Poplar trees, vegetation, and wild animals stopping at the lake to drink.

A warm breeze rifled his hair. It felt like the caress of a woman. The sun beat down. The heat made him drowsy. Eli smiled as the image of the woman in his dreams appeared. Her face was covered with the strange tattoos but it didn't take away from her beauty. Eli named her Iona.

In his daydream, Iona sat down beside him and told him about her people's long journey to China. Her voice was musical and mesmerizing and he smiled as the vivid fantasy unfolded.

"We were once a powerful race and feared by all. Forests and mountains with rivers and lakes belonged to us. Our enemies united and hunted us down. We could never stay long in one place so we traveled far until we reached this place. The land was dying. Our enemies outnumbered us. They drove us to our final sleep." Her voice was bitter. "But you are here. You will help us."

In Eli's imagination she leaned over and kissed him and he groaned. The kiss stirred him. It felt so real.

A camel snorted and Eli felt someone roughly shake him. He opened his eyes and stood up embarrassed. Time had passed. The sun was fading.

"We go back now," the guide said. "Storm comes."

By the time Eli arrived back at camp, it was late. He must have sat by the riverbed fantasizing about a woman who never existed for a couple of hours. The sun was strong and he neglected to put on UV protection before he left. Thankfully he wore long pants and remembered to wear a hat. Any exposed flesh was hot and tender to the touch. He was probably burnt to a crisp. Supper was handed to him to take back to his tent. It was mutton stew and naan bread.

"You've been gone a long time. Was the journey everything you hoped it would be?" Pete asked dryly as Eli entered the tent.

"A sandstorm came up and we had to leave."

"You better put something on that sunburn. It's going to be a bitch tomorrow. I have work to do but don't forget to put your earplugs in."

"I could help you catalogue the artifacts."

"No thanks."

"Why not?"

Pete hesitated. The desire to share struggled with caution. "We're on the verge of a fantastic discovery."

"Another burial site?"

"Better."

"Better how?" Eli demanded. "A tomb filled with gold and jewels like King Tut's?" he asked dryly, knowing it was unlikely.

Pete laughed. "Better. It will change the course of human destiny."

"Bullshit."

Pete smirked as he left, reminding Eli of the camel. The guard took up his position outside Eli's tent.

Eli wasn't sleepy. Pete's refusal to let him accompany him stirred his curiosity. His mysterious allegations of a fantastic discovery, combined with the boy rushing out of the heavily-guarded artifacts tent to be shot and beheaded, had all engendered in Eli a powerful desire to see what was inside.

Stuffing his flashlight in his pocket and removing a pocket knife keychain, he made a slit in the back of the tent and stepped out, grateful for the cover of darkness. The idea of an evil wind calling him to his death was ridiculous so he left the earplugs on the table.

He had to somehow reach the back of the artifacts tent without being seen. His best bet was taking cover behind the scattered sand dunes.

The wind picked up and the temperature plummeted. He should have taken a jacket but it was too late now. He was just glad he wasn't wearing shorts.

Safely reaching a medium-sized dune overlooking the artifacts tent, Eli very carefully peeked over the top. The night before he'd watched amazed as even the guards put their earplugs in. This one was smoking a cigarette. Eli ducked down and waited. The wind blew the sand down his shirt and pants. He was cold and miserable but determined to see it through.

The third time he dared to look over the top, the guard was leaning against a tent pole sound asleep. Eli's hands were numb with the cold. It was now or never. Taking out his knife, Eli passed the snoring guard, made a thin slice in the tent and looked through.

Pete, Professor Eng, Dr. Hunt and Dieter were standing around a metal table. Pete was writing in his notebook and Dr. Hunt was on the other side holding a syringe.

Frustrated at not being able to see clearly, Eli made the slit wider.

On the table was the body of a male mummy, better preserved than the ones in the Bowers Museum. He was at least six and a half feet tall with a large skull and a few strands of gold hair. His flesh had sunk in on itself. Chains were clamped around his blackened wrists. Pete was attaching medical bags of what looked like blood to lines in his arms. Laser lights crisscrossed the mummy's body from his head to his feet.

When they spoke, Eli realized none of them were wearing earplugs.

"We need another test subject," Pete muttered.

"You saw what happened to Ali." Professor Eng said.

Dieter chuckled. "I doubt anyone in camp will volunteer."

"Eli is suspicious," Pete said.

"He'll be gone soon," Professor Eng said.

"Maybe he'd like to be part of our team," Dr. Hunt suggested. "We could use another assistant, someone who understands what we're trying to accomplish."

"Eli never strays from the straight and narrow," Pete said contemptuously. "He'll bring the authorities down on us." After a moment he added, "He has no family and we'll need a new test subject soon."

Outside, Eli listened, horror crawling up his spine like a snake.

Pete released the bag of blood, which sped into the body of the mummy.

To Eli's amazement and revulsion, the man's desiccated flesh filled with life as if it were an inflatable doll.

The mummy opened his eyes. They were blue.

The men watched impassively as he struggled to be free, screaming when the lasers hit his flesh, which sizzled and burned. He fell back moaning. Dieter drew blood.

Professor Eng moved closer. "You will be famous, my ancient friend. When our serum is perfected, your blood will make the human race stronger. We will be like gods. Then you can go to your final rest."

Dieter sliced away a chuck of flesh and the man screamed.

The wind picked up and Eli heard a mournful howl like that of a wolf.

"Did you hear that?" Dr. Hunt muttered.

"We must find her before anyone else does," Professor Eng said as he put his earplugs in. They all followed his example.

Eli turned away sick. Could they really have brought the dead to life? The two missing men made more sense now. They'd discovered Professor Eng's Frankenstein experiments and threatened to tell the authorities. What did they mean by *her?*

The strength of the wind almost knocked Eli down. It whistled and moaned as if it were indeed possessed of an evil spirit.

"Eli!"

Iona's voice entered Eli's mind and fired his blood, driving away all rational thought, leaving only a desire to reach her.

Shielding his eyes from the sand, Eli made his way to where the camels were kept and released one. Mounting it as if he'd done it every day of his life, he took off despite the camel's reluctance to travel at night in a storm. Shouting erupted behind him but Eli didn't hear it.

Beneath the stars with only Iona's sweet voice to guide him, Eli rode to a spot that looked no different than the rest of the desert. He disembarked and joyfully ran, stumbling and falling along the way. He finally stopped, gasping for breath.

"Where are you?" he groaned. He could see nothing but sand and stars.

The wind whipped his face, blinding him. The sand beneath suddenly collapsed. Eli fell into a deep hole, losing his glasses and breaking the spell.

Standing up, a dazed Eli felt around on the ground for his glasses. They were cracked but he put them on anyway and removed his flashlight. He aimed the beam around. Everywhere was broken pottery, carvings and lacquer ware as if grave robbers had been there long ago but left in haste.

"Eli!"

Shaking with terror and a feeling of dread, Eli shone his light in the back where a half opened, stone sarcophagus rested. He shuddered. While Eli's secret pleasure was watching horror flicks, he was a rational scientist. The voice was in his imagination. He moved closer.

Carved all around the stone coffin were faces of demons with fangs. The demons' eyes were rubies and glowed evilly in the flashlight. Overcome with abject fear, Eli turned and ran back. Scrambling, he tried to climb out of the hole but it was deep and there was nothing to hold onto. He kept falling back.

"Don't be frightened."

The voice was haunting, chilling yet compelling. Returning to the sarcophagus, a trembling Eli glanced inside.

The desiccated remains of a very tall woman lay in the coffin. She wore a beaded skirt. Her face was covered by a gold mask carved into the hideous visage of a demon. A few remnants of reddish gold hair peeked out of the top of the mask. A large, wooden phallus rested on her chest and beside her were dozens of skulls.

Eli stepped back as a blood curdling terror gripped him.

Iona's voice was clear in his mind. "You know what to do." The words acted like a drug, calming, reassuring him. With trembling hands Eli removed the mask. Underneath was a large skull.

His will was hers. Eli used the knife to cut his finger and held it over the woman's face.

As soon as the blood touched her mouth, her bones took on a little flesh and began to fill out like the man in the tent.

"More," the voice demanded.

Eli made several more cuts, each one deeper then the next, until the hollows that were the woman's eye sockets filled and her slanted, blue eyes opened. He stared at her, his heart beating wildly from a mix of desire and fear. She was so beautiful. Her lips were pink and full, her cheekbones high, her reddish gold hair now long and thick and entwined with shells.

She sat up and smiled, exposing sharp fangs.

Abject terror broke through the spell. Eli tried to run. In a flash Iona stood before him. Her eyes shone like sapphires. Pulling him to her with strong hands, Iona removed his glasses, crushing them.

Running a graceful finger across his lips, she said, "Your people want immortality. We shall give it to them."

Bending, Iona sank her fangs deep into Eli's neck. He cried out but after the first sharp, savage pain, his fear dissipated as his life drained away.

MUMMY CHIPS

GREGORY L. NORRIS

For nearly two weeks, they kept the creature chained upright inside a refrigerator, one of three high-end restaurant models that blended seamlessly into the acre of cherry cabinets. Three hours before the party guests were expected, Vivianna helped the caterer transfer it onto a length of wooden cutting board, and her sympathy for the creature grew along with her hatred of Gretchen, the rich witch behind the night's gathering.

Wretchin, as Viv called her employer behind her back, had made regular visits to gawk at or taunt the creature since its arrival in a museum van twelve days earlier. The thing continued to struggle against its bindings and a low, throaty moan slithered through the air, a sound felt more than actually heard. Those sobs rose whenever the caterer, a sweaty man with orange hair who'd once appeared on a short-lived reality TV cooking show, hacked off more of its desiccated body. The first tray pass had required taking its lower right leg, halfway to the knee.

No, Viv's inner voice screamed, it wasn't a creature but had once been a woman a very long time ago. And not simply any woman, but a bona fide queen in the day. Or the century. Nepathera, whose remains had gone into a secret burial chamber beneath the pyramids of Egypt, fixed Viv with a pleading, eyeless stare. Like the soft sobs, the sensation of the dead woman's gaze registered in a chill gossiping in whispers across her arms. Gooseflesh rose in response. Viv made the sign of the cross and covered her heart with her hand. The caterer, Chef Mario Minaude, chopped.

Wretchin stormed into the kitchen, reeking of expensive perfume that struck Viv's nostrils like the bitter edge of embalming fluid. If not for the wearer herself, she might have looked chic in her overpriced designer original—a Johnny Van Valkenburg, the witch had made sure to point out to every soul unlucky enough to be present in the west penthouse of the Blayne Building that night, Nepathera included. A frigid smirk spread across Wretchin's thin, sharp lips. She leaned over Minaude's shoulder.

"And how are we, my dear?"

"We are fine, Gretchen."

Wretchin spanked the caterer's enormous ass. "I meant my lovely appetizer here, which is destined to make me the talk of this town—and every other town that matters before the night is through."

Minaude ceased slicing. "I think you are a genius."

"And I agree with you," Wretchin said.

Viv resisted the urge to gag.

"This is greater than fugu fish, in which the dinner can kill the diner," Minaude rambled after he resumed his butchering. "More impressive than glacial ice, so old and harvested from such depths that the pressure has squeezed out most of the air, turning it cobalt blue in color…at a very hefty price."

"You flatter me."

"I meant to. I mean, *Gretchen*…the chance to prepare and serve something so unique! This is a once-in-a-lifetime culinary experience."

Wretchin's smug grin widened. She snapped her fingers at both Viv and the caterer. "Hurry, my guests are due to arrive. Get moving. More chips for the trays, pronto!"

Viv watched as Minaude arranged crispy wedges of Nepathera across sterling serving trays, adding crystal dipping bowls with garlic-stinking gremoulade, honey, and mint jam, plump strawberries, and colorful orchid flowers as decorative garnish.

The usual delicacies would follow the tray passes: lollypop lamb chops, baby quiche, crudités, crab cakes, and crystal flutes filled with bubble water. But the star of this debauched society party would be the *amuse* squirming, sobbing, beneath the caterer's blade.

"You're sure she can't harm me?" Wretchin had asked.

Doubled over the toilet, vomiting up the last of what remained in her stomach, Viv recalled that Minaude had shaken his head, indicating the strands of lapis lazuli stones, brilliant blue, wrapped around the ancient woman's bandaged wrists.

"Not as long as those chains stay on. Don't remove them on pain of death. Or worse."

Viv remembered how Wretchin had leaned over the dead woman, a devious smile on her face. That scared Viv worse than the image of the mummified queen, roused from her thousands-year slumber by a modern day monster with sinister intentions. Wretchin caressed the woman's cheek, the dry rustle of bandages slithering through the kitchen with its restaurant-quality appliances and fortune in gourmet upgrades.

"There, there my dear," Wretchin said.

The dead queen sobbed. Viv heard it quite clearly. Bound by the chains of vibrating blue stones, Nepathera had cried out, seeking mercy. Wretchin stroked her cheek.

"It will all be over soon enough," Wretchin said. And then she clouted her, sending dust into a cloud around the queen's bandaged head.

In the days that followed, Wretchin delighted in torturing her new acquisition the same way she had been known to torment lobsters, crabs, and other catches of the day before the caterer dropped them into a pot of boiling water or hacked through their heads with a cleaver. Only this wasn't some clacking shellfish or squawking exotic variety of poultry; Nepathera was a queen, a woman. Had been once. Still was, after a fashion.

"Isn't this cannibalism" Viv had posed while Wretchin stabbed at the queen's hips with a sterling silver serving fork.

"No, she's a tasty snack for my guests, full of cinnamon and spices, all flaky and delicious, like baklava. The most expensive appetizer ever created! And if you ever dare to question my orders again, Viv, the next party I throw, they'll feast upon *you*."

Viv had hated the woman from the start and didn't think it possible to despise her more. But there it was, the raw, red emotion growing stronger as her stomach, already emptied, lurched again. Wretchin hadn't worked a day in her life. A decade earlier, she'd pitched a memorable hissy fit on the MTV reality show *My Spoiled Sweet Sixteen* because daddy hadn't gotten the shade of pink on her new Mercedes convertible right.

Watching the gluttony taking place had tripped Viv's gag reflex, sending her to the bathroom behind the penthouse's laundry area. Rinsing her mouth, she worried she'd never make it back through the great room, where the pigs and the sinners were chewing and slurping the pieces of human baklava, dunking them in honey, garlic-lemon puree, and mint jam. The penthouse was filled with the same Wall Street devils who'd bankrupted America, sleazy lawyers, the kinds of faux-lebrities that Warhol had predicted would enjoy brief flirtations with fame, corrupt politicians, rich and bitchy pampered housewives, and former one-hit musical wonders, most with their own shitty television shows on lower-tier cable networks. The pigs scrambled for pieces of Nepathera.

"Foreclosures keep rising, and so does our profit," a man in a suit with dead eyes and too-pretty hands said to another, bits of Nepathera's lower leg stuck to his chin. He raised a desiccated chip with a glaze of gremoulade to his mouth and crunched. "The average American family's loss is my gain."

Clutching at her stomach, Viv soldiered forward, toward the kitchen, past a tittering woman in a severe red cocktail dress.

"Of course I didn't stop to help him," Viv caught on her way by. "I didn't want his blood ruining my Fritz Dollienacke sling backs. Besides, he looked *queer*, and it's not like they're real people. Anyway, I was texting Brittany about a sale we just couldn't miss."

Viv's guts pulled into even tighter knots. She almost made it to the kitchen but an ominous flutter of black rolled in front of her. A living storm cloud. Wretchin.

"Where have you been?"

Viv feigned a smile. "Cleaning up after one of your guests."

Guests, thought Viv. She exhaled loudly. Arms dealer and assholes, each and every one.

The lie seemed to work. Though her body language suggested she wasn't entirely convinced, Wretchin said, "More chips, now. More chips for my guests!"

Viv scurried around Wretchin. Over her shoulder, she heard, "Oh, Gretchen, this is extreme eating at its finest!"

"Better than the slop Sam Thurston over there trotted out last week."

"That was certified endangered cuisine, and you didn't bitch about it when you were shoveling it down your yap. Still, I have to agree—this really does taste like pastry."

"Fabulous party, Gretch!"

Viv pushed through the kitchen's swinging door and was greeted by the sad, doomed moans of the dead queen, the loud crunching chops and slices of the caterer's blade, and snapped.

Since the queen's arrival, Viv had heard her sobs and wondered if any of those doing such utter vicious harm had also. If so, it was obvious they didn't care. The queen sobbed. While Minaude cut and Wretchin slapped, Nepathera had pleaded, seeking mercy and finding none, but not giving up hope.

Stockholm Syndrome, thought Viv. The poor ancient thing had become psychologically dependant upon her abductors, only the rest of the gang of deep pocket thugs were beyond compassion. Viv had felt the queen's plaintive moans; worse, she'd watched as the pigs outside devoured the crust of her dehydrated flesh, embalming spices, and bandages.

"Hand me that tray," Minaude said, flicking pudgy fingers that were coated in flecks of a yellow substance that looked like masking tape—more of Nepathera, Viv guessed.

She picked up the platter and struck the caterer over the head with it. Minaude went partway down. He called her an unflattering name for a woman's most sacred flesh and started to rise up, so she grabbed a water pitcher off the counter and clubbed him again. Minaude slumped to the floor in an undignified tangle of limbs, sloshing ice water and cubes, and chunks of mummified human flesh. A terrible silence settled over the kitchen in the wake of the clangs and clatters. There was no telling how quickly Wretchin would tire of waiting for the next tray pass to commence without strong-arming the process along, or some snockered Washington lobbyist staggered in, intending to insert his very much alive, throbbing pink meat-missile into the dead queen's cavities, as more than one male guest had promised. Viv's heart galloped.

Nepathera sobbed and struggled against her lapis bindings. Viv approached the head of the carving board, only a body length away from the pile of blubber and red hair at the base of the counter.

"I'm so sorry for what they've done to you, Your Highness," she said. "If I could go back in time, somehow stop them…"

She inched her eyes toward the ragged, dusty stump with its caramel-candy center of off-white where leg bone protruded out of shrunken bandage and rawhide flesh. Her gaze dipped back up to the dusty hollows of Nepathera's eyes, which were surprisingly easier to face.

"So sorry, Majesty."

The dead woman briefly ceased her struggle, and Viv experienced again the sense of intimacy, dependence, even adoration for the queen's kidnappers. Viv, who'd taken a year of Psych before landing this job to pay bills and getting sucked into Wretchin's high society, low class world, accessed a few of those memory nuggets: *paradoxical psychological phenomenon coined after an infamous robbery case in Stockholm in which bank employees bonded with their captors and even defended them following their release.* It struck her that she, too, had fallen under a similar spell; working for Wretchin, she'd come to confuse the moments of non-abuse for kindness.

"I'm not responsible for you being here and what they've done to you," Viv blathered. "But you probably know that. You're a goddamn queen, certified royalty. I'm just…"

Her gaze spiraled deeper into the queen's vacant sockets, the dead woman's eyes long gone, her brain, guts, and who knew what else yanked out, scooped by the handfuls, and dumped into canopic jars millennia earlier. But there was a spark of warm emotion in the hollows, perhaps an understanding passing between them, telegraphed on Nepathera's low wails.

Viv reached for the strands of lapis and unhooked them from around the queen's closest arm. Vibrations shuddered up her wrists, electric and unpleasant, the phantom chill of bugs walking unexpectedly over bare flesh. Viv shivered. A sour taste of lemon ignited at the back of her throat and over her tongue. The magic was ugly stuff, wretched. *Wretchin'*, which was what Viv wanted to do again. Vomit up the foul air and particles of evil she had breathed into her body all night as a result of being near these wretched people.

She unhooked the queen's other arm. The mummy's bony hands, now freed, reached toward Viv's cheeks. The connection was brief but not unpleasant. Then Nepathera's fingers scrambled toward her own face. A brittle crunching sound, like branches or stalks of celery being snapped in half, croaked through the air. *Bone*, thought Viv, her stomach twisting tighter.

Nepathera's unhinged jaw clicked open, releasing a small cascade of sand. Something moved around inside the grains, dislodging more as it skittered, flicking its legs. A clot of sand and skin dropped out, revealing what was hidden behind the crust: a giant beetle, golden in color. A scarab, said the voice in Viv's racing thoughts. Fear pulsed through her insides, sudden and cramping. She had to pee and worried she might, right then and there.

The scarab clicked and turned about, showing Viv its abdomen. It burrowed into the queen's throat and out of sight, only to reappear in a series of puffs and pulses, throat to chest, its activity lending Nepathera's body the illusion of drawing in breath. Chest to abdomen, it detoured toward the thigh, then to the knee and missing section of leg that the monsters beyond the kitchen door had devoured.

Dust and sand tumbled out of the gap and the scarab's flicking feelers made a hasty appearance as it worked ancient knowledge and attended to its mistress. Another crunch shuddered through the kitchen and then a length of leg bone jutted forward, extending out from the amputation. Five little burs formed on its tip. The burs swelled, becoming toes. Dusty hide coalesced around the bones. Within a minute's time, the leg was again whole, its resurrection choreographed to a hideous croaking noise that unleashed goose bumps across Viv's arms and caused her to let go and wet herself.

Nepathera cast both legs over the edge of the counter and stepped onto the floor, straightening amid a cacophony of popping knuckles and joints.

Viv's paralysis broke. She dropped beside Minaude, her head bowed. "Your Highness."

Nepathera placed bony fingers on Viv's shoulder. The dead queen's sobs evaporated completely. So did Viv's fear that there might be blind vengeance doled out against her. Nepathera caressed Viv's cheek, and no stinging slap followed.

The relief was short-lived. "What the fuck is going on here?" Wretchin barked.

Viv rose and turned. Wretchin stood at the kitchen door, rage written in red strokes across her throat, cheeks, and forehead.

"What the fuck did you do? You let her go?"

Wretchin made a move toward Viv, the murderous intention clear in her eyes but her own life's jeopardy not. Nepathera surged toward Wretchin and seized hold of the other woman's head. The two faced off. Wretchin screamed a wild animal sound, until her head caved in between Nepathera's hands and the peal shorted out. Blood spilled across the Von Valkenburg original. Nepathera gave a tug and the flattened halves of Wretchin's head separated off her shoulders.

Viv blinked. The animated collection of bandages, bones, and dust was gone. In its place was a magnificent woman with emerald gemstone eyes and bronze skin dressed in diaphanous desert garb, spotless white flecked with jewels and strands of gold chain. Only the grisly image of Wretchin's head in the woman's hands connected the two extremes.

The woman smiled and nodded. "The slave who freed Queen Nepathera is now herself also freed."

Nepathera dropped Wretchin's head and continued on through the kitchen door, into the party beyond. A long moment later, the screams began.

SYMPHONY OF THE ANCIENT GODS

T.G. ARSENAULT

In a town where people walking the streets were rarely spotted, Angus Chatham clutched a bottle of whiskey in one hand and a photo of his late wife in another, contemplating his future, the sun yet to rise over his failing Montana crops. Inside a small one-bedroom hovel, he brooded for another day.

Sweat and other stains better left unnamed covered every inch of cloth that stuck to his skin. He reeked from the knee-high striped tube socks to the Montana Grizzlies tank top with both 'Z's worn away to only horizontal lines. Residual alcohol seeped through his pores, exuding an odor akin to stale urine, a smell as numb to him as the sharp tang of the mold spewing from the walls.

In between sips or gulps, Angus placed the bottle down with a shaky hand then flattened his hair, starting with a sweaty palm to his clammy forehead and moving backward. Thinning gray and white strands surrendered like fallen soldiers against his scalp. He let the tears fall unhindered, needing the release as his chest hitched with congested sobs. Snot ran free, reaching his upper lip. Sometimes, he'd cover one nostril and shoot the contents of the other into the cold fireplace before picking up the bottle again.

He wiped away a drop of whiskey from the corner of his mouth just as a knock on the door lifted his head in a lazy wobble on the skinny stalk of his neck. His eyes blinked hard and tried to focus through a haze he always struggled to break through before deciding to rise from his chair with unsteady steps and a favored tilt to the right.

The knock came again, louder, and more insistent with a *rap rap rap,* the wood seeming to split within its rotting frame. Angus sought balance against the fireplace mantel, grumbling a slur of discontent as he weaved a path toward the front door. Though the sweltering heat rained perspiration into his eyes, an arctic blast plunged icy daggers into his bones when he opened the door with just enough space to see through.

The stone-like expressions of the two individuals on the other side of a tarnished brass chain—mouths squeezed into slits; jaws clenched tight enough to see their temples pulse—launched an irrepressible shiver. Angus placed his drunken weight against the doorknob, refusing to believe he was terrified of the strangers standing on the porch, staring from behind mirrored sunglasses. Simply holding himself up was all, or so he wanted to think.

Sobriety came with a painful swallow.

They could have been twins. As if they had been run through an assembly line, the same fine threads could have been used to weave the suits they were wearing. Identical shoes, probably cut from the same side of cattle, shone with a blinding gloss at the tips and heels. Bolo ties were slipped snug under pressed white collars, fastened with oval obsidian medallions. They even had the same lapel pins displaying a symbol he had never seen before. Looked like a glaring eyeball with a long tongue unfurling below its lid.

Weird, he thought.

Stranger still was the way the two stayed in place on the porch. Somehow, they filled every inch of empty space in the shack he lived in with a loathsome film that stuck to his skin more so than the boxers clinging to the crack of his ass.

Both men held a silver suitcase in his left arm, a four-digit combo below each handle, as though they carried the launch codes for the missiles underneath the Treasure State. If Angus were lucky enough to have a missile installed on his property, he might not be in this predicament, what with the government funds it would have brought as it did for a few other successful farmers. Merv Baldinger, for one. Asshole bragged about his settlement for not one but *two* nuclear missiles tucked a hundred feet under his property, miles apart. Had the finest equipment and crops you could ask for. Not Angus, though; his tractors did little else but cough and gag and piss and shit all over the place with leaky valves.

Their right arms hung at their sides, fingers curled into loose fists. Their chests were still, as though they didn't need to draw a single breath. Maybe they just lived on the air they'd sucked from his lungs. When one of them swallowed, Angus almost slammed the door on his own face, so captivated he had leaned forward to see if he had imagined the small event.

He felt drawn into them, pulled from behind the mirrored glasses and into the orbs he knew were penetrating his brain. Without knowing he was doing so, his right hand slid the brass chain from its slide and pulled the door open. He heard the relentless creak upon hinges for the first time in a long while, so hushed was the air encompassing their arrival. Their heels didn't click on the wood floor; their arms and legs didn't swish against fabric as they took long strides into his abode. Nor did the heavy dust on the floor curl behind them as they passed.

As soon as they were in the house, cringing pains twisted in his stomach and exploded through every one of his arthritic joints. A blast of pure agony centered between both eyebrows and dug deep into his head. His knees wobbled, swayed, and then collapsed. He tilted forward, the force of his body closing the door behind them. He slumped to the floor in a fetal ball, chewing back the pain with teeth that chirped as he ground them together. The taste of blood slid down his throat as he caught the inside of a cheek.

Just as the sudden pains began to fade and he felt himself relax, two loud booms shattered the air as both briefcases slammed onto the kitchen table. Rigid with tension, he managed a peek from under one arm, daring not to move an inch.

As if they knew he was looking, both men accomplished slow synchronous facing movements—worthy of any soldier's respect—to either side of the table, coming to rest behind it with hands clasped across their waists. Waiting. For him.

Knuckles scraping the wood floor, Angus crawled a few paces serenaded by the creaks and pops of aging bones. Pulsing aches riddled every joint. Exhausted, he dug deep for the energy to stand upright. His toes were last to drag upon the floor, one sock getting caught on a loose splinter of wood and coming off as he stepped up on its shaky leg. Swaying upon knees that fought to hold his weight, Angus raised his head and met their icy, robotic stares.

An intense moment of anticipation spread the distance between them across the table, as though the suitcases were a main course ready to be served at the appropriate moment. Fearful, yet an intense curiosity gnawing just beneath his chilled flesh, Angus gawked at his two guests, wishing something, *anything* would happen. Anything to unravel the knot that coiled in the nauseous pit of his stomach.

A slight twitch came from the man on the left, almost imperceptible as a single hair fell out of place and across his gleaming forehead. But it was enough for Angus to swallow against the broken glass that seemed to coat his throat, each dry shard crunching within his ears with a cacophonous rattle.

With long, manicured fingers, the same man opened the first suitcase on smooth hinges.

A brilliant shade of green filled Angus' world in stark contrast to the drab colors and stains covering his walls. The pungent smell of crisp new bills pervaded the air and drilled into his nose. Eyes wide and olfactory senses snapping to attention, he stole a deep breath. Angus took the first step forward.

When the man on the right opened the second suitcase, a musical note launched into the air. A beautiful tone twirled in the air and could have been the beginning or the end of a melody, but captured an entire symphony within its short-lived sound. His body was suddenly free of any aches and pains, flushing his system with a comfortable numbness no drug could ever compare to. He smiled, ecstatic at this ability, so unfamiliar were these muscles to be set into motion.

With the second step, he tripped over lagging feet, but the grin that revealed his yellow teeth and receding gums never left his face.

They watched, devoid of emotion, as he inched his way toward the answer to his troubles.

The farmer stumbled, but his eyes never left the suitcase full of fresh currency, still stiff from the press. His pace increased in moments, spears of hair bouncing on his scalp, knees almost clashing together, drool all but cascading from both corners of his mouth. With every step closer he raised his arms at his sides, fingers trembling, reaching.

They let him peruse the contents—the bills so much less important—even remove a stack and place it to his nose, chest expanding with a heavy, quivering inhalation. Then another. With straight-line grins, they waited with the patience of centuries. Luring, expecting. *Knowing.* Refusal was not even an option for Mr. Chatham, the first of their customers. The first of a select few, but they were all the same: destitute, hollow, empty of anything save misery.

The perfect candidates.

The first whiff wasn't nearly enough for him to believe. He pressed the stack of bills hard against his nose; if he could have managed to shove the whole thing inside, he would have. The scent alone was almost enough to quell the hunger boiling within him.

Ignoring their cold glares, he picked up another stack with hesitant fingers, turned it over, and flipped the edges with a thumb to fan against his face. A shiver flickered through his body as the slight draft touched droplets of sweat forming on his upper lip and brow. Only then did he let his gaze travel to the contents of the other suitcase, the musical note now in the forefront of his mind. His brows connected above the bridge of his nose and his forehead creased into canyons as he wondered where the sound had come from.

Four ceramic jars lay in the open suitcase, each one different than the next.

Ancient, was the first word that came to mind as he peered into the suitcase and at the fine layer of dust that covered them. Then at the scraps of dirty, gauze-like material that still adhered to one jar. He marveled at the designs adorning each, apparently engraved by unknown hands so long ago. A few of the etchings almost matched the symbol pinned to the men's lapels.

While the oval shape of the jars resembled similar rotund bodies, each jar was topped with a unique head. Odd looking things really, requiring more than a second glance to capture the details of their faded colors, weathered surfaces, and strange features. Lonesome hours in front of the television watching the Discovery Channel began to make sense as these jars climbed from his subconscious and into familiarity. Considering their origins required even more time to wonder why they were sitting on his kitchen table.

Each man grasped the first canopic jar with tender fingers, removing it from the suitcase and standing it upright at the far end of the table. Angus took a step backward when dust fell down the sides of the canister and the head of a jackal wobbled on its perch. Resting inside, the stomach of something older than them all was finely ground into a special concoction.

A jar displaying a baboon came next. Some of its snout was chipped away and a piece of gauzy linen clung to it as though searching for another breath from the dusty lungs inside the weathered jar.

The head of a falcon, buried within the faded turquoise stripes of a headdress was placed on the table next. It appeared to shift its gaze upward as though ready to take flight, possibly trailing the intestines that the jar contained—a ghastly kite made of papery flesh. Pale fingers rushed to keep it in place, as small vibrations shook the ceramic top.

With even more care to prevent the effigy from breaking along a seam—Imsety, the human-headed god; even the names were starting to come back to Angus—glared from the top of the last canister once released from the confines of the suitcase. Its motionless grin appeared to rise at the corners. Faded pupils emerged from the layer of dust with a sparkle that caused Angus to step back again. Something else lay hidden within that gleam of a past life, something that brought a chill to the room.

The man on the right removed the lid and placed the top carefully behind the canister. A musical note—a bass rhythm that thrummed through to the floor—issued forth from the first jar. A shadow skulked from the lip of its base then curled around its bottom as if in wait.

He repeated the process with the baboon—Hapi, who once protected the throne of Osiris, Angus remembered— and a higher note was unleashed from the jar like a call from the wild. Its shadow curled around the base then crawled up and down the sides, pulsing and frenetic, as if it couldn't stand still. Almost anxious, as though the lungs in the jar were near bursting, begging for release following a lengthy submersion.

The falcon head followed—Qebehsenuef—releasing a note akin to the ear-piercing call of its species, its shadow zipping upon black wings. Shadows cast upon the walls as it flitted up and then down before folding its wings into a circle around the jar.

Only Anubis remained, the jackal, the original god of the dead, its obsidian face as black as the rotting flesh it represented, protecting a centuries old liver inside the jar. Anticipation loomed inside the kitchen with even the coiled shadows trembling. With the removal of that jar's top, a scream wailed into the room, a mixture of pain and ecstasy. Its fluid shadow enshrouded them within sheets of darkness, leaving only the dim sparkle of mirrored sunglasses and the whites of teeth behind wicked smiles.

The combination of sounds silenced at once as the darkness receded from the corners of the room and surrounded every jar in a pool of ink-black, pulsating shadows.

In perfect harmony, both men then began to recite words only they could understand, and with each syllable brought forth by foreign tongues, the music rose in pitch and volume.

Soon, the walls of Angus Chatham's hovel began to shake.

Feet locked into place, Angus pressed his palms hard against his ears and braced himself against the possibility that the very walls of his home could come crashing down around him. He placed his feet farther apart, settling into the undulation beneath him. When the murky lighting returned inside, all motion ceased and, somehow, four shiny metal canisters now rested on the table, tucked to the sides of each jar. He didn't wonder how they got there as the sweetest of melodies, so exquisite a sound, found its way into his ears and lifted him to the tops of his toes.

With a tool resembling a large turkey baster, the suited gentleman on the left dipped the utensil into the first canister, giving the end a slow squeeze around black rubber. Dusty fibers, glowing with scintillating green particles, flowed into the clear tube, resembling miniature versions of the lightning bugs he used to catch as a child. Angus drew a nervous step forward, a profound elation seeping into his bones, his feet just skimming the dust on the floor. Mesmerized, he gazed at the particles flowing into each metal container before the lid was secured into place.

The suitcase filled with everything Angus had ever wished for fell deep into the recesses of his mind, all but forgotten, the activity being played out before him, enthralling. Something unknown to the world as he knew it captured his full attention.

Alluring. Something…so seductive.

He felt a rising in his boxers at every thought that flooded his system in silent wonder of things to follow. He shifted his position to allow himself more freedom, pride not even a consideration. In his throat and ears, a heartbeat pumped hard. He touched himself then and squeezed. In one fluid motion, he released an energy that could not be restrained any longer, and ran down his thigh in the form of hot and sticky trails. His body shook with ecstasy then sagged around bones that were strangely livid, as though a new Angus Chathum had spawned and continued to grow within molten innards. He felt taller, thinner. Stronger.

Deep breaths inside clear lungs propelled him two steps closer. He stood at the edge of the table and looked not at the two individuals behind it, but down. The music still twirled around him like a siren's call from the distant depths of clear blue waters, beckoning.

Words were unnecessary, as complete understanding came with nothing more than a glance at the contents splayed before him. Transferred from the canopic jars and placed into the small metal containers with whispers of a distant language, seeds of some sort now rested inside each. Somehow, he knew this, the melody in his head a glorious symphony of instructions. All he had to do was plant them and let them grow. Grow. *Grow!*

His head bobbed, nodding in agreement to whatever would be asked of him. There was no other choice.

They left the money in a haphazard pile on the table with a quick turn of the suitcase and packed the canopic jars back into the other, leaving the four individual metal canisters where they stood. With two simultaneous motions, both suitcases clasped shut and locked then grasped by identical left hands. Both men exited through the same door through which they had arrived, neither saying a word.

At the end of his walkway, both men stopped and turned toward him with the same nondescript expressions and then continued into the distance. They walked toward the blazing horizon, between the sunburned crops.

Angus watched until the tops of their heads glimmered above the road like a distant mirage.

When he awoke amidst the bedding of unwrapped piles of bills—one bill stuck to the side of a cheek with a dried patch of spit—Angus yawned, stretched, scratched his balls. He had never felt so good. So full of energy that his skin seemed to have stretched with it, now lining his bones with taut, growing muscle supporting what used to be drooping flesh. Even his senses seemed stronger as colors appeared sharper and more focused, and his nose—*Good Lord*, he didn't realize he stank so much. What felt like fur lined his entire mouth and tasted of stale whiskey in need of Listerine, maybe some peroxide.

At that moment, he knew life since his wife had passed had been a complete waste. Pissing away everything—mostly whiskey and bourbon out the end of his dick every morning in noxious yellow streams—but the simple stuff as well.

He knew *exactly* how to fix and maintain his farming equipment, but could never summon the urge, and instead just watched it rust and decay like prehistoric beasts starving in the fields. Just like he knew the trash gathered into every corner of his poor excuse of a home needed to be removed. He had grown so accustomed to the smell and the critters that sometimes crawled beneath and around the piles that he had confined them behind the sealed doors of his mind. The frantic scurry of little feet after he kicked another piece of refuse into a pile was nothing more than distant raindrops on fallen leaves.

Even the last breakfast his wife had consumed before she took her final breath on the couch was still in the back of the refrigerator, existing now in varying shades of pallid colors, beneath plastic wrap that had become part of the breakfast itself. He just couldn't get rid of it. Her fork lay in its center, a touch of lipstick on the base of its tines.

No more.

The sun had set and was rising again to greet a day with clear skies and a gentle breeze, the horizon pink on the underside of distant clouds. He stepped onto the uneven porch and took a deep breath of crisp air. A new day surrounded him with an ethereal embrace as he organized his thoughts before embarking on long overdue spring cleaning; something that had to be done before tackling a task that provided a new and *oh-so-welcome* purpose to his miserable existence on the planet.

It didn't take as long as he thought with newfound energy encapsulating every muscle, the fibers within immersing themselves into the work, relishing in the release. Within a few short hours, trash rested in heaps outside and disinfectant permeated the inside of his home. He had poured every bottle of whiskey he owned down the drain and buried them outside. Everything he needed right now rested on the kitchen table.

One phone call to the tractor supply was all he needed. Just making the call, fingers at first fumbling over the numbers, made him swell with a joy never before experienced, and amazement at how fast things could happen if you only had the money. After a few questioning looks when he produced nothing but sweet cash upon delivery, Angus had spotless and shiny equipment idling in his yard that put that fuckstick, Merv, to shame. For good measure, he even had them install a spongy-gripped steering wheel. He felt something was missing, however, and solved the dilemma by hanging a pair of fuzzy dice on the console.

Angus couldn't climb aboard fast enough. With a quick push of a button, the tractor's engine—so smooth, so *alive*—made his balls tingle.

He tilled the first row and then another, changing direction when required, led by an image branded deep into his subconscious. He smiled until his cheeks hurt, raised his face to the sky and felt the day's heat produce beads of sweat that fell as languid drops between his shoulder blades, stirring the hair on his arms.

When he caught Merv peeking from behind his pickup, no doubt perplexed about his sudden good fortune, Angus flipped a middle finger high into the air and cackled until his lungs hurt. Attention diverted, he weaved a serpentine path in the row, but didn't give a sweet shit. He sprinkled more and more seeds wherever he felt like, knew it just didn't fucking matter. The tractor turned beneath his loose hands when it knew it needed to turn.

Plant. Water. Grow.

So fucking simple.

He wondered how he ended up so fortunate when suicide was his most recent solution, a shotgun at the ready. More than a few times in recent months, the taste of Hoppes oil had seeped into his tongue while a big toe trembled on the trigger. Pulled from the abysmal depths of depression by something he still could not fathom, but dared not question. His world now existed in brilliant shades of green and the canisters resting between his legs, one already empty, the silver sheen on its sides quickly fading into a tarnished shade. The lid itself fell away in flaky fragments. Angus discarded it and opened the next canister.

Destiny.

He loved the sound of the word and the music that still reverberated through his gray matter, notes bouncing off nerves and synapses with pleasant rings that dug ever deeper, into his inner being. Like the flicker of a streetlight before illuminating, the notes sparked then thrummed as one, creating a commanding sensation that demanded attention. The second, third, and fourth canisters followed into more rows that were, for the most part, even.

As the sun began its descent, he marveled at the fresh dirt spilled over the surface in moist clumps. With a swelling of pride that squared his shoulders, he admired the pattern that mimicked the unfurling pins he saw on lapels a short while ago, a design delivered to him with musical tones. The smell of sweat enlivened his senses like a good day's work, unlike the alcohol-reeking poison that exuded from his body in thick, pungent waves most days.

Smells of earth and sweat; hints of a future where before there was none.

Angus took off his faded Broncos hat, wiped his brow with the back of a forearm, and smiled. A cold iced-tea, a shower, and a nap waited inside.

Angus slept with a clear mind and body, relieved of all tension and toxins, smelling of lavender and Old Spice. So deep in sleep that he didn't feel the god-like things invading his mind. From another time and place, they lurked among his brain cells, cutting into memories, slicing away bits and pieces of him with frenzied breeding. Their fervor burned cells away on contact, consuming, devouring. Their parasitic gene allowed them to multiply in feverish waves, sending parts of Angus to linger as dust inside the shell that surrounded his essence.

The nap on the couch absorbed the last of his day and bled into the evening with a gibbous moon shining on his face, which twitched in response to the chaotic visions playing out behind closed lids. His lips trembled, muttering things he did not hear and in a language he didn't understand. Yet he slept peacefully.

When he woke, Angus looked at a home he had almost forgotten he'd cleaned from top to bottom. Confused at the light finding its way through his blinds, he cast a glance at the clock, expecting *p.m.* to appear in the lower right-hand corner.

"Holy fuck," he said to the room, amazed at seeing the sun just climbing above the trees.

Aside from momentary confusion and a mild headache, he felt pretty good, fantastic even. With an entire day available for him to...

To do whatever the hell he wanted, he realized after looking at the bills again stacked on the kitchen table in clean, even rows. A content sigh expelled from his lungs. His pulse jackhammered with excitement, not sure what to expect, but knowing something existed outside that he just had to see. *Now.*

Still dressed, all he had to do was walk onto his porch.

The screen door slammed on his finger but Angus ignored the jolt of pain. He reached for the outside wall with a groping hand as his vision tunneled into darkness. Forcing his legs to remain upright with pure willpower alone, he drew a deep breath, letting the tunnel fade into his periphery.

He beheld the most brilliant crop that had ever sprouted from his crappy plot of land. A little odd, in germination as well as appearance, but so lush, the brilliant shades of green gleaming with moisture, the rising sun making leaves sparkle with new life.

Offering an ecstatic hoot to the farming gods, Angus leapt off the porch with the strength of someone much younger than his years and sprinted to a crop that had grown overnight to a height that had him on his tiptoes should he want to reach the very tops. But not yet. He halted his hand as it reached to touch the nearest thorny vine, inspected the stalk, turned his head sideways when he saw a vine stretch in a rhythmic pattern. Others were doing the same.

Breathing, he thought. But...

The plant's skin gleamed. Infantile skin. Beads of yellow liquid steamed in the morning air with heavy drops falling toward the root—its source. Huge leaves hung from all vines, some bigger than his arms, open and bent upward as though to catch the toxic rain. Their edges rippled and swelled as something buried just beneath the surface traveled around and around, like sine waves cruising a perimeter. With every passing, each leaf quavered on its vine and the edges curled upward a little more, like fingers twitching and grasping for purchase. Entire stalks were littered with these gigantic leaves, to the tops, where—

"Well, I'll be a monkey's fucking uncle," he said, exasperated, removing his cap and preventing the glare from the blinding sun.

At the top of the stalks, a conglomeration of congested vines, leaves, and thorns almost formed a face within an abstract design. One that looked more alien than earthbound, but the structure was still there. Eyes, ears, nose...and a wicked mouth filled with thorns.

A shiver flooded his body as one top bent over—*wind...had to be the wind!*—and seemed to peer at him.

Two brilliant red flowers in the shape of a star had grown equidistant from each other and appeared to scowl down at him, turning a shade darker as they were tucked in shadow. The weave-work of vines opened a little wider, revealing even more teeth-like thorns.

A drop fell away from its open maw and landed on his forehead.

Angus heard the sizzle of his skin before he felt the pain, shock at first holding his feet in place. He shook his head, jumped away and smacked at his brow as though an ember had glued to his skin.

God, it burns!

Shrieking, turning in circles as his flesh seemed to catch fire, he sent hard slaps against his forehead with both hands, squeals pumping from his throat, dust kicking up around his feet in small clouds.

He ran to the house, tripping over the first step of the porch, and then continued inside to bury his face under the kitchen faucet. The screen door slammed against its frame just as the water started flowing.

Though cold water soothed the immediate burn, his forehead thudded with a pulse of its own. Using the reflection from a mirror he hadn't taken down since his wife's feeble attempt at Feng Shui, he dabbed around the swollen redness, outlining a symbol stark against his tanned hide.

That same unfurling eye.
Marked.

Shotgun resting on his lap, Angus sat by the window, where he had perched himself when the first notes cut into the air and dusk encroached. Aloe dried on his forehead and every few minutes he would touch the burn then apply more after the previous coat had dried into sticky blotches.

The music continued to play, the volume so high the floorboards beneath his feet sent vibrations through his core and made his cock stand upright. Voices were masked within these notes, but he heard them just fine. A luring melody pulled him toward the front door with its subtle commands. But he wouldn't be fooled. A quick slash from his straight-razor across his forearm gave him something else to focus on. He let it bleed, dripping onto the shotgun, his lap, the floor. And the shadows continue to grow.

His fireplace burned with bills that curled, ignited, and turned to ash.

Merv was the first person he saw, prefaced by a long shadow. Angus's first instinct was to aim the shotgun at the man's head—so swollen with conceit his eyes appeared to bulge—and pull the trigger. Damn that fucker for trespassing on his property.

Maybe he's jealous, he thought. Yes, maybe that prick just came to wallow in jealousy.

Angus smiled.

He got as far as raising the shotgun to his shoulder, sights on the target—how could he miss that *giant* head?—when he hesitated. Placed it back onto his lap, thumb caressing the hammer in slow circles.

Merv's distended eyes were blank and twinkling with the last of the sun's rays. His mouth hung open as he shuffled forward. An uncomfortable sorrow grew within Angus at the sight of him. *God* he hated that bastard! But something was happening that went beyond neighborly spats. Almost.

Merv teetered unbalanced as his toes caught an uneven patch of earth. He continued forward with jerky paces, heading for the new crops, and disappeared behind the first row. The entire crop swooned at his arrival, the stalks leaning over, toward the exact spot Angus last saw the man. Leaves shook on vines and, as one, erupted into a tumultuous rustling.

Merv's name lingered on the end of his tongue. As hard as he tried to form the shape of the word with his lips, he couldn't bring himself to mumble never mind shout or scream a warning. The music pulled at his feet with invisible strings, calling to him from within a piercing crescendo. A longing for the crop's embrace, a desire to wrap himself inside the emerald sheen of its vines, brought tears to his eyes.

In the midst of this raucous, a piercing scream briefly rose but was choked away at its peak. The stalks again straightened, and the music grew impossibly louder.

A second individual appeared. Then a third.

Emily Twitchell, the cashier at Buttrey's—he'd known her since grade school. She always had trouble scanning his items without casting blatant looks elsewhere, unable to meet his gaze. A nightgown revealed more than he cared to see and rollers clung in disarray in her hair. The same distant stare as on Mel peered out from a mask of green mud. Barefoot, she entered the crop. Close behind, Freddy Simmons stumbled like the drunk he was, a bottle still clutched in his hand. Angus licked his lips until the bottle vanished along with its owner.

From the shadows, the rest of the town followed—all fifty or so of them in total—some bumping into each other, heads cocked to one side or the other as though trying to focus on a beacon with ears pointed in different directions. But the music was everywhere, inside them all, and drew them forward.

He knew he should act—yell, scream, something—to warn them. But a dubious pleasure coursed through him born from the way they had ignored him since his wife's passing. Year after year of the same, without even a simple nod as he walked past neighbors on the street and in the grocery store, as though he didn't exist at all. Every one of them could suck on the hind tit of one of Richard Bailey's hogs as far as he was concerned.

The last of the town's inhabitants disappeared, and the music drowned out his thoughts and filled his head with his own screams.

Oh, God, the voices!

The pull was almost unbearable, wrenching at his resolve to stand fast, the commands powerful. His mouth grew slack, his body numb, surreal with its intoxication.

The shotgun fell to the floor as he rose.

The muscles in his legs expanded and contracted as they pushed him toward the door. He tried to fight it, hands clamped over ears, but the raucous din powered through and into him in painful waves.

Out the door.

Onto the porch.

Down the rickety stairs.

He found the straight-razor from his back pocket and slashed again, harder this time. Blood spilled onto the ground and his brain became less fuzzy, the music falling to muted levels, the voices restrained to whispers.

Something else was happening, exposed in the glowing arc of his porch light.

The crop was now lower than he was tall, wilting before his eyes. Completely curled and wrapped tightly around whatever was inside, leaves fell to the ground with gentle thuds, some falling flat and empty, others stretching against green fibers. Every stalk had drooped to a tangle of leaves and vines. All save one.

He needed answers; of his own volition, he walked ahead with uncertain steps.

Angus entered the dying crop, stepped over tangled vines, then climbed atop a pile of leaves. Some crunched beneath his feet, while others oozed from splitting sides. Angus picked up the largest leaf he could find, this one much lighter than it appeared. Turned it over within his hands, examining the almost weightless creation.

He struggled to uncurl the leaf, its contents so large the green surface split down the middle like the spiny burr of a chestnut before it fell to the earth. He poked below the thin surface with a fingernail and pried an edge away. After a few more yanks and pulls, his chin unhinged to meet his chest.

He stared at a mouth frozen into a silent circle, flesh and eyes shriveled into yellowed, papery skin, and at the mummified face of Merv Baldinger.

Angus heard the patter of his blood upon the leaves below and almost swooned. His stomach plummeted at the realization of what—*who*—he was stepping on.

As Merv's desiccated face fell through his fingers, something wrapped around his feet.

Angus tried in vain to crawl away, jerking his legs against thorns that had already pierced the flesh of his ankles. He raked at the ground with clawed hands, fingers exposing the small pile of bottles he had hoped to never see again. One still had at least a sip of sweet, golden elixir resting at the bottom. He clutched it as his body scraped against the earth, pulled and dragged by the tethers of ancient gods.

He slammed the bottle into his mouth, knocking out a tooth. The fluid burned his throat. Continuing to drink would have been a much safer alternative, Angus chuckled before bursting into fits of psychotic laughter.

Vines coiled around his thighs, sliced into his flesh with serrated, thorny teeth, and pulled. Hard. They climbed his torso and burrowed into his throat, scraping the insides raw.

A probing tentacle buried its way deep into Angus' guts.

And into his soul.

A trial.

A test of new possibilities existed in complete success with the ravenous crop allowed to propagate upon Angus Chatham's land. A crop presently satiated and disintegrating beneath the moon and into the finest of particles with the last of its victims. Come morning, only a sunburned plot of land would exist once again. An entire community withered to nothing more than dusty flesh scattered on the breeze.

The perfect weapon.

Across the borders of countries and oceans, an entire civilization awaited its demise.

DEAD FOR SUPPER

ERIC S. BROWN

"Jeb," Zeke tried to get his brother's attention but it was intensely focused on the road ahead of them. The downpour had came out of nowhere, blotting out the last rays of the twilight sun. The rain fell in waves, washing over the truck's front window faster than the wipers could shove it aside. This road was supposed to be a short cut according to the gas station attendant they'd hassled an hour or so back. They were on a tight schedule with this run. The museum that hired their fledgling company, mostly because they were cheaper than a lot of others when it came to this kind of gig, would raise holy Hell if its new prize exhibit wasn't there on time. Zeke knew they were running behind but that was no big deal. They could make up time on the interstate if forced too, even if they risked a ticket. The truck was equipped with gear to let them know if the *doughnut pigs* were on the lookout for folks speeding.

The back road had changed to from pavement to dirt and Zeke was mightily worried they were going to wreck if Jeb kept on pushing it the way he was. The truck shook and bounced as its wheels rolled over the rocks and holes beneath them. Puddles splashed, throwing even more water onto the windshield when Jeb hit them, making it impossible to see during those moments.

"Blast it, Jeb!" Zeke cried. "Pull over before you get us killed!"

"Ain't doing it," Jeb said through gritted teeth. "You might be okay with that thing we got in the back but I sure as Hell ain't. That thing's just wrong."

Zeke sighed. He could hear the heavy coffin-like box sliding around in the trailer behind them. It thumped off one wall then the other.

"Jeb, I promise you, if you don't wreck us, you're going to mess up the cargo and that's an unforgivable sin bro."

The truck slowed some as Jeb let off the gas a bit. His stubbornness was waning.

"Dang it, Zeke." Jeb brought the truck to a full stop and glared over at him. "Why'd ya have to take this job anyway?"

"Because it's a job, Jeb," Zeke shook his head. "We gotta keep rolling or we'll lose the business. That museum met our price didn't they? The pay from this job will keep us going for another month at least even after expenses. That'll give me time to find us some real work."

The cargo shifted in the trailer with a dull thud.

"That thing ain't right," Jeb warned him again. "When we was loading it, I caught a whiff coming out of its box, Zeke. Don't care how long you say it's been dead, nothing in this world should smell like that."

"Ease up." Zeke reached over and placed a hand on Jeb's shoulder as if to steady him. "It's a mummy. What ya expect it to smell like? Cherry blossoms? There ain't no such thing as curses, Jeb. That's a fact."

Jeb frowned. "You believe what you want, Zeke. I'll do the same."

The rain was letting up a little though that wasn't saying a lot. It was still a hard rain with drops that didn't just fall but exploded on contact.

"That was a lot of shaking about there," Zeke pointed out. "I reckon we ought to go have a look in the back and make sure the thing's all right. Better we know it now than when we get there if it ain't."

Jeb shook his head. "Not on your life."

"Fine. Be that way," Zeke said. He opened his door and stepped out into the rain. It was cold. His flesh broke out in goosebumps as he headed for the rear of the truck. Fishing around in his pockets, he produced the key to the chain-lock that secured the doors. Lightning flashed in the sky and, for a second, Zeke thought he saw something huge and monstrous watching him from the woods. The Jester boys weren't no fools. They never left home without packing a weapon. He slid his hand inside his coat and unholstered the Jackal hidden underneath it. The Jackal was one tough pistol. The sucker was a fully automatic 9 mil. and illegal in a lot of places. Feeling its weight in his hand gave him courage.

"Who's out there?" Zeke shouted at the woods, trying to

outmatch the noise of the falling rain on the trees. No one answered him. He swept his eyes up and down the sides of the road looking for whatever it was he thought he'd seen but there was no sign of it anymore. Keeping his pistol ready, he shrugged and went back to work on opening the doors. As he did so, something inside the rear of the truck slammed into them. The impact sent the doors flying apart and him sprawling backwards onto his butt in the mud. He looked up to see King Amon towering over him. The king was out of his coffin and his bandages hung loosely over his decaying flesh.

"Holy heaven!" Zeke screamed, not believing what he was seeing. It was like something out of a bad horror film. King Amon lowered himself out of the truck to the road, the rain already soaking the cloth wrapping his body. The king made a noise like a muffled growl. Zeke stared at the red glow coming from where the king's eyes should have been and tried not to pee his pants as he brought the Jackal up. His finger squeezed the trigger and the pistol jumped in his hand as it spat a stream of rounds into the king's chest. The bullets struck home, tearing cloth and rotted flesh alike. The king didn't even stagger though. He slowly lurched his way towards Zeke.

Jeb rounded the corner of the truck, shotgun in hand. "What the Hell's going on back here?" he yelled as the king whirled on him with a speed no dead man should ever have.

Zeke saw Jeb's eyes go wide with fear as his mouth fell open in pure shock. The king grabbed hold of Jeb and pulled him close. Jeb's shotgun went flying and splashed in a nearby puddle as one of the king's hands closed over Jeb's head, caving it inward with a wet, crunching sound. Blood exploded from Jeb's eyes, ears, nose, and from where the king's fingers pressed down on it through both skin and bone. Gray brain matter slicked King Amon's fingertips. He withdrew his hand and let Jeb's corpse collapse onto the road.

"Jeb!" Zeke cried as he got to his feet.

He leveled his pistol at the king again but never got the chance to fire. Something huge that stunk as bad as the mummy came plowing out of the trees, snapping limbs and branches as it moved. The beast smashed into the king, knocking him from his feet. The beast leapt onto the mummy. King Amon's fist bashed into the beast's jaw with supernatural force. Blood flew from the beast's ruptured lower lip but it shook off the pain. Zeke watched as the hair-covered giant went into a fury driven rage. It pummeled the king's face over and over with its massive fists. When it was done, there was nothing left of King Amon's head. The beast stood. Its breath came in ragged snorts through its nostrils. Zeke backpedaled, hoping to get away before it remembered he was there. The beast's head swung around to look at him and Zeke knew he was dead. He'd seen looks like this before on rabid dogs and animals so starved they'd gone insane from hunger.

Giving it all he had, Zeke sprinted for the truck's cab, the pistol he clutched forgotten. The engine was still running. If he could get inside the truck, he might have a shot at getting the Hell out of Dodge before the beast could catch him. He threw himself into the driver's seat, his hands clamping onto the wheel, and glanced in the side mirror, wondering how he'd managed to make it. He saw that the headless body of King Amon was on its feet once more. It and the beast had their arms locked together like wrestlers, trying to tear each other to pieces. Zeke didn't really give a crap though. All he cared about was living to see the sun come up in the morning. He floored the gas. The truck fishtailed about, throwing mud with its wheels before they caught and it got moving. He didn't have a clue where the Sasquatch came from but the thing had saved his life.

To Hell with the museum, he thought. *If they want their mummy bad enough, they can come have words with Bigfoot themselves.* And it sure looked like Bigfoot was going to be having some *aged* meat for its dinner tonight.

WALKING WHITE DEATH

KAREN DENT

Thick, white density undulated through space, searching, flowing, knowing eventually it would find what it sought. Its imperative pushed the swollen mass. *Time, it was time!*

Before it could begin, it needed a host. A conduit. Something it could mold, coat with its seductive promises, and veil its eventual plans.

Pulling its massive vitality through nothingness, it used the gravitational waves of each galaxy, each planet and sun, to repel or pull it ever forward. It had an agenda. It had purpose. And it was incredibly hungry.

TV's blared about a mysterious cosmic curtain of dusty debris floating through space, close enough to possibly enter our atmosphere. Anchormen and women waxed poetic about the chance to see awe-inspiring shooting stars. The world held its collective breath, waiting, hoping to see a spectacular light show on a cool, clear October night.

It didn't disappoint. Sixty to one-hundred and twenty blazing arrows of light flashed across the northern hemisphere.

A worm, a doorway, at last!

Oddly there was one particular section of New England that was heavily dowsed with what radio stations called, "Arcs of falling luminosity."

Nearly every person in Massachusetts interviewed declared the Sox were a shoe-in to win the Championship.

"I'm telling ya, any fan worth their *beep* used their extra wishes for that." Big shit –eating grins and thumbs up abounded. "Go Sox!"

The scientific consensus on the downpour just in the New England area was, "Not to the naked eye, but there must have been a dense cluster of debris within a portion of the cloud that was caught by the earth's gravitational pull." Still it was a bit disconcerting to some who wondered.

Not long after, a dry wind swirled down dusty streets, burrowing into corners, following the cracks etched into the red brick of two and three story buildings lining East Boston. Reaching a dead end, it still whispered its song of need.

No one heard; no one listened; except CJ.

The first time she heard it, her name had been Charlotte and she was playing in the community sandbox. Her mother, Mary, hated her digging obsession, calling it a filthy, disgusting disease trap.

Since that day in the sandbox, Mary grew to loathe Charlotte. Despite her outward, over protectiveness, she realized, *something's wrong with my baby.* She was revolted by her pale lumpy body and pudgy cheeks. She could barely bring herself to touch her.

Only once did she confide in anyone. "I'm a terrible mother," she told Sofia. "Charlotte's just so…" she shivered, "*squishy.* And no matter what I do she always smells like rotting cabbage. I can never get the—" Looking up she caught Sofia's expression. *Oh my God, she thinks I'm crazy.*

Sofia had lots of experience with new mothers and some of them, like Mary, imagined things. She patted her hand. "Bambinas are supposed to be soft. And here," she got up and walked over to her own baby's crib, grabbed the Johnson and Johnson Baby Wash and powder, and brought it back. "Bathe your little girl all over with this, then lots of powder. She'll smell so good you'll want to eat her up."

"Sure, sure, you're right." She looked hard at Sofia, "You…never noticed anything wrong with Charlotte?"

Though Sofia shook her head adamantly, she had to acknowledge, if only to herself, that she, too, was repelled by Charlotte. Something was definitely off with that child, but didn't tell the mother. "No, no just your imagination. Now go and enjoy your little girl. Maybe you're sad she grows up too fast, eh?"

Mary nodded, smiled, and took Sofia's advice to heart. She washed Charlotte five to ten times a day, all the while thinking, *this is God's way of testing me. I will prove myself worthy. I will protect, care and love this child.* But no matter how hard she tried, she could never quite bring herself to hug Charlotte. She bathed, diapered, dressed and fed her; then ran to Church to pray.

Mary abhorred Charlotte's love for the sandbox. No matter how much she admonished her daughter, she would find her digging in one when her back was turned.

Charlotte didn't know why she loved the tiny oasis of sand; maybe it was the pretty music which filled her up and made her happy. In defiance of her mother's stern lectures to stay away, Charlotte would slyly watch her mother; and when her attention was distracted, she would bee-line her stubby little legs toward the enclosure to gleefully dig up the buried cigarette butts and chewed balls of gum.

Sometimes Charlotte would get a full twenty minutes to uncover the little jewels hiding beneath the shifting sand. She would place each one in a neat row by her feet before her mother caught her and descended, roughly plucking her up, ignoring her screams of protest.

When the transformation happened, Charlotte insisted she be called CJ for Charles John and Mary told no one. Even her hardworking, hard drinking husband never noticed. She actually felt relieved thinking it wasn't her but something in that tainted dirt all those many years ago that contaminated Charlotte. In a way she was right. CJ heard the seductive song the first time while sitting in the sand and after that everything changed.

When CJ was six, Mary insisted they move. She made arrangements to home school and prayed, begging for guidance. Exiting church while rubbing the thick, reddened calluses on her knees, she bumped into Dr. Chekinov, a new pediatrician and saw it as an act of God.

Haunted by a symphony no one else heard, at the age of sixteen,

CJ grew dissatisfied with his life, the suffocating suburbia that surrounded him, and the stifling intelligence of both his parents and four sisters.

Tall and stout he lied about his age and experience, enlisted on a barge headed for the oil rigs in Saudi Arabia, and sailed away, telling no one and leaving no note.

Gestation is complete. Time to begin the process.

Labor was hard on the rig, the men rough; and while CJ grunted and laughed at their jokes he spared little time socializing before escaping up top to close his eyes and listen to the concerto surrounding him. When certain peculiar notes rose and fell, it gave him goose bumps and he swore there were dainty fingers rubbing, massaging, tickling his flesh.

On those days he'd rush to inspect his skin, searching for a sign, anything to indicate he had indeed been touched by something so glorious, so magnificent he could show others how special he was.

On close examination he detected small white patchworks that layered across a bicep or thigh. But seconds later they would disappear, leaving only muscle fatigue and a deep tingling within.

At those times his lungs hurt with unshed disappointment. He wondered, *if I stop everything, close my eyes and truly listen, maybe the Finger Tipped blessing of White will stay.*

Eventually the men on the rig resented him not doing his work, and gazing at the sky. Loud grumblings filled the rec room.

"Shit, not two months out and he's shirking work already."

CJ noticed a few workers followed him to the deck, found their own private space, and sat while the sea roiled and coated its thick salt on railings, planks and upturned faces. He'd watch while their eyes rolled up into their heads, the whites showing just beneath eyelashes, and smile.

The first time he noticed a silent exodus it was only Karl Syedyjiian. He realized, *he's hearing my song!* Initially pleased, he was shocked when his throat shut while his thoughts whirled with possessive murder, streaked in red and black. His first jealous pang overwhelmed him when oceans of blood rose, suffusing his neck, face, bulging his eyes with pain; engorged with the single need: slaughter. Caught in the rip tide that sucked him down, down, he had no sense of time, no sense of self.

The soft gurgle and punching fists of Karl brought him back to conscious thought. He dropped his strangling hands from his neck and watched as Karl fell to his knees, gasping. "You," he choked, "you fucking maniac!"

CJ looked around. No one else was on deck. He leaned down and flung Karl overboard, mildly surprised how far he pin-wheeled before plunging into the raging sea.

He knew he should feel regret, but instead heard: *He would have told.* A melody so peaceful embraced him. His hands unclenched, his body relaxed and he gave himself up to the *Song of Submission.*

Two months and twenty-one days later, the rig went totally dark. The mainland was ordered to send helicopters out to see why communications were down but they had other more disturbing things to look into.

Half the world's population had fallen into a coma. Two days after infection a thin, sticky white substance appeared on their skin, as if they had spun themselves their own cocoon. Impossible to remove since the coating appeared to have absorbed the skin beneath, it would leave the victims skinned alive and awakened—screaming with pain. But even scrubbing off the white layer was not an option, since the substance, once removed, returned thicker and quicker as if sprouting from within.

Doctors and scientists studied the phenomena to its conclusion. Once the hard shell was cut open they found body parts in varying stages of decomposition. Hysterical mothers and fathers stormed the hospitals, demanding help, begging for answers.

The President of the United States shouted at his cabinet, "*I don't know* is bullshit! Find out, damn it! It's disgusting," he ranted, storming around the Oval Office. "People are being digested, turned into fucking soup!" Froth had gathered in the corners of his mouth as his revulsion mounted. "And for some horrifying reason, you're telling me MRI imagery shows they have cognitive brain function?" He shivered, feeling like he was coming down with a cold. "No bone, muscle, tendon or even teeth, for Christ's sake, but they are aware, thinking, feeling. How is that even possible?"

No one mentioned if left alone to gestate, the *Walking White Death* would leave its victim with the ability to move. How? Especially when the casing was opened up by a hopeful family member, thinking they were cured, and found nothing but putrid, sloshing, liquefied flesh.

The remaining untouched, uncontaminated humans stopped slicing open their loved ones and waited, hoping if they left them alone, maybe—just maybe—they would become whole again. After all, if left alone, they responded to simple word commands, gave comfort just by awakening, sitting up, walking, being there.

They didn't. After incubation, one moment they were passive, the next, they became violent and would rip a loved one's head off, fling it away, then proceed to split that human being in half, plucking arms out of sockets, legs from joints. The pieces would quickly sprout a white sticky coating and begin the process of gestation.

It was a worldwide pandemic.

Scientists frantically looked for a cure. How did it start? What was it caused by? Was there a Ground Zero? Somewhere, somehow there must have been a beginning point.

CJ walked the ship, orchestrating the sounds around him like a professional conductor. His joints felt funny. He never slept but otherwise felt pretty much the same as he always had

The gray sky above was perpetually beautiful, undulating with streaks of pinks and blues, flame orange and purple-reds. The sea below him heaved with shades of greens, blues, blacks and gold. He saw colors he'd never experienced before. Colors with no earthly name. Screaming winds buffeted his body but brought with it none of the numbing cold or heat he'd experienced before. CJ was finally and completely happy.

Until he pushed harder to feel, commune with his Source of Nirvana. A cloud of music parted and, long last, he saw. He stumbled into the truth, in all its gory, glorious detail. Reality was heartbreaking. Hard to grasp in all its deceptive, selfish, greediness.

He tried to not see it. Pretend it wasn't there. He struggled to open his physical eyes but knew he couldn't. He was as *they* were.

I know there is nothing solid left in this white shell that encases me. Even my mind is just a series of synapses and strings of electric currents that have no mass. But, still it is my mind. My thinking.

Why?

The soothing sounds that once calmed and invigorated now left him panicky and sickened. He knew the truth, the beginning and end. Humanity's end.

Never one to be introspective, CJ stiffly walked the parameter of the rig, keeping part of his mind focused on movement, part on thinking.

I've been used, vetted, cultivated. It took years, but for that one simple moment where I said 'Hi' all those many years ago, It would have been forced to move on. In a rush, CJ realized, *It never would have been able to contaminate me—and through me, other humans if I'd only ignored that first knock.*

"Hello: just a telepathic message to your DNA of health and goodwill. May I come in?"

Fuck! he raged. *It's spent millennium doing this to other species.*

CJ had no true mouth. Nonetheless he choked back a sob. *Fucker! You're not a harmonious symphony of sound. You're just a parasite who will eventually leave to find other compatible energy to bleed dry.*

With the realization he would be left, there was no 'special' place for him in the master plan, he became incensed. *Had it not been MY contaminated neuro-pathway, changing my DNA so It could utilize my genetic link and feed, suck the life essence from all living things?* He stiffened. *What will I do once It's gone and the music stops? My own ecstasy terminated?*

At this point, CJ's emotions were of little consequence. Especially since It was busy feeding. However, feeling his anger, It still sent him the obligatory serenity to calm and sooth. Unfortunately, It didn't take the time to understand why he was upset. *Humans waste too much of their precious energies on useless struggles. Besides, right now I'm busy gorging—and dividing.*

Ignoring the sweet melody cocooning him, CJ remembered something from the early days of contact. He was eight and found his mother's matches on the side table. Sneaking into the bathroom he struck match after match, enjoying the sulfur smell and the little sizzle it made when tossed into the toilet. He had three matches left and decided to burn them all. When he lit them he was startled by its sudden flare and singed his hand.

His mind rang, "No! Fire bad."

The pain in his hand and the sharp shout in his head caused him to lose balance, fall against and into the tub, crack his head. He started to cry. The music tried to sooth but he was hurt, scared, and angry. "Why," he demanded. "Why why why why why?"

It felt CJ's negative emotion. *It would not do to break the bond yet.*

More was needed. "Energy that consumes itself is energy dissipated. Focus is lost. It becomes elemental. One of all."

That one telling memory cheered CJ up. *So—fire could dissipate It.* CJ ignored the swirling colors, the restful tones vibrating around him; in him. *If It's turned back into elemental energy maybe it will stay and I can hear It forever.*

CJ didn't put the clues together. Fire, extermination, destruction of The Host, The Conduit, would effectively break the bond.

As all good connections will do, realization, understanding can go both ways.

A quiver brought CJ a warning that he should focus on enjoying the enveloping sounds surrounding him, the beauty and joy of just existing. It was a sham, a lie but he took pleasure in it nonetheless. Peace. Tranquility. Understanding,

CJ's comprehension allowed 'all' to understand. The scientists still unaffected locked onto the location of the 'Source', told the remaining Armies and Strike Forces and they nuked CJ's floating oasis.

With it went the connection. Those already contaminated were burned in pyres. The world had been reduced by three quarters of its population. But finally was able to repair itself.

When the mushroom cloud lifted, no one noticed a small, white ashy blob float away and rise toward the heavens, like the proverbial Phoenix. Tentative, bobbing up and away from the chaos. Away from Mother.

Lazily, it followed an updraft and rose steadily toward the open blue sky. Pulled up by gentle fingers it vaguely understood, it latched on and allowed the radiating energy from the sun and the stars beyond to pull it free. Free to grow and get stronger.

It would remember this place, no matter how far it roamed for food, and it would return smarter than Mother, stronger, and feast till all was consumed.

But now, it must sleep, stasis till it finds food elsewhere.

Tired… but I will become.

JARS

LAWRENCE SANTORO

> "They are lean and athirst!" he shrieked... "All the evil in the universe was concentrated in their lean, hungry bodies. Or had they bodies? I saw them only for a moment, I cannot be certain."
>
> —Frank Belknap Long, "The Hounds of Tindalos"

This began in circumstances ordinary for 1945: a boy and his mother leave home, travel north to be with a wounded soldier, their father and husband. Ordinary. But when the end comes, I will not have prepared you for the rest.

A cab brought us from the railroad station. The driver squinted in the dark and through the rain for the address mother gave. When we got there, the man said, "Why didn't you just say it was the Cornelius?" He sounded annoyed, barely helped with our luggage, most of our summer things. *Yankees*, I thought to myself.

The house stood apart. There were others on the block but our rented place stood alone, taller, deeper. "Row homes," mother called those others, first I'd heard the term.

Inside, she and I stood dripping just beyond the vestibule. The place stank. *What houses are like in the north*, I figured.

"Stale air," mother draped her arm over my shoulder. "We shall air it out."

I called, "Hello," to the empty rooms and the house welcomed us with an echo that was nothing I'd said. Later, there was singing somewhere far away, high-pitched voices and low drones like sacred harp back home but singing words I did not know. Still, they sounded like home and I cried.

When our things arrived, the house swallowed them. Our rugs were islands, our chairs, tables and lamps huddled on their shores surrounded by splinters and varnish.

I exaggerate.

I should tell you about Terry. He could not fly, he did not jump. He was an ordinary, skinny, blond kid. Not a bad guy, he just did what people he clapped onto wanted from him. When he hung around with "Bluto" down the way, whom I will mention only here, Terry was forever in Dutch.

"What Bluto expected," Leslie told me.

Terry was not a smart kid but, like Grampa used to say, "Some people just know which way the wind is going." Maybe that was the problem.

I met Terry right after I met Leslie and I met her on the day mother made me go to Fifth and Hawk elementary where I told everyone I was temporary and would be heading south soon as daddy got better. Daddy was in the big hospital in town, a special place. Burns from the war in the Pacific. He was a pilot.

My first day, Leslie walked me home. She'd run ahead then skip backwards to talk. She knew where I lived. See, while I had noticed no one, everyone had noticed us. Course they did. We were new, the ones in the big place, the Cornelius.

Leslie followed me onto the porch, still talking. She petted the woodwork. She watched the carpenter bees buzz the porch ceiling and not land anywhere. She kept trying to look in the window.

"What's it like? Living in the gods' house?" she said. I had no idea what she meant. "Living under the Mark?" Again, no idea.

She ran backwards to the sidewalk and pointed to just below where Tudor half-beam wood began at the third floor. A flat stone, about a foot on a side, was let into the brick. I had noticed, figured it was something Yankee houses had.

"Doc Cornelius put it there. Before my time, back when dad was a kid. One day Doc got out on the porch roof, right there, put up a ladder, measured, chopped out some bricks and cemented that thing in. The Mark. Something he found out there in the world. An expedition. Said it would bring the gods. What people said he said."

"God?"

"Gods. The gods."

I squinted. There was a head with horns cut in the stone. Too many horns or too many arms, more arms than any animal I knew and I knew octopuses. We starred at it until afternoon heat began to make the head and arms wiggle. When I'd had enough, she was still looking.

"Yep. It moves now," Leslie said. Then she ran down the block to her place.

Mother asked why didn't I invite my little friend in. I said, "Well, I guess I will."

Her first visit, Leslie could not stop touching and looking. And talking. She talked a streak about the house and Doctor Cornelius and the things he did.

"Cornelius was sta-range," she wiggled her fingers and drew out the word. "Here is one of the best hospitals in the world. Right here…" She spun 'round to take in the whole town, "…and Cornelius would not doctor there, nuh-uh. He saw people here." she spun 'round again. "Down there." She pointed to the floor.

"The basement?"

"'S'what they say." She was amazed at my ignorance. "Cornelius dug things up in ancient Egypt, Mesopotamia and Ultimate Thule. Went with Byrd to Little America—that's the South Pole—chopped his way through the Darien Gap! He was a medicine doctor but he was a doctor of other things, too. Things from old books. There any old books here?" I shook my head. "Well, he went on trips to find more books and maps and things."

"Maps?"

"Not like from the Esso station. Museum maps, old books maps, maps dead people pass down in families from time immemorial. That's a long time. He kept them up there." She pointed to the ceiling.

"Up?"

"In your attic. With his books and his things."

"How do you…?"

"'S'what people say!"

We went from room to room. Leslie looked on tip-toe or squatted down and looked under. "He had things. People say."

"You keep saying, 'things,'" I got in edgewise.

"Things like the Mark stone and more. People say he found lost

Atlantis. That's at the bottom of the sea. The Atlantic Sea I guess but some say it's somewhere in the Greek Sea or the Arctic Sea. Imagine the things he could've brought from Atlantis? Right into your house. You know Atlantis, right? That's the Ante…"

"Antediluvian continent. I know that much." And I did. Antediluvian times were the old olden times, times before Noah's flood, before God and everything.

She stopped talking and looked at me. "Antediluvian, indeed. People say he found relics and remains."

"What people?"

"People. They say he found relics, remains of the great old ones. The ones who came before real people got created. Things! What's in the attic now?"

"Nothing," I said.

"No books, no maps?"

"Just grandparent's stuff, silver cups from…"

Of course we went to look. She talked and talked and ran her hands over the flowered wallpaper in the side hallway and up the stairs. At the top of the steps, the air was gray and dusty.

"You get splinters going barefoot here?"

"I don't go barefoot. I almost don't come up here ever."

"Huh."

"Well huh, right back," I said.

The attic light bulbs had clear glass with little tips on the ends. Right away he saw those things, Terry called them "titty-bulbs." The light they threw was hard. But I will not get ahead.

The few boxes we'd put up there were shoved into the middle of the room. Last I'd been there they were to the side under one of the angles of the roof. Or maybe not. I don't want to make things up.

By the time Leslie'd gone through grampaw's skeet shooting cups and such, mother called dinner and did my little friend want to stay?

"Can I use your phone?" she yelled and was already halfway downstairs, hands trailing the flowers on the wall.

"But I'd love nothing more!" she almost cried into the phone. "Please." Finally she hung up and said, "I can't." On her way out she turned to mother like she'd forgotten something. "Thank you so much. I can't tonight and maybe could I have a raincheck?"

"Why, of course," mother said. Leslie was gone and the house was quiet.

I'll get to Terry in a bit. That night, another sound began. The sound was in the hallway wall or maybe in the stairway to the attic. I heard it half the house away. This wasn't singing like before. First, I thought it was a cricket. A cricket's a hard little bug rubbing itself. But in the dark, this became less and less cricket-like and more and more like stretched skin might moan forth if bowed upon. Never heard the like. I followed. The noise stopped in the side hallway to the attic. The big flowers were gray and black in the dark. I put my ear to them and felt their soft roughness. Underneath was that one-string fiddle, faint beneath the flowers and plaster. Then the sound was inside me, inside my head.

Of course it was not. The sound was in the wall, in the stairway wall. I stood alone in the dark, a big space for my barefoot self to fill. Then—I don't know why—my mind went to that Mark, the stone in the bricks just above mother's bedroom window. The thing moved. I could not see it, but I felt the horns, arms or whatever they were writhing round that head and turning, turning inward, reaching inside and for us.

Then the sound was gone and I had a splinter in my foot, which I pulled out in daylight digging with a needle, pulling with the tweezers.

Leslie and I began sharing nickel pops at Engquist's Drug Store after school; did that pretty much right off. Terry joined us. Then he started walking home and going with us to the Saturday matinees downtown. Then that was us.

Terrence Adolphus, to name him fully, got bad grades. He lied. We knew that. I knew because he was a bad liar. Leslie knew because she'd known Terry forever and knew what was so and what wasn't. He stole things—from our house now and then, but always gave them back a day or so after. He stole a funnybook from Enquist's, a

Classics Comic Leslie and I wanted and couldn't afford. We yelled at him. Then all three of us sat and read it in the shade of our house. *The Mysterious Island.* Vèry good. Terry let Leslie keep it. He would have gotten a licking he brought it home. His old man—what Terry called his daddy—gave out lickings ("Beats the snuff out of him," Leslie said) for everything, things, if I had done them, mother would have just looked disappointed about. After one visit to Terry's place, I never went back. He got a licking. The old man heard him cuss or maybe because he'd brought us there, but he got a licking like one I'd never had; got it as though we weren't even there. Probably got one later for coming home with band-aids on, I don't know. That was Terry and he started the real troubles at the Cornelius, but maybe that wasn't his fault.

The House? There were still smells. Stale air? Mother was mostly right. We aired out the place and most of it went. Not all. Something alive-smelling remained. Probably from the basement.

We still had echoes and noises at night. "Old houses have old sounds," mother said and put her arm over my shoulder. No idea what that meant but it made it better.

Sounds in the walls? I pretty much convinced myself of mice, bugs and such. But the echoes never went away. Every night-sound in that big old place brought its whole family of cricks and answering cracks with it, like some small and hard-footed thing was wandering.

Leslie and Terry liked the attic, two big rooms and a hallway. The front room looked through a maple onto the street, the other looked down on the two-story 'row homes' that filled the rest of our block. The only things we put up there were the gramparents' things I mentioned and some board games.

The attic's smell was sweet and thick.

"Flour paste and horsehair," mother said after one sniff, "flour wallpaper paste and hair-plaster that lies beneath." The paper was rough and smooth. The big green and red flowers Leslie loved running her hands over felt alive under my fingers.

"Huh," Terry said.

"Old ways of making things, *cher*," mother said. "Open the windows, young sirs and madam, the odor will depart."

We opened them. The smell departed. Her arm on my shoulder cured my worries and embarrassed me in front of Leslie and Terry.

The basement really stank. Not like anywhere else I knew except the hospital where daddy lay, a place full of rotting limbs. Those stinks were alive.

"Why...coal dust," mother suggested. I knew coal to be long-a-gone ferns and dinosaur bodies squeezed into black rocks. Daddy told me when I was young. So I credited mother's assessment. Coal dust it was. Mother had ways of removing the dark from the world.

Apart from that, the cellar was jim-dandy, wide and deep as the whole house. Bigger, I thought. And three bulbs to light it all; each hung from a cord with a pull chain that dangled at tip-toe height. First time down there, Terry ran the length, leaped and swatted all three bulbs, set them to swinging. Shadows dipped and spun, light and dark traded places, back and forth alive, each changing for the other. I didn't like that.

The smell up where we lived had mostly departed but that living odor lingered below even when the outside hatch was opened to fresh the air when we played submarine, rocket, or bomber plane down there.

"Coal dust," I insisted, defending my mother's honor.

Leslie sniffed. "Cockroach," she said, "maybe rat. Probably Cornelius's patient's bodies." She laughed.

Terry, who loved rumor, laughed. It was at the back of the basement, past the last bulb, where I was later found hugging the "crate of gut-jars" as Leslie called them, but I will not get ahead.

School eased us into October, then November. Leslie, Terry and I went to the Saturday matinees. We improved the movies on our way home. Terry liked playing bad guys but was too nice for it. Leslie would not be the girl. None of us liked girl parts, anyway, so she was mostly the buddy who dies.

Four blocks shy of home was the bridge that carried our street over the railroad yards. We hung over the cement balustrade to spit into the locomotive's smokestacks. That was good and we came up sooty and smoked.

On our side of the bridge was a little triangle park. The park was thick with trees and tall grass and had a cannon from the War of Northern Aggression. We frequently stopped there and used it for our improvements.

When we got home, we went to the attic and read aloud from *Tarzan* and such or played Monopoly, Parcheesi, or Mr. Ree. Terry found the hidden closet up there pretty soon after autumn had shortened our after-matinee time outside.

The door looked just like the wall with flowers and baseboard. But looking close, there was a thin line, a break that rose from the floor to about four feet, then over, then down. Right off, Terry started working to get it open. Why? Have to ask him, and you can't. He worked on that for I don't know, sliding the blade of his Barlow knife into the crack and working it up and down. He was devoted, as mother might have said. Finally, he stopped playing Monopoly and just worked. We called him back for his turns and at first he came, then he stopped.

"What is wrong with you, Terrance?" Leslie yelled.

"Get this Goddamn thing open," he yelled back.

"Why!" she shouted.

"It's a goddamned door and goddamned doors should open." There were other words, lots of cussing.

The hours he spent after-school and after-matinees cutting at whatever held the panel closed and the "bastard," remained steadfast. I bet Terry had never worked so determined on anything in his life. He'd get it almost open, fingers halfway in, then it would slip and snap shut. He'd cuss and be back at it.

November. Leslie and I were settled into evening gloom, scaring each other reading A. Conan Doyle's *The Lost World*. Terry worked.

"Goddamned cursing," Leslie said.

"Son-of-a-bitch," I said.

We'd just finished the chapter, "To-Morrow We Disappear into the Unknown," when Terry, on his knees, shouted "Jes-us Fuckin' Christ!" He'd gotten his fingers inside the panel. "Have the Goddamned thing. I got it. Now I got it." The door and its flowers creaked and cracked.

"You're fixin' to break something," I said.

"I'm okay. Sum-bitch…"

"Don't give a fig about you, you're fixing to break the damn wall."

Then he stopped shaking with effort. The door stopped cracking and creaking, as though they'd come to an agreement. Suddenly Terry's right arm—he was a south-paw—slid to the elbow into whatever was on the other side of that panel. At the same time, the titty-bulbs in our room and the hallway went out. All the lights in the attic so far as I could see, maybe all the lights in the house went out. With the dark came autumn shadow from the street. I saw Terry's shape, and that not so well. He looked to be hugging the panel, his ear against the door, his head turned so I saw nothing of his face. But he spoke and he spoke in whispers; not the usual Goddamn sum-bitches, now there was a smooth flow of whispered nonsense. Down home we'd call it 'speaking in tongues.' But this was quiet, personal.

"You all right?" Leslie's spoke over my shoulder.

First, there was Terry's quiet voice; then there was another, another voice, another presence in the shadows with us. I may be wrong when I say voice. But someone was there who wasn't us. And, this may not make sense, but a darkness lay between Terry and me. Between where he was and where Leslie and I stood, a great gulf was fixed, as they say.

Leslie pushed the light button on and off. I jiggled the titty-bulb in its socket. But that was us. And there was the other place where Terry and that other someone were.

Then the darkness between went away. Lights came on—all over the world for all I knew. The windows were black mirrors and Terry, Leslie and I were alone.

Terry's arm slipped slowly from that little closet, like someone disarming a bomb in a movie. I expected horror and there was some blood, but nothing more than might happen to any boy on any day of work or play. For a moment, the skin of his hand and arm was bone-white and runneled, like he'd been too long in water. He held the edge of the panel with his fingertips.

"Terry," Leslie said, "your hand."

"Hell with it. I gave it. Almost. Shit. We got to find them jars. They're in there, somewhere. Jars of guts then the gods."

The panel slipped from his fingers and slammed shut. Could have heard it all over the house. Mother was at the hospital, though.

"Guess not." Terry whimpered with a sigh.

Forgive me for it but I was thinking, 'That is Terry, *almost* but *not quite*, never all the way.' And whatever eluded him was always the goddamned importantest thing in all the wide world.

"I wanted? Maybe something. Shit, you know?"

"Sure," I said.

Leslie steered Terry downstairs to the bathroom and ran cold water on his hand. With the blood washed away, the damage was, as I said, nothing that didn't happen to a boy every day. The dead whiteness of the flesh, the wrinkles, that was almost gone.

"You've been bit; bit by something with tiny teeth. Something bite you? And who were you talking to? I could not understand a word, Terrance." Leslie talked until the cold water stopped the blood. Terry dried his hands with toilet paper and she stuck three, four Band-Aids where he still oozed but that was that.

Terry shook his head and had no goddamn idea what the hell.

"Yeah, a goddamn bite," he said, "you got something in there that tasted me."

"S'what I said," she said.

"Probably splinters, Leslie! Anyway, you'll keep the hand." Visiting daddy I'd seen people didn't keep hands and other parts. I loved daddy but did not like to visit that place. They did not like me being there, either.

I am now at the kernel of this. After being 'tasted' Terry was different. We played, still went to the matinees and improved them coming home, but Terry was more grown up. Mother said. I thought he was just queer. Leslie said he listened more.

"Not to us," I said.

Okay, I have avoided this, this strange, impossible part. I'm not pulling your leg, though. Here. The kernel. The horror.

We were coming up from town. Late November. A wonderful day, chilly but warm enough to stay outdoors until darkness came. Darkness was coming. Leslie and I were riding the cannon—something we'd seen in a movie. Terry wasn't on the gun with us. He was walking around the little park watching the sky.

"I wonder," he said, "what'll they give back?"

"Huh?" we said. He'd been queer all day.

"I fed them. Gave them up, gave them me."

"Queer," Leslie said.

"Time you noticed," I said.

We'd rutched almost to the muzzle of the cannon when Leslie screamed. I thought she was fixing to fall and, since we were making like the barrel was pointed over a cliff, I turned to save her life. She wasn't falling. She was staring, eyes-wide. The sun had just set and shadows were coming for us, crawling from under the trees by the west. There were lots of trees and wind enough to make the autumn grass whisper.

Terry stood on the bridge balustrade. He often threatened to walk the bridge's narrow ledge, a good thirty-foot drop to the tracks. Leslie always talked him out of it. There he was standing on that cement rail, his back to us and I don't know if he heard Leslie's scream or not. I didn't peep for fear he'd lose his balance. When Leslie drew breath to shout again, I turned to hush her and we both fell off the cannon. Not hundreds of feet to the rocks, just three, four to the grass. For half a second she gave me mad-eyes then her face got bigger. I turned.

I know what I want to say: from where he stood, Terry just seemed to float on smoke or steam that huffed around him from a passing train. I want to say that but, no. He was lifted, borne aloft on swirls of spark and soot. He was awash but not in train smoke. There was something—that dark something I saw when the panel had held him in its mouth, when he spoke in private tongues to the darkness. That something held him now.

We called. I think he did not hear. Leslie ran toward. I followed. Terry was still awash, lifted above and beyond our reach, over the tracks. He looked not at us but somewhere else, I don't know where, but not at us. The long arms of darkness wrapped him. They were alive. Sparks—what I thought were sparks—swirled and crackled like Christmas tinsel on the Lionel tracks. And there was a smell, that alive stink of something that had rotted its way from another world into ours, the stench of something from beyond and long ago. This was the full-out reek that lay under what the Cornelius sometimes fed us until mother made it depart through open windows.

Terry dissolved into the arms and the sparks. Leslie reached for him and failed. She began to climb onto the railing. I dragged her off. We argued, sure, but I was proud of her that she tried, and disgusted with myself that I hadn't.

In a moment, the arms, the sparks and Terry whisked away, a meteor trail up the sky toward our house.

We ran. The Cornelius was just a half-mile but I'd never run that far, so fast. What was I going to do? Tell mother? What else does a kid do? The long wall of row homes passed in slow motion, our breath and legs held and slowed us. Ahead, where Terry and whatever it was had gone, time ran regular. Our feet were lead, our chests filled with sand and cement. When we reached the Cornelius we died for breath.

The Cornelius was utterly black. We breathed.

"Your mom? Not in?"

"Hospital," I remembered, "daddy…"

"Then us…?"

"Us."

"We're it. The rescue."

I never liked the house. That evening, it did not like me. Silly. Not the house, no. Houses do not like or not. They are. But something was there that wore the house, and that did not like me. Us. Leslie and I leaned on our knees and breathed and breathed and did not pass out.

"Look." She pointed.

The streetlight on the corner was out and the house showed little more than angles, black brick and gray wood. Still…a thing moved across the face of the Cornelius. A moth flickering on the screen is something like it. The whole rest of the block was dead. If not dead then sleeping, silent, except for the flap of that growing many-limbed thing that was trying to enter our world from the Mark. I do not mean to be dramatic. I have tried not to be, but that is what it seemed. This thing rose and fell back, rose again, stretched, beat itself against the dormer above or strained down to where it rattled mother's bedroom window. It was smoke learning to have muscle and teeth.

"Terry's in there," Leslie said.

I knew that he was. I just did not want to go in.

We went in. No lights, nothing worked. We ran upstairs into a darker place, down the side hallway, darker still, then climbed the attic steps. We climbed into a downpour of stench, a breath from some Cornelius place where his maps and books had taken him, maps and books that had been part of this house and had lived in these rooms. The thoughts ran through me. How? I do not know. The light ahead was not the hard-edged brightness of titty-bulbs but soft and smoky, a curling light that threw gray shadows. There were voices in that light, far-off but clear and foreign. The walls hummed with them, those flesh-strung violins sang. The sacred harp in tongues fed our ears.

In the front room, the little closet stood open, a gap in the wall's black and gray flowers. Something moved inside, a thing our size that crawled away from us.

Leslie called but Terry did not respond. She dove.

I hesitated. Something urged me stay. The cricket in the wall, I now guess. I pictured Jiminy Cricket. Jiminy Cricket was in my hand, small with long antennae. He said, "Stay."

No. I gripped him hard and followed.

The door closed behind us.

I'm older now. I didn't then know what being a child in the womb was like. I still do not, I suppose, but I do know now that at our beginning we are alive in the body of another, close and embraced by wetness and meat; outside is an alien world, untouched but at-hand.

That experience is probably kin to what Leslie and I felt crawling in that darkness, incomprehensible sound surrounding us. I also know that at our end, the earth will enwrap and hold us forever. A baby has no sense of beginnings or endings or of the world and I suppose a corpse hasn't, either. We did. We knew we were inside a place both alive and utterly alien. The house? No. Was it a creature, one of Cornelius's "old gods"? I do not know.

Jiminy Cricket wiggled in my hand. We crawled, we walked, we ran. Light of a sort aimed us. We moved through rooms—or caverns—walls like slabs of meat rose around us, stars aloft and distant above. We kept on. Winds came. Icy arctic night roared from a side space. We went on, following Terry. From another side, a fetid corruption strangled me, heaving screaming jungle birthsoup belched on me then vanished. We followed Terry. He'd been invited. We'd not.

Jiminy buzzed reminders to my hand. "Not wanted ("needed," "fit," "required")," it sang. His antennae augured their way out of my clenched fist. I called to Leslie but she would not stop. We kept on. Places passed on either side, a black depth of water, living lights moving in it. Sometimes, the way narrowed to a few inches and thousand foot drops gave way to either side of our running feet. And always and ever, alien winds arose from here and there. The smell was what a spider looks like.

Hours and miles later, the way ended. Ahead, Terry knelt by a pit. A greasy light arose around him. Terry reached into the light and, one after another, withdrew a series of glowing jars.

Leslie and I had stopped. I could barely move or breathe, but we stopped, how to explain this? We stopped because Terry seemed to know what he was doing. This not very smart boy had gathered around him a half-dozen of these jars. Various colors played over him, colors I knew and others I had no name for. Quickly, he opened one jar, put it down, reached, opened another, placed it at what seemed a measured distance from the first.

So it went, a pattern being made, colors and life oozing from the open jars.

"What in the hell…" Leslie said.

Jiminy squirmed and screamed.

"Jars of," Terry said. He didn't look but he was speaking to us. He continued to work. "Hearts, lungs, parts there ain't no names for. God-parts, waiting.

"Leave now," Terry said, "we have it to do." Jiminy said, both of them said. "Leave now and the gods will be reborn. They have lain await here in parts and in many places. They begin again. Here the world begins. Anew."

Jiminy gave me a jab. I opened my hand.

"Hell!" Leslie said, seeing the thing for the first time.

I don't know, grabbing him had seemed natural. I'd loved his movie and he was a good little fellow.

"What the hell?" Leslie screamed.

Jiminy's tail fired like a glow-worm. The air lit. Every mote in the world glowed. The Jiminy bug spread wings and flew.

Why? I don't know why I knew but I did know Jiminy was not Jiminy Cricket but something from Doc Cornelius's dreams. The bug's right name popped into my head but I have long forgotten it. I knew, too, that Jiminy must not get to those jars of lungs and parts and...

…and, well, I knew things and among the things I knew, I knew I couldn't let that little bug go. I grabbed him.

Which did not stop him. He flew higher and higher, me with him, holding him.

Now, I was not a heavy boy but I should have been more than a cricket-sized bug could haul aloft.

Leslie called. Her voice and she were dwindling below. Jiminy screamed in the tongue of the old gods. From below, Terry looked up. His face was as full of ancient hate as his old man's had been that one time I saw him reach for his son and beat him out a licking.

How high? Don't know. What was I doing? Don't know. Light and smell oozed from the jars Terry had opened. In them life crawled, craving substance and bawling like babies. I knew (How? Don't know…) that if the parts managed to gather and touch, the critter fluttering from the Mark would be with us in the world. And I knew that would be a very bad thing.

Then I fell.

Did I let go? Don't know. From how high? Don't know. A long drop, sure. Not as far as daddy falling from the sky in the Pacific but the light, colors, the jars, the pit rushed toward me and then I was in it all and overwhelmed.

Terry's mom and old man were dead. Terry killed them the night before, killed the old man first, sleeping. A butcher knife. Many times. His mother fought but she was very small and he killed her, too.

They found Terry on the tracks below the bridge. People said he'd jumped. A train had run over his body but he'd probably been dead before.

I woke, Leslie screaming and shaking me. She'd found me at the far end of the cellar. The lights were on and swinging and I was hugging a box of jars. Looked like old preserves in Ball Jars. But I did not look closer.

How'd I get there? You know by now.

Leslie verified everything I remembered: following Terry, the thing from the Mark, the opening in the attic, the trip through…?

What? Through to the pit. She watched me fly, she said, she saw me drop from on high. Then light like the sun and she awoke in the basement. I was a mess. We never told mother.

Leslie and I watched the Mark that night before we knew about Terry and his parents. After we knew, we watched the Mark for days in the cold winter sun. It did not wiggle.

My daddy passed soon thereafter, a war hero. Everyone was sad. And so soon after the shock about the Adolphus family, a whole family done in like that!

We were sad, Leslie and I. I still am. But daddy could not have been whole again, and like I said, Terry wasn't a bad guy, just someone who knew which way the wind was going. Sad, but I rushed to help mother pack the place because we were going home with daddy.

When we left, I wondered what to do with those jars I woke up hugging. I would not open them even to flush or burn them or whatever. The box was almost full. Just a half dozen missing.

Sometimes I wonder about Doc Cornelius. What happened to him? To his patients, the ones he saw in the basement, to his books and maps, his 'things'?

The jars? I left the decision to Leslie. I still miss her and sometimes wonder.

THE ASPS

JUDI CALHOUN

At three o'clock in the afternoon during the summer of 1942, one of the hottest on record, a large ford truck squeezed through the alley and backed up to the loading platform at the Alexandra Chantal Emilien Museum of Rare Artifacts, on 1200 Thirty Fourth Street in New York City. A crew of three workmen labored in the heat to deliver eight heavy crates.

Eldon Cooper, who had enjoyed more than a few beers the night before and was suffering a massive hangover, struggled with the last. He ignored the knocking sound that came from within the crate, believing it a hallucination born from alcohol. All Eldon wanted to do was go home and have another drink, a little hair of the dog to solve his problems.

The other men reinvigorated themselves with water as they sat on the front fender and waited for Eldon, the new guy, to finish off-loading. Sweat ran down his neck as he lugged in the heavy crate. He didn't see the low conveyor belt that wound around the room like a snake and tripped over the contraption. The crate smashed against a metal rack and cracked open like an egg.

Pain spread across his belly. His head pulsed, too. Then a voice, soft and melodic, wove a message through the jolts.

"Open me if you dare!"

He tracked the voice to the crate. *I'm going rum crazy*, thought Eldon. He ignored the voice and focused on his mistake. He'd be in trouble if he just left it and walked away, but if it looked as though someone from the museum had opened it, Eldon wouldn't be blamed. His pudgy fingers tore into the damaged crate and pulled the wooden ribs fully apart. Buried inside the packing straw was a single ceramic jar with Egyptian hieroglyphics and illustrations crudely painting on cream-colored glass. He set the jar on the metal rack, only briefly acknowledging the disparity in the weight of the broken box and its near-emptiness, and started to leave.

"Open me! Set me free and I will make you my prince."

Eldon shuffled back to the jar. A prince? Crazy, yes—rum or otherwise. But considering his rate of pay, the notion sounded pretty darn good. His trembling hands turned the lid three twists. Mist seeped out of the jar and struck his flesh, cold as winter ice.

The moment the dizziness and weakness hit his legs he knew he'd made a mistake. Eldon dropped the jar and ran. The voice chased him back into the summer heat.

"A curse be upon your family!"

Over the years, 1200 Thirty Fourth Street saw many new tenants. When the museum closed, an off-the-rack dress stop named Maxine's opened and struggled for five years. Sandy's hair salon business went the same way after ten. In the '70s, a dreadful novelty store named Tiny Tim's hung out its tile; later, it was the campaign headquarters for a liberal group. In 2012, Franklin Girvinburger opened a pet store named Franklin's Furry Friends and Fish. The customers just called it 'Frank's'.

Franklin was under the dreadful delusion that he was Italian by birth, perhaps from his close association with his Marconi Hall friends. He was in fact, German. He hired two sales associates—Steve Manzenee and Nick Cooper.

"Hey clerkies—snakes!" yelled Franklin, a squatty guy with a typical New York attitude who struggled to remember his new employees' names.

Nick squinted. "Snakes?"

"Sweet little pythons coming in today. I need you to make sure those delivery goobers don't drop 'em. Got it, kids?"

"Sure," said Nick.

"Which means one of you two clerkies got to open the crates, get them in their aquariums, give them each a mouse for dinner."

Steve rolled his eyes and turned away.

"I've got an important date to keep," Franklin said and soon left the store in the hands of his de facto assistant manager, Nick.

"I don't get paid enough for this, crap," said Steve, hiking up his droopy cargo shorts. Steve was thirty, heavyset, and wore shorts even in the winter. He kept a mustache comb in his shirt pocket and habitually brushed the small caterpillar that lived under his nose. "Handling snakes is not in my contract. Frankenstein's a cheap mofo—we should be getting hazard pay for this." He walked around the side of the kiosk and flopped his butt down on the low counter where customers generally visited with dogs. "You'd think he'd get a clue. We're not animal handlers—we sell pets and supplies, end of story."

"Pythons aren't poisonous," said Nick. He bent to fill a row of rabbit cages with food.

"Tell that to the mice." Steve shuddered. "Doesn't matter. They're still *snakes*."

As Frank's unofficial right hand, Nick figured he'd be the one to handle the snakes; Steve got squeamish even around the store's lizards. "Fine, you feed the dogs and I'll deal with the shipment."

"Damn straight you will. And just so you know, I'm leaving early tonight, too, so I'll need my paycheck."

The back door buzzer sounded while Nick was en route to the office for what Steve often referred to as his, "Weekly insult." Instead, he headed down the back stairs, switching on lights. When he reached the metal delivery door button, he punched it once playfully with his fist. The metal grinding sound echoed throughout the storage room and the door rolled up.

"Nickolas," said Garvey Gray. Their regular delivery guy held a thick bunch of papers. "How we doing today?"

Nick smiled and exchanged the usual pleasantries as he signed the delivery paperwork. Garvey then wrestled the box into the storeroom, a big pet crate containing one dozen snakes.

Once Nick finished placing all twelve pythons in the glass case, he gave them live food and locked down the grate, knowing Franklin would handle bringing them upstairs in the morning. That's when he heard the knocking. At first, he thought someone was outside on the loading dock. He again raised the door but saw nobody.

Shutting the door, Nick followed the sound to a bump out in the storeroom wall and placed his ear against the cold sheet rock. Sure enough, the knocking originated from behind. He stepped back and realized, according to the layout, there was a hollow space back there, the size of a closet. Why would someone build such a small room without a door?

"Hello? Is somebody in there?" he called.

No reply came, and Nick put the knocking down to either pipes or his imagination.

"Yo, Nick!" Steve called, coming halfway down the stairs, "a customer wants to know if the Batfish and those other colorful things will kill each other if she buys two of them."

"No, Blennies are peaceful, however the Batfish are going to get huge. Ask the customer how big her tank is."

Steve started to turn.

"Hey wait, come down here a minute," said Nick.

Steve glanced back up toward the shop then walked down and reluctantly past the empty snake crate, his eyes cutting sideways glances at the occupied tank. "Are you sure you got all those things out?"

"Of course I did," said Nick. He wagged the snake stick and made a point to return it to its hook beside the snake bag and handling gloves. "Do you hear that sound?"

Steve shrugged. "I don't hear nothin'. Look, Nicky boy, it's my break time—why don't you finish up with this customer and I'll take my thirty. And while you're up there, you can get my paycheck."

Nick reluctantly followed Steve back up the stairs.

Steve left early, and the knocking jumped from behind the walls and into Nick's skull. The continual knocking quickly drove him crazy. He couldn't understand how he was able to hear it inside his head.

In the storeroom, Nick found a crowbar in Franklin's toolbox and started digging into the wall. After only a few minutes of work, he made a large hole and sold himself on the explanation he planned to deliver to his boss regarding the unscheduled demolition. Grabbing a flashlight from the toolbox, he shined all around the empty tomb, at first seeing nothing. But then the light flashed over a glass jar. It was close enough for Nick to grab. He pulled it from behind the wall.

"Open me if you dare!" said a voice inside his head.

Nick reluctantly turned the lid. Just as he opened it, something crashed behind him. Nick spun around. The glass tank that held the pythons tipped over, and the snakes spilled out, loose in the storeroom. Only the escapees were different than those he'd transferred with ease from the delivery crate.

These snakes were green, *mean*—like African mambas he recognized from magazine articles and TV documentaries. A toxic cocktail of revulsion and fear embraced Nick as he jumped onto the stairs. His mind raced. The snake stick and bag hung on the nail across the room. If he could round them up and bag them...

Yeah right, his inner voice taunted. How was he supposed to get all of them before they got him? There was nothing sweet about this slithering mass.

"I will get my revenge," the voice said.

"Who's there? Who's talking?" Nick yelled.

"The curse is upon your family," answered the voice.

"Why? What did my family do?"

"Cut us to pieces and cursed our name."

"No I didn't! Or *we* didn't," said Nick. "You are mistaken, whoever you are."

"Your kind always tells lies. We killed your grandfather and we will kill you."

"My grandfather?" asked Nick.

"He brought us to this strange land."

"I think there must be a mistake. Grandpa Eldon never left this city. He was born, raised, and died here in New York."

The voice laughed.

Mist floated out from inside the jar and filled the storeroom. The mist surrounded Nick, and invisible hands lifted him off the stairs. He struggled as he dangled in midair, fighting the fog, but it was useless. His feet touched down on the cement floor in the middle of the snakes.

Nick tried to remain calm because he knew fear was like an aphrodisiac to venomous snakes. Of course, it didn't matter, the snakes were on him in seconds, hissing and curling around his legs, just as the storeroom door opened.

"Hey, Nicky, you down there, buddy? You gave me the wrong envelope—I got your weekly insult, dude."

Steve skipped most of the way down, saw the snakes, and

screamed.

"Dude, help me!" yelled Nick.

The mambas had coiled around him and it felt as if his feet and legs were encased in cement. Not one had bitten him…yet.

Eyes wide, Steve said, "I'm not risking my life for $101.87. What do you want me to do, Nick?"

"Get the bag and snake stick!" Nick shouted and rolled his eyes toward the wall, afraid that even the slightest of movements might prove fatal.

All at once, the snakes rolled off Nick's legs and darted toward Steve. The first to reach him sank its fangs into Steve's sneaker. Steve stumbled and fell the rest of the way to the cement floor. Within seconds, the mambas covered him.

"Why did they do that?" Nick shrieked.

"He was annoying us."

Now free, Nick glanced from the snake stick to Steve. The downed man convulsed and had swollen well past his usual bloated appearance. One of the mambas had bitten the mustache off his face.

"No," Nick moaned, and darted toward the loading dock door.

He slammed his fist into the big red button twice, knowing the door would roll open and then back down. He slid under the door before it closed, ran to his car, and dialed Franklin on his cell phone.

Franklin and the police found what was left of Steve's dead body on the storeroom floor. Even though the shipping door was sealed up snugly, all the snakes were gone. Escaped through holes in the wall was the popular explanation

At night, Nick dreamed of the mambas. They never attacked, only stared at him, their hateful, unblinking eyes somehow worse.

Two weeks after the incident, while Franklin was clearing out the last of his stock, a knocking sound drifted up from the basement storeroom.

"What now?" he bemoaned to the empty walls.

Franklin shuffled down the steps and noticed the ancient jar sitting among the wreckage of his failed business. The knocking seemed to issue from within the odd addition to the storeroom, scene of so much misery.

"I'll make you my prince. Open me if you dare!"

A prince? Present circumstances had left him a pauper.

Franklin twisted the lid open.

RUN-OFF 31

M.J. PRESTON

1.

Chicago, Illinois
Summer, 2013

The bodies started turning up in late July. Before long, police began to think that this was not the work of one serial killer, but two, possibly even three. The only flaw in this thinking lay in the fact that every victim had been left with an identical incision from solar plexus to belly button. Some of the detectives called them the 'X Killings', because carved into each victims belly was an 'X' that was not a symbol but the end result of evisceration. The reason they speculated the killings couldn't possibly be committed by one perpetrator, the sheer number of victims. To date there were forty-four, and the dead weren't more than a day or two old when they began turning up. Now, into the end of August, meant only one thing: the killer or killers, were claiming a victim a day on average, with the odd double.

Sean Woodman was not assigned to the case, he wasn't even a cop anymore, but he followed closely through the papers. It reminded him of a case he'd worked back in his days as a Chicago Police Detective. A case that was never closed. He'd been young and cocky back then, but along with his damn-the-torpedoes attitude, he also had a talent for seeing things others missed. And with the exception of that one unsolved case, he'd cleared a lot of murders. Those cleared cases garnished a respect which would eventually pave the way to a door plate which read: Deputy Chief of Police. That was the end of the line for Woodman. He wasn't a cop anymore, just a PR man who practiced politics with the best of them. Truth was, he hated it. He missed the smell of an unsolved case and made it his business to poke his head in on a task force or two to get a whiff of that scent. At first they thought he was some crazy micro-manager from upstairs. But Woodman proved a great help to his fellow officers; and even better, he took zero credit. Word got around, and after a while the task force cops started coming to him for insight.

Chief Jorgenson didn't like it though when Woodman got down in the trenches with the troops. Woodman thought that dislike was born out of resent. Jorgenson had been a career pencil pusher and had no cred with the cops he commanded. Although Jorgenson disapproved, there was no real reason to put a halt to Woodman's actions. Woodman had balanced his position while Deputy Chief with an occasional task force consultation quite well. When a case cleared, the Chief did what any politician would do: He held a press conference, congratulated his officers, and basked unabashedly in their success.

Then the unthinkable happened to Woodman. The unthinkable being, a car accident that resulted in the death of his wife, Jesse. Then there was the trace amount of alcohol in his bloodstream that hardly registered .04 on the breathalyzer. He hadn't blown enough to be charged, he wasn't legally drunk, but Jesse was gone and when word got out, the media hooked onto him like a pariah. They dogged him about the accident, and about how much he'd drank after someone leaked the blood alcohol tests.

His career ended in much the same way Jesse's life had—abrupt and without mercy. He found himself standing before the Mayor and Chief Jorgenson. On either side of them, like book ends, a Public Relations Bitch and the City Lawyer. Set neatly on a table before them, a stack of paper roughly an inch and a half thick.

That's 'The Big Fuck You,' he thought. Somewhere through that he heard the Mayor offering words of regret, and there was even a round of condolence. But it was hollow, the papers on that table spoke more about what was at play than these four assholes put together. In the end he did the only thing he could do. He signed his resignation, took a handsome buyout, and left them to pat each other on the back. That was the end of Sean Woodman's career in the Chicago Police Department. And though he was gone, he never forgot that one big case that got away. The one with the Indian named Blackbird and the bodies of woman they found in the Chicago sewers. They had also been eviscerated, but the bellies of those girls had been torn open. They called the case Little Big Horn, because on the evening of the last murder there had been an exchange of fire which included the use of a cross bow. Considering that Daniel Blackbird had been of Native descent and was the one firing the arrows, the name stuck.

Scott Emmett showed up on Woodman's doorstep with a case file thicker than a city phone book. He liked Emmett, but he was adamant that his days as a cop were over. Emmett was the son-in-law of his partner and best friend, Brad Rosedale. Coincidentally, Rosedale had been a part of that forgotten case as well. Unlike Woodman, Brad moved on. In fact he moved all the way on down to Tennessee, somewhere between Nashville and Memphis with his third wife.

"I can't do this, Scott. In fact if Jorgenson found out you were on my doorstep you could find yourself in deep shit. You could lose your job."

"Well, normally I'd say fuck Jorgenson, but to be honest, he sanctioned this visit," Emmett replied.

"Don Jorgenson told you to come see me?"

"Yeah."

Woodman laughed, not because it was funny, but because he couldn't believe the bastard would have the nerve. "Nothing personal Scott, but you can tell Jorgenson to go fuck himself."

"We need your help Sean."

"Why should I care? I'm not a cop anymore."

"The last one was a ten-year-old girl."

"Jesus Christ." Woodman sighed and pushed open the screen door. Emmett stepped through the doorway and followed Woodman down the hall of his two room bungalow. "You know that the whole 'last one was a ten-year-old girl' is pretty fucking lame. Little girls get murdered all the time."

"There's something else."

"Yeah, what's that?"

"We have a suspect."

"You've made an arrest? I didn't read anything in the papers."

"No, not exactly, but we...*I* need your help."

"So, you want what? Me to sit down with this guy? Jorgenson can't be agreeing to that. This is all over the papers. I could see the headline—'High profile case pulls disgraced Deputy Chief out of retirement.' As much as I would love to make that fuck-stick squirm, I still have my daughter to think about."

"How is Stacey?"

"I don't know, she hates my guts. I killed her mother after all."

"There's one other thing, Sean."

"What's that?"

"The suspect says he knows you."

"What? Who is he?"

"He doesn't have a name, but he says he knows you and won't talk to anyone else."

2.

They rode in Emmett's car. Woodman leafed through the case file, Emmett briefing him as they rode. "He's approximately forty-years-old, no tattoos and he's huge."

"You mean fat?" Sean was staring at one of the crime scene photos. It was the body of a woman. She was nude, her stomach unzipped.

"No, tall. Stands like seven-foot-three. Scary-looking fucker."

"Where did you pick him up?"

"That's where we're going now."

"How would he know me?"

"I don't know, but we found something."

"What? What did you find?"

Emmett turned toward him, his face serious. "It will be better if you see it. This guy identified you by name. He said you would know him if you met him and he said one other thing." Emmett turned his attention back to the road.

"What?"

"He said, 'I am Number 4.'"

"What? Where? What the fuck? Where the fuck are you taking me?"

"We're going to the run-off." Emmett glanced over then back to the road. "Run-off 31."

Woodman fell silent, but his mind raced. *Run-off 31. Did they? Was it possible? After all these years? Had they finally caught him.* His teeth clenched, turning his cheeks out into hardened contours of meat.

3.

Being back down there, plodding through the sewers, sent tremors through Woodman. It wasn't just the claustrophobia, it was the smell, the dripping sounds, and below the pungent order of methane and human waste lay something darker. Woodman thought about the Nazi death camps and the smell associated with them. Real or imagined, those who visited those dark satanic mills associated that smell with death. This place was very much the same and though it had been almost fourteen years, he still recalled the bloated headless corpses in Run-off 31. They got more than they bargained for when they, Chicago PD, went down below. A log jam of bodies, all headless and eviscerated, crammed into that run-off, like...

"Spoils." Rosedale called from the past. "Like a bunch of fucking discarded chicken carcasses."

Up front, Emmett plodded through the sludge, stirring the septic slew with his hip waders, creating a tide of lurching waves that lapped against the scum-coated walls of the underground tunnel. Woodman felt the pressure of the liquid pushing his own waders against his legs. Emmett had come prepared.

"You boys are going to bring the suspect through this shit, seriously?"

Emmett stopped, swung about, the beam of his flashlight gliding across the glistening walls. Facing Woodman, he said. "He's already there."

"I thought you said that you guys had him in custody."

"Not exactly. He's contained."

"What the fuck is up here, Emmett?"

Emmett chewed his lower lip, eyes losing focus momentarily. Then his gaze hardened and he turned to continue on. "It will be better if I show you." Woodman considered protesting, but his curiosity had the better of him and at this point complaining would accomplish little, if anything. So, he did the only thing he could do; he followed the young officer and they continued on toward the run-off.

They reached the mouth ten minutes later. The arch of concrete was a little over eight feet high. This section of the sewer was as old as the city itself, the walls pitted and worn, falling victim to the elements and toxicity of gas vapors. Emmett halted, tracing the beam of light up the wall until it fell upon a rectangular plate stamped out of brass that had long since faded and turned green.

It read: RUN-OFF 31.

Woodman didn't need the sign. This place was etched into his memory. Through that archway, thirty feet ahead bobbed the horrific memory of his cold case.

"Are you ready?" Emmett's gaze was neutral, even distant.

"Yeah, let's do this."

They waded forward; sloshing liquid bounced off the conduit walls, announcing their presence to the subterranean wildlife. A rat scurried along the edge and dove into the slew, dog-paddling away from them. Thirty feet in Woodman stopped, listening for the ghosts of his past, wondering if they were watching him now. Emmett said nothing, waiting patiently for the moment of silence to pass. It did and Woodman whispered, "Let's go."

Sixty feet in, they came to a Y-Junction. To the left, the run-off continued its course to wherever it was the water flowed. To the right, the path began to climb out of the murky liquid. At its base slimy cobble awaited, but farther up it looked dry. The archway was still high enough to walk upright and for this Woodman was thankful. His back was thankful as well.

"What do you make of this?"

Scrawled into the cobble by their feet was a single word: CHARON. The inscription was not old, weeks, perhaps as long as a month, and it was done free-hand, chiseled into the cobblestone and blotted with what looked to be blood.

Woodman studied it, something in that name struck a chord, but he couldn't put his finger on it. "I don't know. Could it be the name of your Perp?"

"No, I don't think so."

"Okay, that's it! What in the name of fuck is going on here? First you tell me you want me to speak to a suspect, then you drag me down into the sewers. Now I'm taken back to the scene of an old case and you've been...well, *cryptic* seems to be the operative word."

Emmett's gaze was trained upon him, but he said nothing.

"Okay that's it!" Woodman swung around, ready to wade back into the septic stream.

"Wait."

He stopped.

"Almost everything I told you is true, Sean. We need your help."

His back still turned, Woodman responded. "You want my help. Start talking."

"Okay."

He pivoted back around to face Emmett. "I'm waiting."

Emmett took a long, deliberate breath then exhaled. "We tracked our suspect here this afternoon after the body of a ten-year-old girl turned up in St. Paul Woods. This was a fresh kill, crime scene puts it down to hours. The mother wasn't even aware yet that the daughter was missing, let alone dead. She's a latchkey kid, with a single mom working two jobs. Some old homeless guy picking bottles and cans came across her, and he saw the murder."

"He didn't intervene?"

"As I said before, the Perp is huge, I don't think our witness could have done much."

"Never mind, carry on."

"The old man, he's a mess. He said that the girl was screaming when the ghoul cut her open. Screaming and begging for her life." Emmett stopped, took another deep breath and then continued. "So, when it's over, the old guy says the Perp removed her organs and put them into some kind of carry bag then starts out across the park. The homeless guy decides to follow at a fair distance I might add, but God love him for showing some balls. He follows the Perp out of St. Paul over to Oakton Street all the way into Skokie. Two fucking miles, Sean. Guess where it leads him?"

Woodman said, "Little Big Horn."

"You got it. Same place your guy was dumping bodies down the sewer. Same alley. Same fucking manhole. Except this guy pulls back the manhole cover and goes down the hole like a fucking...what did they call those underground moles in H.G. Wells' *The Time Machine*?"

"Morlocks?"

"Yeah like a fucking Morlock. Not far from there, there's a community Precinct. After the Perp goes down the hole, the old guy makes for the Precinct. Takes him about twenty minutes to convince the community cop he's not a loon, twenty more to locate the body, and another ten to call us. We were mobile within an hour and a half. I figured he was long gone. Then, on a hunch I decided to check the Run-off. That's where we found him. Where he is now."

"Why isn't he in the tombs under lock and key?"

"Because we don't have him in custody. We just have him cornered."

Anger bubbled up. "Cornered! You brought me to an apprehension? I don't even have a gun! What the fuck is the matter with you!"

Emmett reached into his jacket and produced a Desert Eagle 9 mm. "You can have this if it makes you feel better, but you won't need it. He's behind some kind of plexus-glass barrier."

"Barrier?"

"Sean, please. Come with me, it's only another sixty yards. He says he knows you. Says that he is Number 4, he won't talk to anyone but you. The others are waiting. We've got ten armed cops down there, you have my spare gun. I need you to talk to this guy, he's up to something, but I'm not sure what. I can stand here and debrief you for another hour, but it will be easier if you just follow me the rest of the way."

"Is it the man from Little Big Horn? Do you think this is my guy."

"I really don't know. That's for you to decide."

Both men carried on into the darkness.

4.

"This is Detective Emmett! I am entering the scene with former Deputy Chief Sean Woodman!" Emmett shifted impatiently from one foot to the other. "Answer, God damn it!"

"Okay Detective, it's clear for you to enter."

The light at the end opened up into a pumping station that had been cut in half by a barrier that indeed looked like plexus-glass. On one side, strategically positioned, police officers stood, weapons drawn and at the ready. On the other, a lone silhouette sat staring out at his captors over a sea of clay pottery. The lighting was dim, but Woodman caught the grin that suddenly formed on the stranger's face and knew that this sudden show of pleasure was due mostly to his arrival.

"What the fuck is he doing here," Woodman cussed when he saw Jorgenson walking toward him.

"I'm sorry Sean, I didn't think you'd come if I told you."

"You're right, I wouldn't have."

"Thank you for coming Sean," Chief Jorgenson stuck out his

hand.

Woodman turned his attention from Emmett to Jorgenson. "Put it away, Jorg, I'm not shaking your fucking hand," he said then, raising his voice just slightly, added, "Would I be correct to assume that that pottery contains what was taken from the victims?"

"Yeah, that would be correct." Jorgenson lowered his hand and placed it into his pocket. He took a cursory glance around to see if his subordinates had noticed; they had.

"How did he get in there?"

"We don't know."

Then from behind. "Wood Man."

Startled, Woodman pivoted to face the Perp.

He rose, strode forward, coming into the light. He was a giant of a man. His hands hung like machinery at his sides. His clothes, still stained with copper, gave testament to the last killing. His face was hard and angular, bone and muscle pulled his skin back making him look gaunt.

"I have been waiting for you?"

"You have? Why?"

"Because you have seen him."

"Who?"

"Keh Run, of course."

"I don't know any Keh Run. Who are you?"

"I am Number 4."

"How did you get in there? Who is Keh Run?"

The stranger frowned. "I do not like games, Wood Man."

Woodman thought back to the inscription in the cobblestone. Charon. "Was that his name at the base of the tunnel? I thought it was pronounced Charon, not Keh Run."

"Yes, Charon." He smiled again, revealing uniform planks of yellow teeth, looking more like old fence boards stacked on top of each other. He folded his hands neatly in front him, tilting his head downward.

"You said you knew me." Woodman decided to ask the question that was eating him alive. "Have you done this before? Back in 2001? Was that you?" He brought his eyes up to meet the stranger, steeling his expression and waiting.

The stranger's smile melted back into his milky complexion. He turned and moved back between the pots, settling down on his pedestal; arms crossed. From there, shadows fell upon his face, making it look skull-like.

"What now?" Emmett whispered.

Woodman cocked his head right, catching Jorgenson and Emmett's attention and glanced toward the opening of the pump room. They took the hint and followed. Once out of earshot, he began talking. "This isn't my guy."

"How can you be sure?"

"The girls back in 2001 were torn open, their heads literally twisted off. This wacko is emulating that, but he wouldn't know the state of the victims were in. Does anyone have a cell phone that works down here?"

Emmett pulled out his iPhone. "Yeah, I have a signal."

"Okay, Google Charon."

From above, a muddy drop of water fell downward and splashed across the screen.

"Fuck." He wiped it with his sleeve or he tried to then stopped. "It's going to take a second, the touch screen doesn't react well to liquid poo."

Woodman and Jorgenson both laughed, but stifled their amusement when they saw the other sharing in the joke. "So what's your contingency plan?" Woodman asked.

"I've got a SWAT team coming down with a fixed charge. If you can't talk him out, we'll go tactical and take the fucker out." Jorgenson nudged Emmett. "How are you making out?"

"Give me a second, the signal is pretty weak."

"There has to be another way in. Are you looking at that?"

"I've got a city works guy coming with blue prints, but these are some old fucking tunnels. When I called over the Chief of Operations he asked me if I was kidding. Said that finding a blue-print of this section might take a lot of hours."

"But he found them?"

"Yeah, he's conferring with the SWAT Lieutenant."

"Got it! Holy shit, if this is right, this dude has some serious expectations of you, Sean."

Woodman reached over, took the phone and began to read. He didn't have his glasses, but the font was large enough that he didn't struggle too much. After he finished, he passed the phone over to Jorgenson and said, "Well, at least we know who Charon is."

"He's certifiable," Jorgenson said.

"Really? You needed Google to figure that out, eh, Jorg? The whole evisceration thing didn't tip you off?" Woodman regretted letting that out only a second after it spilled from his mouth. Bitterness would accomplish nothing here.

Jorgenson glanced up, his face red and angry. "You don't want to be here. I'll have an officer escort you out. I didn't end your career, you did."

"Could we save this for another time?" Emmett interrupted.

Woodman didn't give Jorgenson a chance to respond. He walked out of the pump room back to the plexus. "The boatman. You're waiting for the boatman to arrive?"

The stranger rose. "Charon, yes. I have a tidy sum to give him."

"Who are you?"

"I told you, I am Number 4." He reached down and lifted the lid from one of the pots. "One left to fill then Charon will come for me."

"What is this? Why did you ask for me?"

The stranger smiled. "You will see."

From behind, Jorgenson whispered, " I just got word, they found another tunnel that'll lead them in. Tactical will be here in five, keep him talking."

"Why do you call yourself Number 4?"

"Because I am not the first." He stood, walked to the back of the enclosure. "I am the fourth servant, cast down to earth. But to find my way back to the Master, I must first do his bidding and payment must be made."

"Payment to Charon?"

From behind, Jorgenson again. "Four minutes."

"Yes, but he is also a servant. He will take my payment, but the cargo will not be his to keep." The stranger reached up onto the wall and flicked a switch. The room lit up, shadows retreating into the walls and in their absence Woodman saw it all.

There behind him, amongst the many clay pots smeared with copper that could only be coagulant, formed a new source of concern. Was it? Beneath a tarpaulin standing upright was a figure that could only be...

"Behold, Wood Man!" The stranger said and pulled away the tarp.

Horror cut through him like rusty barb wire. Woodman's eyes

widened, his thoughts spinning and as shock melted over him he could hear himself screaming. "No! No! No! No!"

From behind, Jorgenson again. Panicked. "Keep him talking. Tactical is close."

"Stacey!"

She was barely conscious, not a strip of clothing on her body, her arms tied behind her back, her belly exposed. Like a witch on a stake.

"Jesus Christ, no! Let her go, please. "

"Forty-five is the number, Wood Man."

There below her, a pot was waiting, its lid removed.

The officers at the scene raised their weapons. Safeties clicked off.

The stranger reached down and produced a knife, its blade long and curving into a hook. He stepped forward and blew into her face. "Wake, child."

"You fucking psycho, let her go!" Woodman was blubbering. "Please, take me instead!"

Suddenly conscious, Stacey whimpered, "Daddy?"

"It's time, Wood Man." He grinned and raised the blade.

"Shoot! Shoot the fucker!" Jorgenson ordered.

The underground room exploded in a barrage of gunfire. Bullets ricocheted off the plexus, one zipping past Woodman's head. Another struck Jorgenson in the throat opening his jugular. Blood spurted out of the wound, splashing upward against the plexus; first defying gravity then it began to flow downward. Another officer was struck in the ankle, bone fragments splintered from skin in porcupine fashion.

The stranger seemed not to notice.

Woodman begged—pleaded—cried and then fell to his knees when the knife cut up into her belly on its first diagonal pass. Stacey stiffened, her eyes locking with her father's. Then, after the second cut, she screamed, but only for a second; the peal drowned out by her father's howls of anguish.

Emmett ordered, "Hold your fire! Hold your fire!" Then a bullet cut into his guts, turning his knees to rubber. As if in prayer, he dropped and let loose a groan that exemplified agony.

Woodman could only hope a stray bullet would take him, but the barrage fell silent, replaced by ringing disbelief. Stacey's chin rested against her chest, her mouth opening and closing, her pupils dilating.

Woodman prayed, *Take her, please take her now.*

Then, with one hooked hand, the stranger who called himself Number 4 reached inside to eviscerate her. She was gone before the audible plop, her insides warming the cool clay jar.

The stranger came to the glass, and with one bloodied finger wrote the word: Charon.

"Your soul for hers," he invited.

"You bastard, you fucking psycho piece of shit!"

From the headset that now lay beside a dead Jorgenson, he heard, "One minute to breach!"

The stranger returned to the center of the pots and stood on his pedestal. Then he began to pray aloud in some foreign tongue. It was rhythmic, rising and falling. Woodman had never heard the language, but it was indeed a language.

"You're going to get the needle for this, you sick fuck!"

"*Shay-gra-che-Keh-Run-la-a-Jee*," he prayed, a chant of psychobabble. "*Keh Run-la-a-Jee! Charon! La-a-jee! Charon! La-a-jee!*"

Something began to happen.

From each pot a light began to bloom, first growing then pulsing like a heartbeat. All of them, all forty-five glowed in a myriad of color. The temperature plummeted, frost forming on the walls, turning breath into vapor.

"What's happening?" someone asked.

The stranger began to change as well. His face hardening, the milky skin turning first to serape and then ashen. The radiance from the pots increased, the stranger raised a hand, his skin crumbling away like cigarette ash leaving only an accusing boney talon. "Behold," he said.

Behind him, the wall began to ripple and then fade. Light dissolved the matrix of reality and the wall was no more. Reality buckled and came apart. A corridor materialized; a long wide passageway set in stone bookmarking each side, halfway filled with water. Down that passage was a place that those who feared for their eternal soul would not dare look.

Woodman, mouth agape, remembered what he'd read: *Dark and dismal, the River of Acheson and across the Styx cometh the boatman: Charon to collect the payment for safe passage to Hades.*

The light inside each of the pots rose and materialized corporeally.

First he saw a man then woman then a child and then Stacey. Behind them, the stranger continued to decompose, muscle degenerating, skin tightening, until only mummified bone remained.

"Oh my God," the officer whose ankle had been shot called out.

Down the corridor, pushing against the current, the boatman was coming.

The ghostly forms gathered about the one who called himself Number 4 and followed him to the shoreline as the boatman approached.

"Hades," Woodman mumbled.

"What?" Emmett grunted.

"Your soul for hers," he had offered.

There's still time. I can save her. I can stop him from taking her!

Woodman reached into his jacket pocket, felt the gun, wrapped his fingers around the pistol grip. "I can't let this happen! I can't let him take her!"

Almost at the shore now, soon the boatman would be ready to take them aboard.

"Sean! What are you doing?" Emmett cried.

Sean Woodman placed the gun barrel under his chin, closed his eyes and squeezed.

UNWRAPPED

MICHAEL M. HUGHES

He woke up in a circle of candles in a dark, windowless room. A woman loomed over him. The candle flames bobbed and swayed in her pupils like serpents.

"You're alive," she said.

He tried to speak but couldn't. Bandages covered his mouth. His body was numb, and beneath the numbness was a deep, icy ache.

She leaned closer and kissed his lips. "My love. It's okay now. I'll take care of you."

His head felt like an old, empty pot. No memories, nothing but a hollow void. He tried to move his hands. To reach out and touch this strange woman's face. But nothing worked. Only his eyes moved, peering through the openings in the fabric.

She had a pleasant, rounded face, despite its strange paleness.

He struggled to speak, but his tongue was as still as a rock.

He dreamed of the golden sun dancing on a river, but when he woke up he was still lost. He couldn't even remember his name. Whatever had happened to him—trauma, illness, or accident—had taken away his tongue. Words would not come to his lips, nor would thoughts form themselves into words. He felt as if he were a boat, unmoored and drifting on an endless, ink-black sea.

At least the woman was taking good care of him. She moved him to a bed in a sunny room, which cheered him immensely, and spent much of the day praying by his side and reading aloud from a little book. A spotted, silvery cat sat in her lap, purring loudly and paying him little notice.

One evening, after she kissed him goodnight, he pushed his mind as hard as he could and lifted a bandaged finger from the bed. Held it, then let it fall. It was all he could muster, and when she saw it, tears ran from her eyes, and he knew that, whoever she was, she loved him. No matter that he was near-death and couldn't speak or even understand her—she loved him. And that made him cry, too, even if his lips didn't move and his eyes stayed dry and his sobs echoed in the empty cavity of his chest.

Every morning, after she opened the curtains to let the sun warm him, she settled into a chair and began with his lessons. She held up cards with symbols and pictures and spoke slowly. At first it was all gibberish, but over the days and weeks he began to understand simple words. Bird. Sun. Eye. Triangle. Boat. Feather. Heart.

It was strange, learning to think in language.

"Bee," she said, holding up a picture.

Bee, he would repeat silently. Bee. Bee.

And then a flash of something—a taste. Sweetness. Sticky, dark, and cloying, scooped from a hive and smeared on an old woman's burned face.

A sound emerged from his dry throat. "Mmmm."

Her eyes widened. "Yes," she whispered, crawling into bed next to him. "Talk to me. I'm listening." She stroked his forehead with her thick fingers.

But nothing more came from his lips.

One morning he awoke to find the cat sitting on his chest. It moved its face into his and sniffed, from his eyes to his nose and his mouth, then let out a high-pitched chirp.

It lifted its paw to his cheek. He felt its claws, like tiny needles, sinking into his flesh.

He tried to scream, but the muffled grunt was barely a whisper.

The cat pulled its paw away, and with it came a strand of his gray bandages. It looked at the fabric caught in its claws, its huge, gooseberry green eyes registering surprise, and pulled harder.

He tried again to cry out, but only a low hiss of air escaped his lips. The cat stared. Its head pivoted, as if confused, and raised the other paw to his face.

When she finally arrived she saw the cat, sitting on his chest in a pile of bandages, and screamed.

The cat was banished from his room.

He marked time by the passage of the sun and stars outside the window. Sometimes strange, horseless chariots passed outside, making thunderous noises. But the days were otherwise punctuated only by her questions and drills. *Priest. Scarab. King. River.* And then she showed him exquisite drawings, so detailed and real they seemed magical—images of temples and carved stone. As the days passed, his body grew stronger, with sensation moving from his extremities into his limbs. She would sometimes unroll his bandages and delicately rub his desiccated skin with oil while far-off musicians played. The music sounded strange to him at first, but he grew to associate it with the pleasing touch of her soft hands.

Her name was Helen.

As his body warmed and healed, he remembered more. He'd had a wife, but her name danced just out of reach of his tongue. She was dark-skinned, with sharp features, and much more pleasant to look at than this woman, who was soft and much too round and dressed in strange clothing. And with his wife he'd made two children—boys, with shaved heads and wide, mischievous brown eyes. He'd been a physician, wealthy and well-respected, never lacking patients, grain, or oil.

And as he recalled these things, she asked him questions about his life—yes or no questions that he answered by grunting or raising his index finger. If he had treated kings (yes). If he fixed teeth (no). If he used camel dung and goose fat on open wounds (yes). She wrote the answers in a book, smiling, patient, and always attentive. He didn't understand why he was of such interest, but she seemed eager to know even the smallest of details.

Sometimes she asked him so many questions his mind would lock up. When he could no longer answer, she would climb into bed with him, carefully, and whisper in his bandaged ear, telling him how much she loved him, and how one day they would walk together in the sun.

One night, as he lay staring at the moon through the window, she came to him without knocking. She was naked and her flaxen hair, which was normally tied up tightly, fell about her shoulders. The candlelight softened her features, and he remembered the first moment he'd seen her face, hovering above him as he returned from death, with snakes weaving in her pupils. A witch woman, her lips painted the color of blood.

And then he remembered his wife.

Serket. Her name was Serket.

And with her name came a thousand recollections: her thick, black wig weighed down with beads of lapis lazuli, her kohl-rimmed eyes and polished gold jewelry against her dark brown skin as she brought him bread and cakes and roasted quail on a silver tray, and the sharp taste of pomegranate on her tongue. Their boys, naked, kicking and punching and pulling at side-locks, fighting over a painted toy boat. Cutting the foreskin from a young man with a polished obsidian blade.

Then he smelled Serket's pungent, spicy perfume, which filled him with a crushing sorrow.

Serket, mother of his *khered,* his *hemet.* Where was she? What had happened to her, and why was he here, far away from her and his life and his children, trapped in this godforsaken sickroom with a pale woman who ripped into his memories like a hyena tearing the entrails of an ox?

He grunted in agony, but she took it for his pleasure at the sight of her nakedness.

"One day soon, you will get out of that bed. You will have me, as you see me now. And I'll have you, my love."

My love. In her filthy, alien tongue it sounded like a curse. When she bent to kiss him her breast brushed his shoulder. It felt like the touch of a viper.

At first, she was alarmed. She prayed constantly, keeping vigil at his bedside until she was too tired to go on. She begged him to lift his finger, to blink, to make a sound. She held up pictures and words—*House. Reed. Breast. Beer.* She played his favorite music and rubbed his cracked skin with oil, her eyes searching for a reply. Finally, she threw her notebook in the floor in disgust. "Why are you doing this?" she screamed.

Serket smiled at him from somewhere far away, and the melody of an old chant rose in his ears like a thousand whispers: *Fall, lie down, glide away, so that thy mother Nut may see thee.*

She grew to hate him.

First, she let the cat back in the room and shut the door. But after leaving strips of his dirty bandages scattered around the room it lost interest and sat chortling at birds outside the window, flicking its banded tail and licking bits of his flesh from its claws. He and Serket had had many cats, and he understood that this one was just doing what the gods had made it to do. He wished it no ill will.

She left him alone in the dark for days, with the curtains drawn, but he found the darkness preferable to the sight of her. And in the darkness, he was rediscovering his essence. Serket came closer, her rich scent of myrrh, balanos oil, and resin carrying with it brighter and more vivid memories. He was dying again in this world, but he welcomed the transition to the world that felt much more familiar.

She cursed at him, spat on him, and smashed him in the face repeatedly with her unfinished book, her eyes wild with rage.

In silence he went deeper and closer to the abode of the blessed.

When she finally gave up and returned him to where she had found him, he was no longer merely a *khat* bound from head to foot in linen wrappings. While the parades of children pointed and gaped and stared at his body through the glass, he had already put on his loincloth, his panther skin, and his jackal-tailed girdle. Serket stood by his side as he received his long-promised bread from the hand of Osiris *Pepi Nefer-ka-Ra.*

CHAMBER OF THE GODS

GORD ROLLO AND BRETT A. SAVORY

"For Christ's sake, Sims... get a grip, will ya? I told you already, there's nothing the matter with you that a good hour in the tank won't cure."

"I don't know, Doug," Sims stalled, halfway down the plush carpeted walkway exiting the cockpit of the Air Transat L1011 wide-bodied jet, flight 407 from JFK in New York, having just touched down at Terminal 3 of Pearson International in Toronto, Canada. It was 2:25 p.m., Friday May 26, the temperature a gorgeous seventy-eight degrees Fahrenheit, and the sun shining brightly in a cloudless, azure sky. Another picture-perfect spring day in Southern Ontario, other than the fact that Captain John Benjamin Sims, veteran pilot with twenty-four years of impeccable service, had just come within seconds of killing all 193 souls aboard his aircraft.

"Do you really think it will help? I've heard they're dangerous."

"You read too many science fiction novels. Relax...this isn't *Altered States*, John, this is the real world. I've been using them for years. They're harmless."

Bowen had been yapping about the sensory deprivation tank throughout the flight, but Sims had been far too busy warding off an impending nervous breakdown to put any serious thought into what his friend was suggesting. One thing was for sure—he had to try *something*. He'd been flying wild for some time now, nervous and on edge for weeks.

Sims would be fine one minute, feeling alert, confident, and in full control of himself and the aircraft, then he'd suddenly zone out, his mind drifting away without a care in the world. In the beginning it had only lasted for a few seconds, just a harmless little daydream now and then. Unfortunately, things had gotten much worse, to the point where Sims would 'lose' time up in the sky. Ten minutes, twenty, sometimes more. Worse still was how disoriented he was once he snapped back to reality, when he couldn't remember where he was or why he was strapped in a chair looking out of a tiny window at a bunch of clouds.

Today, Sims had already begun his approach into Toronto when his attention drifted away. His fugue only lasted a moment this time, but when he came back to his senses, he couldn't for the life of him remember how to land an airplane. With all those lives in his hands and the ground less than 300 feet below him, he drew a blank. Panic had set in—total, complete, mind-numbing panic. Landing this bird should have been as easy as tying his shoelaces, but raw fear blazed through him, burning up every scrap of information he'd ever learned about aviation.

With no time to spare, with the ground practically scraping the plane's belly, Sims had faked a stomach cramp, pretending to be in such severe pain that Bowen had to take the stick and land the plane. If he'd hesitated a few seconds longer, or had been alone for whatever reason, they'd all be dead right now.

Forty minutes after checking into the Sheridan, finding their rooms, and getting unpacked, Sims found himself down in the hotel's health and fitness center dressed in baggy green bathing shorts he'd purchased in the lobby. He felt like a fool, all knobby knees and elbows, standing half-naked by the Olympic-sized swimming pool waiting for Bowen. He was on the verge of sneaking back up to his room and forgetting this nonsense when his friend arrived looking equally silly in a tight brown Speedo, his flabby belly flopping over the top of it.

Together they strolled around the pool and entered a room labeled Therapeutic Isolation Chamber. Sims liked that name much better than sensory deprivation tank. It seemed less hostile somehow.

The machine itself looked surprisingly like a giant bird's egg. The isolation chamber—as explained to Sims by a friendly, red-haired attendant named Larry—was a black-enameled oval measuring nine by six by four feet high. It was lined with aluminum, with a hinged lid on the top half nearest the door to the pool. There were numerous other lights, dials, bells, and whistles—all of which Larry was happy to point out—but what it boiled down to was that the tank was nothing more than a hi-tech bathtub with a lid, not nearly as intimidating as Sims had imagined it to be.

Bowen went first, and since he was an old pro at this and wanted to show off in front of his friend, he waved away Larry's attempts to aid him and confidently climbed into the chamber. He winked once and pulled the lid shut. Larry set the timer for sixty minutes then he and Sims settled down on two plastic deck chairs to wait.

"Is it filled with salt water...or something, to help you float?" Sims was bored and figured he may as well make conversation to pass the time.

"No, not salt. It depends on the chamber's size, but this one is filled with a ten-percent solution of magnesium sulfate in twenty-four inches of water. That mix gives you just enough buoyancy to hold your mouth, nose, and eyes above the water line. There's a footrest to hold your feet up, but your head, body, and arms float freely. The water's heated to ninety-three degrees Fahrenheit, the temperature a floating body feels the least amount of gravity."

"So all you do is, what...lie around? What's so therapeutic about that? Sounds boring."

"Different people have different experiences, but being bored isn't usually one of them. You have to understand that your brain is used to being constantly assaulted by external stimuli. We see, hear, taste, smell, and feel things, right? Well, all of that information has to be sorted out, evaluated, prioritized, processed, acted upon, then stored away in memory. We do this 24/7, even while we sleep. No wonder our minds sometimes get a little scrambled. Our brains are too busy processing external stimuli, keeping our hearts beating, and regulating our other body systems to give a damn whether you've had a shitty day at the office."

"So?" Sims shrugged.

"So...the brain's an information junkie. When you suddenly take all the stimuli away, cut the brain off cold turkey from its normal fix, so to speak, it goes searching for other ways to occupy its time. Inside the chamber, it's effectively cut off from the normal five senses, so it turns inward, starts dealing with the things it didn't have time for before."

"And this relieves stress?" Sims asked, genuinely interested now, feeling hope that maybe this weird-looking machine really might be able to help get his life back on track.

"Right. The brain does a complete internal audit, hopefully resetting everything that's out of whack. The only problem is that our brains aren't used to this forced downtime. Some people can't handle it. It freaks them out. Some people experience intense sensual fantasies or have really vivid hallucinations. Dark, crazy stuff that's been suppressed and locked away in their subconscious. Not a lot of people, though; most just come out filled with renewed energy and a deep sense of rest."

When the buzzer sounded, Bowen popped out of the tank, whooping with delight, bursting with energy. "Wow! Terrific, John! Nothing like it, nothing at all! Get your butt in there and enjoy yourself."

Larry helped Sims into the chamber, pointing out the submerged footrest, and giving him some last-minute advice. "Okay, you'll probably feel weird for a few minutes, but that's normal. Once your brain accepts it really isn't going to get any incoming stimuli, you'll settle down and be fine. Questions?"

"Does this thing really cut out *all* the senses?" Sims asked.

"Near enough. It's soundproof, lightproof, and there's nothing to smell or touch while you float. The darkness bothers people the most. Even in the darkest rooms, there's always at least *some* light; after a few minutes your eyes adjust and you start to see things. Well, you won't in there. With the aluminum-coated interior, the insulation, and the rubber seals, no light penetrates this shell. I'm talking total darkness...deep space black. Don't worry, though, I'll check on you in half an hour, just to make sure you're okay."

Sims nodded and lay back in the surprisingly hot water. Bowen appeared at the hatch, towel-drying his hair, still grinning like a loon. "Just relax and let your thoughts drift, John. Oh, and try not to freak out!"

With those encouraging words of wisdom, he slammed down the tank lid, plunging Sims into instant midnight. He waited for his eyes to adjust, but just as Larry had said, they didn't.

"Deep space black." He laughed nervously, took three deep breaths, and tried to relax.

Sims lay as still as he could, settling into the comfortable embrace of the heated water. It felt really nice for a few minutes, peaceful, like the first soothing moments you stretch out in a hot, freshly-run bubble bath. The tranquil sensation passed quickly, though—too quickly—and soon Sims started to feel different, light-headed, slightly nauseous, and totally disoriented. Sims was starting to think that maybe this hadn't been such a great idea after all, but decided to give it another few minutes before packing it in.

He concentrated on nothing, yet couldn't stop thinking about everything that had been going wrong lately: his mind racing, turning, spinning, and threatening to careen out of control. He was close to hysteria, and the last thing he wanted to do was freak out in front of Bowen. Sims would never live it down. Thankfully, as sudden as the panic attack had come, it was gone, a spreading inner peace cooling his feverish thoughts. Sims began to feel comfortable again, losing his fear of this strange artificial environment.

He also began to lose his sense of confinement. The walls of the chamber seemed to recede into the pitch black at an alarming speed, the space around him expanding exponentially, leaving Sims suspended in the epicenter of an infinite black void. The void filled with liquid, but not the water he'd originally laid down in; this was a sticky, warm liquid with the viscosity of blood. His body rose on the crimson ocean, vividly imagined in blazing red Technicolor behind his tightly closed eyes. Something latched onto his feet, preventing Sims from rising with the tide, and when he opened his eyes, he was surprised that he could see his surroundings clearly.

"What the hell is happening?" Sims whispered.

Above him, the sky was yellow, and seven immense orange suns were spread across the endless horizon. Sims was shocked to find that he really was afloat on a sea of glowing blood, and he just managed a glimpse of the shackles and chains binding his ankles to the submerged metal footrest before the rising blood raised another ten inches.

"I'm hallucinating," Sims said.

Although fully cognizant that he was John Benjamin Sims, a veteran airline pilot lying completely still inside a sensory deprivation tank in Toronto, Canada, he couldn't help but panic when the blood continued to rise. Sims swam into an upright position, perching precariously atop the footrest he was bound tightly to. He tried bending down and yanking his feet free, but no matter how hard he pulled, the chains held.

The blood continued to rise, covering the waistband of his baggy green shorts, inching its way steadily toward his nipples. Sims frantically looked around, desperate for help, but for miles in all directions there was nothing but the red ocean—no land, no ships, and no one to come to his aid. The glowing blood rose past his shoulders, tickled its way up his neck, then crested his chin. In vain, Sims stretched his neck skyward, but within seconds the blood was over his head.

Sims struggled like mad, holding his breath for as long as he possibly could, then holding it some more, but eventually he was forced to gasp for breath. He sucked in a huge lungful of sticky blood, and it took him another two panic-stricken gulps to realize he could breathe just fine.

"Still hallucinating," he reminded himself.

He'd just started to relax a bit, when he felt another presence in the red ocean with him. Sims couldn't see it yet, but he could feel its powerful aura buzzing all around him, an electric vibe in the warm liquid, moving rapidly closer.

A small blue dot appeared in front of him, displacing the sticky blood, expanding bigger and bigger as something mammoth propelled itself through the ocean toward him. Sims felt a tug on his chains, and looked down to see the small metal footrest growing, transforming into a large rectangular stone block. Two more heavy chains snaked out from under the block, and latched securely onto each of Sims' wrists, pulling and stretching his body taut against the cold stone. Sims started to panic again, feeling the first stab of real fear—strung up so tightly he could hardly move a muscle.

He didn't have to wait long.

Sims thought his mind would snap, almost wished that it would, when he finally realized what he was seeing. A colossal semi-transparent animal, larger than a football stadium, filled Sims' entire field of vision. It had the body of a turtle, its armored shell thick and scarred, yet it was translucent. Inside, things slithered and shifted, serpentine things coiling and uncoiling around a bloated, neon-blue pulsating heart.

A huge, bulbous head pushed out of the shell, its jelly-like brain throbbing in time with the heart. It had one massive blue eye in the center of its head, with twelve smaller, multi-colored eyes surrounding it like a distant solar system orbiting an alien sun. All thirteen eyes swiveled to lock on Sims, and he cringed under their omniscient gaze.

From out of the feet and leg holes of the turtle shell thousands of tentacles burst free like entrails from a gutted deer, and began moving purposefully toward Sims. Some were covered with tire-sized suction pads; others layered in scales with needle-sharp bone spurs protruding in all directions; others still were smooth and unblemished, just greasy looking flesh fingers feeling their way closer, closer, until they touched him.

It was only a brief moment of physical contact, but that was all it took for Sims to finally realize that this thing filling his vision wasn't an animal; it wasn't some 'B' movie monster, either. The intelligence that radiated around him, into him, filling his mind with things he'd never even dreamed before, told him all he needed to know. One touch, one blazing flash of insight, and everything became crystal clear. Sims stood in the presence of a god, the rock he was chained to its altar stone, and he its sadly inadequate sacrifice.

A flesh finger tentacle swished back and forth in front of Sims' face, seeming to move to some unheard rhythmic beat, and it wasn't until the tip of it began moving down to his chest that he realized the beat it was homing in on was his triphammering heart. A narrow slit opened at the apex of the tentacle, and a barbed steel hook pushed out, its razor point touching Sims' scrawny, exposed chest. With one twitch of its muscles, Sims' sternum was split wide open, his still pumping heart torn from its protective cage, skewered on the steel hook.

The gargantuan head of the god moved closer to Sims' flayed body, opened its cavernous maw, and shredded Sims' tiny heart between its jagged teeth. It swallowed, savoring the sweet meat for a moment, then spoke directly to Sims in a language he'd never heard before, but somehow understood:

"I AM TUL OORTHU," it said, "AND I ACCEPT YOUR OFFERING."

Sims woke up screaming, flailing in a shallow, watery grave, staring up into the face of a red-haired man he couldn't remember having ever seen before in his life. He clutched his hands protectively to his chest, remembering the dream, but still not quite sure where he was. Then it all came back to him: The near miss at the airport, Skyline Towers, Bowen, Larry the attendant, and last but certainly not least, the isolation tank.

"I'm so sorry, Mr. Sims," Larry said to him, helping Sims out of the tank and giving him a couple of dry, white towels. "I should have never let Mr. Bowen talk me into it. Never! Please...are you okay?"

Sims felt terrific—better than terrific, actually—but still wasn't quite with it yet, and he wasn't at all sure what Larry was talking about. Why was he being so bloody apologetic?

"What are you babbling about?"

"I tried to tell him it was too long...especially for your first time, but he...he gave me five hundred dollars to just let you stay in there...and, and now..."

"What was too long?" Sims interrupted. "Me? In the tank? Was I in there more than half an hour?"

All Larry could do was nod.

"How long, then? And where the hell is Bowen, anyway?"

"He went up to his room a long time ago. Oh hell, Mr. Sims, I'll just say it. You've been in the isolation chamber for a little over four hours."

Four hours can be a very long time, or it can flash by in the blink of an eye. It all depends on if you're enjoying yourself. Sims had enjoyed himself very much in the tank, more so than even he wanted to admit. Tul Oorthu had eaten of his soul and Sims was now a part of the beast, and it a part of him.

Larry was afraid Sims would get him fired, but Sims said he wouldn't report him...if he let him go back into the tank, back into his chamber of the gods. Even after Larry's shift was over, Sims paid his replacement handsomely to fuck off and leave him alone.

By morning, he'd spent well over fourteen hours in the tank, relishing every pain and pleasure-filled minute. He would have happily stayed forever, but he had important things to do. He had to meet Bowen for breakfast. And he had a plane to fly.

"Wow!" was the first word out of Bowen's mouth, when he and Sims met in the hotel restaurant at 8:00 a.m. Saturday morning. "You look...well, great!"

Sims looked calm, rested, and focused for the first time in a hell of a long while. They both ordered the all-you-can-eat buffet, but Sims ate at least three times the amount his pudgy friend did, ravenous from having skipped supper the previous night. Bowen just accepted his hunger as another good sign that he was back to his old self again.

Four hours later, they were in their seats, back at the helm of the Air Transat L1011, one hour and forty minutes into their flight to Nassau, Bahamas. They had cleared the U.S. coast a while ago, exiting the mainland over Hilton Head, South Carolina, then easing the throttles back a touch as they caught the strong trade winds helping push them south over the Atlantic Ocean. The sun was shining, the sky was clear, and the plane was humming along nicely. Captain Sims was in fine form this morning, handling the plane and issuing instructions and orders with authority and confidence. Bowen was pleased to see his friend back in control, and even more pleased that this was turning into just another routine flight.

"I told you, all you needed was an hour in that tank to get you back on your feet again, didn't I? When I'm feeling stressed, it works for me every time."

"Yeah, thanks for the tip, Doug, you were right. I feel like a whole new man today."

"Great! It's about bloody time, too. You were getting pretty miserable to fly with, buddy. Say, I've gotta take a leak, and I was gonna grab a coffee...you want anything?"

Sims just shook his head, kept smiling.

Bowen went out the door, leaving Sims alone in the cockpit for the first time since takeoff. A single tear slid from Sims' left eye as he rose out of his seat, possibly a tear of regret for the life that had once been his own. A tiny thread-like tentacle slithered out of the blue iris of his eye, gently swished the offending tear away, then retracted back out of sight. Sims was smiling ear to ear by the time he walked to the cabin door and flicked the steel lever over to the locked position.

There was no turning back now; nor did Sims want to. He was thrilled to serve his god. At a speed in excess of four hundred miles an hour, Sims took the plane into a nosedive, headed straight for the glistening blue Atlantic.

Having always wanted to try some of his old Air Force tricks in a commercial bird, he managed to pull the nose up just before impact and rolled the plane onto its back. Throughout it all, he never heard a single person scream. 209 passengers, six stewardesses, a flight crew of four, and one captain—all torn into little lumps of charbroiled fish food, and scattered over a debris area three miles square.

Well, not all of them…

There was one survivor.

"There! Over there, damn it!" the soaking wet search-and-rescue specialist screamed into his hand-held radio, pointing to a man bobbing with the waves about two hundred yards off the Coast Guard cutter's starboard side. "You heard me...I said it looks like he's alive. Yes! He's waving at us...get me over there, quick!"

The powerful boat throttled up its twin diesels, and the sole survivor of Flight 818 on route to Nassau was quickly but carefully hauled aboard. The man was bleeding and injured, but alive.

"Can you speak, sir? What's your name?" the ship's medic wanted to know.

"I'm John Sims. Captain John Benjamin Sims."

"Captain? Did you say 'captain'? Were you flying that plane, sir?"

Sims looked the doctor straight in the eye and said in his most sincere voice, "No. No I was not."

They never found the plane's little black boxes to dispute Sims' claim. Some speculated they'd sunk, others said they'd turn up if the search area was widened—but they never did. Sims blamed everything on Bowen, saying how he'd been in the toilet when Doug had gone berserk in the cockpit, that he'd locked everyone out and was screaming and breaking things in a fit. Next thing he knew, he said, he was bobbing about in the water, struggling to retain consciousness.

They had no choice but to believe him, and soon, really soon, he hoped, they'd clear him and let him go back to work. Things would be harder to explain after the *next* big crash, and he doubted very much any airline would let him pilot a bird again.

No matter.

There were other jobs.

LUXOR DECANTED

MARIANNE HALBERT

I can't say with any sense of precision when a lark turned into obsession. I can, however, tell you the moment we first laid eyes upon the obelisk.

We arrived at the Louvre an hour before it opened. We'd inadvertently gotten off the Metro one stop too soon. Marlene had this mischievous grin as we raced for the museum, my hand tight in her grip. Entering the courtyard, she let go and ran forward. She turned, the early morning sunlight glinting off her light brown hair, and she waved me forward. *Come on, come on.* When I reached her, she flashed our museum passes in my face.

"See? Straight to the front of the line, just like I told you."

She leaned up onto her toes and kissed my cheek then rested her head against my shoulder. I could feel her heart beating. I draped my arms around her waist and let my gaze wander. I saw it in the distance. The obelisk. It seemed a strange sight, in the heart of Paris. But then again, we were about to enter a pyramid. Sure, it was a glass pyramid. Marlene had told me about the urban legend. That it contained six hundred and sixty-six panes of glass. I felt tempted to start counting them, but there was too much else to look at. The architecture of the Louvre was impressive. Looking toward the obelisk, I could see the Eiffel Tower—or *la Tour Eiffel*, as Marlene had begun calling it—off to the left, and the Arc de Triomphe in the distance. We'd talked about this second honeymoon for years, and a part of me still couldn't believe we were actually here.

We spent the weekend following our wedding at her uncle's cabin in Kentucky. My rusted-out pickup got stuck in the weeds twice before we decided to walk the rest of the way. The only music in the cabin came from an old turntable and a stack of vinyl albums. Patsy Cline, Buddy Holly, Ritchie Valens type of stuff. That first night, on the rotted back porch, exchanging swigs from a bottle of Strawberry Hill, we pretended we were in Paris. Marlene pointed out the Eiffel Tower, cleverly disguised as a dying silver oak. I told her what looked like a mosquito-ridden crick was really the River Seine. The buzzing of the cicadas was actually the ringing of the bells of Notre Dame. There was a pause in the music as one album finished and another one dropped. The needle hit vinyl and through the open screen door I could hear the hiss and pop as it worked its way into the grooves.

"See the pyramids along the Nile..."

I ran my hand up under the back of Marlene's tank top and pulled her close.

"Watch the sunrise on a tropic isle..."

She tasted like cheap, sweet wine, and I'd never been more in love with her.

Fireflies lit up the Champs-Elysees. As Marlene straddled me, her eyes a little glazed, and the rickety loveseat threatening to give out beneath us, I whispered to her about Paris.

"Just remember darlin' all the while...You belong to me."

As she unzipped my pants, I promised her I'd give her the world.

And now, ten years later, here we were. A group of local teens stood behind us. A man in a raincoat walked toward one of the fountains near the pyramid. He stood on the rim, hesitated, then stepped into the water. He kept his eyes down, as though he were searching for something. He shuffled, his stride through the water slow but steady. I hadn't remembered seeing fish in the pool of the fountain when we'd run past it, but something seemed to be swimming, or slithering, swirling, near his feet. The man finally looked up, looked around. Dazed. He seemed completely unaware of the hundreds in the courtyard, yet he *was* searching for something.

"What do you make of that?" I asked. Marlene glanced up from her tour book and shrugged.

One of the teenagers behind us spoke up. "The Romani? Never mind him. He descended from the Italian Alps."

"Or arose from the depths of the Mediterranean, depending on who's telling the tale," another one said.

The first one continued. "Anyway, he took up residence in the Tuileries, and developed Paris Syndrome."

"Paris syndrome?" I'd never heard of it.

"Ah, *comment dis tu*, how do you say...hallu...hallucinations?"

Just then they began accepting visitors into the Louvre. The crowd moved forward and we descended beneath the pyramid. We didn't need to ask where the Mona Lisa was. Hordes of people were streaming toward the stairs. Just looking at that crowd made me claustrophobic. They brushed past me as though I weren't even there.

"Come on," Marlene said. I looked at the swarm of people and shook her off.

"You go. I'll wander around and meet you near the Venus de Milo."

I could tell she wanted to give me that disapproving look of hers for a longer period of time, but the swell was only growing, bottlenecking near the stairs. So she scurried off to see the lady.

I wandered, walking in the direction of the fewest people. Chatter faded until all I could hear was the sound of my own footfalls. I stopped in front of a marble bust of Osiris, staring into the cold empty eyes of the god of the dead.

"Where have you been?"

I shook my head, and saw Marlene staring at me, her face a mixture of annoyance, embarrassment, and concern. I was no longer in the hallway with Osiris. I was in an alcove, standing on the wrong side of the velvet rope. My eyes focused, and I saw a crowd of people staring at me on display. I had one hand on a cold stone. I took a step back and realized it was an enormous sphinx.

"Come on," Marlene said, pulling me away. People gave me a wide berth.

"What happened to you?" she asked in a harsh whisper.

"Nothing," I said. I didn't know how I'd gotten there, or how long I'd stood there. How long had all those eyes been staring at me?

"You don't look good. I knew you should've eaten before we left this morning. Let's get lunch."

We emerged from the pyramid and walked toward the Tuileries. There was a fountain at the center of the garden. I couldn't help notice the wet footprints that led away, toward the Place de la Concorde.

"If we keep walking," Marlene said, "we'll get to the Champs-Elysee. There'll be plenty of cafés there."

As we got closer to the obelisk, I felt my heart racing. There was a buzzing in my ear. Then my wife's voice.

"On second thought, you sit. Rest. I'll grab something and bring lunch back."

I waited for some tourists to take a photo. Once they moved away, I walked up to the obelisk. I felt shaky, like I needed to steady myself. I raised my hand and leaned against the cool red granite. It was not long before I let my fingers trace the grooves of the hieroglyphics. Images of an Egyptian temple played throughout my mind. Then I heard a voice.

"Pardon, but I think you dropped this."

I looked. It was the man from the fountain. He held his hand toward me. In his fingers he clasped a golden ring that twinkled in the sunlight.

Instinctively I looked at my left hand. My wedding band was missing.

"She belongs to you. Take it," he insisted.

I felt guilty, worrying that Marlene would see that I'd lost it. I snatched it from him and shoved it back on my finger. It seemed tighter, biting down on me.

"You like the writing," he said, nodding toward the inscriptions on the stone. It wasn't a question.

Something dripped from the hem of his coat. It seemed too thick to be water. Then it slithered up his leg. "It's a shame it's here. The Luxor Obelisk. Ripped from the Luxor Temple, leaving its fraternal twin behind. Five years it took them. Ah yes. Five years to build a ship shallow and narrow enough to navigate the Seine and the Nile, yet strong enough to survive the Mediterranean with the weight of the monolith she'd brought inside her. To sheath it, fell it, slide it into the ship, ride it over the swells and to erect it again."

This had very quickly turned into a one-sided conversation. For a moment, the Romani seemed to be talking more to himself than to me. People had begun pointing at him again, and a little boy ran for the comfort of his mother's embrace. Enraged, the man was physically trembling as he continued his diatribe.

"The natives of Luxor swore the magic of the sun wouldn't allow them to tear it down. As the sun scorched them, those same men dug the trenches for the ship that would carry it away. And after the drunken French men defiled their virgin daughters, those same men beheaded their daughters out of shame. They tossed the heads into the Nile so the girls' eyes could look upward to watch this great phallus depart at the hands of their French lovers. So five years it took the French. But this obelisk had stood there for *millennia.* With Egypt's dust in their lungs, those men swore The One would rise again and seek vengeance for this blasphemy." Sated, his anger seemed to dissipate for the moment, and he laughed. "You know what stood here before the Obelisk of Luxor?"

I shook my head. The sun was rising higher, searing the images he'd described into my brain.

He laughed again, heartier this time, almost giddy. "The guillotine." He spread his arms out to the sides. "Heads rolled right where you are standing. Louis XVI. Marie-Antoinette. Three thousand others. They say the smell of the blood was so thick, even the horses refused to draw near."

The smell of copper thickened in the air. A falcon flew overhead, screeching, and my guts twisted, cramped. I felt moisture soaking into my socks. I tried to convince myself it was just sweat, but I couldn't shake the vision of my feet soaked in blood as heads rolled all around me.

"Did you know Dr. Guillotin was a pacifist? Abhorred the death penalty." He chuckled, but then his face took on a more serious countenance. "You want to thank Salvolini for the ring."

Hadn't I already said thank you? I couldn't remember.

"My people have a chateau along the Cote d'Azur," he said. "Still in France, but almost to the Italian border. They send me to Paris seeking guests. Everyone who visits the coast wants to see Cannes or Nice, Monte Carlo. But we have the most spectacular views of the Mediterranean in all of France. It's the top of the world."

"I don't know." My wedding band seemed to constrict even tighter. "We've got a hotel booked already. Nonrefundable."

"Then I don't charge you. We have a working vineyard. You do a small bit of labor in exchange. You will be our, *comment dis tu*, our 'word of mouth'. Also, you admire the hieroglyphs. You like history, I can show you more. We have our own Book of the Dead."

"I don't know. My wife—"

"Will be happy that the ring stays on your finger." He shoved a small card into my hand. "You want to thank Salvolini." It wasn't a question.

A few minutes later, Marlene came back with lunch. She raised a paper bag. "Croque Monsieur?" Of course she'd gotten mine without the ham. She was always thoughtful like that. The grilled cheese sandwich hit the spot. We sat on a bench while we ate, sunlight glinting off the pylon atop the obelisk.

"I know we planned to leave tomorrow for Normandy. But I've been thinking—"

"Uh-oh," she said, giving me a skeptical look.

"We should go to the Cote d'Azur." I didn't want to seem too eager, but in reality I felt compelled to go regardless of her answer.

"The Riviera?" she said, still chewing a bite of her sandwich. She swallowed and wiped some Dijon from her lip. "I thought you hated that idea."

"I never hated it. I just wanted to find history. I met a guy who said his people have a place with the best views in the region." I took her hand. I did my best to remember the tune of that old doo wop song. "*Let's watch the sunrise on a tropic isle.*"

Marlene giggled. "It's tropical, but it's not an isle."

I needed her to say yes so badly I could feel tears starting to sting my eyes. I kissed the back of her hand and whispered, "I still want to give you the world."

The next morning, we took the bullet train to Nice.

Marlene had fallen asleep about two hours into the train ride. We made quick time from Paris to Marseille, but then progress along the coast was slow as the train stopped in coastal town after town. I leaned over Marlene to get a better glimpse out the window. Vineyards stretched on for miles, and I wondered at all the wine, all the future headiness it was waiting to cause. Then I caught the first patch of blue. My head swam as though already drunk on wine, and my breath caught. There it was. The sea.

If Marlene had been awake, she'd have said the sunlight sparkled off it like diamonds. But it sparkled like scales. There was movement. There was life. And a more magnificent blue than I'd ever imagined.

We picked up a rental car after we got off the train in Nice. Marlene insisted on driving. I programmed the coordinates from the card into the GPS app on my phone. Soon, we were driving along the coastal highway. We veered seaward, then back toward the mountain over and over in a dizzying rhythm. Like a snake. Serpentine, serpentine.

I saw people on the beach, wading into the water. Splashing, oblivious to what might lie beneath. Houses dotted the mountainside.

Some perched on cliffs.

My heart quickened as we neared our stop. "Turn here."

It was an impossible road. It veered up away from the highway, but seemed askew, as though the dimensions, the angle didn't quite fit with the rest of reality. Marlene took the turn and something scraped along the bottom of the car. She let out a small yelp. The tires spun and dug in. I told her to downshift to get a better grip.

The drive was unfeasibly narrow as we ascended. On my side was a steep drop-off, on hers, the jagged rocky mountain. It scraped along her door more than once.

"This can't be right." I heard the fear in her voice, and somehow got satisfaction from it. "Are you a hundred percent sure? This just can't be right."

"I'm a thousand percent sure. We're almost there."

The car continued to climb. "There's got to be a place to turn around." Her voice was quivering.

We continued on for five minutes. Ten. Twenty. Marlene was trying to hold back the tears as her hands gripped the wheel tighter, and even I began to feel the suffocating pressure of my claustrophobia begin to close in as the road seemed to narrow even more.

"I'm not staying up here. We're switching hotels as soon—" A creature dropped onto the hood of the car. Marlene screamed and slammed on the brakes. The car veered toward the drop-off on my side, and the front tire left the road. I could feel it as that corner of the car dropped with a *thunk*, leaving the car listing badly. I looked at the animal and realized it was a baboon. It used its long shaggy arms to pound on the windshield, which cracked under the pressure. The beast lunged its face forward and screeched at Marlene as its jaw seemed to come unhinged.

Marlene began hyperventilating, her wide eyes frozen on those long curved, razor-sharp teeth. "I can't…breathe…"

"Get out of the car," I commanded.

She struggled for breath. "But the—"

The ring on my left hand squeezed my finger. "Get out!" The creature seemed to take an interest in me. At my dominance.

Marlene opened her door and scrambled out, tears streaming down her cheeks. I followed her, feeling the car shift beneath me. The creature scrambled up to the roof of the car and stood, screeching at us. I shoved the car, and it toppled over the edge. We heard the sound of angry metallic scraping and crunching. I could also hear the baboon screaming as it receded into the trees.

Marlene looked at me as though I'd gone mad.

"Why did you do that? Our luggage…my purse? The car!"

Annoyed, I responded, "You wanted to be rid of the baboon, didn't you?" She continued to look at me like I was crazy. I took a few paces, and then looked into her eyes, and softened my voice. "All of those things can be replaced." I approached her, and brushed my fingertips along her cheek. I meant it, too. I could get through the rest of this without the luggage. Without the car. But I needed her. She must have seen that truth in my eyes. Marlene was still upset. She shook her head in that *what am I going to do with you?* gesture, but drew my hand from her cheek to her lips, closed her eyes, and kissed my palm.

We began walking up. Sweat was dripping down my back, my shirt clinging to me. My legs were aching, already strained from all the stair climbing we'd done that week.

Salvolini came around the corner.

"Ha! My friends. I was beginning to worry."

"We had a little trouble with the car," I said.

Marlene stopped and glared at me. "To put it mildly."

We climbed the rest of the way up the hill. Eventually, the path leveled out and opened into a courtyard. He stopped. Too exhausted to be polite, Marlene ignored him, walking into the entrance of the chateau.

The door was an open archway, letting in the warm summer breeze blowing up from the sea. The floor was made up of large flat stones. Marlene took her shoes off and walked across the room. She collapsed onto a couch.

"*Vin rouge*?" our host asked.

"Please," I said.

Marlene seemed in a daze. Shell-shocked. She hadn't even acknowledged Salvolini's question. I said, "Marlene, do you want some wine?"

She lifted her gaze and her eyes met mine. She nodded.

"Let us go to the cellar."

"Be right back," I said.

He led me into a tunnel. It was dark at first, but with each step a light began to glow ahead of us. Motion sensor lights, I guessed, although I didn't see any bulbs or cords. The light glowed from crevasses off both sides of the tunnel. As we descended, the air became dry and cool.

I couldn't help noticing the writings along the walls of the cave.

"The Book of the Dead?" I asked.

"Yes. If you continue down, there is much more of it along the walls in the cavern. That is where our guests enjoy the grape stomping. I'll arrange everything in case you care to partake. After some nourishment, of course. Here," Salvolini said, his arm sweeping the air in front of hundreds of bottles. None of them were labeled.

"I'm really not an expert. Maybe you should choose."

"No. The grapes were stomped under the feet of previous guests. You choose. You will know the one."

I pulled one out. The bottle was huge. It had to hold at least four times as much as we were used to. We ascended and walked toward the kitchen. He opened the bottle.

"Soon, I will have everything prepared for you and your bride on the veranda. But first, we must transfer this to another vessel." Salvolini opened a cupboard, and pulled down a decanter, setting it on the counter. As he gingerly poured the wine from the bottle into the large glass carafe, he continued to speak. "This is a critical part of the process. The *most* critical. All of the work that has been done before—tending to the vines, harvesting and stomping the grapes, fermenting, storing it in darkness—it means nothing without decantation." He poured the last few worthy drops into the carafe. With a wide grin, he swirled what was left in the bottle in my direction. "Leaving the sediment, the bitterness, behind." In another one of those moments where I felt he was talking to himself rather than to me, he said, "And now, it needs to breathe."

I walked back into the foyer, where Marlene was pacing.

"I don't like it here."

"We've got the sea, wine, each other."

"You shoved our car over a cliff—"

"It was a rental car, and it's insured."

"We could just walk down the mountain." Still pacing, my wife was talking to the floor now. Chewing on a fingernail, she was mumbling, trying to convince herself. "Find another hotel. There's got to be some other place."

“Babe, we are both exhausted. It would be dark before we even made it to the base of the mountain. Let’s rest up. Relax. Enjoy some wine and the view. I predict you’re going to fall in love with this place. In the morning, if you’re still able to tell me you want to leave, we leave.”

I took her hand. She surrendered, and I led her to the veranda. A table awaited us. White table cloth. One plate of smoked salmon, and another of beef tartar. Two over-sized glasses of wine had already been poured.

“How did you—?” she began. “Never mind. I’m starving.” I held her chair out for her and she took a seat.

We were well over a thousand feet above sea level, and had a view all the way to the horizon. Before I took a seat, I peered over the rail that ran part way along the veranda. I could see grapevines below, thick, and twisted, and choking the hillside.

Marlene had never converted to my pescatarian diet. After I sat down, I watched as she broke the yoke of the raw egg that sat atop the raw minced beef. It was blood red. She sprinkled capers, pepper, and finely chopped red onion over it, then drizzled the dish with olive oil.

I saw a flash of movement behind her and a golden jackal slinked out of the brush. It sniffed the air, smelling fresh meat. I stood with a fork in my hand, and growled. The jackal laid its ears back. One trembling lip curled up for a moment before it snuck away. I lowered my arm, and my stomach cramped as I sat back down.

I took a hunk of the fleshy pink salmon sprinkled with dill and plopped it into my mouth. It was so fresh, I began salivating. I could picture the fish when it had still been alive, swimming and darting across the current in the depths of the ocean. I pictured how it must’ve desperately attempted to avoid the net. How it must’ve suffocated when there was nothing to breathe but air. The dill tasted more like seaweed, but that only added to my enjoyment.

Marlene didn’t say a word until she had finished half of her plate of beef, taking long languid sips of wine after each bite. In her light blue sundress, she looked as though she belonged here.

She finally looked around to appreciate our surroundings. She reached up, and her fingers played with palm fronds that draped over her head. She finally realized there were palm trees all around. Where the railing ended, a long trough of water separated us from the drop-off, hundreds of pink flowers floating on the surface.

"Water lilies?" she asked.

"No, they're lotus flowers. See the rounded leaves?"

"They're beautiful."

I imagined Salvolini stepping out of the center of one of these at the bottom of the ocean.

Now on her third glass of wine, Marlene had a playful, tipsy look on her face. One bare foot began to rub against my ankle. She scootched her chair closer to mine and kissed me. She tasted of wine. Only this was no back-road Kentucky cabin wine. She tasted rich. Smooth. Full bodied.

"I've got a better use for those feet," I told her.

"Oh really?" I filled up her wineglass and lifted it up.

I took Marlene by the hand and led her toward the tunnel. Again, those dim lights glowed as we passed down the corridor. We moved past the wine bottles, and descended farther. The air grew even cooler, and Marlene ran one hand along her arm. Then there were stairs. Steep, carved stone steps descending into an abyss.

When it came to a platform, glowing firelight from torches shone around. A throne-like chair. I set her glass down on a small table.

"My lady."

She sat, and I took her foot. I dipped a cloth into warm liquid. It smelled of incense. I ran the cloth slowly over her foot, her heel, her toes. I moved it up her calf and her muscles flexed, eliciting a small laugh from her. I could sense her breathing, shallow, anticipating. I took her other foot. I repeated the ritual, only more slowly. Torturously slow. There was no more giggling. Just an animal lust in her eyes. She was the queen, and I her slave.

I lifted her from the throne, not allowing her feet to touch the ground. I carried her toward the vat. I kissed her, her eyes reflecting the flames that danced all around us. I lifted her over the rim of the vat. Her arms clenched tighter around my neck.

"What the—"

"Grape stomping. We drank wine those before us stomped. Now we do the same in turn."

"It's work," she pouted.

"It's a privilege. Besides, everything involves sacrifice."

I brought her the wine glass, and she took another sip. "Now walk, my queen." I sang the first line of our song. "*See the pyramids along the Nile.*"

Marlene took a tentative step. I could hear the fruit squishing beneath her, and the scent began to take over the room. At first she was squeamish, but the more she moved, the more she seemed to enjoy the sensation. She lifted the hem of her dress, but even so, it became soaked in red. She closed her eyes, and moved almost dance-like, swaying to a rhythm only she could hear. But she began to hum our song and in my mind I sang, '... *you belong to me.*' She passed by me and opened her eyes, holding her arms out to me to steady her.

"You know, when I saw you walking through that fountain and then later leaning up against the Sphinx, I thought you'd lost it. Especially when you were jabbering to yourself near that obelisk and insisted we come here. But this is amazing."

"Me? In the *fountain*?"

The drumbeat sound of a heart began a distant hum. I thought back to that morning. Standing on the edge of the fountain, wanting to feel the water. Something swimming, slithering at my ankles. The kids pointing at me.

"*How do you say...hallucinations?*"

I remembered the ache I felt as the Luxor obelisk passed fathoms overhead as it crossed the Mediterranean. How it had guarded the tomb of Ramses II who had waited for the return of The One. How I'd cried out as I tore and broke free from the lotus, slow motion stomping across the sediment in the bed of the sea, always in the shadow of the ship far above me. The years I'd followed the obelisk, first on sea, then on land. Watched as they hoisted it up. Congratulated themselves on the location, not knowing it was the monolith itself who chose this spot. If it must remain in this foreign land, let it be in the heart of the blood bath.

I looked at my beautiful bride, in the heart of the blood bath.

I could sense The One in the belly of the mountain. The falcon had come from the west and provided him intestines. The baboon from the north, breathing air into his lungs. The jackal from the east, providing his stomach and, along with that, a long overdue hunger. It was gaining strength. All that was needed now to restore The One to its full power and glory was the human from the south to provide the wine-soaked liver.

I heard a roar and the rocky walls surrounding us shuddered as something began to slurp up from below. Marlene's eyes shown wide.

To comfort her, I sang a few more lines from our song.

"*But remember, when a dream appears, you belong to me.*"

I could tell by the way she gripped me, she couldn't understand why I was singing when the world was crashing down around us. "Sal? Get me out of here." She was pleading now.

Tentacles slithered out from my sleeves and pant legs. Out from *me.* I held her fast.

I could hear those doo wop boys harmonizing in my mind as I sang one more line to her. It was hard singing and stifling a laugh at the same time. "*I'll be so alone without you.*"

The woman I'd been married to for ten years let out a scream then. But this wasn't your average 'spider in the shower' scream. This was guttural. This, I'm quite certain, shredded pieces of her esophagus. This was sincere. I was so proud of her. And as that pride swelled in me, I reassured her.

"Straight to the front of the line, my love."

She struggled and shrieked some more, the sound echoing through the chamber and into the abyss. An even louder roar rose up to meet us. The walls trembled again and I could hear rock cracking, splintering. Dust fell down from overhead. You'd think with all that, my claustrophobia would have reached its limits. But I'd never felt more liberated. Claws scraped along the rock floor and walls as euphoria enveloped me, and The One slithered forward. In the light of the torches, a thousand pulsing yellow eyes stared up us. When it roared again all I could think was that it put the baboon's teeth to shame. I'd never loved Marlene more than I did in that moment. I could have covered her mouth, but I liked the raspy sounds of her dust-filled screams.

SANDCASTLES

HENRY SNIDER

The Wyoming wind whipped against the car's right side, threatening to force it into the neighboring lane. Teri over-corrected and felt the vibration strips bordering the shoulder. A second jerk of the wheel pulled the car back between the painted lines.

"Damn it," she muttered and stole a glance to the passenger seat. Melanie didn't show any signs of waking up. Her wife stayed neatly curled as if a cat in a warm ray of sunshine, dark curls masking naturally caramel-colored skin.

Her wife.

The thought rolled through Teri's mind. Not even married a week and the two had settled on a cross-country adventure for their honeymoon. They'd flown hours to Los Angeles and rented a car so that the landscape would be new from day one. Angry urban lifestyles gave way to equally-angry suburbanites as they tore through the land of actors, aspiring actors, and would-never-be actors. That first day had come to a close and the second nearly half-gone before the couple happened across someone who wasn't hoping to make it on the big screen...or little screen for that matter. That person, Ted, seemed to be the breaking point from actor-land to the rest of the world.

Teri leaned her head from side to side, stretching tense neck muscles.

A semi blasted past them doing at least ninety and the car shuddered in its wake.

"Damn it," she repeated and adjusted her glasses. A bit of blonde hair escaped her scrunchie and tickled the front of her face. She tried to tuck the strands back, but felt the elastic in the hair tie pop. With a grumble, Teri pulled her hair loose.

"You gotta get a new curse," Melanie mumbled, then shifted and stretched her legs out.

"Sorry. Didn't mean to wake you."

"Well," a yawn escaped her as she rubbed sleep from her eyes, "you wouldn't have if you didn't keep thumping my head against the window."

"Sorry." Teri gripped the wheel a little harder. "It's this damned wind. It keeps tossing us all over the place." She blew at the free strands, trying to get them away from her lips before giving up and tucking them behind one ear.

"You know, we could have stayed another day in Salt Lake City and rested up a bit more."

"Pass."

"Oh, it wasn't *that* bad."

"Once we were on the outskirts it wasn't that bad, but the hotel...and right across from the compound."

"Teri, it was the Latter Day Saints and no one said a single negative word to us the entire time we were there...even when we toured the place."

"It wasn't what they said, it was the men." Teri's grip went from tight to white-knuckled. "You know what I mean."

"What?" She smirked and crinkled her nose. "Seeing two beautiful people in love?"

"No. The men seeing us as if we were two porn stars about to go at it at any moment."

"Well, after the dancing last night—"

"Stop it," Teri said. A smile played at the corners of her mouth.

"And that trick you did when we got back to our room."

The smile wouldn't be refused and grew. "I mean it." Her grip on the wheel eased a tad.

"Listen, Em, most men are just going to do that. They can't help it. Besides, I think I can keep the assholes at bay for you."

Em. Short for 'emerald' – the dark green of Teri's eyes. A name to be whispered in her ear where no one else could hear. A name given to her.

The perfect name.

"I know." Teri reached over and squeezed Melanie's leg. "You did take care of the 'Boy Wonders' at the club, didn't you?"

"Yuppers."

In fact, she had. Last night they'd enjoyed an evening of dinner and dancing up until around ten, when Steven and Cal cornered them at the bar and offered to buy them drinks. Melanie politely refused and one of the men – Teri couldn't remember which was Steven and which was Cal – noticed their wedding rings and said he was sure it would be okay to steal a dance or two until the girls' husbands showed up. Without missing a beat, Mel replied that they were on *their* honeymoon then snatched Teri by the hand and whisked her back to the dance floor before the statement sank in with the would-be Romeos.

Melanie massaged her scalp vigorously, trying to wake up before reaching into the back seat to pull a water from the cooler. "Want one?"

"Still on my soda."

"Munchies?"

"Nope."

"Shit."

"Uhhh...cute, Mels."

"No. Check out the rearview."

Teri glanced at the mirror and saw the razor-straight stretch of interstate behind them disappearing into a dusty beige landscape. "Looks dusty."

"Dusty, hell."

Teri gave a second look. The shifting beige background went from the ground to so high in the sky it disappeared out of sight at the top of the back window. She checked the side mirror. Same thing.

Mel stayed turned around in the seat looking from left to right. "It goes as far as I can see both North and South."

Teri waited for the wind pounding against the side of the car to ease then craned her head to look over her left shoulder. A wall of dust and debris pushed from the West, swallowing everything in its path. "Christ. How far back is it?"

A canary-yellow SUV shot past going the opposite direction and straight toward the dust storm. "Tell you in a sec." She felt Melanie tapping her fingers on the driver's seat as seconds became minutes.

One...

Three...

Five...

"Almost six minutes behind us," she blurted out. "That storm's so dense the Hummer was there one second then gone the next."

"Guess we're going the right direction then, huh?"

"Creepy." She was still turned around and staring out the back window.

"With all this wind I'd be a lot happier if you'd buckle up."

"Don't wanna be a widow before the honeymoon's over?"

"There are times..."

Melanie slid around clutching a bag of Cheetos and a water. She dumped both onto the seat between them and locked her safety belt in place. "Better?"

"Much."

They peaked a small rise and noticed cars coming the opposite direction flashing their lights. The distant sound of horns overshadowed their music playing. Ahead of them, maybe five miles away, twinkling reflections of cars jammed bumper to bumper met their eyes.

Melanie slapped the dash. "A traffic jam?" She tore the Cheetos bag open without looking down.

"Out here?" Teri added.

The multi-colored threaded line of traffic went as far as they could see, disappearing over a rise ten or so miles ahead.

Melanie pointed to a sign as they shot past. "There!"

"What?"

"An exit coming up in a mile."

"But we don't know where it goes."

Melanie motioned to the road ahead. "The evil we know, or the evil we don't?"

Teri looked around at the landscape. Ground so dry even scrub brush refused to grow met her gaze in every direction. She glanced at the fuel gauge – three quarters of a tank. Butterflies danced in her stomach at the thought of being stranded in such desolate territory. "I don't—"

"There it is. Take it."

"I—"

"Em, just do it!" Melanie aimed an orange-stained finger in the exit's direction for emphasis.

Teri rolled her eyes and sighed, but flicked on the turn signal. She braked hard because the off ramp was shorter than expected, and the car went from sixty to fifteen in a short span before skidding to a dusty halt in front of the stop sign. There was no on-ramp across the road, only a crevasse serving as the final resting place for old tumbleweeds. To the left took them under the interstate on a single-lane access barely big enough for a car to navigate. Shadows contrasted sharply in the midday sun, making the underpass appear darker to the naked eye. Their other option bore little in the way of promise. To the right a dust-encrusted blacktop ended a dozen or so yards from where the car sat. Granted, the road continued but appeared to become more washboard than access before vanishing over the rise a quarter-mile away.

Teri sat and stared first at the underpass and then to the rough stretch of road before settling on Melanie. "Well?"

"Well what?" She took a long drink from the bottle of water.

"Which way, oh great adventurer?"

"No idea."

Teri reached over, popped open the glove box, and grabbed a scrunchie. She fumbled with it, pulling the sweaty mane off the back of her neck. "No one's come down after us. Maybe I can back up."

"And wait who knows how long before traffic gets moving again? I think I'll pass."

The air hung heavy in the rental car with Teri struggling not to lose her temper and Melanie obliviously content to follow her Zen approach to the situation.

Teri looked at Melanie then straight out the front of the car. "What did it say?"

"Hmm?"

Words came from Teri's mouth both slow and quiet. "The sign for this exit. What did it say?"

"Free beer." Melanie sat a little straighter when the comment fell flat. "Sorry, Em. I didn't mean to..." The words trailed off.

Teri continued to stare out the windshield for nearly a full minute when she said, "I know. I'm just hot, tired and not really looking forward to any of the options before us right now."

"Hot? The AC's on."

"I'm baking in the sun."

Wind buffeted the car, rocking it from right-rear to left front.

"I don't remember what it said. I just caught sight of the thing as we went by." She furrowed her brow and pinched the bridge of her nose with a forefinger and thumb. "I *think* it said something about a rest stop."

Teri chanced a look over her shoulder. “You'd think with a sandstorm coming there'd be a line of cars following down here after us.”

“There weren't that many behind us.” She stuck a thumb out to the right. “I doubt the rest stop's that way.”

“Good. I don't think my back could handle that.”

“So,” Melanie said with a renewed grin, “our adventure takes us to the left?”

Another sigh escaped her. “To the left,” she agreed.

Her wife leaned over and stole a quick kiss, leaving a Cheeto-encrusted orange print on the side of Teri's mouth.

“Keep eating those and I'm going to start calling you Chester.”

“Chester?” Melanie's eyes lit up “Oh, the cheetah. Cool. I can be Chester the cheesy Persian lesbian cheetah.”

“Quite the name. Sounds right up your alley.”

Another gust of wind hit the car, causing them both to crane their necks and look out the rear window. The sky still shone blue, but the onset of the storm was evident. Air pressure increased and they both yawned in an effort to get their ears to pop.

Teri turned left. “Pillow talk later.”

Melanie sat back and stared at her. “Pillow talk? After three years your pillow talk's still about as Disney as they come.”

Teri cut her a look and stuck out her tongue.

The bridge loomed overhead. Two slices of shade and then the road curved left and out of sight. Sand peppered the car along the driver's side, leaving residue a darker hue of orange than Melanie's kiss. She stepped on the gas. Shade engulfed the vehicle and the bridge shielded them from the worst of Mother Nature's assault. Both women looked at the narrow access. Graffiti covered the concrete where the hill's slope met the underside of the structure. All of the writing and artwork was too small to make out and lacked the general soft-cornered touch that spray paint offered.

“Creepy,” Teri breathed. She strained to make out some of what marred the slate-gray surface. Words and drawings stayed just out of focus. Her eyes watered, causing images to blur into ant-trails and deny her any sense of enlightenment.

A low rumble filled the car as the wind whipped up ahead of them. Tumbleweeds and loose clumps of dirt whipped past at crazy speeds.

"Em," Melanie said while gripping the car's door handle, "we better get moving. Looks like the storm's about here."

Teri stepped on the gas and moved the car into the channel between the bridges. "Only fifty feet. Only fifty feet," she repeated. The Buick rocked as they left the relative safety of the underpass. "Come on." She stepped harder on the gas pedal and felt the tire slip on the sand.

"Easy," Mel said, raising her voice to be heard over the gale.

Fifty feet fell to thirty and then to ten. Just as quickly as the wind assaulted them, it blew past as Teri stopped the car once again, this time directly beneath the road.

Melanie grasped the door handle and slid her flip-flops on. "Will you look at that," she said, staring at a new batch of graffiti up high on the concrete.

Teri clicked the lock button just before her wife pulled on the handle and was rewarded with a motherly look.

"Come on, Em. Let me out. I wanna see. I mean look at all this graffiti...in the middle of nowhere!" She grinned. "Aren't you at least a little bit interested what people had to say out here...under a bridge? It could be like some kind of prophetic poetry."

"Not as interested as you might think. It's probably a limerick about a man and his horse."

"Let me out," Melanie said playfully. "Let a girl have some fun."

"You could have fun at a funeral."

Her smile broadened. "Depends on the funeral. Five minutes – I promise."

"How about we get to the rest stop and you can look at all the urban hieroglyphics you want after this blows over?"

"Deal!"

"And," Teri added, "you drive the next leg."

"But it's so *boring*!" She stressed the last word in such a salute to teenage years past that they broke into laughter.

"That's the deal. Better take it before I add a foot rub in for good measure."

"Fine," Melanie relented. "But hurry up. I've got to pee."

Teri urged the car from their relative safety and back into the storm. She followed the road around to the left. The car faced back in the direction they'd come and full fury of the forthcoming storm came into view. A wall of wind was nearly upon them. Good-sized pieces of sand pitted the glass as seconds passed.

"Em, go." Melanie gripped Teri's shoulder hard. "Go! Go, go, go!"

Teri stomped on the gas, spinning the tires as they raced toward the cluster of brown-painted structures just ahead. Something swung across the middle of the road, blocking their path. She hit the brakes just as quickly, but not fast enough to stop short of the heavy duty chain barring the road. Headlights shattered and the hood popped free of the clasp, only to have the wind jerk the plate of metal up, straining the hinges and blocking any view of what was about to hit.

CLOSED, the sign read before disappearing from view.

"No," Teri whispered.

"Back!" Melanie went from gripping her shoulder to smacking it repeatedly. "Back under the bridge!"

Teri put the car in reverse and backed as quickly as she dared. Bright blue sky fell to an angry orange then darkened even more. The underpass appeared as little more than a mirage through the coated windows. She felt the tires spin, not from speed, but from the air pressure urging the car faster.

She heard herself say, "We're not going to make it."

Melanie reached in front of Teri, grabbed the wheel and jerked it counterclockwise. The car's rear end turned toward the bridge then the wind caught the front of the car and continued the spin free of road for the tires to grip. The newlyweds screamed as the Buick turned in a slow 180, but mercifully still overall in the direction of the underpass. Tires gripped pavement again and Teri put the car in drive and pulled the last few feet back under the interstate.

Minutes passed and neither said a word.

Then Melanie grabbed the door handle again.

"No!"

"Em, we have to get the hood down before the engine clogs with dirt!"

"Don't...please!"

Melanie reached out and gently ran her fingers down Teri's jawline. "Have to."

Before Teri could object a second time, she watched Melanie slam all her weight against the door.

Nothing happened.

Another slam.

Metal groaned and the door pulled out of her hands.

"Mels!"

Teri reached out and felt her fingers drag along Melanie's T-shirt as she forced her way free of the car. The door slammed with the finality of a kettle drum. Wind tossed Melanie against the hood of the car, her head striking the open hood's edge. Red joined the orange hue, muddying an area half the size of a softball in the second before dust clotted the wound. Teri scampered across the seat to the passenger side of the car, less than two feet from the woman who'd been at her side since they'd met at the coffee shop just a few short years ago.

"Melanie!" Teri's scream sounded little more than a whisper.

Clumped hair whipped around the woman's face, dirt clotting both eyes and crusting them shut in seconds. Still, she managed to stay on her feet with hands gripping the hood for balance. Melanie's face turned in Teri's direction as she pressed down on the hood. It resisted, bobbing down briefly before popping up again.

She watched as Melanie pushed down on the hood again, this time locking both arms and pushing down with all her might. Metal bobbed down a second time. Peppered red patterns appeared on the Persian woman's arms and shoulders.

Teri bit her lip. "Just come back," she pleaded to no one, to anyone who might answer her prayer.

Wind caught again, thrusting Melanie across the top of the Buick and onto the road. Teri grabbed the driver's door handle and pushed with everything she had. The door refused to budge.

Teri saw Melanie struggle to her knees, a crimson gash already scabbed across her forehead, her black hair now sporting deep dust-orange highlights. Blood crusted below both eyes, telling of her mistake opening them. "Mels!"

A silent scream came from her wife as she sat back on her haunches. White teeth went first red with blood then orange and layers of sand, dirt and clay worked to clog the woman's airway. The peppered areas on her skin grew as blowing dust blasted layers of skin off. Olive skin opened to pale pink before blood welled and crusted over every exposed inch of flesh.

She smacked against the door rhythmically—first the door, then the door glass, then again against the door.

The roar's volume smothered all other sound.

Melanie reached out with one hand to the car when the wind knocked her over and rolled her up the slope to the bottom of the bridge. Fingers grew bloody as she scrabbled to find a grip along the wall of graffiti-strewn concrete.

Teri pushed her way back to the passenger side of the car to follow her spouse outside.

Suddenly the car rose.

She was weightless.

Ground sped by the windows wrong.

Then the car folded in half, wedged tight into the underpass.

She looked from what felt a million miles away out the passenger door window. Cracks spider-webbed the glass, expanding as she watched.

Teri blinked.

The wind howled.

Teri blinked.

It was dark.

Teri blinked.

Bright sunlight shone on a lobster-red patch of her shin.

Her neck hurt.

"Mels?"

It came back to her in waves...their vows...the dancing...playing on Hollywood Boulevard...

...and the storm.

"Mels!" Her voice sounded small, devoid of the panic rising in her chest. Teri shifted and white fire shot from her left elbow up to the shoulder. She wormed herself free from under the driver's foot-well, gritting teeth against tears. Each breath faster than the previous until effort brought success and after two kicks to the cracked window, Teri found herself sliding out of the car and spilling, not unlike a pile of clothes, onto the slope.

Air hung heavy under the bridge, abandoned by the winds that drove it the day before. It had to already be nearing a hundred. Teri looked back at the car. From it's awkward angle Teri felt vertigo wash over her. An empty stomach churned.

"M-Mel!"

Legs shaking, she backed up a couple of feet and sat down against the concrete base of the underpass. Teri's insides tensed and vomit rose to her throat. Her insides churned and she clenched her eyes shut. A moment passed with no resolution to the feeling.

"Shock," she said. Stating the obvious did nothing to help. Another minute passed as she waited for the nausea to erupt or abate. The latter won out and Teri swallowed hard, choking down crusty bile.

She opened her eyes and looked to her left—along the four foot high wall. Dates, limericks, declarations of undying love covered the concrete in paint, marker, fingernail polish, and even etched into the man-made rock itself.

I should put Melanie's name here.

Teri scooted down the slope a little and stood again. This time her stomach held firm. She turned and looked at the graffiti. A few feet farther down dusty lines marred the years-old—in some cases decades—artwork.

Lines that reminded Teri of sheet music.

She heard herself starting to hum a tune.

Wait.

Teri stopped, shook her head in an effort to try to clear it.

The lines.

Feet moved of their own accord, passing where the lines began and continuing to the side of the underpass.

Fingers. Blood from Mel's fingers. Oh, God. "How much blood?"

Drag marks continued to the corner then vanished, much as Melanie had.

Teri stepped from the shade and looked up the short man-made valley between the interstate lanes. Its upward slope appeared empty. She staggered to the middle of the dip and started walking up, moving in the direction the wind had blown Melanie.

Silence, like the air, hung heavy. No rumble from cars whizzing by...no horns beep beep beeping as they blew past her. Not even birds squawked.

The blurry world fell into differing levels of an impressionist painting mere yards away. Teri reached up to push her glasses higher on her nose and found them missing.

"The accident."

She continued walking the center divider between the interstate lanes and looked at the twin strips of pavement.

"Mels?" She parroted the call every minute or so. Teri turned around and looked behind her. The bridge was nothing more than a dark blob in an equally blurry world.

"Fuckin' eyes." A laugh escaped her as a bark. "Well," she said to herself, "Mels wanted me to find a new curse." Another laugh gave way to sobs and Teri cradled her injured arm and kept her slow pace.

Time passed.

Teri wasn't sure how much had gone by, but at some point she'd fought and finally succeeded in pulling the scrunchie from her hair and let it fall free.

Not as good as a hat but at least it's keeping some of the sun off of me.

Teri looked down and discovered she'd left the center divider and walked along the right road's shoulder. The back of her legs burned as did her left shin, bringing to mind her injured arm. A quick glance down showed her left elbow an angry purple.

"Broken...got to be."

Another look back yielded nothing other than blue sky and brown earth.

Sand started crunching underfoot. Asphalt vanished under increasing layers of dust and sand. Ahead the black lines thinned, became spotty and ultimately vanished from view.

"Mels?" she called for what felt like the thousandth time. The tears had long-dried, but anguish rang fresh in her voice.

Still no answer.

The sand grew thicker. Heavy grains covered the ground, barren of the lighter dust that wind ferried farther away. Something else was in the road.

Shapes.

Shades of brown, black, even green met her gaze.

"Cars!"

Shambling footsteps became a half-hearted jog, each step a jarring painful reminder of her arm.

"Help!"

Like her cry for Melanie, the call went unanswered.

Teri reached the rear car of the traffic jam—a green Taurus. The storm had removed most of the paint, leaving only the plastic and door seams to tell what the color was supposed to be. She smacked the trunk.

"Hello?" she half-yelled. "I need...I need help!"

She banged on the door.

It was empty.

The car's front end was wedged under the rear bumper of a black SUV. It, too, was missing its passengers.

"What the hell is this?"

Thoughts of her church upbringing came back. Warnings of the Rapture and what happened to those who didn't follow God's plan filled her mind. She shook them off with a shudder.

"They were outside when the storm hit...or in another car."

Teri crouched down and looked underneath the vehicles as best she could. Nothing human shaped was wedged between any of the cars' tires. Only sand and other cars.

Her shirt was drenched with sweat.

She staggered to what had once been a white Subaru and opened the back door. A cooler sat in the middle of the seat. Inside rested half a dozen beers floating in ice-filled water. Her right hand left an orange ring as she ignored the beers and grabbed a handful of ice. The first chunk swished around Teri's mouth. She resisted the urge to swallow and spat it out onto the ground. The action was repeated with the second and third chunks as she worked to free her mouth of caked dirt. Droplets from the fourth slid down her throat like mother's milk—an icy pleasure cooling her from the middle-out.

A fit of coughing followed. Inky-brown droplets of mud fell from her lips and she reached in, scooped a handful of water and brought it to her lips. She swished and spat then took another handful and swallowed it.

Teri looked around, suddenly feeling guilty.

"Hello? Is anyone there?"

Nothing.

"Mels?"

Not even the wind answered.

"Maybe there was an evacuation."

She looked down and considered the beer a moment before taking it and setting the wet can on the car's roof. Three tries and one broken nail later she'd managed to open the can. A full can became half in a quick series of swallows.

The belch came with such force that it hurt her throat. Teri tried to wipe the leftover beer from her lips with the back of her good arm, but only succeeded in creating a dirty smear.

Tossing the beer can aside, Teri dug into the vehicle and looked for anything that might shield her from the unforgiving sun. Nothing.

She repeated the process on the next vehicle and was rewarded with an umbrella, a backpack, and bottles of water.

Her trek continued as Teri did her best, one handed, to manage both the backpack and the open umbrella. An hour passed before she tired of looking into the never-ending line of cars in the hopes of finding someone. Her elbow throbbed in time with each step, creating its own painful rhythm.

Teri blinked away sweat and squinted at the road ahead. Reflections twinkled in the afternoon sun. Ant-sized shadows shifted at the horizon. The shadows moved a second time.

"People," she gasped.

As before, her steps quickened, each landing with more reckless abandon than the last.

Shapes grew and what were once blobs solidified into vehicles lining a intersecting road. Farther on, beyond her limited vision's capabilities, stood a structure she couldn't quite make out, something resembling an oversized mound with so many sunlight reflections coming from it that even looking in its general direction hurt.

Teri stared first at the road before her then off at a forty-five degree angle to the mound. Heat radiated through the soles of her shoes and rivulets of salty sweat cut trails along the dust on her skin.

"Stay on the road or go cross country?" Words from all the reality survival shows flooded her memory and better judgment won out against desire. "Damned road," she muttered and started out following the barely visible dotted yellow line. A distant thumping resonated throughout the Wyoming flats, working its way into her eardrums.

Voices and the groaning of metal wafted on what little wind the day offered. Teri passed the sign for the upcoming exit.

WHAGEENEE ROAD NEXT LEFT

"Whageenee," she muttered. "Melanie will be there."

As she got closer she heard a myriad of voices overlapping, some crying, others barking expulsions of anger, all of which were still unintelligible by anything other than their tones.

"Must..." Teri gulped air as a new wave of pain shot through her arm, "be...an...emergency tent."

Another scream rang out and her steps faltered.

The off ramp had become a blurry reality, a sandy slide slipping off the highway to Whageenee Road. A crowd stood at the edge of the ramp. Sand blew across the distance between her and them, whipping a dust devil of debris into the air. Six figures broke away from the cluster, surrounded an SUV and began moving it down toward Whageenee's underpass.

"Hello?" her voice rasped as little more than a whisper. She tried again, putting a lungful of air behind the word this time. "Hello?"

Figures stopped moving and looked up. Two, standing a full head taller, broke from the group and walked toward her.

"Thank God! Oh thank—"

"Oph!"

The first figure came into stark reality. Leathery flesh clutched bone in a stiff embrace. Nose, eyelids and lips were all drawn back in an exaggerated manifestation of dehydration. Dry, empty sockets each held a beetle as emerald green as Teri's eyes. In lieu of a shirt, the cadaver wore an Audi leather seat cover as a tunic, its shriveled genitalia exposed with each step.

Teri stumbled away from the thing, falling hard on her rump.

It towered over her as its companion, similarly garbed in an unknown seat cover, stood at Teri's feet. The first reached down and grabbed her by her broken arm and she howled.

The creature eased his grip but didn't let go. It leaned forward and studied her eyes before presenting her to the second.

"Ehmet tont phu," the first said.

"Pok tont phu," came the reply and it drew a tire iron from its belt.

"Ehmet tont phu," the first insisted.

Teri watched with horror at the exchange going on between the two.

The second replied, "Dah!" and stiffly waved at her arm and walked away.

White fire shot through her arm as the corpse jerked her to her feet.

It forced her beside it. "Toh!"

She stayed at its side, slowing her pace to match. They passed the cluster of people at the ramp's edge. Teri counted nine, mostly children, surrounded by five of the walking husks.

"Please," she uttered, fearful of some supernatural wrath, "you're hurting me."

It jerked her arm hard in reply, bringing forth a raspy scream from

Teri.

They left the ramp and stepped into the bridge's shade. Children lined the underpass, scrawling on the concrete with everything from crayons to makeup. Sobs sang out in chorus as Teri passed them. One sat up straighter and she glimpsed eye sockets as empty as the thing leading her. A green glint caught her attention and Teri looked away just as quickly, seeing a beetle's exoskeleton wet with blood as it peeked between the child's ruined lids.

They left the shade of the bridge and continued along the shoulder of Whageenee, moving ever toward the reflective mound. Vehicles were pushed by groups of four, occupying both lanes of the road. Bordering them were more of the husk creatures, each wielding fan belts as if they were whips.

Teri looked up at the mound and lost her breath.

"Cars."

Cars, trucks, in one place even a house door, were stacked neatly, creating an ever-growing mound. The flow of vehicles never slowed, only kept the same steady pace. Sun reflected off dozens of windshields and car doors, catching the vibrant green of thousands of beetles, all pressed against cracked glass.

"I don't understand."

"Toh," the thing leading her repeated and shoved her toward the line of vehicles. It pointed casually to the cars and made a pushing motion. The beetles moved around in its eye sockets, shifting for a better position.

Teri looked to her left at the caravan of metal. Two cars up, a familiar clutch of hair caught her gaze. Though dirty and clotted, it could only belong to one person.

"Melanie!"

Teri scrambled out of the husk's reach and broke into a full run, clasping the broken arm to her chest, toward Melanie. She passed the first vehicle and was nearly to the second when her head snapped back and her feet shot out before her.

The husk jerked Teri back to her feet by the fist full of hair it clutched. "Pok tont phu," it said and reached for a wicked-looking length of rusty metal wedged in its belt. She smacked at its arm with her good hand and pulled free, running the last few steps behind Melanie.

"Stop!" she yelled and pointed at Melanie's back. "I want to be here." She made a pushing motion to the car.

Suddenly her back lit up, hurting as bad as her arm. Teri looked over her shoulder and saw another of the husks pulling back on a fan belt it had just lashed out at her with.

"Ehmet tont phu," it said and pointed to the car.

Teri wedged herself between Melanie and some man that sobbed quietly to himself. Her bare arm brushed against Melanie's.

Too rough.

Melanie's mane of ebony hair covered her face and most of her body to the waist. The narrow bare patch along her upper arm was leathery, nearly as dry as the husks.

Voice half-hitched in her throat, Teri whispered, "Mels?"

Melanie's head lifted slightly, but she never stopped pushing.

Teri tried again. "Melanie?"

A quiet rasp came from beneath the hair. "Ems?"

"Yeah." Teri shifted so she was still pushing with her shoulder and reached out with her good hand and put it over Melanie's. "I'm here."

Melanie's hand slowly pulled away. "Don't look at me, Em. My eyes—"

"I know, baby. I saw in the storm."

"But I'm not blind anymore." Melanie's voice rose. "I can still see...they show me...oh, God, I can see the most horrible things."

Teri stayed silent but kept staring at Melanie, waiting for her story to continue. No more was offered.

"What's happening?"

The man next to them said, "We're pushing."

"No, I mean...all this. What's going on?"

Melanie laughed a bitter bark. "We're in Hell, that's what's going on."

The man cut in. "You know what this pile of cars is starting to look like to me?"

Teri ignored him and said, "Mels," then fell silent as Melanie looked up. Ruined sockets that once held chocolate brown eyes now housed two large green beetles. Mandibles quickened in agitation.

"My..."

My what? My God? My goodness?

"Oh, Mels."

Melanie's head looked back down. "You don't know how horrific you and—hell, everything looks now. It's all so alien and...." Tearless sobs broke free. "I can't hardly move. Everything's so stiff. The skin on my neck split right before you found me. I...I didn't even bleed. They're...they're inside me."

They pushed in silence for a while longer before Melanie asked, "What do I look like to you?"

"The same. You're the same beautiful woman I fell in love with."

The man next to them stopped pushing and grabbed her by the arm. "Wait—you still have *your* eyes?"

A crack of the makeshift whip brought their fellow captive to his knees. Another strike followed the first. Then a third. He threw up his hands in supplication and pointed back at Teri.

"Oomph," the husk said and closed in on him.

"She still has her eyes!" He motioned with two fingers to his beetle-filled sockets then back to Teri.

"Pah?" It bent over him then craned it's head to look at Teri and Melanie.

"Chelah neh pah!"

Teri quit pushing, grabbed Melanie by the hand and backed away. "Can you run?"

"What?"

Teri hissed, "Can you run?"

"Ems, I can hardly walk. They...they won't let me."

Melanie's arms began to shake. Leathery skin stretched, showing miniscule hands gripping muscle from deeper within her body. A small hand—doll-sized and the same leathery hue—stuck out of the tear in her neck. It probed the rip a second before retreating from the blistering sun.

Three whip cracks struck Teri in quick succession, bringing her to her knees. The husk in front of her stepped closer while shadows from three others approached from just out of sight. They pinned her, even pulling her broken arm out and pressing it into the dirt. A splintering sensation, like a stick wrapped in steak being twisted, radiated up her arm into the shoulder.

"Gah," was all Teri could manage to mutter.

"Oomph Tallah?" One of the other three husks leaned in close and forced her left eye open with a bony finger and thumb.

Teri froze when a second lowered a beetle down beside her opened lid.

A finger, impossibly big from Teri's perspective, pointed first to the beetle then to her eye, his fingertip actually pressing against her orb.

"It's not so bad, Ems," Melanie said from behind the car.

The beetle fell from the husk's grasp, landing on Teri's cheek. Talons dug into her sunburned flesh as the insect righted itself before crawling toward its new home.

"You'll see."

"Mels!"

"You'll see."

JARRING LUCAS

KRISTI PETERSEN SCHOONOVER

Sometimes all it takes is a push. To be born. To kill your asshole father. To convince the parole board that you are, to your very *core*, remorseful for what you did. To assure the astonished realtor that you're so desperate to put the past where it belongs that yes, *really*, this broken hulk of a mansion in Murrells Inlet lying just beyond a state preserve is *perfect*.

My childhood friend Leza's excitement that I'm back makes her even more beautiful than I remember, and I wish I'd taken the time to shave and look decent, although it seems she doesn't notice. She wrinkles up that cute little nose of hers, folds her arms across her form-fitting yellow sweater and says, "Really, Lucas? Why didn't you pick something in better shape?"

I'd hoped she'd instantly fall in love with it. "This was the most out-of-the-way place I could find." A ghost crab scuttles across a patch of sand in front of my car; they're nocturnal and beach-dwellers, so I take this as proof. I survey the weather-beaten stones, the rotting door, the broken stained glass window that overlooks the foyer. "Plus, the owner died, the family wanted nothing to do with it, and it's been sitting here like this for years. So I got it for practically nothing. I can fix it up." I'd always worked construction and had returned to the job I'd left, thanks to the fact the company's owned by a family friend. I have income and inexpensive access to materials. "Wait 'til you see the inside."

She moves next to me; I can smell her, a faint hint of cucumber and melon. That's when I see the scratches on her neck: five neat lines, like a claw mark. I reach out and brush back her hair to get a better look. "What's that?"

She shifts the collar of her sweater to obscure it. "You know me. Always getting into things."

Although I sense something's off, it's true. When I was in prison, she sent me a letter just about every week, chronicling her volunteer activities at Huntington Beach State Park, sharing high jinks at her for-fun job at Whales pushing three-dollar towels and sand art, and familiarizing me with the strays she feeds after her daily runs.

"It was just one of the cats." She moves across the arid, sea-grass choked lawn and hesitates on the stone steps. The cicadas are so loud she almost has to shout: "Come on, I haven't got all day. My husband's done at five."

Kent is a pilot and inherited his dad's tourist-shuttling scenic flight business. He's always been possessive of her, and I notice she's nestled her red Miata beneath a cluster of palmettos, up against the untamed tangle of woods that separates us from a cliff overlooking a beach.

She's right. We don't have much time.

The massive door is padlocked. I fish the ancient, scroll-worked key from my pocket and work inside the rusty hole; when, at last, it pops open and the door gives way, it creaks like the grinding of worn brake pads.

There is the smell of camphor, mildew and wet stone, and the sound of the ocean echoes in the cathedral-ceilinged main hall.

"Jesus," she says. "How are you going to sleep? It's like being inside a conch shell."

"That's part of the charm." I reach for the light switch; the wrought-iron chandelier spits to life, sheds orange-gold shafts on a paling mural of a river and desert beyond gold columns and palm fronds; in front of that is a dusty—but solid—intricately-carved Cleopatra-style sofa. The teak banister along the stone stairs to the second floor is still in good shape, just gossamered with cobwebs. "See? Not too bad. A couple things, but, really, it's mostly clean-up and updating. She's structurally sound."

She frowns.

"Come on, I'll give you the tour."

We begin in the sitting room to our left which, like most of the rooms, is full of ancient rattan and mahogany furniture, curiously none of it covered by sheets.

She points to the stenciling on the wall: a repeating rose-navy-amber series of large symbols. "What's with that? It looks Egyptian."

I regret not having made more accurate mental notes when I was with the realtor, but I remember a few things. "This place was built in the twenties when the Egyptian revival was going on."

She steps forward, looks more closely. "I get the pyramid and the sphinx and all that, but what's with the vases with the heads on top?"

Every fourth symbol is crowned with a head wearing a smug countenance: a man. A monkey. A dog. A bird of prey. No, the monkey is a baboon, the dog is a jackal, and the bird of prey is a falcon. That's right. The realtor had explained it when she'd noted if I didn't like them I could remove them. "Those aren't vases. I think those are…" I dip into my memory, but can't remember what they're called—only what they're used for. Embarrassed, I just say, "funeral jars."

"What?"

"When Egyptians made mummies, they took the innards out and put them in those."

"Why?"

"So the person could use them in the afterlife."

"Ew. They couldn't pick staffs or suns or something like that?"

"I think the last owner was like…he studied burials, he'd been to Egypt a bunch of times. The same thing's in every room in the house."

"They're looking at me."

Actually, they hadn't bothered me when I looked at the place. "There's a way to get rid of them."

She considers me for a long moment, steps forward, and sets a hand on my arm. "I know you wanted to start over, but…at least consider staying at Pop's hotel until it's…restored to its former grandeur."

I flush at the feel of her hand, so I look at my feet. "Nah. I'll be fine."

She looks disappointed.

A furious beating noise surrounds us, drowns all else. Leza thrusts her hands over her ears and crouches down, and out of instinct I pull her against me. Huddled together, I am less focused on the ungodly pounding than on the thrill coursing through me.

The sound recedes, and I realize it was a helicopter passing overhead.

We don't move for what seems like several minutes. At last, she looks up at me. Something hangs between us.

"I...I have to go." She breaks our embrace, stands up. "It's late." She retreats to the rectangle of gray and palm trees that is the front doorway, and I follow. "You're *sure* you don't want me to get you a room."

I know I should say yes, but something is tugging at me: *this is where I belong*. I shake my head.

"Well," she says. "I'm not crazy about it, but I guess I'll just have to visit you out here then."

She turns to go, and I watch as she fights the dense growth around where she's parked, gets into her convertible, and drives away.

In her absence, I am drawn once again to the wall stencils.

My mind gropes for the jars' proper name; I'm gravitating toward words that start with 'C', words I realize I'm making up: canic? Conundric? No. Something *like* that, though. I stare at the falcon-shaped one a bit longer. Its eyes seem to pierce through me.

Canopic. That's what they're called. Canopic jars.

I wonder what Mom—the *queen* of jars—would have thought.

I grew up in a one-thousand square-foot trailer on a permanent site in the KOA Campground in Myrtle Beach, and it was crammed with jars: buttons, change, safety pins, everything you could think of was stored in blue glass, pink marble, stoneware, metal; some shaped like chickens, fish, cottages. Mom combed estate sales and thrift shops on a regular basis to find more, and when she wasn't doing that, she was pickling, jamming, canning: Lemony Cauliflower, Spiced Plum Jam, Roasted Corn Salsa. She'd put everything in Ball Jars, fleece them with gingham, and sell them anywhere she could, sometimes even at the State Fair all the way in Columbia.

When I was in elementary school, my birthdays always fell during a themed week—Fire Prevention Week, Ecology Week, Dental Hygiene Week. When I was in second grade, my day landed in the middle of Personal Safety Week, and it was so hot it felt like even our vinyl siding would melt. I was supposed to go to Leza's pool—her parents owned the Polynesian Golf and Beach Resort—but Mom wanted me home right away. Although we didn't have air conditioning, and the simmering menagerie of fruits on the stove made the kitchen a sticky, mango miasma, I was more disappointed I wasn't going to see Leza.

Mom sat me down at the table. "Now, honey, I know you've been learning at school about when to tell adults certain things that you see or hear." She slid me a honey-colored ceramic castle jar; the bottom was the building, and the top was a pagoda-like spire. Needless to say, I was a kid and would have rather been given a toy, so I just sat there, and saw what I swear was the slight sag of disappointment in her deep blue eyes. Still, she smiled. "Go ahead, now! Open it."

I wrapped my chubby hand around the spire and lifted the top. It was empty.

"Do you know why it's empty?"

I shook my head.

"Because it's meant to keep your secrets. See, we don't tell other people outside this house what goes on here. It's…private. So instead of telling someone at school, you come home, and you whisper into the jar, and then you put the lid back on, and no one will ever know. And if you want, you can keep your secrets about other things in there, too. Okay?"

There was the bang of the sunroom door, and I knew what that meant.

My father was home.

"Go, go." Mom shooed me to my room.

Jar against my chest, I was ear to wall for the usual: the insult ("Love those flowers you put out there. If only you were that pretty."), the reprimand ("It stinks like a whore's cheap perfume in here!"), the slap, the slam ("Jesus. I'm going out!"), the tears, and later, when I would alight the rickety spiral staircase that lead to our sundeck atop the kitchen to find her, the excuse: *I fell, I cut myself on a broken jar, clumsy me—I burned my arm on a hot pan.*

That night, before bed, I whispered a secret into my jar. But I'm sure it wasn't the secret Mom'd had in mind.

The house *is* like a conch shell—the *hish-roar* of the sea permeates every nook, overwhelms every space. I'm successful in drowning it out only when I'm immersed in various renovating tasks: for now, covering the damaged stained glass window with thick plastic; ripping out the ancient cabinets in the kitchen; removing the stencils: pressure washing and using a solvent.

The rooms in the house are also oddly-shaped. Most are hexagonal or octagonal, but there's always one wall that has a closet-sized protrusion which ruins the flow; like a buck tooth in an otherwise perfect smile. Since it's not stone—it's fake brickwork, in some places deteriorated enough I can see there's horsehair plaster underneath—I've assumed there are probably pipes and electric inside, but today, I feel like someone is standing in there, watching me.

Don't be a jackass, I tell myself. I rev up the pressure washer and move for a hose-down on one of the jackal-headed jars.

I swear he's leering at me.

My father rarely deigned to acknowledge my existence, so I wasn't afraid; I was, instead, angry. Which wasn't an issue when I was eight, but became one as I grew. Thanks to Mom's Hungarian heritage, I towered over that squat pepper-shaped Italian; the image of us abreast was a Sasquatch vs. Man illustration. By the time I was seventeen, my physical presence in the house was enough to keep things from being incendiary.

Until the night I came home to the violent sounds of shattering glass.

I rushed into the house and found Mom cowering in the corner on a bed of what amounted to her entire jar collection and its contents; my father was hurling them at her, and blood covered the refrigerator, the stove, the cabinets. She could do little more than duck and scream for him to stop.

Everything inside me boiled over. I clocked him, picked him up by his belt and his thick little arm that had swung at Mom for the final time, and made for the spiral staircase to the sundeck.

"Lucas, don't!" Mom yelled after me, but I was deaf to everything save the sound of his body landing on the crack-riddled shellstone of our parking area; I wanted to hurt him the way he'd hurt her.

As it turned out, I killed him.

As a minor with no priors and the mitigating factor that I was under duress, I was given half the normal sentence and released early for good behavior. But every night I spent in J. Reuben, I thought of Mom, whose last words to me before she died of her injuries were "We could have kept it a secret."

Sweat pours into my eyes as I chip away at the stencils; the sitting room is almost completely clear of them, and although the pressure washer stage drowns the noise of the ocean, the solvent-and-brush stage doesn't, so I buy a cheap radio and work to whatever's spinning on 94.9 The Surf. When I was a kid it played beachside oldies most of the time, but now it's a mix of everything, not all of it worth hearing.

As far as stencil removal's concerned, it's the falcon-headed jar's eyes that are particularly difficult; it's like someone used tar. After I've wiped out the jar, the beak, and the feathers on the head, I'm always left with the eyes. I'm about to tackle a pair when the radio turns to static.

Dammit, that's what I get for buying a five dollar special. I put down my brush and crouch to play with the antennae. I bend it left and there's a high-pitched sound; I bend it right, and I hear something that curdles my blood.

Voices. Gutteral, sinister, low.

Who would listen to this crap? I think, but I can't help feeling that there's something not right about this. There's no melody. It's spooky. Frantically, I spin the dial both ways, trying to get another station to come in. Nothing. I try to turn the volume down. Nothing.

There's a loud knock at the door, and I jump.

The radio pops to the 4 Jacks' 'Bobcat Woman.'

More knocking. "Coming!" I switch the radio off, wipe my hands, and tuck the rag into the back pocket of my shorts.

Leza stands on the front steps, haloed by the afternoon sun and in a peony-patterned dress—appropriate for the heat, although she's wearing an olive-colored sweater that completely covers her arms.

She holds up a reedy basket laced with green gingham. "My

husband's at work, I have the day off and I thought we might celebrate. Champagne? I brought your favorite. Or at least it used to be your favorite. Cold lime chicken?"

As glad as I am to see her, I wish I'd had warning so I'm not a sweaty mess.

She blinks expectantly. "Well?"

I open the door wider. "Come in."

She does, peers into the sitting room, and I note she looks tired. Not sleep-tired. Done-with-life tired.

"Lucas? Did you hear what I said?"

"Oh…sorry. What?"

"I said, 'you've done a beautiful job erasing the stencils, but how come you left the jars?'"

I'm confused and follow her gaze. It's true. The other symbols—the pyramids, sphinxes, and scarab beetles—are gone. But the jars are back. It's as though I never touched them at all.

At first my stomach wrenches. Then I remember the nature of things like paint coverage jobs. Why would this be different? "They're…probably ghosting. They look like they're not there when they're still wet, but when they're dry…"

"Like a stain on a carpet?"

"Yes, that's it." They probably, I figure, need a few more applications.

Another helicopter passes over the house, and although Leza reacts, I've gotten used to it. Still, I say, "Let's go eat in the courtyard."

The jar Mom had given me held my secrets, most about Leza. Somehow, I'd always understood—from a first glimpse of her in kindergarten—that I *wasn't* just friends with her. That there was more than that.

But I also knew I wasn't good enough for her, not like that, anyway. My family didn't own a motel, restaurant, bar, or attraction. I was the son of a trucker who drank away his paycheck. She could never feel that way about me. And I remember the day Kent became all she talked about.

We were at our favorite spot on the beach, the sun a glowing red orb sinking into a swatch of fuchsia, violet, and tangerine.

"So what would you like, Lucas?" Leza dug her toes in the sand. I'd brought her an ice-cold Bud, and she sipped it even though I could tell she didn't savor the taste.

I wasn't sure what she was getting at. "What do you mean?"

She rooted her beer in the sand and leaned back, propping herself up on her elbows. "I mean, what do you want?"

I knew what I really wanted, but my jar carried that secret, so I just said, "Someday I'd like to live in an out-of-the-way place. Somewhere private and where I don't have to deal with any arguments."

She laughed. "No, I mean, like, *now*. Like…something more."

I was confused, so I just shrugged. There was only the crashing of surf; in the blue-gray water, a dolphin leapt not far from a phosphorescent patch of plankton.

She shifted, looked away. "Well, Kent really loves me, you know. I've never had *anyone* care so much about where I'm going and who I'm with—I mean, not even my parents ever did!—and he even lets me take his dogs for walks. He's teaching me how to be more affectionate." She drained her beer. "He's really good for me."

"Leza."

"What?"

"Are you happy?"

A long silence. "Sure."

We stayed until the dark descended and the ghost crabs emerged. Then I went home and threw my father off the sundeck.

The day before I was carted off to prison, she came to say goodbye. I remember her sad expression as Kent, copping a satisfied look, stood behind her.

We're halfway through our meal in the weed-choked courtyard when a violent afternoon downpour moves in from the sea. Squealing like we used to when we were kids in her beach-side pool, we toss everything into the basket and bolt for shelter.

"Come on!" She tugs me along. Her hand feels small and fragile.

In my back hall, she stands, staring at me, seeming expectant.

I let go of her hand and move toward the kitchen. "We can finish in here. It's dusty still, but doable."

She patters behind me. "Actually…I should go. With these storms I'm sure Kent'll be checking in."

"Are you sure?"

"I don't want to, but," she sighs, "yes. I should. You know, I'm soaked, anyway. Don't want to catch a cold."

"Why don't you just take the sweater off? Let it dry?"

She rubs her arms. "No…I'll…I'll be fine."

I notice her shoulders seem a bit slumped as I show her out. Just before she steps across the threshold, she hugs me. And she holds on.

I let her, feeling things I know I shouldn't, a warmth in my extremities, an incredible calm.

At last she pulls away and looks up at me.

"You," my voice cracks. "You need to go."

Her lips part, like she's about to say something; then she nods.

After I secure the massive door behind her, I'm unsettled, but not sure why. I'm overwhelmed by the sounds of the crashing ocean waves, the thrum of the deluge, the rumble of thunder.

And something else.

The voices I heard before, like a group of old men having a conversation. But this time, the radio isn't on.

Is it possible there's someone in the house? "Hello?"

No response. Champagne wells up my throat, and I force it back down as I clamber for something to carry as a weapon. I settle for the broken base of a lamp in the shape of an Egyptian goddess.

I make my way from room to room. Through the kitchen with its water-damaged outer wall, the dining hall with its broken mahogany table, the sitting room with its web-canopied chandelier. I ascend the staircase, but there's nothing in any of the rooms, not the strangely painted nursery, the two guest chambers, my bedroom with its unusual brick floor. No matter which room I'm in, I'm goaded to the next.

A crack of thunder and a *smackrash* makes the second floor buck beneath my feet. I fall backwards, wrench my knee.

What the hell was that?

I recover from the shock to find the voices have stopped. But it sounds as though it's pouring inside the house.

I limp downstairs and a moist breeze blows from behind the stairwell: the library. When I get there, I see that it *is* raining in the house. A palmetto has plunged through the glass ceiling.

The voices begin again. This time, though, they've melded into a single voice, and it's somewhere in this room.

Everything inside me screams *run*, but I'm strangely compelled to go inside. The rain pelting my eyes makes navigation over the broken glass and around the metal girders sticking up at precarious angles difficult.

I'm lured to the tree's fronds, and then I see it: the tooth wall, that odd chunk that juts into every room, has been compromised. Pieces of brick façade and plaster litter the area around the tree.

The voice is definitely inside that wall. Some kind of speaker, maybe? That doesn't seem likely, but I need to find out.

Ax. Get the ax.

The air is heavy with the smell of mud and palm as I work, and the voice continues. I hack off frond after frond, throw it aside. When I've got most of them gone, I'm still blocked by part of the trunk. Undaunted, I get my chainsaw.

Halfway through, the blade hits the tree's core and gets stuck. I try to force it, but the machine squeals and grinds, the smell of scorching metal and gas getting stronger. I stop and try to shift the tree. My arms burn, but I manage to make a wide enough gap to get close to the wall.

The storm is moving away now; the thunder is trundling off in the distance. But in the voice, I can almost identify words now—almost. I wedge myself between the tree and the wall and press my ear against it.

Pain shoots through my right ear. I scream and cup my hand to it, feel a warm trickle, but glance in time to see the bas-relief of...a bird, that's a *beak*, fade back into the wall. My ear stings like someone has poured alcohol on the open wound.

What the hell IS that?

Enraged, I throw everything I've got into rolling the tree away, and succeed. It feels like I can't get enough air, my arms throb and my ear pulses, but I'm too pissed off now to stop. I seize the ax and hack at the plaster. Eventually, I see the sand-colored curve of an object, a glint of gold, a hint of navy. I fling the ax aside and reach my hands into the hole, dismantling carefully, not unaware of the scrapes and cuts I'm putting on my fingers. Piece after piece snaps off, white powder puffs into the air, sifts onto my boots, skins the puddles. When I'm done, I take an abashed stumble back.

Leering from the gloom is a three-foot falcon-headed canopic jar. It stares right through me.

Not one of these weird spurs in the house is for pipes. These were put here to conceal the jars. And God knows what's in them.

No wonder the family wanted nothing to do with this place. "What do you *want*?" I ask.

Behind me, something skitters. Ghost crabs. Scurrying for cover.

A deep male voice says, "Open me."

It laughs.

"Open me."

I knot in fear, but I've come this far. I close my eyes to summon my strength, step forward, and reach.

"Oh my God, Lucas, what happened? Are you okay?"

It's Leza. Still soaked, still in her olive sweater.

"Jesus, your ear!" She takes a step forward, touches my cheek.

The deep male voice: *Open me open me open me open me.*

She has no reaction.

My God, she didn't hear that, I think. I pull away from her.

"What? What is it?"

"Leza, I have to tell you—"

She sets her hands on my shoulders. "I have to tell you something, too."

"Something isn't right and—"

"Listen. Did you think no one knew what was going on in your house? Did you think we were blind? Our Moms shopped at the same Piggly Wiggly. I know you did what you had to do. You were protecting your mother." She puts her arms down, steps back, and unbuttons her sweater.

"Leez, please, just listen to me for a second—"

"And now you need to protect me." With one deep breath and a look of determination, she pulls back the cardigan.

I gasp. Both of her upper arms are mottled with bright purple and blood red bruises ringed in sickly yellow, and now it all makes sense—scratches on her neck, sweaters in the heat, cloaking the car and how, how did I not see this? If there's anyone who should have known it was me. "He did that to you."

She is so quiet and tearful I almost don't hear her. "He has been. Since after you left."

Instant anger. "Why did you *stay*?"

She doesn't respond. Instead, her mouth, warm and tasting like champagne, is on mine. A surge courses through me. She pulls back, breathes the words "I was just waiting for you to come home. I've *always* been waiting for you."

The voice: *Open me open me open me open me…*

The front door bangs open. "Leza? I know you're in here!"

Kent.

"Answer me!"

We separate. I help her back into her sweater even as she winces.

"I'm here!"

I feel ill. I follow her out to the hall. Kent was always a big man, built like a string base. But who he is has, over the years, taken a toll on his body; he is lean, corded, wolf-like.

And he's brandishing a crowbar.

"I'm here, Kent," Leza says. "I was just stopping by to see how—"

"My ass. You been here a couple of times, I seen it from the air."

Jesus, I think. *The helicopters.*

"Get over here."

"Honey," she says.

"Get. Over. Here."

It breaks my heart to see her head bow in obedience. She folds her hands in front of her and walks dutifully behind him.

"Go home, baby," Kent taps the crowbar against his palm. "Now."

She doesn't move.

"Do what I tell you!"

Her lower lip trembles. She looks like she's about to cry.

I'm having visions of what he's going to do to her later. "This isn't what it looks like—"

"Shut up."

I glance back into the library.

I could swear the falcon's expression is different: pleased.

"Look at me, coward!" Kent screams at me.

I look at Leza. She looks small. "It's okay, Leez. Go on home."

She hesitates, then pivots and flees.

Kent and I remain locked in quiet, seething opposition until the car engine fades.

The voice: *Open me open me open me open me.*

There is an awful burning inside me, as though someone's poured scalding water down my gullet. I have the sudden urge to get the hell out of the house. "Kent," I can barely talk. "Let's take this outside, man."

"So you can run, chicken?"

"No. This place is under construction. There's stuff around here that could get you hurt."

He laughs. "Oh, I'm not the one getting hurt. Somebody's gotta teach you not to come near my property."

My fingers tingle. My face gets hot. *She's not property,* I think. *She's a woman, dammit.*

Openmeopenmeopenmeopenme.

He's advancing on me. He's pushing us back toward the library.

"Listen, I swear to God, I will never talk to her again. Just, don't come closer."

He comes at me with the crowbar and I duck. He ends up standing with his back to the library, and I notice that the falcon-headed jar is not where it was a minute ago.

It's sitting in the doorway.

Openmeopenmeopenmeopenme!

"You really don't want to do this, Kent."

He leers at me. "I can do anything I want. She's the one with the problems, you know. She provokes me!"

It boils over in me, then, the things I kept inside. The things I should have told others. The things I should have said to my father's face. "You're a sissy little man, that's what you are, a fucking pansy-ass, picking on her! Now I'm gonna show *you* what it's like to be picked on!"

I lower my head and plow into his stomach. He falls back over the jar, the crowbar flies from his hand, and a spritz of blood peppers the air as he's impaled on one of the giant girders that used to cement my glass ceiling.

His legs spasm, his arm drops to his side, and his body goes limp.

Everything is still, and I'm numb.

Jesus. I killed him.

This can't be happening. It can't. I won't get such a lax punishment this time. I won't finish this house. I won't be with Leza.

I break down into tears.

For a while there is only the sound of my sobs and the surf. Then I hear the voice:

Open me open me open me open me.

I remember what Mom said. Her last words: *We could have kept it a secret.* I think of the jars in the walls all over this house, the jars that were made for holding human body parts, the jars no one will ever know are there if I do it right.

I know what Mom meant, now, and I pick up the ax.

RETRIBUTION

D.B. POIRIER

"I'm not going to shoot him!"

Old Man Kittredge thrust the shotgun into the hands of the red-haired man. "Goddamn it, Red, just take the gun! He's got one himself and he's been smashing up the place for hours."

The pump action shotgun was lighter than Red expected. Its black stock and fore-end fit perfectly in his hands.

Red looked at Kittredge. "Abe's my brother-in-law. I won't kill him."

"Your sister's been dead for nearly a year. He ain't your kin no more." Kittredge changed his mind and placed strong leathery hands on the gun. "Give it back then. I'm old but I reckon I can still shoot."

The old man's words struck Red hard. His sister had passed a year ago this same month but his grief was still fresh. With controlled rage, Red yanked the weapon from Kittredge's hands, almost knocking him over.

"Take care how you speak about my family, old man."

"Red, that man up there is not the same person who married your sister. He's changed—and for the worse."

"Then why did you rent him a room? Why take him in at all?"

Kittredge looked to the floor and shook his head. "Because my Penny was a good friend of your sister. She misses Amy as much as the rest of us. Frankly, you taking down that Ministry group, well it helped the town. Heck, it probably saved my Penny. I saw her hanging around with some of those people more than once. Damn it, it just seemed like the right thing to do, but lately he's been nothing but trouble."

"You think he's responsible for all those missing animals? Really, are you still on that kick? Look, if it's more money you want, I'll give it to you."

"Just 'cause you're the District Attorney doesn't mean you can intimidate me. Even the magician up the road thinks he kidnapped his monkey. It's time for Abe to leave my home, and no amount of money is going to change that. Penny is scared of him and I ain't in no shape to be combatin' young psychos."

Red's expression twisted. "Magician? You mean that washed-up drunk down the road? His monkey assaulted a half dozen people this year alone. Someone probably got the good sense to put it down."

An enraged howl came from above, accompanied by the scuffle of feet and the sounds of furniture being upended. Then came the banging. Plaster rained down from the ceiling. A long wail followed in Abe's familiar voice. "No, no, *no!*"

When the commotion stopped, Kittredge looked at Red and scratched his gray stubble. "See what I mean. Still think he should stay?"

Red answered with a scowl and led the way through Kittredge's centennial home. The decor was as old and out of date as its owner. Handmade furniture passed down for generations filled the halls and rooms, impeding their progress. When they came to the stairs, the two men ascended with caution. Each step complained under their weight.

Red noticed that he was gripping the shotgun hard, the whites of his knuckles evident.

Old man Kittredge motioned around a corner. "His room is the last on the left, just past the attic door."

Red turned the corner and saw the door to Abe's room hanging from its bottom hinge, the top leaning awkwardly into the hall. Beyond was Abe, sitting on the floor, his back braced against the foot of a twin bed. His expression was distant, his eyes unblinking. Blood dripped from his face. Half a dozen lacerations peppered his cheeks and forehead. His right hand clutched an old hatchet. His left held a revolver, the muzzle pointed at the floor.

Red leaned the shotgun against the door jamb just out of site, but still within reach. "Abe?" he asked in a soft voice. "Abe, what's going on?"

When Abe didn't answer, Red lifted the door out of the way and placed it against the wall. Furniture was scattered about, some of it damaged beyond repair. The floor was covered in divots, fresh chunks gouged from the planks—clearly the work of Abe's hatchet. Abe's right calf rested on top of a large silver pot turned upside down. Blood dripped from the bottom of his shoe.

Red gasped, "Dear God, what happened?"

For the first time, Abe noticed him. "Red? What are you doing here?"

"Kittredge called me, said you were having an episode or something."

Abe let out a cynical laugh. "That old shit's been on my case since I got here. Sticking his nose into my things." He looked up at Kittredge, "Ain't that so, ya old fuck?"

Kittredge sneered at the younger man, his retort held at bay by Red's piercing glance. Red was taken aback by Abe's demeanor. His brother-in-law's eyes were wild like an animal. *Maybe the old man's right about him. He has changed.*

Abe noticed Red's reaction and drew in a cleansing breath. "I'm sorry, Red. You've always been so good to me. Even after Amy..." He choked out the words. "After she passed you still treated me as family."

Red nodded. "You know I always thought you a good man. Amy truly loved you and you treated her well in return."

"It's my fault," Abe said. Grief washed visibly over him.

Red shook his head. "No, it's not. It was the cancer that took her."

"The Ministry took her," Abe barked. "They took her because of me, retribution for my betrayal."

"Abe, your turning states evidence helped a lot of people, probably saved lives. It was a cult full of very bad people and they're all gone away now. They have been for two years, ever since the Fed's raided their compound. Amy's death ..." Red took a breath and held in his own grief. "Her death had nothing to do with the Ministry. You're suffering survivor's guilt."

Abe laughed again. "It *was* them. I've seen their rituals, the demons they have called forth. Many members of the Ministry have power—power to reach across the world and strike a person dead." His eyes grew distant. "And now I have some of that power."

"You're talking nonsense. No one has that kind of power."

"We found books, Penny and I, at the abandoned compound. I've been studying them."

"Why would you go back there?" Red demanded, anger sharp in his question. "After everything Amy did to save you from those people."

"For the books. I needed the damn books! It was Penny who found them, under a pile of stones. I've been practicing, but the power got away from me. It's difficult to master."

"What got away from you?"

The pot jumped up several inches, lifting Abe's leg, then fell back to the floor. Abe's focus returned to the pot. His demeanor changed and he struck the pot several times with the back of the hatchet.

"No you don't, you little devil! I killed you once, I'll do it again." Abe smashed the pot again.

Red took a step back on instinct. "Abe, what the hell do you have under there?"

Abe's breath hitched with a sob. "It ain't important. It's what's in the closet that will really interest you."

Red looked to the closet door. It was painted white and covered in scrawls of a strange script, one he was not familiar with. As he navigated around Abe and over to the door, he saw that nails, bent and twisted, secured the door to its frame. He reached for the knob. Something slapped it from the other side.

Red jumped back. "We have to get you help. I know doctors," he started.

Then the pot jumped. This time, a small hand with black fingernails escaped from beneath. Pinned by the rim of the pot at its wrist, the hand clawed at the wooden floor.

"Stop it!" screamed Abe.

The small hand shot back and out of view.

"Dad, what's going on?" called a female voice outside the room.

"Penny? What are you doing here, girl. I told you to go somewhere safe."

Red hurried past Abe to the hallway, where Kittredge and his daughter were huddled. "Penny, you need to get out of here. It isn't safe."

"Oh really, now you agree with me," said Kittredge.

The thunderclap of a gun's report shook the hallway. Instinctively, Kittredge shielded Penny. Red braced the wall. He looked back at Abe, who held his revolver over the pot, his leg still covering half of it. Smoke rose from a bullet sized-hole in its upturned base.

"I told you I would kill you again!" Abe fired two more shots down into the metal. Bullets ricocheted.

Kittredge took the shotgun from the wall and chambered a round. "I'll kill him! Before he kills us."

Red reached for the gun as Kittredge fired, sending the shot astray. Instead of striking its target, the blast struck Abe's foot, blowing it clear off. Bloody chunks spattered the floor. Abe screamed and reached toward the bloody stump. His leg came off the pot, which flew into the air, its prisoner freed. A murky streak bolted across the room on two legs and skittered towards the wall, tail trailing behind.

"It's the damn monkey!" yelled Kittredge.

But it was like no monkey Red had ever seen. Its body was covered in linen strips, tufts of hair protruding in gaps. More disturbing were its dark and empty eye sockets. The creature moved with unusual speed and climbed straight up the walls and across the ceiling.

"Kill it!" cried Abe.

He climbed to his one good foot and hobbled across the floor on the remnants of his other leg, firing repeatedly as the monkey darted from ceiling to wall to floor with unnatural speed. Every shot missed. After the last shot, the horror leaped into the hall and onto Penny's head. She let out an unholy scream as it mauled her face.

Kittredge tore the shotgun from Red's hand and brought the butt of it down on the monkey's bandaged head. As though anticipating the attack, the thing jumped away. Kittredge crushed his daughter's nose, knocking her unconscious.

When they turned to find it, they discovered the monkey savaging Abe, biting at his neck. Kittredge chambered another round and fired. Again the monkey leaped away, and the shot took off Abe's head. Blood and bone painted the room. The monkey skittered from wall to wall, leaving a trail of crimson footprints as it charged toward the hall.

Kittredge pumped and fired in quick succession. None of the shots hit, but the barrage kept the monstrosity contained in the room. "One shot left," he said, breaths coming hard.

Red took the weapon and fired at a window. Glass burst into the yard beyond, but the thing did not take the easy exit and instead came at him. Stepping into the room, Red grasped the barrel of the shot gun. His skin sizzled as he touched the searing metal and swung it at the vile creature. The stock connected with a crunch, launching the monkey out the window.

Kittredge cradled his daughter's head. "By all that's holy, what was that thing!"

Red punched the old man's shoulder. "Why did you shoot him? You killed him!"

Abe laid on his back, most of his skull gone, its contents oozing across the floor. Red turn to rebuke Kittredge again, but a loud bang from behind the closet door drew his attention. He remembered Abe's words, minutes-old but feeling like part of another life in the aftermath.

"Leave it be. It's probably another animal or monster," moaned Kittredge.

The sound of breaking glass and movement overhead caused both men to look up. The Attic.

"I think that damn monkey's back," said Kittredge.

Red knelt beside Penny and examined her wounds. "It's bad. Get her downstairs and call for an ambulance. I'm going up to the attic to find that little demon."

"And what are you going to do, club it back to the after-life with the butt of my shotgun? Give it here." Kittredge pulled out a handful of shells from his pocket and motioned for the gun. "Hand it over."

Red was reluctant to but did anyway. The old man loaded all the shells into the weapon. "You got five shots plus one in the chamber. Don't waste them cause I ain't got no more."

"How do you kill something that's already dead?" asked Red, doubt in his voice.

"Can't say for sure, but you hit that sucker at point blank range and there won't be much left, I'd bet."

Red nodded. "Take care of your daughter and call for help. And you'd best be prepared to answer for what you did in there." He tipped his chin toward the bedroom, now painted in Abe's blood.

Red opened the attic door and ascended the stairs. The place was dusty and smelled of mothballs. When he reached the top, he could see the naked frame of the house. The joists were spaced out evenly supporting the slanted roof, the gaps stuffed with yellow fiberglass insulation. The floor, where one existed, consisted of one-by-five planks. Boxes, crates and old furniture littered the place, most of it draped in dust and spider webs.

Red listened for the monkey as he slowly walked deeper, shotgun aimed before him. He heard nothing, but somehow sensed the creature's presence. Behind a wall of boxes and drop cloths, he discovered a knob-less door. With the barrel of the gun Red pushed it open. The scent of exotic spices assaulted his nose.

Light streamed in from a lone window, partially opened. The room was slightly smaller than Abe's rented space below. Planks covered half the floor, plywood the rest. Dark stains coated most of it.

Red made out several tables. Each supported the carcasses of animals in various stages of mummification. Dozens of painted jars arranged in quartets lined the spaces beyond the grisly displays, their sculpted lids depicting the heads of what appeared to Red as those of birds, dogs, snakes, and humans.

Red nudged one of the carcasses with the nose of his gun, what appeared to be a small dog of the yippy variety. Its leg kicked and he jumped back with a start. He almost pulled the trigger but the thing stopped moving. He let out a breath, grateful he had not wasted the shot.

One of the tables had three worn books bound in black leather on top of it. The first two appeared to be written in Greek and Arabic respectively, the third in English. It was titled simply, *The Ministry*. With one hand he flipped through the dark tome. Each page was more grotesque than the last, photographs depicting rituals of animal sacrifice and the step-by-step process of mummification.

A dark foreboding came over Red. He looked up. There, perched on a split wooden beam, was the monkey. It sat unmoving, the empty sockets of its eyes fixed upon him. Red took deliberate aim and fired. The monkey jumped clear and the blast blew a hole in the roof, revealing a patch of blue sky.

The monkey bounded out of the room and into the greater attic. Red shot at the thing in midair, another miss. A cardboard box burst into confetti.

"Damn it. How does it know when I'm going to shoot?"

The door at the bottom of the stairs opened. "Did you get it," called Kittredge.

"No, the thing keeps bouncing around."

Red walked behind stacks of dusty boxes and discovered a crude wooden sarcophagus between them and the wall. It was hand-carved and partially-painted, its lid propped to the side. Opposite the lid were four canopic jars detailed like the others in the back room with the animal lids, but larger and more ornate.

Something darted across the back wall. Red quickly grabbed one of the smaller boxes and emptied its contents across the attic floor. The thing leapt box to box and wall to floor before attacking. As the monkey dove at him, Red pulled the box up, caught the little fiend, and trapped it against the floor.

The box jerked and jumped as the monkey fought its captor. When it couldn't force its way out, it started to chew through the cardboard. Red realized he couldn't hold it for long and lifted an edge of the box slightly. The monkey took the bait. Its head appeared from under the box and, lightning-quick, Red stepped on it, pinning it beneath his boot.

He tossed the box aside and the monkey's body flailed wildly. Red pressed the barrel of the shot gun against its abdomen and fired. Linen and fur exploded in a cloud of dust, along with the searing, close-up pungency of those rare and exotic spices.

Red shot the body two more times, blasting holes in the floor, and then took his foot off the head and shot that, too.

"Did you get it?" called Kittredge again.

"Yeah, I got the damn thing."

"Good jo—" the other man started then Kittredge's voice shorted out with a gasp of pain.

Red moved in the direction of the stairs. "What's wrong?"

The stairs creaked as someone slowly climbed up. When no one answered his call, he raised the shotgun on instinct but realized he was out of bullets.

Penny, her nose crushed and face still bleeding from the monkey's attack, crested the top of the stairs. Piercing eyes regarded him and her face carried an expression that was not her own. In her hand was a carving knife that dripped blood.

"How far you have fallen," she said.

The voice was not fully Penny's; it was deeper and its cadence, its inflections, activated Red's memory. He knew that voice, knew its speaker.

Penny's head cocked to the side awkwardly. "You recognize me, no?"

Fear slithered over Red's flesh. "You're one of the Ministry elders. Pratt, Simon Pratt."

"It is time. A reckoning is upon you," said Pratt with Penny's mouth. "Prepare yourself."

Red stumbled backwards. "Prepare for what?"

Pratt did not answer. He stabbed a nearby box with the carving knife and left it there lodged in the corrugation. He waved Penny's hand, and all the boxes in front of her slid against the wall, exposing the sarcophagus and canopic jars. A second wave drew the canopic jars into perfect formation at her feet.

The fear of being mummified drove Red to action. He held the shot gun like a baseball bat and charged. *One good swing should knock her out again.*

Pratt raised Penny's hand and Red flew into the wall. The shotgun fell to the floor beside him. Dazed, he looked up and found himself held fast in a kneeling position, dominated by a will other than his own. Pratt. He watched in confusion as Penny disrobed.

"I don't understand—how is this happening?" cried Red.

When Penny was naked, Pratt answered, "You underestimated us and overlooked many things. Penny is an initiate of the Ministry and thus shares a connection with us."

Red reeled at the news. Suddenly it made sense. That's how Amy met Abe, through Penny. For some reason, Amy had hidden this fact from him.

Pratt continued, "Penny, like Abe, abandoned us, turned on us, but unlike Abe she did not reclaim herself. She had no one to believe in her and did not believe in herself. She remained a vessel for us."

Penny's left arm reached out and grabbed the knife. Two steps forward and she stood over the canopic jars, with Red less than a foot away. Red cringed as she brought the knife high, but found no relief when he saw it plunge into Penny's side. Blood gouted from the wound. Even more rained out when the knife was withdrawn.

"What the hell are you doing! Kill me, not her."

"A career man, you have no family. No wife and no children, you should consider yourself lucky. There is a truly unique pain that comes from watching one's child tortured to death."

Now he understood. With no family of his own left, the Ministry would torture others close to him. Penny was his high school sweetheart. He thought of marrying her once but decided against it. The daughter of Old Man Kittredge would have been a hindrance to his chosen career path.

He looked up at her, tears streaked down her face. Somewhere deep inside, Penny was conscious, aware of everything, even the pain.

"Penny, I know you're in there," Red gasped, his emotions stretched beyond breaking. "I know you can hear me. This isn't your fault. I'm sorry I didn't try to make things work between us. I should have married you. I love you and I—"

Pratt drove Penny's hand into her body cavity and ripped out part of her stomach. Her other hand cut away viscera and dropped the bloodied mess into one of the canopic jars. It landed with a sickening splash. A foul smell joined the rest of the odors in the attic. Red gagged.

"Love is such a weak thing. It inevitably leads to the opposite of its intended outcome," said Pratt.

The elder of the Ministry plunged Penny's fingers back into her body, this time up to the elbow, and tore out the dark mass of her liver. This, too, went into one of the canopic jars. Red could only watch as the light left Penny's eyes. She was dead, he knew, her body sustained only by the dark power of the Ministry elder. Deep crimson continued to pour from her wound.

Pratt spoke again, this time with a commanding voice, more like the one Red remembered, the soft feminine tones of Penny completely gone. "You will be disgraced by this. There will be no reasonable explanation. They will see our bible, our works, and their District Attorney as part of the Ministry. Soon after, we will go free and when we do, I will see everyone in your office dead, slowly over time. Such is the punishment for interfering with us."

Penny's abdomen collapsed as Pratt pulled her intestines free, placing them into one of the jars, which overflowed. The lungs followed next. Penny gestured. Long strips of linen rolled from a box and wrapped themselves about her defiled body. When she was covered head to toe, Pratt walked Penny over to the sarcophagus, laid her down inside it, and pulled the lid over the top.

It was many minutes before Red realized he was free. His arms, legs and back ached. He looked at the sarcophagus but didn't dare touch, let alone open it. Slowly, he stood and walked to the stairs. His body shook with exhaustion and he nearly collapsed when he saw the body of Kittredge sprawled at the bottom, in a pool of his own blood.

Red made it down and checked Kittredge. Dead. Everyone was dead except him. Pratt was right, he would be disgraced. How would he explain what had happened? A sharp knock sounded from the direction of Abe's room and Red turned. The noise repeated—someone was trapped in the closet. He didn't want to go in there but knew he had to.

Slowly he walked into the room. What was left of Abe's body remained where it had fallen, coagulating pools of blood around mangled top and bottom. Red crawled over the bed to reach the closet. A slight vibration telegraphed through the door, as if the someone or something on the other side were moving against it. Rethinking, he slowly stepped back. He needed to get help before going forward.

A loud bang thundered from the door. A crack appeared lengthwise in the wood. Another savage shove from the other side caused the door to buckle. The nails holding it in its frame gave way. Red retreated backwards and stumbled over the bed.

The door burst fully open. A desiccated and half mummified figure emerged. It fell on him, jaws agape. Red knew, even with its empty eyes and emaciated face, that it was Amy, his dead sister.

THE HANDS OF TIME

B.E. SCULLY

"You said having something that belonged to Ray would help. Maybe this will do the trick."

The woman who had introduced herself as Dora pulled something brown and withered from a plastic shopping bag. When she laid it on the table between them, there was no mistaking what it was: a perfectly mummified human hand.

Griff McGillis, Great Clairvoyant and Speaker for the Dead, made his living finding whatever words his clients came looking for. But now the only ones he could manage were, "That's not… that can't be…"

She flashed him a smile full of jagged yellow cliffs and empty pink valleys. "You'd best believe it is."

Apparently Dora had taken his instruction to bring along one of the departed loved one's most cherished possessions a bit too literally.

She leaned across the table and dropped her voice to a whisper as if she feared the tiny room concealed spies. "Ray never went in for that all that funeral business. Had it right in his will to be cremated A.S.A.P. Fine by me, but ending up with only a little pile of ash after almost forty years of puttin' up with the flesh and blood man—and believe me, we're talkin' a *lot* of flesh here—well, that just didn't seem fair to me. My cousin Ruthie heard about an undertaker over in Paradise Valley—let's call him Joe for the sake of conversation—who's willing to bend the rules a bit in exchange for a little extra slipped into the bill, if you know what I mean. So when I wanted something of Ray to take home with me, Joe worked out a fair price and there you go. Way it's turned out, it's a good thing I'm sentimental, eh?"

"Uh, good thing, indeed," Griff said, stalling for time. He was trying to think of a way to get rid of Dora without involving the police. "And, ah, how did it end up so…well preserved? Did Joe take care of that, too?"

"Why, no, sir! I did that all by myself, thank you very much. Makin' a mummy is easy if you know how to do it. Go on. Pick it up. It won't bite ya."

Maybe not, but Griff wasn't so sure about Dora.

One of the most important tricks of the clairvoyant trade was to let the client do most of the work. All Griff usually had to do was throw out a few vague hints about events likely to have occurred in the lives of ninety-nine percent of the adult population and wait. He had learned long ago that most of the people who came to retrieve the last 'lost' conversation of a loved one didn't really believe their husband or sister or mother had died suddenly with some extraordinary thing left unsaid. Most of them really needed to get out what *they* had missed the chance to say.

Dora, though, was a different story, a clairvoyant's worst nightmare—the client in search of a very specific piece of information. For the past twenty years Dora and her husband Ray had been setting aside money to fund a Winnebago trip across country. Dora, however, being something of a compulsive spender, had asked Ray not to disclose the place where he kept the money hidden. The system worked fine, only neither of them had thought to write the location down in case Ray went to his untimely grave first. That's where Griff the Great came in.

The only problem was that Griff the Great had not one clue, earthly or otherwise, where the departed Ray might have hidden the money.

It wasn't as if he was a complete fraud. Even as a little kid he could sense things that other people couldn't. Sometimes a feeling of panic or even sheer terror would take hold of him, and he'd later learn that someone was sick or had died or been in an accident. Sometimes he could tell a person's mood or hidden thoughts without being told. When Clarence Lubisich had become Griff McGillis the Great, he'd genuinely wanted to help people. But people, he'd discovered, weren't willing to hand over hard-earned cash for a feeling. Every now and then something big would come through, like the time he'd told that young man to call in sick to his factory job and the very next day a gas explosion killed everyone inside. But most of the time it was pretending to figure out winning lottery numbers or telling people what they already knew about their spouses or lovers or whether or not they should invest in that piece of real estate.

It was a decent enough living, though, and he'd probably have kept at it until he had enough to retire if not for the heart attack. As his doctor sat there saying how lucky he was and running down a list of life style changes he was supposed to make, Griff had known as certainly as he'd known that young man should stay home from work that this had been a prelude to The Big One that would eventually kill him. He'd gone home, pulled all the shades, and finished off his best bottle of brandy. Lying on the floor staring at the ceiling fan turning circles into nowhere, he'd had an epiphany: if he was soon set to join the dead, he damn well wanted to find out where he was going. Maybe his so-called gift would finally pay off at the end. And in the meantime, why not make a little money?

The next day Griff the Great specialized: What would your loved one have wanted to say if Death hadn't snatched the words away too soon? Come find out when Griff McGillis channels the Dead's last unspoken words from beyond the grave!

Only he soon realized that the dead had even less to say than the living. He'd tried communing with pets, clothing, collectibles—you name it, he'd meditated on it, including everything from pacemakers to artificial limbs. He'd laid his hands on stiff, powdered funeral home flesh and shifted through cremated ashes with his bare hands. Once he'd witnessed a pedestrian hit by a truck in a crosswalk; when he'd checked for vitals, the lifeless body was still warm—and as empty and silent as a mausoleum. For the past three years he'd encountered death and its detritus in every form imaginable, yet he'd never once gotten so much as a, "Hello, how are you?" from the other side. Griff had secretly begun to think that the only thing beyond the grave was a great big pile of nothing.

He couldn't exactly tell Dora that, though. Griff leaned over and looked closer at the hand. It actually wasn't just a hand but the wrist and part of the forearm. The shoe-leather skin had shrunken around the bones so that every preserved tendon and muscle stood out like river markers on an ancient map. The end of the amputated stump was wrapped in filthy, once-white gauze. The fingers were stretched outward as if reaching for something. It seemed to Griff as if those searching fingers were crying out as audibly as any human voice.

"Well?"

Griff jumped at the sound of Dora's actual voice. She was sitting across the table with her hands clasped tightly in front of her. As far as Dora was concerned, a lifetime of work and sacrifice was sitting between them in that hand.

"Of course, I can't make any promises..." Griff said. "And naturally there's no charge if I can't channel anything."

Dora sat there staring at him. Griff reached out gingerly and picked up the hand. If the two of them had been on a movie set, the lights would have started to flash, the music would have reached a heart-pounding crescendo, and Griff would have begun to convulse in his chair. Since they were only in the front room of a budget condominium in a questionable part of town, none of those things happened. Instead, Griff was overcome with an unsettling sensation—not of *being* someone else, exactly, but of someone else taking up temporary residence inside his skin. He was still in there, but Ray was, too. It was if Ray had dropped in to knock back a few beers and discuss old times, only instead of his condo, Ray was hanging out in Griff's *soul.*

"The loose tiles in the basement, on the left side of the radiator," Griff said. "A small crawl space and a box...the green metal box I—Ray—used to take fishing..."

Griff shook his head to get his own thoughts back. Unlike the other times, this was no elusive feeling or vague impression; this was as clear and certain as if he'd put the money in the box and pried up every tile himself.

"Hot damn!" Dora jumped up and smacked the table. "My cousin Ruthie, who is the only one I told about all this—you know, in exchange for the tip-off about the undertaker? Well, she said, 'Dora, are you out of your mind?' She said not only was I *not* gonna find that money, I was gonna lose a whole lot more for my trouble! But I just *knew* Ray would come through." She leaned over and placed her hand on Griff's, which still had a hold of Ray's. "It was the *hand*, wasn't it?"

Ray let go of the withered digit. The occupied sensation passed out of him like waking from a dream. "Yes," he told Dora. "It was the hand."

The inside of the suitcase looked as if someone had detonated a pile of rotten beef jerky. Griff knew he should have been more careful about removing the organs. Then again, he was kind of new at this whole 'pulling brains through the nose with a hook' business.

"Sorry, Fluffy," he said to the stray cat who had been his first unwilling volunteer. "I guess you won't be joining the Great Eternal this time around."

Griff had tried to forget about the hand. He told himself that it had been a fluke, a one-time super shot of undiluted psychic vision. But he hadn't believed himself for one second. In fact, Griff McGillis was convinced that he'd finally found the secret of the other side. What if the soul was eternal, but only if it stayed put in its original wrapper? What if the soul was like liquid helium, safe and sound in its container, but evaporating into nothing upon release? Modern embalming was as close as most people got to eternal preservation, but that was only meant to last long enough for a nice-looking viewing. The ancient Egyptians, on the other hand, had been playing for keeps.

Makin' a mummy is easy if you know how to do it.

Griff McGillis believed that he had discovered the key to immortality, but Griff McGillis was nobody's fool. Before he agreed to let anyone pull his brains through his nose with a hook, he wanted proof.

The next cat to go into a suitcase was as clean as a military barracks at inspection time.

After forty-five days he tore open the sealed garbage bag and unlocked the suitcase. He dug through the sodium carbonate, which his research told him was the closest thing to natron, the salt-soil mixture that ancient Egyptians had used to cover their corpses. At the bottom of the suitcase was a shriveled, ugly as sin, perfectly preserved mummy cat.

He reached out to touch it and then drew his hand back. He'd been waiting months for this moment and now suddenly he was afraid. Whether he was more afraid that the experiment wouldn't work or that it would, he couldn't yet say.

"Oh, what the hell," he said to the shriveled cat. "What have I got to lose either way?"

The cat was fresher than Ray's hand. It felt thicker, more newly dead. Griff sat there holding onto the cat for what seemed like a long time. He had decided that Ray's hand must have been a fluke after all when he finally felt it. A warm, peaceful sensation…a *living* sensation of rest and comfort. Of course! The cat wasn't exactly going to talk to him like Ray had. It was a cat, not a human being. Griff realized that he was experiencing the cat's impressions rather than its thoughts. And the fact that it still *had* impressions meant that his mummy cat was alive inside that desiccated skin!

The euphoria lasted about a week before a new doubt crept in. The mummy cat had been a success, but what about higher order animals? What about actual human beings?

Three days and four and a half bottles of brandy later, Griff knew what he had to do. He waited until the early morning hours of a weekday and drove down to the underpass where the homeless people set up make-shift camps. He lured a healthy-enough looking specimen into his car with the remaining half bottle of brandy that hours earlier he'd laced with a lethal dose of antifreeze.

Unlike the cats, a coat closet wasn't going to do it for a human being, so Griff had rented a storage facility with self-controlled temperature and humidity settings in a desolate stretch of desert an hour outside of town. He'd gone to three different swimming pool supply companies and bought out their stock of sodium carbonate. Now he had the final, most important requirement.

A human being, however, was proving much messier than the cats.

The hook Griff had fashioned for brain removal didn't work as well with the three-pound human variety. He couldn't get hold of enough tissue, so eventually he whirled the hook around the head cavity like a whisk in scrambled eggs. When Griff tipped the body onto its side, the liquefied brain matter poured through the nose like a strawberry milkshake left in the sun too long.

Mission accomplished, Griff bolted outside and threw up his breakfast in one great, painful heave.

The organ removal went a lot smoother, especially on his now-empty stomach. He consulted his anatomy chart and made a series of long incisions on the torso: the upper intestinal tract and pancreas were the first to go, followed by the spleen, kidneys, and bladder. He then took care of the stomach, the liver, lungs, and heart. Griff had read that the ancient Egyptians left the hearts in their mummies because they believed the dead needed it to enter the afterlife. But Griff knew something they didn't—the dead didn't need to enter the afterlife. They achieved eternal life just by sticking around in this one.

He piled the organs into a plastic crate. Later he'd dump them way out in the desert for the turkey vultures to finish off. The layers of plastic and old sheets he'd lain down to keep the floor clean were soaked in blood and gore. He stuffed them into a trash bag and cleaned up the rest of the storage unit, adjusting the internal conditions from freezing cold to hot and dry. Fighting back his exhaustion, he then lugged the body into the special mummy crate he'd designed and built himself.

The sun was dipping low by the time he'd unloaded the sodium carbonate and poured the last of it over the body. Every muscle in his body ached and he was parched with dehydration. Tomorrow morning he wouldn't even be able to get out of bed, but it was worth every ache and pain. In forty-five days he would have his first human mummy and a direct line of communication with the undead.

The body was rigid and blackened, but it didn't smell nearly as bad as Griff had feared. The sodium carbonate had clumped around the body like wet sand. It had sucked away all of the moisture and fat, leaving a seventy-nine pound husk in place of where a hundred-and-sixty pound body had been.

Griff had planned to clean out the storage facility and then take his mummy home before attempting a connection. He wanted the moment to have some ritual to it, some significance. But now that his human mummy was right there in front of him, he couldn't wait another second to hear what it had to say.

He reached out and grabbed hold of one withered arm.

The sensation was immediate and far more powerful than it had been with Ray's hand. Griff had expected the mummy to feel some god-like sense of omnipotence, but mostly it just seemed confused.

Where am I? Am I dead?

"You're not dead," Griff said. Despite his telepathic connection with the mummy, he continued to speak to it as if it were a living person. "I mean to say, you *are* dead, but not really."

The mummy seemed even more confused. Griff considered that in its previous form, it had been a derelict living beneath an underpass. Perhaps joining the Great Eternal didn't necessarily increase one's intellect.

"You are *immortal*!" Griff tried again. "Your body has been preserved as a vessel for your now equally preserved soul!"

All of a sudden Griff felt the mummy relax into a state of bliss impossible for most human beings to even imagine let alone achieve. The stresses and cares of daily life didn't exist; the aches and indignities of the human body vanished; and greatest of all, the shadow of death that chills all mortal souls was obliterated beneath the blazing rays of eternity.

I'll live forever! I'll never die!

"Yes, yes!" Griff cried, forcing himself to stay calm. Now that he had discovered the secret of eternal life, he didn't want The Big One to come before he'd had time to do something about it.

There was one thing Griff had to ask. "I hope I'm not getting too personal here, but…did it hurt? I mean, the whole scrambled eggs thing and all."

Nothing hurts. In fact, the last pain I remember is the stomach cramps after drinking that bottle of booze—

A jolt ran up and down Griff's body like a lightning strike. He fell backward and scrambled away from the mummy. Had something gone wrong with the process? Was his mummy somehow dying?

He crept back toward the withered body and took hold of its arm. The jolt went through him again, but now he understood: it wasn't death he'd felt from the mummy but pure, raw rage.

Murderer! Filthy murderer!

Griff let go of the arm. He shoveled the sodium carbonate into buckets and emptied them behind the storage shed, kicking his foot around to blend it in with the dirt. He dismantled the mummy crate and loaded the pieces into the back of his car. He swept out the shed and checked for any suspicious leftovers. He then wrapped the mummy in two sets of sheets and a thick blanket, hoping the barrier would prevent contact. This hope, however, was in vain. The mummy flooded Griff with recriminations the entire time it took to carry it out to the car and dump it in the back seat.

The assault continued up the steps of his condominium and through the front living room until Griff finally stuffed it into an unused storage closet in a back hallway. He had put the mummy cat on display in a special glass case in the front parlor. The mummy homeless man, on the other hand, was staying in the storage closet.

"And here we have one of our more unique possessions." The tall, elegantly dressed man gestured toward the display with a magician's flourish. "A genuine decommissioned electric chair. Apparently it provided the last resting place for over a hundred men and one woman. We don't usually allow visitors near the exhibit, but considering the circumstances, we could make an exception. Would you care to have a seat?"

Griff eyed the wooden contraption with its ominous leather straps and buckles. "Ah, that might not be such a good idea."

"Oh! I suppose not, given your professional abilities. Then how about a tour of our death mask collection? Or perhaps our newest exhibit of human organs preserved in plastic?"

"Maybe after we've taken care of the arrangements. As you can guess, I'm kind of anxious to get things settled."

"Indeed," the gentleman said, eyeing him with the relish of an antique collector at an estate sale. "One never knows when the Grim Reaper will come calling with our name on his card, eh?"

The Reaper's uncertain schedule had been the main reason Griff had wasted no time considering his options. He'd been surprised by how easy it had been. He'd had no trouble locating 'Joe,' the rule-bending undertaker in Paradise Valley, but even that had proven unnecessary. Having oneself mummified was perfectly legal as long as proper arrangements—and payments—were made in advance. The bigger problem had been making sure that his soul storage unit ended up somewhere secure. After all, what was the point of being mummified only to end up destroyed by some careless custodian or caretaker a hundred years from now?

He'd had no idea there were so many museums in the world dedicated to death and dying. There were three possible candidates in his state alone, but geography wasn't his primary consideration. He wanted a museum established enough to make sure that his mummy had a safe resting place for a long, long time to come. It had taken his entire life savings, a second mortgage on the condo, and months of astonishingly expensive legal wrangling, but now all that stood between him and immortality was his signature on a stack of papers. And, of course, his death, which would ruin everything if it arrived even one day too soon.

After all, every minute counts in the countdown to eternity.

The elegant gentleman ushered him into a suite filled with other elegantly dressed men and women who rambled on with explanations of museum policy, the display and handling of his donated remains, and on and on until Griff thought he would perish right there and eliminate the need for the transportation clause of the contract. Finally, the papers were signed and he was shaking hands with the smiling curator.

"Nice doing business, Mr. McGillis," she said. "I look forward to seeing you again—though not *too* soon, I hope, ha ha!"

But for the first time in his life Griff McGillis no longer heard the relentless clock of mortality ticking toward his certain doom. In fact, Griff McGillis heard nothing but the blissful, uninterrupted silence of eternity.

It might have stayed that way until the Big One finally came if it hadn't been for the cat. Griff often admired it sitting there in eternal feline preservation, but he'd never had the urge to connect with it again. As for mummy man, after too many sleepless nights Griff had eventually driven it way out into the desert and let gasoline and a match take care of that particular eternal soul.

Maybe the combination of the brandy and the moon drew him to the cat that night. Maybe he'd needed a reminder that the whole thing wasn't some crazy fantasy he'd dreamed up to make himself feel better about the Big One. Whatever the reason, Griff had unlocked the glass display case and lifted out the mummy cat. Sitting in the middle of the parlor with the cat on his lap, Griff waited for that peaceful, cat-essence of eternity he'd felt the first time he'd touched it.

Instead, he was filled with a howl so forlorn and terrifying that he jumped to his feet and let the cat crash to the floor. It lay there shriveled and dark and silent. Griff circled around it a few times and then nudged it with his foot, but the cat remained quiet.

Griff laughed nervously and wiped his hands on his pants as if he'd touched something nasty. "Must be my nerves getting to me. Gotta lay off of that brandy."

He picked up the cat to return it to the display case. As soon as his hands wrapped around the grizzled body, the terrible howl went through him again. Griff dropped the cat into the case with trembling hands and locked the lid. He went into the living room, pulled the shades against the moon, and downed another glass of brandy. It was almost dawn by the time the memory rose up, unbidden and even more unwelcome: the last time he'd heard howling like that was when he'd been a little boy visiting his grandfather's ranch. One morning they'd come upon a coyote with its leg caught in a steel trap. Griff had stood there in terrified fascination as the desperate creature howled and howled to be released.

After that the mummies showed up in his dreams; they stared back at him from his bathroom mirror in the morning; they whispered to him across the vast stretches of time, but he couldn't quite make out what they were trying to say. Everything sounded like one terrible, tremendous howl.

At night with his brandy and the shades pulled down, Griff thought about the hand. He pictured those outstretched fingers, forever reaching for something they would never find. He thought about ancient mummies buried in desert sand. With his eyes closed and the liquor coursing through him, he could almost hear the hot, dry desert wind. It sounded like one terrible, tremendous howl.

He might have gone on sitting there thinking until the Big One came for him if serendipity hadn't intervened. One morning while working through his third cup of coffee, Griff came across a news article about an exhibit in a museum less than half a day's drive away:

Come unravel the mysteries of the mummy! Mummies of the World is the largest exhibition of mummies ever assembled. This compelling collection includes ancient mummies and artifacts from Asia, Oceania, South America, Europe, as well as ancient Egypt, dating as far back as 6,500 years. What secrets do mummies hold about the past...and what clues do they provide about the future?

For the past six months Griff had been asking himself that same question. The time had come to get some answers, one way or the other.

He got to the museum about an hour before closing. There were no metal detectors or special security measures in place, and Griff breezed past the entrance guard without any trouble. He waited until the museum guides started ushering everyone toward the exit and then slipped through a door marked 'Employees Only.' For a minute he walked in blind panic down a long corridor and into what looked like some kind of lounge or cafeteria. As soon as he'd finished reading the news article, Griff had known what he had to do. Now that he was in the museum, though, he realized he didn't have a plan for actually doing it.

He heard voices approaching in the corridor. If he was caught now, he might never find out in time what he needed to know. Suddenly he spied a large closet along the back wall and ducked into it just as the lounge door opened. The closet was filled with cleaning supplies and paper products. Griff crouched behind a stack of paper towel boxes and waited.

It was hard to tell how many hours went by. When Griff crept out of the closet and back into the corridor, his back was stiff and his knees ached. He'd been afraid the door leading into the mummy display might be locked, but the knob turned easily beneath his hand.

The darkened display room was filled with dozens of mummies. Some were so blackened and distorted that they looked more like horror monsters than humans. Some were so well preserved that they seemed ready to step out of their display cases and have a look around. All of them, however, had something to say that Griff needed to hear.

He had to act quickly. The security guards would have already begun their nightly rounds, and the sound of shattering glass would bring them quickly. Griff had given no consideration to stealth. The only precaution he'd taken was to bring an instrument heavy enough to break what he knew would be the glazed security glass on the display cases. He had known right from the start that he would be caught and arrested, but none of that mattered now.

The first display case contained a small Peruvian mummy coiled into a ball. Griff shattered the glass, grasped its ankle, and waited. At first he felt nothing, as if the mummy had been slumbering too long to awaken. Then a slow, agonizing feeling of dread crept through him like a strangling ivy vine.

Let me out! Set me free!

Alarm bells were shrieking as Griff raced from one display case to another. He had just made contact with his tenth mummy when the security guards arrived.

"Hold it right there! Put your hands were we can see them!"

Griff stood in the middle of the room with his hands in the air, but the human voices were drowned out by the ancient ones still echoing through his soul.

Let me out! Set me free! Release me!

The mummies seemed to be staring at him with wild, desperate eyes; their outstretched hands seemed to be forever reaching for something they would never find.

A spasm of pain tore through Griff's chest and he fell to his knees.

"No! No, wait!" Griff cried, but he knew it was too late. The ancient mummies had told him what the newer ones could not yet know: the preserved body wasn't an eternal *vessel* for the soul; it was an eternal *trap.*

Griff rolled onto his back and groaned. He pictured secrets older than the ancient Egyptians, buried even deeper than the desert sands; he pictured endless cycles of regeneration and decay; he pictured the universe exploding and reforming again and again into eternal time; he pictured his soul somewhere out there among the star dust, reforming along with it.

"No! No, wait!" he cried. But by the time the security guards reached him, Griff McGillis was dead.

"And this is the infamous G.G., folks, a genuine, fully preserved human mummy!" The museum guide stood back as the gaggle of visitors crowded round the display case. Even though the mummy the staff called 'G.G.' wasn't the museum's most unusual artifact, it was consistently one of its most popular. At first everyone attributed the interest to the bizarre circumstances surrounding the death of the donor, which had made headlines nationwide. But years after most people had forgotten the story of Griff McGillis, G.G. remained as popular as ever. The staff eventually decided that the ongoing fascination with the mummy was in part due to its unusual expression. People would sometimes stand for hours staring in terrified fascination at the contorted face and wide open mouth that seemed frozen in the midst of a terrible, tremendous, eternally preserved howl.

PROFESSOR HOWLAND'S ASSISTANT

JONATHAN DUBEY

She wandered the desert alone. It wasn't wandering really, as she knew which way to go, or had at least been pointed in the direction by her guides. They refused to trek any closer to the tomb—a good sign. It meant that Professor Lane Howland had made a discovery. He may not have found a sarcophagus yet, but there was no way Annabelle would know until her arrival, which she hoped would be before nightfall.

The gentle wind smelled faintly of decayed flora. Dust blew into the air, drying it, nowhere near the violent sandstorms she expected. With the promise of only three kilometers to go, she allowed the men to take the camels as long as the mule was left with her. Annabelle was stronger than most girls her age, but there were too many supplies for her to carry by herself. Ahmet was the perfect travel companion for her. He was loyal, didn't complain, and did more than his fair share of the work.

A stone outcropping rose on the horizon. She didn't have far to go now and felt the excitement build within. She wasn't the only one excited, as Ahmet chose the moment to snort with what sounded to her ear as glee. She wanted to quicken her pace, she wanted to break into a full run. But that was not a good idea in desert terrain. Ever since Carter's great discovery a few years before, every archeologist seemed to flock to Egypt, as did anybody with a passing interest in history if they could get the funding. Lane Howland's discovery was different. Though it was still technically Egypt, and most certainly in the desert, it was far from Abydos or the Valley of the Kings or any other well known burial site.

As the stone peak grew higher, attempting to kiss the sun on it's descent, light flickered at it's base. A fire. Annabelle was definitely near the goal of her week's travel. Next to the light that was now certainly a campfire the outline of a tent formed.

The man pulled himself from the newly-carved ventilation duct. As he found footing atop the stone, he noticed movement in the distance. Squinting, he made out the image of a man and a horse on approach. He was alone now, didn't have time to stomp the fire ahead of him before the intruder arrived. Climbing carefully down the outcropping, the man intended to meet the unwelcome arrival head on. But first he needed a weapon.

A hand trowel protruded in the dirt between the fire and the one remaining tent. It wasn't sword nor spear, but would do. Picking it up, the man crouched behind the tent and waited. The interloper walked nearer. At this point surprise was his best ally. He needed only to wait for the perfect moment to reveal and strike. Then the intruder did something unexpected.

"Hello...Professor Howland?" The voice was higher of pitch than he anticipated.

The threat was most likely not what he feared. The man rose and approached, keeping the trowel behind his back.

The intruder was shorter than expected, broader of hip and slimmer of shoulder. The horse was smaller and, in fact, not a horse at all but a mule. The trespasser obviously saw his coming and pulled at the fabric of the turban covering his face. Long curled brown hair spilled forth, revealing that the man he was about to murder was no man at all, but a bespectacled woman who had likely not yet seen twenty years.

He dropped the weapon from behind his back, reconsidering the threat before him. The trowel landed with a dull thud. He remained silent as the woman removed her glasses, cleaning them on the cloth that once held back her hair, and replaced them. She spoke again.

"Are you Professor Howland? Do you know where he is, or where I can find him?" she asked, her voice soft but confident. He racked his brain to think of an answer, but was too long in doing so and she spoke again. "Where is everybody? Do you know of Lane Howland? Can you understand me?"

He found his voice and spoke. "Yes, it is I. I'm Howland."

The man before Annabelle now was not what she'd imagined. Though she'd never seen a picture, and did not know the archeologist's exact age, she had envisioned an older man, short and stout like most of her university professors. There was very little white or thin hair in this man's thick, black close-cropped but disheveled coif. This man was younger, his skin darker, likely from so many days if not weeks spent in the inhospitable sun. His eyes appeared almost mascara darkened, his features distinct, high cheek bones and slender nose. It became suddenly apparent to the young woman that she found him handsome. It would however be extremely unprofessional to allow this opinion any credence.

She wanted to ask her questions again, but decided introductions first would be best.

"Professor Howland, I'm Annabelle McAlister. The University sent me to be your new assistant. I was expecting a larger group. Where has everyone gone?"

"You are very young," he replied, tilting his head slightly, sizing her up.

"Yes, well I've skipped a grade level, and I'm top of my class. I would not have been chosen otherwise. Now, I do not wish to be rude but I've been traveling through the desert for hours, and I'm really quite tired. Not to mention confused. So if you please, sir."

"Apologies. There is no one else here. They've gone."

"The Curse. Howard Carter had the same problems. I'll have you know I don't frighten so easily. Is that the only tent?"

"The others took much with them."

"I have three brothers."

"Do you?" he asked, the confusion now his.

"What I mean is that I've camped with boys before. I'll need to be permitted some time to myself every now and again, though."

"Of course."

"You don't say very much. This is Ahmet. "

Annabelle handed him the reins to the mule and sauntered toward the lone tent. Once inside, it became apparent that either the professor was a slob, or the others had left both recently and hurriedly. Books and papers were scattered about the sandy floor. A desk was upturned and several cots were inside, but only one was intact. She tried to find a mirror and spotted a silver frame.

The picture beneath the glass was of a family with two children. The father was an older man, balding with a neck tie and glasses. The mother and daughters were beautiful and shared the same smile. The picture was dark enough that the glass reflected Annabelle's visage. The desert wind had not been kind to her curls.

The man outside stared at the beast beside him. The mule stared back and let out a brae. Ahmet was laden, but not heavily. There was food and water inside the satchels and they only needed to be unbound. He pulled at the first of the knots and it loosed and started at another. Before long the luggage was stacked neatly beside the animal. He patted Ahmet on the head and stroked his ears. There was a covered watering trough on the other side of the camp. He set the beast there. Ahmet lapped thirstily with appreciation.

He knew that important things still needed to be done, but first there was the matter of the food. When was the last time he'd eaten? The first package contained fabrics and a few papers, mostly blank. The next, metal containers, likely food.

"Excuse me." He turned to see the girl approach behind him. "I appreciate that you've unpacked, but you should not go through a lady's things."

"Again, apologies, Anne Belle. I'm hungry."

"It's Annabelle, but you can call me Anna. There's fish in that can. I'd open it for you."

"Thank you, Anna." He handed her the can.

"Have you found the can opener, Professor?"

There was a pause then a simple, "No."

Annabelle went to a different package, retrieving the needed item, then worked on the can. Perforating the metal with a small hiss, a sweet odor wafted out.

"Most professors talk quite a lot more than you do. On account of they lecture and such."

"I've been alone for a long time, and the fumes cause pain in my head."

Annabelle almost dropped the can. "Sulfurous fumes? You've found a tomb!"

"Yes."

"You must show me."

"May I have the fish first?"

"Oh yes, of course." She made quick work finishing the can and handed it to him. "They took all of the food, didn't they?"

"Yes."

"Would you like a fork or spoon for that?"

"No need."

After a short walk from the camp, the pair arrived at the rough stone that towered above the sands. They worked their way toward an ancient, man made wall of carved brick. One stone was removed, about five feet from the ground. Annabelle ran ahead then stood on her toes, excited to see into the space. The man behind her reached around her face, covering her mouth and nose with a wet rag. She tried to scream, but was unable to breathe.

She reached for his hand to knock it away from her face, but he pulled her back, and the two nearly toppled over.

"Don't breathe," he said. "And cover your face with this when you look inside."

The gas, of course. In the excitement of the moment, she'd forgotten that the stale air from a tightly-enclosed space so long sealed was noxious and possibly deadly. She took the cloth from his hand, nodded, and held it snugly over the lower half of her face. Her eyes adjusted to the dimness.

Inside was a box, the size and shape of a human. Obviously a sarcophagus, but not as neatly carved or ornate as she expected. It seemed half finished, and stood upright instead of supine like in pictures of other tombs. The most unexpected features were the eyes, or lack of them. Two dark round holes were carved in apparent haste where the features were supposed to be. In front of the relic was a rectangular carved stone serving as a table; on it five cylindrical containers. The room was otherwise barren but for the dust and sand, lacking great gold statues, bejeweled furniture, or remnants of tapestry.

There was a sour smell and she needed air, so she pulled away, sat beneath the gap and breathed. Questions flooded her mind for the second time that afternoon and again she started with the most obvious.

"How is it that there is light enough to see in there?"

"I ventilation the rock." He pointed above.

"You mean, you *ventilated* it."

"I'm sorry, the gas."

"I understand, Professor, we don't have to talk."

"No, I want to. At the camp. It will be dark soon."

After the sun went down and they'd taken time to drink water, eat a little, and tend to Ahmet, the two sat by the fire.

"Well, Professor, you certainly have something here," Annabelle started after a long moment of quiet.

He looked at her, pondering his next move. He had never met a woman quite like her before, or maybe there was one. His wife. It had been so long since he'd seen her last. She was curious as well. Always seeking knowledge and truth. Always asking questions. And speaking with such enthusiasm. Until today, she was the only woman not afraid to tell him how to behave. He couldn't just stare at her now, could he? He had to talk, had to make conversation. Language was now a struggle for him but he powered through, or tried to. "You're very young."

"We've been over this, I'm twenty-two. Is your age that important?"

"I don't know." He offered a smile.

"When can we go into the tomb?"

"Tomorrow maybe."

"Excellent. Do you think you've really found the tomb of Ka'Fachee?"

With this question, he was astonished. "What do you know of *Ka'Fa'Yeh*?"

"That's why I'm here. Of all the students at the University I've read the most on the subject. I've studied your work. I've wanted to meet you."

"But tell me what you know."

"Geographically speaking, the location was always thought to be much closer to the delta, but you theorized that..."

"No, the man. What do you know about the story of the man?"

"Very little is known, but I believe I've put a lot of the pieces together."

With that she told him all she knew.

"Ka'Fa'Yeh was a warrior, a general. There was no match for him on the field of battle. He would face multiple adversaries at once and usually came out without a scratch. It is rumored he killed over a hundred men with his own hands, and ordered his soldiers to kill thousands more.

"His lust for blood was matched only by his lust for women. He committed horrible atrocities to his enemies then worse still to their wives and daughters, encouraging his men to do the same. This was not a man to be admired. But in the end he got his.

"When he retired from the field of battle he was named Vizier to the Pharaoh. He advised the Pharaoh well, but overstepped his bounds, setting his sites on his master's young daughter. It is said that he visited her bed chambers multiple times and eventually murdered her when she threatened to tell. He was caught by the royal guard, killed a few of them, and fled into the desert.

"Weeks later he was found nearly dead of exposure. However, there were some laws that even the great ruler of Egypt was required to follow. The death of a man of his office must be dealt with a certain way.

"The priests began the mummification process, removing his organs while still alive. They say that Pharaoh delivered the final deadly cut himself. He was buried in a half-finished mastaba, no treasures to see him well in the afterlife."

"I see," The man said looking not at Annabelle, but into the fire.

"And it all makes sense. Judging by the inside of the tomb. No treasure, but no evidence of it having been plundered. No antechamber, just one room. The sarcophagus didn't appear finished, either."

"Anna, I believe you are mistaken. You and all of the others."

"Why do you say that? Most of what I have read on the subject has been your work."

"Much has changed. Ka'Fa'Yeh was not as you say. He was education."

"*Educator*, you mean. A teacher?"

"I have learned so much in these last few days."

"Tell me about him, please," Annabelle said. "Share your knowledge, I want to know everything."

"Ka'Fa'Yeh was a scribe, what you would call a poet now. He spent some time as a soldier, but almost never saw battle. He was a strategist, and advised the generals, never attaining that rank himself. He was pulled from the army as a young man becoming one of the advisers to Pharaoh. He was never the Vizier, but worked closely with him, and perhaps would have been in time. He educated the children of the top noblemen along with his regular duties.

"The Pharaoh had no daughter, but the Vizier did. Azeneth. She was beautiful and quick-witted. Ka'Fa'Yeh was very much in love. The Vizier was jealous of Ka'Fa'Yeh, knowing it was only a matter of time before the young man would have not only his station, but his daughter as well. He kept them apart and forbade her from his company all together.

"But love has a power much stronger than the mind's ability to make smart choices. The two married in secret and planned to plead their case to Pharaoh. The Vizier kept by Pharaoh's side, filling his head with lies about the young man abducting his daughter. They hid in the desert for a time, sneaked into the palace one night to find Pharaoh, but the Vizier caught them first. Azeneth implored her father to reason, but in anger he murdered his own daughter.

"Ka'Fa'Yeh tried to save her, tried to fight the Vizier but was brought down by the royal guards. He was strung up in the desert and made to watch the rituals performed on his wife. Her organs were removed and placed into the four jars then with little regard for the rest of the sacred process, and her body was burned in front of him.

"When Ka'Fa'Yeh was near the point of death, he was brought to a simple unfinished tomb and placed still alive into his prison casket, the eyes of which were carved away so he could spend eternity looking at the jars containing all that was left of his beloved."

The story was related with such emotion that Annabelle was nearly unable to control her actions. Before she understood what was happening her hand was on his shoulder, her lips upon his. The professor broke the kiss, and she tasted the salt of his tears.

"I'm sorry," she said. "I don't know what came over me. I've never been so brash."

The professor looked with a puzzled expression as fresh tears welled up in his eyes. "I liked it, but we can't," he said eventually.

"I should go to bed," Annabelle said, her face red in the light of the campfire. "I've had a long day of traveling and we've got a lot to do tomorrow, can we just forget that that happened?"

"I don't want to forget," the professor managed a smile. "But it can't happen again."

"I'm going to get some sleep before I say or do something else foolish." She started toward the tent but turned as she remembered something from peering into the tomb. "You said they put her organs into four jars, but in the tomb I saw five."

"That was...I'm sorry." The tears ran down his cheeks again. "That was their unborn child."

For the first time that she could remember, Annabelle had nothing to say. The professor was not even trying to hide his tears. She didn't move until he spoke.

"Go ahead, I'll stay up for a while."

Annabelle fell asleep in the unkempt tent, hearing the crackling fire and the faint sounds of weeping.

When she woke, she was alone in the tent. The mess was gone, books and papers vanished. All that remained was the desk now righted, the broken cots, her bed and the items she brought in. Annabelle rubbed her eyes as she sat up, pressing hard as if to pull away the muddiness of her just-woken mind. She was usually a light sleeper, and must have been exhausted to have slept through Professor Howland's night or possibly early morning cleanup. She stood, still dressed in the clothes she had traveled in the day before. She looked around and when she was sure to be alone, she unbuttoned her jodhpurs to tuck in her still buttoned shirt. She could not check herself in the photograph that was her makeshift mirror, for it, too, was gone. She pulled open the tent to search for the professor. Wind blew in and a paper slid from the desk.

She picked it up. It was a letter written to her, obviously from the night before.

My Anna,

You must do something for me. Take the beast and leave this place. Stay out of the tomb. Tell no one you were here. I could not kill you. You made me think of her.

It was unsigned, but who else could it be from?

She left the tent, desperate to find Howland for some explanation. She stumbled from not allowing her eyes to adjust to the brightness of the daylight. She called out for the professor, to no avail. Ahmet was still tied on the other side of the camp. The provisions she had brought were where she left them, but for the can opener and some of the cans of food. A few digging tools lay abandoned on the dusty desert floor. All else had been moved into the fire which was now burned down to glowing crackling embers. She called out again. No answer came other than a look from the mule.

At the edge of the fire was a book, partially burned. One that she did not recall seeing in the tent before. It was too hot to touch so she stabbed it with a small pick-ax and brought it to the trough, setting it down beside the basin then splashing water onto it. Not much was left as the front cover and at least the first half of the pages were gone. It was obviously a journal, as what was written on some of the remaining pages was by hand. A few words could be made out but nothing more than a half of a sentence until the last page with any writing. The bottom half was almost intact, and short passages could be made out.

> *... learns quickly speaking English almost as well as I in just a few short ... fear him and they have left, sneaked off in the night taking most of the ... with such a great discovery, and potential for learning. I am anxious for other people to meet him. He still seems somewhat confused, and the circumstances are unbelievable ... at best if I hadn't been here firsthand, I don't think I could believe ... he seems reluctant to meet others, becoming almost violent at the very idea...*

Annabelle dropped the book. There was no more to read. Only one small piece of the mystery remained. She picked up the ax and made her way to the tomb.

Rage and desperation for truth proved a good substitute for skill at demolition, and it didn't take long for the single removed brick window to become a hole large enough to crawl through. The sulfurous odor in the burial chamber was far less than the previous day, and did not impede her progress. She passed the five jars and made her way to the upright sarcophagus.

She pulled at the lid, but it did not move. She wedged the ax and pushed it. The lid budged a little and then a little more, until the hardwood handle broke at the neck. She picked up the metal blade, now more of a spear and struck at the unfinished carved face that mocked her efforts. She struck again and again until a small trickle of blood seeped from her hand. One more hit and the lid cracked.

Inside was a body, but not the mummy she expected. It was an older man, one she recognized from the picture she'd seen the day before with his balding head and spectacles, his outer layer of clothing removed. Before her, slumped in the bottom of the coffin, was the real Professor Lane Howland, dead barely more than a day.

PORTRAITS OF THE DEAD

SUZANNE ROBB

"He's perfect, just the way I remember him," Marcy said, "I feel like I can reach out and touch him."

Yvette gave a contented sigh. Another satisfied client, and a few thousand dollars to add to her account. She watched Marcy touch the canvas, an expression of awe on her client's face. Tears had formed in Marcy's eyes, and Yvette felt a twinge of guilt. Fidgeting with the dark blue lapis lazuli necklace she wore every day, Yvette pushed the invasive thought out of her mind.

"He loved that ball. Every morning he would sit beside my bed, tongue lolling to one side because he wanted to play fetch."

"That reminds me." Yvette took the tennis ball and a few other items she wanted in her studio while she worked, including the stuffed Mr. Wiggles.

Marcy, holding back tears, cuddled the glass-eyed version of her beloved pet. She nodded her thanks, and left with her purchase.

Yvette closed the curtains, tilted the blinds, and opened a small door leading to the backyard. Several dog-like sounds greeted her while she ruffled a few dusty ears and tossed toys to their owners. She eyed the animals, ensuring they all moved around.

"Okay, rugrats, I'll see you tomorrow. Try to keep it down tonight."

Yvette locked up the studio and entered the family room of her house. Antiques from all over the world hung on the walls, stood on shelves, and peeked out of overstuffed drawers. Black and white photos filled the few spaces not covered or taken up by knick knacks. The images were diverse: horrific scenes of mass burials, gathered storm clouds ready to release their wrath, children playing in a public fountain on a hot summer day, and various historical sites.

She flipped open her bag and checked her phone. No messages, no texts, no emails—as usual. Seeing the time was too late to deposit the check, she decided to go to the bank the following morning, just before the monthly ordeal of lunch with her mother.

In the kitchen, she made a quick salad and opened a bottle of wine, the glass an afterthought. She settled on the couch with her supper and thumbed the television's remote control, searching through over a hundred channels before settling on an old movie she'd seen as a child, a horror flick about an archaeological excavation and the mummy who roamed it in search of his lost love.

The movie didn't hold her attention for long. Her hand dug out the photograph she kept in her breast pocket, close to her heart at all times. Before the credits rolled she fell asleep, and thoughts of loss consumed her dreams.

"Next," called out the bored voice of one of the tellers at Neighbor National Bank.

Yvette walked up to the counter and slid her bank card, along with Marcy's check, to the woman whose nametag read 'Rhonda'.

"Good afternoon," continued Rhonda, in a voice that implied the afternoon was anything but. "How can I help you?"

"I'd like to deposit that into my checking account, and I'll take a hundred in cash, please." Yvette wondered if she would be able to catch the mixture of boredom and faux perkiness on the face of the woman across from her in a portrait.

"Oh, you're Yvette Castella." Rhonda brightened. "My friend goes on and on about you, says you do the most amazing portraits. I saw the one you did of Sophie, her Shih-Tzu, and I swear I thought the damn dog was going to jump out of the picture and bite me."

Yvette smiled. Her hand went to the necklace in an unconscious gesture. "Thank you, although I do a lot of other things as well. In fact, I have an exhibition at the gallery down the street displaying my photographs of the Tarim Basin mummies."

"That's great. How much do you charge for a portrait? My dog's getting on in years, and I'd love if you were able to paint him while he was alive."

Yvette swallowed the acidic retort that came to mind. "Two

thousand, but I only do deceased…pets, and I need to have a few items that your dog played with. It helps me get a better idea of the animal."

Rhonda's smile froze. "Oh, well…here's your cash and receipt. If you can just sign here."

Yvette left the bank feeling deflated , no one wanted to hear about her other talents. Now she was even less inclined to face lunch with her mother. The monthly meeting would end with Yvette going home and drinking until she passed out. The disgrace of the Castella family.

"Yvette, I just do not understand you. You are a respected academic and artist. With all your talent, you choose to make a living by doing those silly portraits for grief-stricken animal lovers. It isn't right." The monthly ordeal had begun in the usual fashion.

"Mother, do *not* talk to me about grief, you have no right. As for how I earn my living or use my talent, it's my choice. I do what I do for a reason."

Mother picked up a spoon and checked it for spots before turning her attention to the water glass. The waiter dropped off their drink orders, hurrying away before he was chastised for the water being too cold or the creases on the tablecloth not being satisfactorily defined. Yvette sighed. Everyone knew to avoid her mother except her.

"Dear," Evelyn said, "I'm just trying to help you move on with your life. You've still got your looks. Men love the exotic look you have, and you're still young, only thirty-two, you could have another…"

Yvette downed her Jack Daniels and Coke. "Do not say what I think you are going to say. My family is not something I can just replace, nor can I go out and make another one." She stood and snatched her purse from the chair beside her.

"You're making a scene, sit down and behave," her mother hissed.

Yvette ignored her and walked away, wondering if she could recreate the expression of disappointment and shock on her mother's face in a portrait.

Everywhere she looked on her walk home, angles, eye colors,

wrinkles, smiles, and frowns jumped out at her. Faces of strangers plagued her dreams and now they invaded her waking moments. Earning a living by painting dead animals was not on her list of career choices, but the medical bills, not to mention the cost of two funerals, forced her to do something.

The looks of pity she had received from her co-workers at the university led to a sabbatical. The joy she once found in capturing precious moments on film quickly evaporated. Within months, she had emptied her savings. When no alternative presented itself—she'd be damned if she accepted so much as a cent from her mother—she opened up her studio.

Yvette uncorked a bottle of wine and meandered to the sofa. She plopped down and took several swigs. The day the doctors came back with the test results and told her that her three-year-old son had leukemia was the hardest of her life. She and Richard had spent every single spare moment with Jack, but in the end all the love and prayer in the world didn't make a damn bit of difference. She held his body for hours, tears streaming down her face while her husband stared into space.

Six hours later, she had to call 911; her husband had blown his brains out, realizing all their days from then forward were too difficult to cope with. She knelt next to him, memorizing him the same way she had their son.

From that day on, faces haunted her. Bits and pieces caught her newfound artistic eye, and within minutes, she'd formed a patchwork of eyes, lips, and facial contours to remind her of what she'd lost.

Five years later, here she was: painting commissioned portraits of stuffed dead animals. Each day harder than the one prior, and her list of reasons to live dwindled down to one thing: capturing the dead in her portraits.

Yvette did have a valid reason for her madness, but one she couldn't share with others. She set the empty bottle on the table and headed for her studio. Shutting herself in, ensuring the door was locked, she stretched a new canvas.

The rigid material in her hands was a specialty item purchased during her last trip to the Xinjiang province in China—Small River Cemetery No.5, to be exact. A woman had approached her with the canvas, saying it had pieces of material from one of the mummies woven into it. Yvette pressed the woman for more details and discovered, if the woman was to be believed, the ancient textiles came from 'Chärchän Man,' one of several mummies dating back to 1000 BCE.

With care, Yvette folded the delicate cloth over the frame she'd made with wood from the Atacama Desert. Two years after she lost everything, she'd made a trip to Southern Peru when she heard about the mummies there and how they pre-dated Egyptian finds by thousands of years. The embalming process was different in that area. The organs were removed, but in some instances so was the skin, replaced with clay. The end result was both horrifying and beautiful to behold. Yvette photographed these husks of former human beings with a fascination she couldn't explain or even understand. Their angular faces haunted her with portrayals of eternal screams.

After hours of struggling to create the perfect surface to paint on, Yvette felt satisfied with the end result. She went to open the door to the backyard and the sounds of her dogs filled the tiny work space.

Using a lighter, she lit several sticks of incense she'd purchased at an occult shop. Her research indicated *Kyphi* was used during the embalming process, and that a man named Plutarch had combined it with *Ashphaltum* to make a resin. Not a pleasant smell, but certain practitioners in darker circles believed it held magical properties. In moments, it went to work, creating spider web clouds in the corners of the room and her mind. The smell nauseated her and burned her nostrils, but she endured it.

Last, but most importantly, were her paints. She placed the tins on the table next to the easel, with a special spot reserved for Mummy Brown. This item had been the hardest to obtain. Made from ground-up Egyptian mummies, white pitch, and myrrh, production had stopped over a century earlier. However, the artist Edward Burne-Jones had buried a tube in his yard when he discovered its origins. Yvette had spent all her savings earned from her artwork and photography, for what she hoped was the last sample of a rare paint believed long gone.

Sitting on her stool, she pulled the ever-present picture out of her breast pocket and pinned it to the corner of the expanse of white cloth before her. Picking up the tin containing mummia, she popped the lid and pinched a small amount of the substance between her fingers. Calming herself, she snorted it.

A surge ran through her, and she picked up her brush, hands

moving of their own volition. For years, one of her friends had supplied her with the exotic substance. Yvette paid no attention to the warnings of abuse and long-term side effects. Things like that mattered little to her.

Time to paint.

First, the symbols in each corner. Hieroglyphics for life, Kanji symbols for birth, replications of cave drawings depicting fertility. Yvette's eyes brightened, and she snorted more of the ancient ground-up bones as her brush traced the outline with certainty on the canvas. A cramp started in her leg, and she shook it out.

The background appeared: a small chair like the one she placed the stuffed, dead dogs on. A mat full of toys and a soft blanket developed next. Sweat poured off her as she translated her vision to lines and curves, one she instinctively knew would become her masterpiece. Something even her mother would be unable to find fault with. The incense burned, wisps of smoke floating past her, taking the shape of malformed faces that mocked what she was trying to do. She waved them away, her fingers obliterating them. She pretended she didn't hear their screams.

She was aware that the sun was setting, the time to ensure the shadows were just right. There could be no room for error on this piece.

In the center, a large white space remained. She hesitated a few moments before steeling herself to fill it in. She took her special brush, one she had made herself. Nowhere else in the world did this instrument exist, for the bristles were combined with the hairs of her dead son and husband.

She paused, reached for a glass of water and realized she had not brought any in with her. The task called out to her to continue, to deny her thirst.

With a silent prayer, she went back to work. The pain in her hands and ache in her back were forgotten when the image in front of her took form. With the finest of brushstrokes and a steady hand, she painted bright blue eyes with curls of blond hair partially obscuring them. Puffy cheeks, a button nose, and a smile revealing a missing tooth. Jack wore pajamas with robot patterns, his favorite. She choked back a sob, and blood dribbled from her mouth. Wiping it away, she reminded herself it was worth it.

A sigh escaped her as she gazed on the face of her son, almost—

but not quite—real. She dipped the brush into the Mummy Brown and filled in the fleshy parts. Everything she'd learned was true: the color was the perfect tone for skin. She smiled back at her son, tears falling unchecked into her lap, eyes drying out. She yearned to touch him, and before she could stop herself her fingers reached out and smudged his cheek. She worked quickly to repair it and hoped it wouldn't ruin the end result, though she would love it no matter what. Her sides ached, and she felt as if her head was in a crushing vice. She rubbed her temples, and large clumps of her hair fell out.

She continued after another dip into the tin unaware what was happening to her. The painting demanded all of her attention.

Next, she drew in the angular face of Richard. Dark eyes she'd stared into for hours on end during their yearlong courtship. A sexy smile, an air of mystery, the strong jaw line that quivered when he watched her cradle their dead son. The five o'clock shadow, and the small scar on his chin from when he fell as a boy. Dressed in a T-shirt and jeans, his at-home attire, Yvette wanted to cry. The pain inside her intensified with each stroke of the brush, an unseen icy hand ripping her insides out. She wrapped her left arm around her stomach and pushed on. No quitting now, not when she was so close.

She reached out for the mummia, startled to see the tin was empty. Her vision blurred and when she tried to stand she felt muscles stretching, heard bones creaking. A few feet away was her goal, her reward, what would make everything better. She ambled as fast as her wretched body would allow. At the small doorway, the dogs made no noise.

Yvette tilted her head to the side. "Mr. Giggles? Sophie?" She waited for a response but only the echo of her voice answered.

"No," she cried as she fell to the ground. "This isn't how it's supposed to work. I did *everything*!"

For years, she'd been perfecting her ability, honing the talent she had to keep secret in order to preserve its power. Losing her family enabled her to visit the dark places of her soul and make wishes no one in their right mind would. She'd researched, studied, and collected all she could about mummies from around the world and the various belief systems surrounding the afterlife.

The antiques littering her living room and den were the first attempts: pots, bowls, jewelry, and other random objects she would paint and find the next day in her backyard covered in dust and other debris. At first she thought the neighborhood kids had played a prank on her or in a drunken stupor she'd misplaced the items. Taking a closer look, she had realized what they were, and the power she possessed. For hours she'd stare at the things she created in amazement, touching them with reverence. Careful not to break them, despite their recent appearance they were old and fragile.

She moved on to animals when her confidence grew. Her first attempt brought her a pug. He had ambled toward her, his collar with the nametag reading 'Buster' dangling around his emaciated neck, rags trailing behind allowing her to see his empty ribcage. When the full scale of what she could do hit her, she had spent every penny she owned collecting what she needed. Bringing her family back didn't have a price tag.

But here she sat, broken, dried up, and empty inside. All her work gone, even the animals she brought back over the years left her. Her vision darkened. Relying on sound, she heard tentative steps. A hand on her shoulder. A scream. Was that her voice?

Yvette forced her eyes open. Small flakes of dust and dead skin sloughed off of her as she did so. Dark eyes bored into hers and a thrill passed through her, to be replaced with horror when her vision cleared.

Above her stood a desiccated corpse in rags, Richard's angular features unmistakable under the taut skin. In his hands was a small body. Yvette looked away, unable to face what she'd done.

Head rolling to the side she saw her yard for what it truly was: a cemetery. Piles of dust with rusted metal nametags, some of the more solid ones hobbled around in ancient bandages. None barked. None played. None were alive. She'd brought them back and mummified them in the process.

"I'm so sorry…I thought…" she lifted a hand toward Richard.

She watched him step back, still cradling their dead son. She wondered if she could get the right mix of anger and horror on his face. More guilt, another set of faces to haunt her. Shutting her eyes against the onslaught of images, she passed out, the dark eyes of Richard, bottomless sockets, burning with hatred.

With a huff, the older woman moved around the slab. Yvette had missed their monthly lunch a few weeks ago. Worried something might have happened, she had driven to her daughter's home with Marcus, her husband.

When they entered the house, Evelyn fell back into Marcus in an attempt to avoid the smell. Fear gripped her, and she pushed her way through the house while her husband called 911. A thorough search turned up nothing, only the locked studio remained. Two firemen used their axes to break down the door. Thousands of flies swarmed the group, buzzing in their ears, up their noses, and tangling in their hair. The stench of decay caused bile to rise in Evelyn's throat.

"I got a body, or at least I think…" One of the firemen trailed off.

"Don't touch anything, my daughter is a talented artist. Get out and let me make sure you aren't destroying a work of art."

In the center of the room lay a body wrapped in dirt-encrusted bandages. Stringy black hair stuck out of a few folds at the top of what Evelyn assumed was the head. The arms were crossed over the chest in the traditional Egyptian mummy fashion. Moving around, she bumped into the easel and stared in horror at the grotesque family portrait. Three painted bodies, no more than bones and strips of flesh smiled back at her.

"She's gone, probably on one of her photography trips to get more inspiration. This piece here, I don't understand it, but call the gallery to pick it up right away. No questions, pay whatever it costs."

"Yes, Dear," her husband replied.

Marcus pulled her out of the memory. "I think it's one of those expressionist things. Shame she's missing out on the display, she'd be happy."

Evelyn couldn't take her eyes off of the mummy. "Perhaps, I wish she'd told me where she was going. This constant up and leaving with no notice is childish and unacceptable."

Removing his glasses, Marcus motioned with his hand. "She'll be fine, it's not the first time. Now, look at the necklace, it seems familiar."

Evelyn gasped when she saw the blue stone hanging around the thin neck. A single tear traced a pattern down her cheek.

THE PRICE OF FOREVER

JOHN MCILVEEN

Henderson silently smiles as he approaches the immense stairway. The slabs of stacked dark granite loom before him, seeming to expand and steepen the closer he gets. He sprints up the flight of stairs, accidentally spilling some ale from a bottle he carries. He mechanically mouths *thirty-six* as his foot settles on the landing. He wasn't aware that he had counted the treads, and he's a little surprised by the height from the top. Part of him wants to double check the number of steps, but he's in a hurry. He is late for his appointment.

He is a tall man, rugged and athletic, but the huge granite landing and the massive set of heavy oaken doors make him feel irrelevant, a sensation that is uncommon to him.

Medieval Gothic sconces of hammered iron are mounted on either side of the doors, slanted forward like leering condors. A malevolent orange glow oozes through narrow slots in the lamps, contributing too little lighting to the murky landing. The forged iron door handles seem a product of the same mind that created the sconces, cold, weighty, and solid, with a flowing curve that fails to add delicacy. Simple engravings of fish, crosses, and doves adorn the handles and back-plates; iconic symbols of Christianity.

He pulls open the weighty door to the cathedral and enters a silent antechamber, which offers entry to the inner cathedral through a set of sturdy interior doors. A large bulletin board mounted to the dark mahogany walls looms to the left. It is riddled with computer printouts of benefit drives and from parishioners promoting goods or services; blood drive Saturday/Sunday, babysitter available nights and weekends—call Jenny, Dell laptop for sale—software included. Weeds in a rose garden, an obscene testament to a contemporary age. The antechamber is otherwise empty and has the gloomy and cold atmosphere synonymous with churches; especially older ones. He finds it humorous that Christianity, a faith that regularly refers to the light, is represented by so much darkness; *I am the light, walk in the light, the Lord is my light, let there be light.*

He chuckles and pours his remaining ale into a stoup mounted beside the doorway to the main worship hall and thinks, *we'll leave the light on for you.* Challenged as to where to put the empty bottle, he sets it in the stoup as well.

He strides through the doorway and along the nave, his footsteps ringing hollow and as loud as hoof beats in the vast emptiness of the cathedral. A solitary figure sits alone in the dusky distance of the front row of pews. As he approaches, the silhouette becomes a man and then even more distinguishable. A black shirt and white clerical collar materialize.

The young priest crosses himself and looks up as Henderson reaches the first row. He is handsome in an earthy, country boy way, with curly light-brown hair, ruddy cheeks, and a fresh complexion. A baby-face, some would say.

"Father Lowery?" asks Henderson.

The priest stands up, extends a compact hand and says, "Ah yes, you must be Patrick White. How can I help you, Mr. White?" The priest motions for Henderson to have a seat. He obliges and sits hunkered forward, nervously kneading his hands.

"Thank you for agreeing to see me on such short notice, Father," Henderson says.

"Nonsense, it's what I'm here for, Patrick."

Henderson almost chuckles at the comment, but resists. *Nonsense is what I'm here for,* he muses. It's amazing how the smallest of tweaks can completely alter the meaning of words…like in the Bible. He smiles appreciatively and offers a contemplative look. He says, "I hear you're a healer."

"Not me, I am simply a vessel through which our Lord God works." Father Lowery smiles humbly.

"Ahh yes, of course you are. Well, you see, Father, I'm having a little bit of…trouble." Henderson hesitates, considers his words and asks, "Father Lowery, are you an honorable man? I mean, do you live for and by the cloth?"

Father Lowery's brow furrows, a little surprised by the question. He says, "I've always tried to serve our Lord with supreme devotion. I believe in my heart that he is pleased with my service to him."

"In your heart," Henderson says and looks at the young priest. "Good…good. Dedication is important. You see, I've got this…predicament. You might think this is crazy," He repositions himself, turning more to face the priest. "But there's this ancient shrine tucked away in an Egyptian village I've recently visited, and it seems there's a queen who is mummified and entombed there. The locals believe she's a real high maintenance sort of gal, but whoever pleases her most will be rewarded with great wealth and immortality."

Father Lowery sighs deeply and rests a comforting hand on Henderson's shoulder. "Patrick, the scriptures teach us that we are all immortal. Those who aspire to Heaven will reap the wealth of Paradise for eternity. God has promised this to all of us. We don't need to seek other…*pagan* means to obtain these rewards."

Henderson says, "Well, that's all well and fucking dandy, Father, but that's not where my problem lies. What I need is to know for certain is whether you are a truly holy man or not. The last priest I relied on wasn't, he was crooked as a bobby pin, and I think maybe he had a taste for the little boys, which seems a common quandary among your sort, am I wrong?"

Skepticism clouds Father Lowery's face. "I fail to see where…" he starts saying, but Henderson interrupts."Father, you're missing the point. The last priest, he put on a good show, but underneath it all he was a dirt bag; had a soiled heart. Naunet will only accept a holy man with a truly pure heart." Henderson draws a large blade from within his blazer and drives it upward, beneath the priest's ribs. He leans forward and whispers into Father Lowery's ear. "It pisses me off when people waste my time. I hope you're not wasting my time, Father."

The priest's body twitches as his blood runs over the knife handle and into his attacker's hand. Henderson reaches into his left pocket and retrieves two matching emeralds. He rubs his hands together coating the gems with the still warm fluid and drops them into a small pouch.

Utter darkness.

All is silent except for the sound of breathing, slow, tortured, and rattling damply with illness.

A heavy, metallic clack breaks the silence. It is distant, but echoes loudly throughout the vast chamber, startling the sickly breather. A great latch activates, followed by the distinct sound of a heavy door opening laboriously on ancient hinges, the stubborn scraping of stones and primeval rust. An unsteady yellow light is born as the door is wrestled open. A figure enters carrying an excruciatingly bright lamp, though a candle would glare like the sun to the breather, who hasn't seen light in what feels like eternity.

The light bearer moves slowly forward, exposing a great granite chamber, maybe eighty feet long by twenty feet wide, with a comparatively low stone ceiling nine feet overhead. Passing primordial stone pillars lined up like soldiers every fifteen feet, the light comes to a halt before a ten by ten foot cage, constructed of heavy gold colored bars. The air is fetid and damp, and reeks of moss and sickness.

At the center of the prison an old man drifts slowly in small arcs, suspended six inches above the floor by a thick rope tethered to the top of the cage. He is naked and ghastly thin, and his knees are prominent knobs that bisect the thin bones of his legs. Long yellowed and crusted whiskers fall from his skeletal face, washing over ribs that protrude through translucent flesh like surfacing tree roots, and ending whip-like at his waist. His mouth is a gaping oval, revealing sparse and rotted teeth. The man partially averts his head from the brilliance of the light, but the stranger who cautiously approaches interests him. His head twitches in birdlike jerks as he follows the new man's movement.

"Ah, a guest," the hanging man says in a tongue resembling old Latin. His voice is gravelly, yet weedy from long abandonment and the constriction of the rope. Each breath drags in and forces out, sliding from his throat like stone upon stone.

"That's Greek to me, comrade. *No comprende, capice?*" Henderson says. He stops about two feet from the cage.

"Please *(labored breath),* come forward. What is your name?" says the hanging man, switching to a proper English dialect. His limited breath nearly whistles. He raises his head to confront the tall stranger, but it remains awkwardly and impossibly canted to the left.

"That doesn't concern you old man, but you *are* the guy I'm looking for," Henderson replies. He approaches the cell warily. An expression of disgust replaces the unease once he fully sees the hanging man who, still disturbed by the light, tries to focus his odd, pale eyes on him. The baby-blue, nearly white irises do not remind Henderson of the summer skies, but of blubbery, albino creatures that reside in the deepest part of the ocean.

"On the contrary my greedy seeker, *(breath)* you have come here with a wish, which *(breath)* I cannot fulfill without your name."

"Okay. Call me Ken Smith."

"I call you a liar, Mr. William James Henderson *(breath)* of Norton, Ohio."

Surprise crosses Henderson's face, but he quickly regains his composure. He says, "Alrighty, then. What I'm looking for is…"

"Wealth and immortality," completes the caged man. He wrestles another breath in. "It's what they all seek."

"Who're you talking about when you say *all*?" Henderson asks.

"Only a fool would believe (*breath*) that he is the only one who seeks wealth (*breath*) and immortality."

Henderson walks the perimeter of the cage, not liking the hanging man's sickly eyes on him. "How many have come knocking?" He asks.

"Scores…legions." The hanging man offers a shrewd grin.

"And?"

"They leave with nothing," he promises. "They have all (*breath*) come up short, as you will."

Henderson reaches deep into the pocket of his cargo pants and retracts the pouch. He displays it to the hanging man, but well out of reach.

"The flesh of a virgin child. (*breath*) Admirable. But you are not the first."

Henderson opens the bag and dumps the gems into his left hand and displays them.

"You bluff. Those are clearly not Naunet's amulets (*breath*), they are the wrong hue," rasps the hanging man, a surprised change in his demeanor.

"Now who's the liar?" asks Henderson. "What other color does emerald come in? I've done all the work with my own hands, and you know it, pal."

"I know I smell the blood of a saint on your hands *(breath)*. You reek of blasphemy."

"Which means I did what needed to be done," Henderson stresses with a hiss.

The hanging man locks onto Henderson with his sickly insipid eyes. "Then you know (*breath*) what you must do next," he says.

"I have to touch these amulets to your eyes."

"And try to steal from me *(breath)* what all the others have tried to steal."

Henderson smiles derisively. "What good is wealth to you when you're holed up in there?" he asks. "And why in the *hell* would you want immortality?"

"You could free me *(breath)* if your heart is good, but forfeit your *(breath)* prize," says the old man.

Henderson laughs mockingly and moves cautiously to the bars of the cage.

"Ah, I thought not. What is it you fear?" says the hanging man, forcing a horrific smile. "I am bound and decrepit, *(breath)* what harm can I possibly present to you?"

"None. I'm not afraid of you. I'm just disgusted by you, you're a fucking mess. Lean your head over here," Henderson demands, stepping closer to the cage.

The hanging man bows his head and waits for the kiss of the amulets to his eyes. As Henderson reaches into the cage, the ancient fellow grabs Henderson's arms with amazing speed and pulls himself against the bars and towards him. He traps the stranger's arms between his body and the bars of his prison.

Shock and disgust paralyze Henderson as the hanging man moves in on him, face to face as if to kiss him. He fights to settle his rising gorge as the squalid lips brush against his. The hanging man inhales a deep and tortured breath, and Henderson feels something large and serpentine being drawn from deep within. It struggles but fails to stay within him, and carries with it his health, desires, and his sanity. The hanging man takes another deep breath and exhales a fetid smoke into Henderson's mouth. It tastes of death and rancid meat, jarring Henderson and forcing him to collapse weakly against the bars.

The hanging man reels backwards as if dealt a huge blow. He strikes against the far bars and swings back on the rope, gliding in slowing arcs to finally center in the cage. Absolute and abject terror radiates from his hazel eyes, and etches into his wizened features. He claws at his throat, digging for release from the constricting rope.

Henderson smirks at the old man, winking at him with his new baby blues. "Don't look so surprised, my friend," he says, exhaling his words freely for the first time in centuries…millennia, not strangled and not constricted. "You have what you came for. Your wishes are granted. You wanted wealth? These gold bars weigh tons…and they are yours, you are sole heir to this priceless cage." He taps the bars with long sturdy fingers…*his* long, sturdy fingers. He pauses and a slight and contented smile forms on his healthy lips. "And you have your immortality, though I suspect you will opt to trade it in once...make that *if* the next greedy soul finds the keys and meets the demands."

Henderson's form bends over to pick up the amulets from the floor. "I will do my best to hide these well, but it could make for interesting sport, a little game of hide and seek?"

He pauses and stares at the decrepit old man swinging in wide arcs within the cage as he digs at the rope encircling his neck.

"Well, Mr. Henderson. Oh, that's right…I'm Mr. Henderson, now. Nonetheless, as I was saying, it's not all bad. This is not your average prison, though there are *some* forgiving attributes. For one, you don't have to stew in your own waste, because the cursed and the dead do not require food, just an inclusive memory of our transgressions and a full acknowledgement of pain…we feed well on those."

He walks for the doorway, tossing the amulets playfully in the air and catching them like dice. He pauses when the swinging form in the cage rasps.

"No! (*breath*) Wait!"

He pauses and chuckles softly. "I think not. I have waited eternities and I feel no remorse…concerning you, that is. I know what you've done to get inside these wretched cavern walls, beneath that wretched holy city."

In a panic the hanging man jerks violently and retches as the rope bites harder into his neck.

"You might want to mind that," says the man who wears Henderson's body. He points to the collar on his neck. "It only gets tighter, but *never* tight enough. No…never tight enough."

He tosses the amulets up in the air and catches them. "You know, I once sold a pure and holy man for thirty pieces of silver. That was my sin. Maybe your eternity will be shorter than mine, but I doubt it." He grabs the door handle, smiles, winks at the prisoner and says, "Hey! See you later."

He closes the door. The room sinks into blackness as the latch engages with deafening finality.

WRAPPINGS AND RAPTURE

ALLEN DUSK

I wander lost through the desert mirage of her eyes, my throat so parched words no longer come forth. Light gleams from her eyes, their brightness more intense than the midday sun. My flesh boils wherever her gaze sets focus. Evil spirits peer through from doorways, though the light green shades painted upon her eyelids ward their shadows away.

Her face hovers close enough that every warm breath she expels caresses my cheek. Her lips glisten with each passing circle of her tongue. Scenarios of her mouth descending upon my most intimate regions consume all my cognition.

If only I could tell her how she infatuates me, she would certainly swoon into my arms. She would be bestowed with all the privileges of a queen. Temples would be raised in her honor, where priests would kneel in worship of her elegance. Servants would tend to her every whim and I would privately cater to her most intimate desires.

If only I could tell her how much I loved her.

If only I were not dead.

Rudy's rising voice distracts my captivation. In he walks wearing his usual blue jacket, and a badge bearing his likeness. For an instant I envision him as he was five years ago: hair more red than silver, a strong stance with good posture. That was before his wife died, before devotion to his job became the sole remnant sustaining his life. His gray hair appears a little thinner today, his pants a tad tighter.

"Gather around everybody. I want to tell you about one of our proudest guests here at the Arkham Natural History Museum." He summons his flock with an exaggerated wave. "The mummy in the case before us is none other than the great Pharaoh Snowfrue. His body and the treasures you see in this room were all discovered inside a secret tomb below the Red Pyramid in Giza. Even after years of study we still have much to learn about the time when he ruled Egypt."

If I still had eyes in my sockets I would have rolled them. *Snowfrue*, really? My name is *Sneferu*. Is that so difficult to pronounce? I ruled my land for over fifty years, and that tablet over there clearly states that I built far more than the Red Pyramid. Just look at it, you illiterate.

Peeking from behind his mother's thigh, a curly-haired brat sticks his tongue out at me. How dare he disrespect my majesty with such a disgusting gesture! At one time I would have had both him and his parents lashed with reeds for such blasphemy. In my current state I am powerless to do anything but stare. If only I were able to wave a single finger at him, and send him screaming down the hall.

"Let me introduce you to one of our conservators here at the museum." Rudy points his wiry finger at the object of my desire. "This is Lillian and she, well…do you have a moment to speak with the tour group about what you do, or are you busy right now?"

She turns from me, her dark hair caressing my skin, her perfume haunting my desire. A smile lifts her lightly-freckled cheeks. "Sure thing, Rudy. You know I always have time for you."

Curiosity focuses their eyes upon her. Jealously smolders within my bandaged chest. My crooked neck, compressed from decay, leaves me no option to trail her. Rather I must gawk across the hall where ceramic jars filled with my organs are on display. The withered husk of my liver clings to the sides of a jar which has been cleanly cut in half for all to see.

"Hello Everybody! My name is Lillian Howell, and I'm the principal conservator for the Grand Hall of Pharaohs exhibit here at the Arkham Museum. Basically I'm responsible for restoring and preserving all of the over two hundred artifacts we have on display. Right now, as you can see, I'm repairing a few wrapping on this mummy. He's over 4,000 years old, so he's *very* fragile."

Every set of eyeballs glides my way, and every second of this public spectacle humiliates me for its own eternity. The objects gripped in their hands blind me with flashes of bright light.

"Does anybody have any questions?" Lillian turns an ear their way.

"What do you use to preserve the mummy?" A broad woman with

no neck barks from her flowered tunic. "I mean, aren't they already preserved?"

"That's a great question, thank you. Primarily I use paper made from Japanese mulberry trees and a special paste to reinforce weak spots. Sometimes I also use papier-mâché and color it to match. Even though we keep him inside a glass case, for some reason dust still slips past the seal, so from time to time I need to carefully brush away the build-up. Any other questions?"

"Do you know how the mummy died?" The red-headed child steps forwarded, his pudgy jaw hanging in awe.

"We don't know exactly, but medical researchers from Miskatonic University performed a number of tests on his body, which show that he may have been poisoned."

My soul cringes again, even though I have heard the story recounted hundreds of times during my tenure on display. My sweet Lillian recounts the words of fools which are nothing more than a plague of inaccuracies.

So, how did I actually die? How did I come to find myself on exhibit in a foreign land? Step closer, you pack of commoners, so Pharaoh may whisper the truth from his withered lips.

One evening, right after a mighty feast, I had just returned to my chambers when a sudden dizziness forced me to sit down. Panic coursed through all my senses. Cold sweat poured in frigid sheets, soaking my tunic. The great Anubis appeared before me, drool spilling from his jackal jowls. Then I was swallowed down his gullet where calm washed over me, cleansing away my anxieties.

Numerous hands caressed my flesh, and ferried my body to the temple. Muffled whispers joked about my death. If they knew Pharaoh overheard their every word would they have continued their slander?

Oil lamps lit one by one. Soft glowing wicks revealed priests surrounding me, their slow prayers encircling me within the haze of sedation. The high priest approached wearing a mask of the great Anubis. He leaned close to whisper in my ear, "I know you can hear me, my great Pharaoh, and I am well aware you will feel everything we are about to do to you as part of this ceremony."

His mumbling continued about a powerful spell trapping my soul. My attention shifted from his words to the long, slender hook grasped in his hand. Beneath the mask I could sense the priest smiling with disgusted delight as he forced the hook up through my nose.

Agony poured from my lips, yet my screams never echoed from the temple walls. Horror sank its fangs into me, injecting the sudden knowledge that I could scream all I wanted from within this prison and nobody would ever know of my suffering.

Bones shattered inside my skull. White pain filled my vision. Every rotation of the hook, every crack of bone, every sensation magnified itself a thousand-fold as the rod ascended through my brain. Gore wept from me. Tendrils of blood grew from my nostrils like the snot of a hysterical infant. Piece by excruciating piece the High Priest extracted my brain into a golden bowl; bits of its whitish-pink meat tumbled wasted to the ground.

A ceremonial blade glimmered. A brick became wedged beneath my neck, forcing my head toward my torso so I might witness my own disemboweling. My legs felt as if they were trembling, though they remained as limp as cords of rope. My foot twitched. Hope rushed into my spirit—perhaps motion was returning to me and I could run away from this nightmare. Despair settled in when I realized my limbs were only moving as the result of my internal organs being torn away from their connective tissues.

Delirium encircled me, like a pack of Hyenas preparing to feast on carrion—*my carrion*! Staring, laughing, their eyes burning with starlight. Detached from all sense of direction, it felt as if I was floating and falling all at once.

My heart raised out of my chest, clutched by two blood-soaked hands. A wave of grand hysteria swallowed me into its undertow. Without my heart, my soul would never be able to pass into the afterlife. A stone amulet bearing inscriptions from the *Book of the Dead* replaced the presence of my most important organ then the gaping hole in my carcass was stuffed with herbs and bandaged shut.

Bitterly my awareness drifted back to the present. There was no trace of my beloved Lillian, all of her tools gone, the glass around me resealed. The crowd had moved on. Voices dwindled from the great hall until the cleaners arrived with their noisy contraptions. The glowing orbs overhead extinguished in batches. Again I was left alone in the dark. Long fingers of green light reached out from glowing letters over the door, each illuminating portions of my tarnished treasures; all of them entombed within glass just as I was.

Tiles rippled along the floor, swelling as storm-driven waves, yet I knew they lie perfectly still. Lunacy was now my only true companion. It listened to my words, nodded with empathy, holding my hand for the eternity we shall share together.

Time stretched before me as a ribbon decorated with the thousands of faces who have stopped to stare at Pharaoh. Their strange lights flashed brighter than the stars up in the heavens. Itching crept along my nose. I was cursed to tolerate every tickling nerve, wishing in secret I could scratch away the annoyance, even if it meant I would shred my flesh in return.

Finally the week was over. My hollow chest cramped with affection when I saw my desire approaching. Her soft curls bounced with every step; her hips mesmerized me with their slow sway. A golden scarab hung from a chain around her neck, its limbs caressing the supple flesh between her breasts. Her new perfume lulled me with its opiate fumes. What was that dusty box within her hands?

Great Anubis had been mocking me. Suddenly a rapid beating filled my ears. Warmth swelled in my hollow chest, raced through my limbs as if I were again alive. The fool I was would certainly call this sensation *love.*

"Good afternoon, great Pharaoh," she said, her eyes widening at my magnificence. "I'm sorry I missed your cleaning last week, but Dr. Rosewater wanted me to spend some time cleaning out the archives in the basement."

Only two weeks had passed? Eons could have drizzled past and I would have been none the wiser about it. For an instant it seemed as if I had just stepped inside my palace to take refuge from the scorching midday sun. Burning sand intruded beneath my toes, or was it just another insect nibbling away? I stared at her, enduring the discomfort.

"But I think I found something you'll be interested in." Her smile widened, showing her perfect white teeth. "I bet you'll never guess what it is."

She pulled a ceramic jar from the box, and raised it before my face. Vigor slapped me awake. The cartouche on the jar was indeed mine, but she moved it away before I could read the entire inscription.

"According to the documents, this was discovered in a vault beneath your main burial chamber. There's a faded image of the god

Horus on the lid, probably because he symbolizes the life of the pharaoh." Her voice rose, bubbling with excitement. "Well, I had a hunch, so I ran it over to Miskatonic University Hospital and had them do a CAT scan, and, well, I'm pretty *damn* sure I found *your* heart."

Modern felines were capable of discerning the contents of canopic jars? Amazing, but by what magic, I could care less. Joy erupted—there, in the middle of my chest, as if my heart had never been taken. The torture of this statuary Hell might finally cease. No longer would the afterlife forbid my entrance!

"I could see all of the valves and chambers on the screen, and the doctor there confirmed it was a heart. They even took a small sample to run a DNA test." She laughed softly, her cheeks flushing. "It's funny, you know, but I've never had the honor of holding a man's heart in my hands before."

I wanted nothing more than to pull her close. I would have given up all my treasures just to taste her lips against mine. I gazed at her, rapture radiating inside of me, and unable to do a damn thing about it. Torture obtained its long-awaited perfection.

Lillian bounced across the hall, pulling her keys from her long white coat. "I'll just put it in here with your other *insides*. Once we have confirmation from the tests, we should be able to go public with the find."

"I don't know about you, but I think it's very exciting. Mummies usually don't have their hearts removed, right?" She slid on squares of glass which enlarged her eyes to giant proportions, and plucked a brush from her tray. "Why would they do such a thing to you?"

Lean closer, and I'll tell you every gruesome detail of how they did it, I wanted to say. But to this day I still don't know why I was murdered, or by whom.

"Let's get you dusted off, shall we?" Intensity filled her stare. "I can't wait until we get the funds to fix this case. All of this acidic dust is wreaking havoc on your body."

She leaned in closer than ever before, heat from her touch driving me wild. I lingered over every fine hair budding from her neck, every distinctive crease forming her perfect lips. Had I been able to move my arms, I would have embraced her, whispered soothing words in her ear. Centuries of decay allowed only the silent reply of death's grimace twisting my face.

My desire to kiss her summoned only the frustration of impossibility. But improbability alone would not extinguish the fantasy. Walking hand in hand through the desert sands, I would take her to the secluded Oasis, and feed her sweet dates from the palms. I would tear away her clothing, releasing her nude perfection upon me. My fingers could already feel the fabric within their grasp.

After an especially long session of brushing, during which she whispered about her noisy neighbors, Lillian put her tools away, and sealed the case around me. She walked away slowly, turning once more, I presume, to admire a job completed with excellence. Her footsteps faded from the room, the orbs overhead again extinguished. The numbered disc on the wall counted through the dark. Beneath the echo of its ticking, a soft rhythm became apparent to my ears. I listened intently for a long time, doubting the evidence gathered by my frayed sanity.

At first, they were muted, occasional thumps beneath the faintest whispers, causing me to question if they even existed. Volume of the dull notes increased with every passing moment. The tempo quickened, swelling full with the cadence of a hundred drums booming between my ears. Vibrations rattled loose my teeth. Certainly my bones would crumble should the racket continue, reducing me to nothing more than a pile of dusty bandages. Finally, I could no longer deny the source of the sound. It was a heartbeat, *my* heartbeat, calling from its containment.

My heart halted beating abruptly. Again I was left to wonder if this had simply been the taunting of another hallucination.

Foreign accents approached. I welcomed the sight of the cleaning servants entering my grand hall with equipment in tow. They had brought their polishing machines with them this time. While I admired the shine they applied to the floor, they used odorous fluids which burned my hollow eye sockets. They surrounded the cabinet containing my organ jars, and moved it beside my case.

Pulsations moved my ribs, as if my heart was once more within my chest. Again, the sound of chambers and valves formed their musical notes. From my angle I could just make out the collection of canopic jars. The jar containing my heart rocked gently with every beat.

Excitement coursed through me, even greater than the time Lillian stooped over and accidentally revealed her lace undergarments.

Tingling struck my fingertips, steadily spread up my arms, as if I had fallen asleep on them and now the circulation had returned. Optimism overcame me, and a crazy idea filled my head.

I concentrated on moving my fingers toward my thumb.

They met in a soft pinch.

My disembodied heart skipped a surprised beat.

Without a doubt I was again capable of moving—or was madness continuing to play games? There was only one way to tell.

I moved my jaw slowly, aches filling my cheeks as my mouth opened. Dust puffed from my jawbone popping back into its joint. If not for the cleaner's noisy machines I'm certain they would have heard me.

I tipped my head down, exploring these new found ranges of motion, ever so slight as they were. For the first time in centuries I could actually see my toes. Each shriveled black digit wiggled with returning sensations.

My chest lurched on its own, drawing in its first true breath since my death. Though my decayed lungs rested in a jar near my feet, cool air still soothed the inside of my hollow rib cage.

Awe struck me with too much excitement to bear. "Praise be to Amen-Ra," I shouted. My Egyptian tongue echoed about the room.

The closest cleaner—a short, thick man with nearly no neck—dropped his broom, and spun on his heels toward me. His wide eyes narrowed while repeatedly scanning over me. It was suddenly difficult for me to remain still, yet somehow I managed.

"Did you hear something?" He said to a woman polishing a cabinet.

She pulled a plug from her ear which was attached to a colorful cord around her neck. "*Que*?"

"I said, *did you hear something*?"

She shrugged, shook her head no, and returned to her duties. While they were distracted with each other I used the opportunity to turn my head slightly to the right for a better view of my organs.

The man picked up his broom, stared at me with intensity before finally returning to work. Doubt and fear danced in his eyes, even after he turned away. I discovered myself holding my breath, fearing I might burst out laughing.

The cleaning servants continued about their business, and the short man continued to glance at me from time to time. More cabinets filled with my beloved treasures were positioned around where I stood. Leisurely I turned my head, laying my eyes upon talismans which I had not seen since I last strolled through my palace.

Delusion distracted me, wandered away with my mind just as a weary traveler succumbs to a mirage. I imagined leading Lillian through my palace, pointing out each item and boasting about how my wealth acquired them with such ease. She nodded with appreciation, our gazes locked; we descended with a passionate kiss, and indulged in each other's nudity right there on the floor. Her body writhed beneath mine, ecstasy boiling between our stares.

Reality snapped back, the present rushing upon me. My head spun as if I had indulged wine as a drunkard. Most of the cabinets in my exhibit had been emptied. Servants in green clothing were removing my other treasures and packing them in boxes filled with straw. Lillian stood before me with tears streaming from her eyes.

"Well, I guess this is goodbye, Great Pharaoh." Pain filled her every word. "I walked into work this morning only to find out that Dr. Rosewater has sold our entire exhibit to a museum in Cambridge."

I fought to remain still, just as the corpse she had known for years. The affliction of her voice tore a vast wound through my soul. Her lips trembled as if she were about to reveal more words.

"It turns out that asshole asked me to clear out the archives just so he could get a premium price for every last trinket we had."

She burst out crying, and all I could do was watch with absolute stillness as her own despair infected me. Had I chosen to reveal my reanimation at that point it surely would have fractured her fragile state.

"But I told him he could go fuck himself, and then I told him, *I quit!*" She pressed her hand against the glass, and smiled through her anguish. "Take care my friend. Maybe I'll hop on a plane and visit you some time, if I can ever afford it."

She pressed her lips against my case, a soft kiss flattened against the glass. Then she turned and ran away, leaving only a smudge of lipstick behind.

My arm struck the glass as I reached for her. My rotten throat held my words captive until she disappeared through the doors at the end of the hallway. Then I realized the harsh truth. Lillian was truly gone.

All my sorrow poured through a long wail, and for the first time in centuries my own tears once again moistened my flesh.

All my love for her swelled into a triumphant anthem. With strength I never knew I possessed, my arms struck out, shattering the glass which had offered protection from curious patrons for so long. I punched through the canopic exhibit, and retrieved the jar containing my heart. Shards of glass sliced deep grooves through my flesh. The intense pain reminded me how fortunate I was to be alive again.

My legs carried me down the hallway in the direction where Lillian had exited, their numbness preventing me from achieving anything more than a quick wobble. I recall passing several tour guides, one of those being Rudy, who dropped dead against the wall, a sudden landslide of shit spilling from his trousers. Flocks of tourists scattered screaming. Those who paused to take *photographs* were trampled by the crowd.

I burst out onto the street of the grand metropolis. Flocks of pigeons took flight into the cloudy sky as panic rang out in the streets. That day I met hundreds of faces frozen with terror, but none of them belonged to her.

Looking back now, all the centuries blur together, their tattered memories stretching through the void of space. Although if I close my eyes and focus, I can picture Lillian's beautiful face leaning over me as if it were the very first time. The heartbeat from the jar clutched against my chest spreads warmth through me as if I were basking beneath her loving stare. Her perfume lingers all around me, but I know she is not there.

Today I march on, driven by the knowledge that eventually one day I *will* stumble upon my love again, even if it's in the dead of night, or while she's midway through a meal. You mark my words, Lillian Howell will be my queen, and I will be her Pharaoh, even if it takes all of eternity for me to find her.

THE FOLKS ON THE HILL

PHILIP C. PERRON

"How did you know about this place?" Oscar Novak asked.

George Rodriguez placed the set of coasters back on the coffee table after looking them over. They weren't worth taking, just the freebies you got when you bought a bottle of vodka—in this case Skyy. "Driving around," Rodriguez explained. "Just scoping out houses that looked like they'd be worth our time."

"But here?" Novak asked. "What town is this again?"

"Wilton," Harry Borges said. He appeared at the doorway that lead into the kitchen. In his hands was a mahogany box with the word Miyabi lettered in silver.

"New Hampshire?"

"That's right." Borges placed the box in the camping backpack by the wall. "We're maybe twenty minutes over the border."

"Dude, we drove over an hour to get here."

Borges sighed. Annoyance crossed over his face. "I said twenty minutes over the border. Getting to the border from Boston was forty minutes."

Novak nodded. "Gotcha." He appeared as a silhouette as he passed by the large bay windows.

Rodriguez had no idea what he'd call this room but the closest thing that came to mind was rec room. Outside, two and a half feet of snow covered the front lawn and driveway. The prior day, a nor'easter, arguably the worst in ten years, buried New England under two to three feet of snow, and the exact amount just depended on where you lived. Besides Worcester, southern New Hampshire had the highest accumulation.

Borges circled the pool table, reaching into each pocket, tossing balls onto the felt surface. Over against the wall, a loud chime clanged. Novak, who was on the other side of the room, jumped and fell back onto the love seat by the pellet stove.

"Christ," Rodriguez said, "God damned grandfather clock." He looked over his shoulder to see that its face read 4:45 p.m. In half an hour it would be dark.

"I'm telling you," Novak said, rounding the room to stand in front of the clock, "someday we should go bigger. Start fencing the big stuff. Do you know how much a grandfather clock is worth? Three grand, easily. Maybe four."

Over on the wall, a cuckoo clock gave its own squawk for quarter to the hour. Borges tossed the eight ball on the pool table and crossed the room. "These things go for two hundred at least, and we can carry it."

"Take it," Rodriguez agreed. "Wrap it up with some of those magazines by the bar. I don't want it to get nicked."

Borges walked by the bay window and looked out. "The owners should have hired someone to plow their driveway. Now everyone knows they aren't home." He gave out a loud guffaw that drew looks.

Rodriguez bent down and wiped the snow off his denim pants. Both Borges and Novak had been smart enough to wear snow pants and boots. Rodriguez had figured that the snowshoes he picked up for each of them would have been enough. But as they had trekked through the woods up a hill trailing the sled just to get to this four thousand-square-foot McMansion, the snow at points had reached the height of three feet. And unlike the fluffy powder stuff, the snowshoes didn't work all that well with wet snow.

"What type of name is Chatterjee?"

"What's that?" Rodriguez asked. He peeled off the little nuggets of caked snow that clung between his sneakers' laces.

"Chatterjee," Borges repeated, holding up a handful of magazines. "Terrance Chatterjee...Christie Chatterjee... Carol Chatterjee. And look at this—*Golf Digest*, *Saveur*, *Forbes*. Pretentious shit."

"I'd say that's Portuguese," Novak said.

"Italian," Rodriguez added. "Hungarian...Arabic...it could be anything. Hell, it even could be Finnish for all I know. Or care."

"Well, whatever it is," Borges grunted, "they get some shit magazines."

He yanked a bunch from the stack nuzzled within the wicker basket by the bar and headed back over to the cuckoo clock. Standing up on his toes, he reached over the loveseat. His gloved hands gently encircled the clock, and he lifted it from its setting. "Yeah, this will get at least two hundred." He began ripping pages out of a magazine.

"South Asian," Novak said. He held up a framed photograph in his hand. "Chatterjee is probably Indian."

Rodriguez took the photo from him and looked. A well-dressed Indian, his beautiful Caucasian wife, and their three attractive teenage daughters smiled back. The five showed wide, bright smiles, their teeth as perfect as those on fashion models. He tossed the frame on the pool table.

"I've always wondered what type of people lived in houses like these," Borges said, wrapping the cuckoo clock. "I drive by them all the time when I head through places like Lynnfield and wonder, does some hotshot dot-com asshole live there? Maybe a professional athlete, like a Bruins player. Maybe a doctor? How about some organized crime boss? You just don't know."

"Could be anyone," Rodriguez agreed. "Chatterjee could be a banker or an engineer. He could be anything. I wonder...since they're not plowed, is this a summer home? Now, if I were to take a guess I'd say they're vacationing somewhere, like Key West."

"Key West," Borges laughed. "You ever been there? The place is awesome."

At the bar, Rodriguez inventoried the various bottles of liquor. His eye located a Johnnie Walker Blue Label sitting in the back. He snaked his arm through the various flavored Skyy vodkas, grabbed the scotch then let out a satisfied grunt when he discovered it unopened.

"What do you have there?" Novak came up beside him. "You going to open it?"

"Nope." Rodriguez brought the bottle up close to his eyes to make sure the seal was indeed still intact. "This bottle sells for two hundred at any liquor store."

"Sweet, should I wrap it?"

"Yeah. Use the magazines." Rodriguez handed the bottle over.

Borges crossed the room and joined them. As he looked over the bottles, he fitted the cuckoo clock snuggly in his backpack. "Check that out," he said, placing the camping bag on the pool table. He picked up a large bottle and bent it towards the day's remaining light oozing through the bay window. Rodriguez looked over his shoulder and read the label—*Everclear Grain Alcohol.*

"What is it?"

"This stuff is ninety-five percent pure alcohol."

"You're kidding me?"

"No." Borges shook his head. "For real, it's actually pretty good stuff."

"Worth taking?" Rodriguez asked.

"It's opened so no, but to be honest, it only goes for around thirty-five bucks. You want a swig?"

"Forget it." Rodriguez scanned the remaining bottles. None were worth much. "No booze on the job." He took another cursory glance around the room courtesy of the beam of his flashlight. "Anyways, I think we should head upstairs. All the good stuff has to be up there."

"Hey, I already found Miyabis, and over there," Borges pointed, "is one of those hand-held humidors. I bet there's Cubans in there."

"What's a Miyabi?"

Borges laughed. "Are you kidding me? Kitchen knives. They're easily worth $350. And the cuckoo clock, based off this house, I'd bet its worth closer to a grand than the two hundred I said earlier."

"Are you shitting me?" Rodriguez said, his mouth dropping.

"If it's handmade or one of those boutique ones right from Switzerland, absolutely."

"Nice. And the knives? How do you know they're worth that much?"

"An ex-girlfriend of mine was a cook at a fancy restaurant. That chick knew her knives."

"All right," Rodriguez said. "I'm making the executive decision. Let's go upstairs. Novak, you sure the alarms are out?"

Novak laughed. "You could squat here and no one would ever know...as long as these Chatter-whatever-there-names-are don't come back anytime soon."

"They won't." Rodriguez gazed out into the growing dusk. The driveway, the walkway, even the back deck where they had left the sled were covered with two feet of damp snow.

Borges walked around the pool table. He reached into his pocket and turned on a small LED flashlight. Putting it in his mouth to free his hands, he picked up the little humidor and shined the light inside. His half open mouth turned into a smile. "Cubans," he said, his voice muffled. "At least twenty of them. They're worth twenty bucks a pop.

And the humidor itself, Id' say, at least a hundred."

"Take it," Rodriguez said.

Borges took the flashlight out of his mouth and gave Rodriguez a grin. "Consider it done." He grabbed another handful of magazines.

Novak pulled out his own flashlight and shined it about. The light circled about before landing on a deer's head mounted upon the wall. "A hunter?" he asked, looking over at Rodriguez.

Rodriguez shrugged. "Are you thinking what I'm thinking?"

"I think so. Maybe a nice gun collection. Could be worth a small fortune."

"More reason to head upstairs to the bedrooms." Rodriguez watched as Borges finished up with the humidor. He gave the room one last scan. There were a few other things that piqued his interest, like a marble chess set and a whiskey decanter, but unless the score upstairs wasn't worth much, those spoils weren't worth taking.

He headed over to a pair of French doors and looked into the foyer beyond. His flashlight shined up a set of elegant stairs that turned to the left and led to a balcony above. Various family pictures hung along the walls. By a closet door were pairs of boots, stilettos, and shoes.

Rodriguez led the way up the steps. As he reached the halfway landing, a guttural sound came from somewhere beyond the balcony. A metallic rattle followed and the noise carried down the stairway.

"What the fuck was that?" Borges asked.

"I don't know."

"Well, keep going," Novak said. "The alarms are off and no one's here."

"Do we know that for sure?" Borges asked.

Rodriguez's heart pounded in his chest. "I...I mean, how could there be anyone here? The driveway isn't even plowed."

"Just keep going," Novak said. When Rodriguez and Borges didn't move, he walked past them and headed up to the landing. His light source bounced along the walls. The hanging foyer's crystal chandelier refracted the beam and danced rainbow colors against the second floor walls.

"You see anything?" Rodriguez called up.

"Nothing." Novak shined his flashlight down the hall to the right. Rodriguez and Borges finished their march up the steps and joined him.

"So what was that noise then?" Borges asked. Down the left hall behind him, the metallic shuddering came again, causing him to tense. He bumped into Novak before straightening himself out.

Rodriguez flashed his light down the hall. Up against the right side was a bookcase. A large vase sat upon its top. The hall then veered to the right towards the back of the house. Rodriguez walked down the corridor, flashing his light on the numerous titles in the bookcase. Classics, mostly reprints of such works as *Moby Dick*, *The Sound and the Fury*, and *Dracula*, lined its shelves. Though the noise had spooked him, he was still able to concentrate and consider the value of potential finds.

Novak and Borges came up behind him. Leading the way, Rodriguez turned the corner. Two doors, one to the left and another at the end of the hall, stood closed. Even so, the hallway was large enough to give the impression that it was itself a room. Behind the left door, the rattling sounded.

"What the fuck is that?" Rodriguez asked.

"Only one way to find out." Novak reached over his shoulder and grabbed a long black utility flashlight from his backpack. He flicked a switch and a blinding light lit up the entire hall. Reaching his hand out, he grasped the doorknob and slowly turned it. The latch clicked.

With the flashlight's head, Novak pushed the door forward. It quietly swung inward. The flashlight lit up the room, showing feminine, pink decor. Posters on the walls, including a provocatively posed Christina Aguilera and one of a Harley-Davidson, dressed the bedroom.

Novak took a step through the doorway. As he did so, the silence again broke in the metallic shaking. On instinct he took a step backwards, bumping into his companions. Rodriguez shined his own flashlight toward the cause of the ruckus. From the corner, a red reflection glinted. A loud guttural squawk pierced out. Novak flashed his own utility flashlight at the cause and a cat-sized Amazon parrot appeared from the darkness. It jumped up onto a perch within a dresser-sized cage. The animal looked at them curiously before pecking at the cuttlebone attached to the bars. The entire enclosure shook, identifying the metallic sound.

"Christ," Rodriguez said as he entered the room. "Just a fucking pet." He looked about and immediately felt elated as he saw a group of unopened collectable Barbie dolls lining a shelf. He walked across the room and shined his light upon them. "These are worth a good piece of change."

"How much?" Borges asked.

"That one there," Rodriguez said and pointed the light on a box labeled *Let's Play Barbie*, "is easily worth $200." Behind the plastic window stood a doll dressed in a 1950's-style red bathing suit holding a rainbow-colored beach ball.

Borges crossed the room and grabbed the box off the shelf.

"Be careful," Rodriguez insisted. "If the box gets crushed, you can forget it."

"*Forget it.*" The parrot turned its head sideways and repeated the words. "*Forget it.*"

"For Christ's sake," Novak laughed, "go figure. I may be going a bit crazy, but why the fuck would they leave a pet here? And why isn't anyone taking care of it? It makes no sense."

"Don't worry," Rodriguez said. "It's not a dog."

"Dude, who leaves a pet to starve? I don't get it."

"They didn't. Like a cat—you leave plenty of water and food out with a clean litter box and you're good to go. People do it all the time."

Novak bit his lower lip in thought. "Yeah, okay." He walked over to the bird's cage and shined his light inside. "All right, yeah, there's food and the water bottle is huge."

"Or a fish tank," Borges said as he placed his backpack on the queen-sized bed and strategically placed the boxed Barbie inside. "Same thing."

"Same thing," the parrot repeated.

"I didn't know parrots were so huge," Novak said. "It's like the size of a duck."

"All right, cut the shit," Rodriguez sighed. "Let's start clearing this place out. I want jewelry. If there're any perfumes like *Shalimar* or *Chanel No. 5*, bag them. Also, guns, take any you find. Let's get to work."

"Get to work," the parrot repeated.

Borges headed to a doorway that lead into a bathroom. Rodriguez followed Novak back into the hall and the two went their own ways—Novak to the door at the end of the hall, while Rodriguez headed back out toward the balcony. At the bookcase, he took another peak. On the bottom shelf he found a first edition of Jack

Williamson's *The Cometeers* with an original dust jacket covered in Mylar. He flipped through the pages finding no markings. The dust jacket showed a little aging but otherwise was in very good to mint condition.

Easily a hundred bucks, he smiled to himself. *Sweet.* An easy carry, he took off his backpack and placed the book inside. At the banister, he looked down at the foyer and considered going back downstairs to bag the decanter. But he figured there was plenty of time. Instead, he went down the adjoining hall and found another corridor, almost a mirror image of the first. With no bookcase, the hall was empty except for a replica of a John Singer Sargent painting hanging on the wall.

He opened the door to the right and found another bedroom with feminine decor. The walls were painted in a sunflower yellow, with posters of Matt Damon and Tom Cruise. In between two windows was a makeup table with perfume bottles. Rodriguez pulled out the chair and sat down. Sure enough one of the perfume spray bottles was *Shalimar*, barely used.

.05 ounces. Rodriguez shook his head with mixed feelings. To think parents would give their teenage daughter such a luxury was insane. He went through the other items on the table and also took a bottle of *Gucci Première*—worth about a hundred bucks. With nothing else valued over fifty, he got up and went to the dresser. Inside, he found little of interest unless you were a horny teenage boy. He grabbed a couple of pink tank tops and wrapped the bottles of perfume in them.

Rodriguez walked over to one of the windows and looked out upon the snowy front lawn. About forty yards away he could see the plowed road, which was a drastic contrast from the snow-covered driveway. Through the wooded yard, other McMansions were visible, their blue-gray televisions and yellow shining reading lamps casting light into the graying darkness of the new night.

Down the road, headlights shined through the many leafless trees. The vehicle neared and stopped at the entrance of the driveway. Rodriguez saw that it was a pickup with a large plow on the front. The truck turned toward the driveway and the headlights flashed the front of the house and window. Rodriguez jumped out of sight and peeked out to see that the plow was most certainly here for the Chatterjee house.

He bolted out of the room and ran to the other door in the hall. When he opened it, a horrendous smell similar to rotten eggs hit him like a punch to the gut. Light blinded him and he brought his arm up over his eyes.

"Rodriguez?" Novak's voice came from somewhere in the room. "Man, don't scare me like that."

"Shut the fucking flashlight off." The light moved to a wall where a king-sized bed stood. "I said *off!*" The room went dark. "Where's Borges?"

"I'm right here," said a voice in the dark. A silhouette stood in a doorway on the other side of the room. "What the fuck's that smell?"

"Quiet," Rodriguez snapped. "Both of you."

Outside, a rumble resonated as the plow pushed into the driveway. A steel on stone grumble rattled the window. Light from the vehicle's headlights traveled across the bedroom. Decorative muntins outlined shadow crosses, which settled upon Borges. Borges hit the floor and crawled over to the corner.

"Who the fuck is it?" Novak whispered.

Rodriguez crept on all fours to where Novak was and sat himself against a wardrobe. "A plow."

The clanking and banging of the plow continued for a good ten minutes.

Through the doorway leading to the bathroom, the parrot squawked, "Carol is a pretty girl. Carol is a pretty girl."

The sound of the plow truck's engine began to fade. Novak crawled over to one of the windows and looked out. "It's gone."

Rodriguez got to his feet and peeked out. The driveway was plowed but the walkway to the front door was still covered with snow. As his heart slowed, the rotten egg smell took front and center. "What the hell is that stench?"

"Oh, right." Novak turned on his flashlight and lit up what was obviously the master bedroom. "I put it under the covers." He flashed the light over to the California king.

"You put what there?" Borges asked. He crossed the room and stood over the bed.

"I am a Chatterjee," the parrot said from down the hall.

"It's under the covers," Novak said through his laughter.

Borges reached down and pulled back the blankets. Underneath was a half-eaten sandwich with a green mold growing on the bread.

"Bologna sandwich", Novak said. "It was over there on the desk."

"Dude," Borges said turning to him and using his arm to shield the harshness of the utility flashlight, "no week old sandwich would make this smell."

"Make this smell," the parrot said. "Carol is a pretty girl."

Rodriguez circled the room, sniffed. On the desk he grabbed a sterling silver Cross pen. *About three hundred bucks.* As he passed the bathroom door, he heard the parrot cracking open seeds.

"Now here's the problem," Borges said. "While you guys were checking your rooms, I canvassed the floor and there's something not quite right. The thing is, we have a u-shaped hallway, right? And the bottom of the 'u' is where the balcony is."

"Yeah, so?"

"Well, what about the center of the house? Inside the 'u'—there's no doors in that part of the hallway."

Rodriguez thought about that. Borges was right. He looked over at Novak, but the man wore a blank expression.

"Hold it," said Rodriguez, "this room...and the fucking stench… God, this room, the master bedroom, is the only one that would be touching the inside of the 'u', right?"

"So it must be a walk-in closet."

"That's over there," Novak said flashing his light over at an open doorway.

"Did you check it for loot yet?" Rodriguez asked.

"Haven't got to it."

"Okay, so if that over there is the walk-in closet, where is the door to the inside of the 'u'?"

Borges walked into the center of the room and looked about. "Do you think…?"

"What?" Rodriguez asked.

"Could it be one of those panic rooms?"

"Holy shit!" Novak said. "Maybe." He walked over to the inside wall of the master bedroom and began taking down the framed Sargent reproduction.

"Help me move this wardrobe," Borges said and grabbed one of its edges. Rodriguez and Novak moved to help and the three pushed it across the floor. Immediately the rotten egg stench increased.

"For Christ's sake," Borges said. He pulled his shirt over his nose.

Novak picked up his utility flashlight and shined it where the wardrobe had stood. They had exhumed a white door, no higher than five feet, stenciled with the outlined figure of a human pouring liquid from an urn.

"A panic room?" Borges asked.

"A panic room," the parrot repeated. "Have a cracker, have a cracker."

"I don't think so," Novak said. He traced the stencil with his fingers. "That's an astrology symbol. Aquarius."

"How do you know that?" Rodriguez asked.

"Because I'm one."

"That smell is coming from in there," Borges said through the shirt tight around the lower half of his face.

Novak looked over at him and then turned to Rodriguez. A neutral expression remained on his face. He shined the flashlight to the right of the stencil. There was a sliding lock, presently unlatched. He pushed the head of his flashlight against the door. It swung inward with a loud creak. Stale air billowed out, along with another flourish of the putrid smell. The three men stepped back in disgust.

"What now?" Borges asked. Their eyes met. "Novak?"

Novak rolled his eyes. He shined the light through the doorway. Inside was an unfinished room. Above hung a single unlit bulb on a string. The walls were open studs and the backside of drywall. Over to the right sat a small table that looked much like a tool bench. Laying on top of it was a hardbound book with no dust jacket. A folding chair stood opened on the other side of the room with a small covered ceramic jar displayed upon it.

In the middle of the floor lay the decaying bodies of five people, their faces, dried and mummified. Four were clothed in skirts and blouses, the fifth dressed in slacks, white dress shirt, and red tie.

Borges spoke first. "What the fuck is this?"

"The Chatterjees," Rodriguez replied.

"But what-?"

"I don't know." Rodriguez stepped into the room and crossed to the bodies. He scrunched up his face as he began checking the pockets of the male corpse. His hand came out with a wallet. "Terrence Chatterjee."

Novak moved over to the tool bench and picked up the book. "Borges, shine your flashlight here."

Borges turned on his LED light. On the cover of the book was the circle of the Zodiac. Novak pulled his shirt down off his face and flipped through the pages, which were decorated with symbols and writing.

Rodriguez moved forward to get a better look. "What language is that?"

"I don't know, German maybe?"

Novak stopped on a page displaying the eleventh symbol of the zodiac, Aquarius.

"It could be Danish...maybe Dutch." He slowly mouthed one of the sentences phonetically, stumbling on the words.

The parrot repeated, "*Verbruik van de put van wijn die Pan u zal geven.*"

Borges eyes widened. "What the hell?"

"That's written right here," Novak said. More words spilled from his lips. The voice from the other room spoke them, too.

"*Om zo te doen zal vele naties gegeven worden.*"

The folding chair collapsed behind them. Borges jumped. The small jar rolled along the floorboards and settled against the far wall. It's cap lazily slipped off and circled to stillness.

"I think we should get the fuck out of here," Borges said "There's a family of stiffs in a hidden room. Dude, this is a crime scene. The wardrobe was even pushed back in place blocking the only exit out."

Another rattle sounded from the cage in the other room. "*Maar toch het leven zal nog eens terugkeerde naar hem zijn,*" the parrot sang in a shrill voice.

The door slammed shut. Rodriguez ran over and found it locked. A mist began to slither out from the tipped over jar. Borges pushed Rodriguez to the side and slammed his shoulder against the door. The barrier held, denying escape.

"It's poison," Novak said, his voice shaky. He circled the bodies, stepping on the folding chair. "I'm telling you, it's poison gas!"

"It's poison gas," the parrot sang.

Borges picked up the folded chair and turned the legs out like a weapon. He slammed it into the drywall between two studs. Plaster broke up into powder and dispersed into the air. Borges slammed the chair a second time against the wall before letting it go. It bounced on the floor and settled by the dead father's feet. He then began grabbing chunks of the wall and ripping them from the frame. Rodriguez caught on and hurried over to help.

"Get out of the way," Novak said. Rodriguez turned to the side and watched as Novak swung the utility flashlight down upon the drywall. More pieces dropped away. The hole in the wall widened.

Rodriguez glanced behind him and was shocked to see the mist taking shape. When Novak moved from the hole, Rodriguez stepped forward and shoved himself partially through the opening. He shined his flashlight to find the way blocked by the back of the hall bookcase. He pushed forward with his shoulder and the barricade crashed over. Books spilled across the floor. Rodriguez pulled himself through, sliding on the bookcase's angled back and landing hard beside the shards of the broken vase. Behind him, Borges struggled through the opening with Novak quickly following.

"Oh my God," Borges said, his voice cracked from fear. "What's that?"

Rodriguez looked back through the hole in the wall and saw the corporeal form of something tall, human in form but with the head of a moose. There one second, it was gone the next, fading back into the mist.

"Let's get the fuck out of here," Borges said.

He led the way back through the corridor and down the stairs. Rodriguez followed. Novak's footsteps pounded behind them. Rather than heading out the way they came, Borges simply opened the front door and ran into the night. Novak barreled through the arch and landed in the snow. Borges was already racing up the driveway, out to the street.

As Rodriguez darted into the cold, the parrot shrieked, "Monsters in the mist. Monsters in the mist!"

Rodriguez pushed along through the deep snow. He trekked far through the woods that lead to the other neighborhood, where his Chevy Cruze was parked. As he broke through the last snow bank to the street, he saw two silhouettes standing at the vehicle.

"Rodriguez—that you?" Novak asked.

Rodriguez straightened himself up and moved into a huddle with his two cohorts.

"We've been waiting for ten minutes," Borges whispered. "Open the fucking car." Rodriguez reached into the pocket of his snow-covered jeans for his keys and pressed the fob. The squeak of the vehicle broke the stillness of the night. The other two jumped in. Rodriguez opened the driver's side door and slid onto the seat.

"So what now?" Borges asked from the backseat.

"We go back," Novak said.

"Are you fucking kidding me?"

"Novak's right," Rodriguez said. "Our sled's still on their back deck. And we left our backpacks."

"I have mine," Novak said. The inside car light lit up their faces.

Novak undid his backpack and flopped it onto the seat beside Rodriguez.

"I'm not going back," Borges said. "You saw the same thing I saw. And I'm not even talking about the Chatterjees."

Novak swallowed hard. "I'll go. I'll get what we left behind and then we can get lost of this place for good."

Borges looked at him, eyed Rodriguez, and then glanced down at the backpack. He reached over the seat and unhooked the latch. Opening it revealed the spoils wrapped in magazine pages and woman's underwear.

"What the hell?" Rodriguez asked.

Borges pulled out the object, the only thing not wrapped. Novak gasped out a swear. In Borges' hands was the small ceramic jar from the hidden room. He dropped it, and it rolled onto the front seat.

Also in Novak's backpack was a book. Not the prized first edition, its cover was decorated with the circle of the Zodiac.

JARS OF HEARTS

MELISSA M. GATES

The first heart Jave took belonged to his dog, Ralph. Jave's parents thought a companion would be good for their son, who was named after a great uncle that lived in a tiny nation in Europe. The puppy, Ralph, arrived one morning in a cage with a large red bow wrapped around it. Excited as the boy was, Jave was very cruel to Ralph, kicking and beating him for no reason when others weren't looking. And yet despite this, the dog loved his master dearly.

One morning the two were in the woods behind their home. As usual, Jave played his favorite game: throwing rocks at the dog. When Ralph was bloodied and bruised, the boy knelt to inspect the dog's injuries. When he caressed Ralph's fur, an unexpected thing occurred. His hand disappeared deep under Ralph's coat, Jave's fingertips encountering little resistance as they snaked past flesh and muscle. The dog whimpered, looking at Jave, but was much too weak to lift its head from the shroud of dead leaves and branches.

Adrenaline rushed through the boy's mind as he viewed his buried hand deep within the dog's chest cavity. He felt blood and tissue sloshing between his fingers. Its warm and thick texture reminded him of melted chocolate on a hot summer day. The dog whimpered and stared up at the boy.

Instead of disgust, curiosity possessed Jave, and he pushed on to see what would happen. He felt the prickly bones of the dog's ribcage. They separated quite easily. His fingertips slipped inward, where he located the vibrations of the dog's heartbeat; slowly, he encircled his fingers around the beating life force. With a quick motion, Jave squeezed. The dog howled in pain, startling the boy. Just as quickly, he let his grasp go. The harsh wail turned into a muffled breath.

Interesting, Jave thought. He enclosed his fingers once more around the pulsating heart but this time pulled upon it. The organ resisted only for a moment. Slowly, his wrist reappeared, colored crimson with blood. Moments later his hand slipped free, holding the dog's heart. He examined it with a peculiar interest. The heart beat once and then a second time before it stilled.

Returning his gaze to Ralph, he realized the dog was dead. Its blank eyes stared up at him the same as those wax cavemen and animals he saw at museums. Strangely, the opening along Ralph's chest had vanished. The only evidence that remained of what he'd done was the heart in his hand.

Can others do this? Jave wondered, with no remorse.

He put the organ in his coat pocket and left the dog lying in the dirt. When he arrived home, his mother asked where Ralph had gone and Jave responded he didn't know. He stole a bottle of cider vinegar and one of her mason jars then ran to his room like a child on Christmas day. He pulled the heart from his coat and sealed it into the jar. Sitting on his bed, he admired it, turning the jar in his hands.

That was his first piece, his first prize, his first heart.

Jave's excitement over Ralph's heart was short-lived. He loved the heart sitting in the jar, but he longed for the sensation and power he felt in taking it. He needed another, and thoughts of how he could possess one consumed him all the time. He begged his parents for another pet, but after the sudden disappearance of Ralph, they refused. Finally, he discovered a stray cat. He fed the animal secretly, day after day, until it finally trusted him. Quickly he pinned it down with one hand, and reached between the front legs with his other. The cat cried out, spitting and scratching him.

Ignoring the pain he pushed on with excitement, watching his hand disappear under the fur and skin, like he had done with Ralph. His body tingled with the delightful feeling of the warm innards that ran through his fingers. The cat's ribs didn't part as easily as they had with Ralph, but he pushed hard enough and felt a pop as they gave way. Behind the bones, his fingertips felt a quick rhythmic pumping. Slowly he enclosed his palm, encircling the heart. The little organ beat much faster than the way Ralph's had. With ease, the muscle dislodged from its cradle as he pulled his fist back. Jave was intrigued as he watched the life of the cat dwindle and it gave up the fight.

The heart was smaller than Ralph's. After twirling it between his fingers, he looked back at the dead cat. Just as with Ralph, the hole that had been made had vanished. Unlike Ralph, who had been bloodied and beaten from the rock game, the cat looked peaceful, like it had died naturally. Jave knew better. The animal had suffered. Knowing this filled him with happiness.

Returning his gaze back at the tiny heart, any joy he felt dissipated. The heart was too small for his liking. Jave realized the scrawny organ wasn't worthy to sit in a jar next to Ralph's. He squished it in his palm, watching it ooze between his knuckles. He shook the broken membrane from his finger tips and dropped it by his feet.

Jave walked out of the woods. Though unsatisfied, he replayed in his memory the cat's suffering. As he wandered he came upon the fence of the Entwistle Farm. In the distance, cows grazed nonchalantly. Such a peaceful image couldn't dispel the anger that grew within him over the cat's pathetic heart. Jumping over the fence, Jave walked up to a large Holstein. The animal looked upon him with disinterest. Jave reached just below the cow's neck. To his surprise, the flesh didn't part as he expected. His fingertips simply pressed upon the animal's large neck muscles. He pushed harder but couldn't get his hand to disappear. Defeated, he punched the cow in the throat.

Why doesn't it work this time? he wondered.

The cow looked at him unfazed as it continued its grassy meal.

The second jar Jave added to his collection finally came when he was sixteen. After almost four years since his dissatisfaction with the stray cat, his hand itched for the day when he could figure out how to control his power. *Power?* he wondered. *What else can it be?*

A loner in high school, he was deemed a freak by classmates. Jave kept his head down and sat quietly in the back of many of his classes. By his sophomore year, he had alienated himself from everyone. He ignored those around him; stupid, simple people talking about sports, proms and the newest boy bands.

Like many days walking home from school, Jave was lost in thought about his unique power. So much so that he didn't notice the four boys from the football team approaching from the corner of the school field.

"You're on our turf, loser," the largest one said, a jock named Philip.

Jave mumbled an apology and tried to walk past. Two of the others, Peter and Michael, blocked the way.

Philip grabbed Jave by the back of his neck and spun him around. "Where do you think you're going, freak?" Drops of spit rained over Jave's face.

"I said I'm sorry." Jave said, fresh fear consuming him. All the boys were taller and weighed more than he.

"Guys, I think he wants to join the football team," Philip laughed while Peter and Michael circled around him.

"Come on, Philip," the fourth boy, Brian, chimed in. "We're gonna be late, and coach will kill us."

"Dude, I think we could practice right here. Four players." Philip looked at Jave. "And a ball."

Before he could react, Philip kneed Jave hard in the groin. Pain shot all the way up to his chest. Queasiness blanketed over him that almost made him unload his lunch. Immediately Peter and Michael joined in; a kick connected with his tailbone causing a shudder to shoot up his spine.

Philip caught him from falling. "You ain't leaving yet, asshole."

The bully looked Jave in the eyes and grinned. Jave reached out and placed his hand upon Philip's chest, meeting solid muscle. He pushing hard with his fingertips but nothing gave. Jave didn't care if the others saw his *power*; the hatred that burned within his own heart gave him desire to take the bully's.

Philip looked down at Jave's hand. "You think you can push me, dickhead?" The bully pulled his fist back, swung, and connected across Jave's nose.

Jave fell to his knees and vomited. Blood trickled down, mixing with his vomit.

"Come on, coach is gonna kill us!" Brian urged.

The final blow was unexpected, a punch just below his ribs. Jave doubled over. Between his tears, he watched the four walk away, laughing between their derogatory remarks. Jave remained on the ground, drooling, bleeding, unable to move. His fury deepened. He staggered up and quickly headed into the forest.

"Hey, Jave, you okay?"

He recognized Brian's voice behind him. The other boy caught up and placed a hand on his shoulder .

Expecting another attack, Jave quickly whipped around. He grabbed at Brian's chest. A rush of ecstasy came over him. His fist disappeared through the football player's shirt. Brian's eyes shot open. The rage within Jave grew. Pushing forward, he felt ribs move.

Jave beamed as his own pain turned to joy. In a mirror reflection, tears fell from Brian's eyes as he tightened his fist around the surprisingly large heart. Without ceremony, Jave ripped his hand back, pulling the organ with him. He held it high above his head in triumph as Brian slowly slid to the ground beside him. Drops of blood dripped out of the organ and mingled with Jave's. As the wave of emotion began to subside, he looked over at the dead student. Just like the other two times, there was no evidence of what he had done. A boy, unharmed, seemed to be lying asleep on a bed of leaves.

Regaining his composure, Jave ran home, flying on adrenaline from the good luck at taking Brian's heart.

He pulled back the clothing in his closet and picked up the empty jar that sat next to the one containing Ralph's heart. Jave massaged the smooth glass like it was a precious stone then reached into his jacket pocket and put the now lifeless heart inside. As he sealed the cover, Jave smiled, turning the mason jar around and around, inspecting the size, shape, and color of the dead teen's heart. He carefully placed the jar on the shelf next to the one that held Ralph's and craved more.

How did I take Brian's heart so easily but not Philip's? he wondered.

Jave was still baffled over this strange inconsistency. And such a question didn't even answer what the power was in the first place. As dusk crawled across the evening sky, he waited for darkness to head out and find a burial spot for the boy.

Two days later at breakfast, Jave watched the news anchor report the tragic story of the missing football player. Back at school, students wept. Cheerleaders set up a memorial by the football field.

Rumors flew that Brian took performance enhancing drugs and had gotten involved with the wrong people. Jave, however, knew the truth and went about his day as usual, trying to ignore the throngs of girls he passed in the corridor crying on each other's shoulders.

As lunch began, Jave was cornered by Courtney, a bubbly blonde cheerleader who hadn't spoken two words to him since second grade.

"Hey," she whispered quietly, sitting beside him.

Jave looked at her. She seemed like she hadn't slept in a month. "Yeah?" he asked.

Courtney leaned in, tears flooding her bottom lids. "Look, I have something to tell you. It's important."

Jave waited for his boxers to be grabbed from behind and his body to be lifted painfully off the seat. Instinctively, he put his hand upon his lower back just to make sure he wasn't ambushed. "What is it?"

"Everyone believed Brian and I were dating."

"I thought you were."

"We made a pact in sixth grade to pretend that."

"Huh?"

Courtney looked down; her perfectly manicured fingernail scratched at some graffiti on the table. "We made a pact to pretend we were together. Brian and I…" Courtney stopped and sniffed. Tears tumbled down her cheeks. "Brian knew he…knew he wasn't like that. I knew it, too."

Jave looked around again, waiting for the punch line. He expected someone to run up and dump lunch on his head. "What does this have to do with me?"

She snapped, "Look, Brian liked guys. We grew up together, and are—*were*—best friends. We told each other everything, things we wouldn't tell other people." Her words rushed out between sniffs. "I liked girls, he liked guys but that doesn't work when you're a cheerleader or a football player. Are you getting what I'm saying?"

Jave stared at Courtney, confused why she'd tell him such useless information. "No," he finally admitted. He really didn't care.

"Brian and I are both gay. We didn't want people to know, so we said we'd just always pretend we were dating until we got to college and could be more open about it. We didn't want to risk our reputations and be considered losers like—" Courtney frowned. "Like you."

"So?"

"First, if you tell anyone this, they won't believe you." Courtney smirked, knowing she was right. "Second, I have no idea why, but Brian had a thing for you. He liked you. I think he was going through some kind of bad boy phase or something. Anyway," she sniffed through a whisper, "since he's gone, I thought it was important to tell you the truth."

Jave was untouched. He wasn't stupid enough to believe a dumb cheerleader. There had to be a punch line...or a physical punch coming from somewhere.

"I swear if you tell anyone, I'll deny it," Courtney hissed and walked away.

Jave thought about Ralph's heart, the cat's, and his newest acquisition, Brian's. They'd cared for him. The wild animals, the cow, and Philip didn't. And then it all made sense. *The more they love me the easier it is to take the heart! That's it. That's the connection...I'm the connection. It has to be.*

When he got home, Jave ran to his room and opened his closet door. He pushed clothing back, revealing the shelf. No, the *altar* with jars of hearts upon it. He sat on his bed, staring at his prized possessions. That was it—if someone loved him, he could collect their heart. Jave's smile quickly disappeared. What if others could do this?

If I loved someone, could they take my heart, too?

He vowed never to love anyone. His only love would be his collection of hearts.

As time passed, the only two people he had ever let close to him passed away. Unlike others that he loved, his parents died of natural causes. As a result, the house and property were all left to Jave. By the age of thirty-five, he had collected nineteen jars; thirteen of them human. He spent his days working at a local paper mill, always thinking about his next target, his next heart. Jave had plenty of room in the house now, and had decided to display his jars in the basement instead of hidden away like a dirty secret.

Jave never took a girlfriend except when it suited him to find a new heart. He never allowed himself to really get to know a girl; they were all dumb, worried about their hair, or how fat they looked in their cleavage-revealing dresses. Jave was determined never to care about any of them, but he let them all care about him.

One Friday night after his shift, Jave went to his local watering hole as usual. Taking his regular seat at the bar, he was shocked to see that Barbara wasn't working. In her place was a curly-haired redhead with cute little freckles across her cheeks. She gave him a very warm smile and asked if she could help him.

"Who're you?" Jave asked.

"I'm Angie. I just started."

"I've never seen you before."

"I just moved to town. Boyfriend trouble at home," Angie said, winking at him.

"Really? Beautiful girl like you, I can see why."

Angie smiled "What can I get you?"

"Beer, draft."

Jave watched the petite redhead as she sashayed from one patron to the next. He'd catch her looking at him and her smile made his heart flutter. *Not good,* he thought, *protect your heart, but take hers.*

After sixth months, Jave finally got the nerve to ask her out. He had flirted before, but she never fell for his lines like others had. She was special, he agreed. She didn't reveal much about herself, and that intrigued Jave even more.

On their first date, Jave found himself nervous, fumbling to help her into her seat, saying stupid things, and when she looked into his eyes he felt his stomach doing flips. At the end of the night, instead of just leaning in to kiss her, Jave asked permission. To his surprise she said no.

"I don't kiss on the first date." She smiled and walked into her house.

Weeks of dates, and finally kissing, Jave realized that he didn't want to take her heart. He wanted to share his collection with her.

But would she turn him in, or even understand his special ability?

Jave spent weeks wrestling with what to do. Since meeting Angie, he hadn't seen any other women and hadn't added to his collection. And while his mind thought of her, his hand itched for a heart.

"What are you thinking about?" Angie asked between bites of salad one night.

"Huh?"

She laughed a heavenly laugh. "You, you're lost in thought. What's on your mind?"

"You don't want to know."

"Yes I do. Try me."

Jave stared at Angie and pondered a way to tell her about his marvelous collection. "It's dark."

Angie leaned in, her V-neck shirt dipping lower, revealing heart-shaped cleavage. "I like dark," she whispered.

"Have you ever thought of killing someone?"

Angie stared at him, her face paled slightly. *Shit!* he thought. *You just freaked her out!*

"Who doesn't think about it," she finally answered, color rushing back to her face.

"Yeah, I guess you're right." Jave gave a small chuckle of relief.

"You know, I've always found it fascinating. What drives people to kill? Not like a husband killing a wife, but serial killers. The people who do bad things just because." Angie flashed a sly smile and leaned closer. "It makes me hot thinking about that kind of passion."

"Really?"

"Yeah, does that make me a freak?"

No, it means you're the one! "It makes me think we should go home to my place," Jave said, flashing a suggestive smile.

Jave tried to concentrate on the road while he drove. Between Angie's head bobbing between his legs and his eagerness to share his most prized possessions, it was nearly impossible to hold onto the wheel. When they entered the house, Angie started for the bedroom, but Jave turned her toward the basement.

"I want to show you something," he said, taking her hand.

"Where are we going?"

"I want to show you my collection."

"Collection?"

"I've never shown it to anyone. You're the first. The jars are my passion."

"You collect jars?" she snickered.

"It's not the jars; it's what's in them. Trust me," he said, taking her hand. Jave flipped the light switch and led the way down the stairs.

Angie gazed around the room at his life's work. "Holy fuck," she gasped.

Jave moved behind her. Angie picked up one of the jars. Even without a label, Jave knew exactly who its heart belonged to.

"Her name was Sara, she was an easy one. I enjoyed chasing her through the woods behind the field of her parents' home in Vermont."

"You took her heart?"

"I was twenty-seven. She had fallen for me after only three days together."

Angie put the jar down carefully and looked at him. "Why do this?"

"Because I can. The more someone loves me, the easier it is to take their heart. Sometimes, I enjoy when they don't love me enough, because it's more of a challenge."

"You killed all these people?"

Jave felt an unfamiliar feeling in his stomach. *Is she disgusted? Will she have to be the next?* "Yes, but don't you see, Angie? I have a gift."

"Were they bad people? Did they hurt you?"

"No, they were just ordinary, simple. I have a power. I was chosen to be able to do this."

"Why are you showing me this?" she asked waving her arms at the jars. Her eyes lit with fear. "Am I next?"

"I wanted to show you because I want to share this with you. You're special to me, Angie. I've never felt this way. You're the one I've waited for."

Angie crossed the room. He thought she was going to storm out, hit him, leave. Another strange feeling washed over him. Sadness? *She'll have to be my next heart,* he thought.

Instead of leaving, she wrapped her arms around his neck and kissed him deeply. When she finally broke their embrace, she looked at him and smiled. "I think you've been a very bad boy, Jave. Have you ever been punished?"

She took his hand and led him up the stairs and into his bedroom.

He flicked Angie's nipples as she bounced above him, riding him like a cowgirl. She smiled at him and leaned forward for a kiss. He wrapped his arms around her slim frame and rolled over and back, never breaking their embrace. Jave looked up at her, brushing a strand of hair from her face.

"I love you," he whispered. That was the first time he had ever said those words to anyone, and he meant them.

"You do?"

"With all my heart. I've never loved anyone until I met you, Angie."

"Oh, Jave, I've been waiting to hear you say that."

Angie reached up and pulled his lips to hers, kissing him deeply. She trailed her hands down his back, moved up to his shoulders, rubbing deeply into his muscles. Her touch was amazing. Her body pressed into his. Her hands moved to his chest. Jave closed his eyes, reveling in the intimacy. Her warmth felt incredible on his skin as her fingers traveled down his stomach.

Suddenly pain exploded at his groin. Angie's smile widened.

"What the-?" the sentence went unfinished as agony rang through his body.

He shoved Angie off him. Jave's balls had been set on fire, and his dick felt like it had been dropped in acid. He couldn't breathe, couldn't speak.

"What did you do?" h spurted as his mouth filled with blood.

"You were an easy one, Jave. You must really love me," Angie said, smiling down as he tried to breathe. "I admit, you were tough to hook, making me wait six months. You see, I'm a collector, too, and you were a perfect specimen."

"Wha-?"

"Shhh," Angie put a finger to his lips. She held up her other hand. Blood dripped down her wrist. "Don't talk, you only have another few seconds to live. Let me just look at you."

"Hey, I'm Cindy. Can I help you?"

"Yeah, thanks. I'm Angie."

"You moving into Unit Two?" the young woman asked.

"Yeah, just moved here from Maine."

"Awesome, we're neighbors. I'm in Three. Maine to Washington, huh? All the way across the country?"

Angie smiled at the girl. "Yeah, well, boyfriend trouble. You know, had to get away."

The girl gave Angie a sympathetic smile and reached to pick up the green plastic tub Angie had just unloaded.

"I'll get that one," Angie said. "It's full of breakables."

The girl helped Angie carry her boxes into the new place and left her to unpack. When she was alone, Angie carefully lifted her jars one at a time into a shelf in her closet. Smiling, she remembered how she had obtained the testicles of her victims, and how easily each of the men fell in love with her.

A TRIP TO EGYPT

TRACY L. CARBONE

Jerry didn't know how long he had been walking, or where his shoes were. His feet were numb and had blood on them when he arrived in front of the *A Trip to Egypt* attraction at the carnival. The blaring music and bright lights from the fair snapped him out of whatever kind of trance he was in.

He patted his pockets for his phone but it wasn't there. His wallet wasn't either. *Where am I? Who am I? Jerry. My name is Jerry.* The air was sticky and heavy, and a mosquito buzzed around his head, trying to land so he surmised it was summertime. He wore a black concert shirt and jean shorts. Track marks riddled his arms.

"Step right up, step right up! Enter here to find your way home!" A black-haired midget in a faded magenta tuxedo yelled to passersby. His short hair was parted down the middle and held in place with hair wax. For a small man, his voice bellowed through the crowd. His presence fit perfectly in a dusty country fair, if indeed that's where Jerry was. He looked around. *Where the hell am I?*

"Hey Mister!" The little man called to him. "You need some help?"

"Yes, I, I'm a little lost."

"Well, Mister, you are at Bart's Carnival. The oldest family-run carnival on the East Coast."

"Oh." That didn't help. What Jerry should have asked was, "What town am I in?"

"Say," the man said as he walked to Jerry and looked him up and down. "Where are your shoes?"

"I don't know. I was, I was nowhere at all and then I was here. Right here on this spot."

"Well that can't be. You must have walked in the front gate. Let me see your right hand."

Jerry offered up his hand, which the man examined.

"Oh yeah there it is. See that?"

Jerry looked. "What is that?"

"It's your wrist band. It's got a scarab on it. Come to think of it, I remember you now. You came by a few hours ago, took a tour through *A Trip to Egypt* and asked for the special treatment."

"Did I get it?"

"Yeah, but it didn't take. Come with me. I'll get you home." Jerry felt the man's stubby little fingers grab his hand. Jerry yanked them away. "Someone's sensitive about his disfigurement," he heckled.

Jerry didn't reply to that. Damn straight he was sensitive about it. "How are you going to get me home? You don't even know my name much less my address," Jerry protested.

"Do you know your address?"

"No, dude, but I must be tripping. Took something and got confused is all. None of this is even real, I bet."

"It's real, all right. Come with me." The man took his hand and they walked like a father son team toward the fun house. "Name's Merle."

"Don't think I ought to be going into a funhouse when I'm high like this. Feel freaked out. Can you call an ambulance?"

"Aren't you afraid of being arrested for the drugs you took?"

"No. Not right now. I'm just scared, dude. Something's seriously wrong with me."

Merle furrowed his brow. "What goes around comes around. You go on right ahead of the crowd, right up to the front. Tell the man I sent you. Tell them the scarab didn't take and you need a blue one."

"A scarab? Like those little beetles?"

"In a sense, yes. It's what you need. It will help you find your way."

Jerry felt relieved. This was clearly a bad trip. He didn't remember taking mushrooms or acid but something was racing through his blood, messing with his mind. Better to run with it. He knew what happened when you panicked during a bad trip. A friend of his bit his own lips off on bath salts, screaming the whole time that he wanted to wake up. Jerry wouldn't make that mistake. He'd stay calm and go with it.

"I don't have any money. My wallet—"

"Now isn't the time to worry about that. Tell you what. You go in

A Trip to Egypt. Humor me. Ask for a blue scarab. While you're in there, I'll call an ambulance. It will take them awhile to get here what with all the 4th of July traffic and all—"

"It's the 4th of July?" Jerry asked.

"Sure is. Independence Day for you. Just go in the house. It'll get your mind off things. When you get out, the ambulance will be here and you'll be home in no time."

Suppose there's nothing to lose. Jerry walked to the head of the line. A chubby little girl in a too-tight sequin dress glared at him and whined. "Hey, where are that guy's shoes? How come I have to wear shoes and he doesn't? It's not fair!"

"Hush," her look-a-like mother said. "It's not polite." The sequins in the girl's dress sparkled like they were electrified. Her whole body glowed like an angel. *A little bitch of an angel. Yeah, I'm tripping.*

Jerry walked past them and up the short metal ramp. Ahead lay a trailer painted black with poorly-drawn camels and pyramids decorating the outside. A worn recording of tinny sitar music bleated over the loud speakers. Ultraviolet light peered from behind the door where blue and green fluorescent paint illuminated murals of giant eyes and mummies. Jerry was intrigued.

"Can I help you?" a young skinny kid asked him.

What's up with his eyes? White-blue eyes and pale skin. Vampire? Yeah, totally tripping. Hold it together, Jerry.

"Holy shit, what happened to your hand?" the kid said, breaking Jerry from his messed up thoughts.

"Afghanistan happened. U.S. Marine at your service." He saluted but with half his hand missing it didn't garner the respect it once had. *I was a Marine.* Bits of his past dribbled in.

"I get it. So you get in for free, right? Don't have to pay?"

Jerry shrugged.

"Policy. Armed services, they get the special treatment."

"I don't know about that but Merle said I need to ask for a blue scarab. Said the other one didn't take."

The kid gave him a hard stare. "Hold on." He walked away then came back and handed Jerry a small plastic bag.

"Not for human consumption," Jerry read. The small, typed black letters marched across the white label like soldiers. He shook his head and looked again. This time they stood still.

"Yeah, we have to state that disclaimer. You remember, right?"

Jerry shook his head. "Don't remember anything."

"Just pop what's in there and go ahead through that door."

Jerry held the bag up to the bright carnival lights. A small bright blue beetle glowed inside the back like a firefly. It wiggled its tiny legs and Jerry flinched when he felt the sharp legs scratch against the plastic. "I'm not taking this. It's alive."

The kid smiled at him, and again gave him the hard stare with his snowy eyes. "Look again, Jerry."

How did he know my name?

Now the bag contained a small blue pill. "Not a bug?"

The kid leaned in to Jerry, whispered in his ear. "Bath salts formed into the shape of a scarab. You know, the whole Egyptian theme. Makes the ride a little more fun."

Jerry opened the bag and poured the bug into the palm of his hand. "The little guy, Merle, he said I did a red one before. Did I get it from you?"

The pale kid smiled but didn't answer the question. "Go on, step right on in." He called out to the crowd then. "Everyone, step right on into this attraction and take your own trip to Egypt."

Jerry popped the bug-shaped pill into his mouth and swallowed. He felt its legs tickle his throat but ignored it. *Not real.* He turned around to see if Merle was indeed calling an ambulance but the midget was nowhere in sight. *Just need to go with this. Soon I'll wake up and I'll be on my couch or wherever I was when this started. I'll get myself home.*

He stepped through the entrance and a door slammed shut behind him. He took a few steps, turned a corner, and was plunged into utter darkness. Jerry's heart hammered in his chest. He turned around the way he came but now there was a wall behind him. A wall to his left and right too. He felt along the plywood. His only choice was to move forward.

"Hello!" he called out. He saw others walk in before him, so where did they go? And where were the ones behind him in line?

The texture of the partition changed from wood to brick. Big stone blocks, like in a pyramid. He felt along the grooves, at the gritty sand left on his fingers. Hard insect legs scratched his esophagus: The scarab, crawling back out. He coughed to dislodge it but to no avail.

He stepped cautiously, heart beating too fast, breathing too shallow. He felt his forehead. Wet. Sweat poured into his eyes. He wiped it away. "Let me out!"

No one answered. He carefully placed his foot in front of him. *Yes, the ground is still there. Another step. Yes, still there.* His arms flew in front of him but there was no way to know how long he would go on before the ground gave way, or the walls. Suddenly the right wall was gone. He stepped to the side. When he reached back, all the walls were gone. *No!* He flailed his arms, reaching for anything, but there was nothing but vast darkness.

He screamed as loudly as he could but the music outside was so loud. Damn twanging sound, increasing in volume. He covered his ears and screamed. "Help me!" No one came.

Jerry stepped forward and the ground disappeared. He screamed with all the power and terror he'd ever possessed, and prayed someone would hear. He fell through the air until he hit the floor hard and passed out.

"Mommy, I smell popcorn. Can I have some popcorn?"

It was the voice of a child. *Someone else was here*! Jerry flailed his arms, reaching for anyone. He was still alone in this dark funhouse but people were nearby. He sniffed. *Not popcorn.* It was acrid, horrible. Burnt.

"We'll see," a woman's voice replied.

"Hello! Is anyone there?" Jerry called out. "Are you in here with me?"

Neither voice answered him.

"Help me! Please, help me!" Jerry yelled. The mother and child walked by in the darkness. He could feel the cool whoosh of their bodies; smell a trace of cotton candy on the child's breath.

He ran after them, groping the endless wall for an exit, but all he felt was more stone dust on his fingers.

"Mommy, where did the man go? The one who came in before us? The one with the funny hand?"

"The crazy man with no shoes?"

"Yes," the girl answered. "No shoes, and that hand. What happened to him?"

"I'm right here!" he screamed.

"Don't worry about him. You don't talk to strangers."

"Okay, Mommy. But how did his face get like that?"

Jerry leaned back against the wall. *My face? What's wrong with my face?* He brought his good hand to his cheek. But— *Where the hell is my face?*

He ran. It was pitch black and Jerry couldn't tell if his eyes were open or shut but he pushed himself forward. *Just a bad trip. I'm not a monster. Not a monster. This isn't real!*

The wall changed from stone to fabric. A curtain! He pulled it open and bright lights blinded his sensitive eyes. The carnival music grew louder. People stared at him. Whispered. Pointed. He turned and saw the little girl and her mother emerge behind him. Sticky pink cotton candy framed the girl's mouth like anemic blood.

"What happened to you?" she asked him. "What happened to your face?"

He saw the ambulance parked ahead, its lights mixing with those from the carnival to illuminate the summer sky like a '70s disco. *Thank God.* Jerry ran toward it. Merle awaited. "Do you remember?"

"No," Jerry answered. "I'm tripping. I need to go to the hospital. It's all a hallucination. I just need to come down."

The little girl was beside him again. She tugged on his shirt. "*I'm* not a hallucination, Jerry. I'm real."

"Come along, Lisa," her mother said.

The girl smiled at Jerry and waved with a bloody stump of a hand. "I'm just like you," she said. Her face began to melt like a plastic doll in a house fire.

"Where the hell is the paramedic?"

"Come this way, Jerry," Merle said. The little man took Jerry's good hand and walked him toward a waiting stretcher. Merle's hand was tiny and soft, like that of small child. *An innocent child.* He looked for the girl in the crowd but she was gone.

Jerry opened his eyes. His right hand was covered in gauze, as well as his left. He saw his surroundings through a white patchwork filter. One stray piece of cloth fell over his eye, partially obscuring his vision.

"Do you remember, Jerry?" a man asked. He didn't recognize the voice.

A bug crawled on his neck. He tried to lift his hand to swat it away. *Can't move my hands.* The tinny sitar music blared. "Am I mummy?" *I ate a scarab and now I'm a mummy? I get it. Still tripping.* "What was in those things?"

An Asian man in a paramedic uniform adjusted a dial on a machine. "What things? I need to know what you took."

"A scarab. A red and a blue. From the little carnival barker," Jerry said numbly.

The man shook his head. "There's no carnival, Jerry. Tell me what you took."

Jerry tried to sort out the reality from the fantasy but his brain was fried. "I only remember being at the carnival. And taking a trip to Egypt. The little man. The drugs."

"Temperature is one-oh-four," a woman said. He turned his bandaged head to see the other EMT. She was ragged and about fifty. Her hair was boy-short and she looked tougher than nails.

"You a lesbian?"

"How did you hurt your hand?" she asked.

Good. I didn't ask her out loud.

"Afghanistan. U.S. Marines."

"No," the guy said. "You're not a Marine. Do you remember your accident?"

Jerry closed his eyes. He didn't feel any pain but his injury was a year ago. Didn't make any sense they were wrapping him up but he attributed it to the hallucinogens. *Just go with it, man.* "A little girl came up to our tent. Strapped with explosives. She asked what we were doing." *The little girl in the sequin dress.*

"We?" The woman asked.

"Me and my buddies. She asked and then—"

"What *were* you doing?" Another voice. He looked to the foot of his stretcher. He realized then he was in a hospital. Not in the ambulance, not at the carnival. *So mixed up.*

A cop stared him down. "When the little girl approached, what were you doing?"

The memories were clouded. "She walked into our tent. Said she was looking for her puppy."

"Are you sure it was a tent?"

"No. Not anymore. I can't—Why am I here? It was a long time ago. My hand is healed over now. They sent me home. Government sent me home with half a hand and a big thank you for my service."

"His fever and injuries are blurring his memory. Can you ask him later? We need to stabilize him," a man said. Dr. Nino, his nametag read. Named sounded familiar, but… .

Jerry was back at the carnival. Good. He liked it better here. Bright lights and good smells. If he was going to trip, this was a better place than a hospital room. He looked down at his right hand. Still there. Awesome! He felt a cold spot on his butt and reached back. *Shit.* He wore only a hospital johnny, tied at the back. No underwear.

Need to hide somewhere. A Trip to Egypt beckoned. He gathered the fabric tight to cover himself and ran to the front of the line once again.

"Back for another ride?" the vampire kid asked.

Jerry didn't answer, just darted behind the curtain.

He looked around and was shocked this time. Not utter darkness, but dingy lights and a kind of laboratory. It was filthy. It smelled like ammonia. The gurgle of boiling water and the warmth of steam reminded him of—

"Have you seen my puppy?" asked the little girl in the sequin dress.

"No, get out of here!" he said. "You shouldn't be in here!"

She was frightened by his rage but it was for her own good. A kid didn't belong in a meth lab.

Meth lab.

He looked around again. A trailer, not a tent. *His* lab. His coworkers were here, one cooking, one taking up space. Dennis showed up bragging he'd gotten some bath salts on the way in. He'd showed Jerry and Smitty the package. "Went to pick up some smokes at the Shop and Pay, and Nino pulls me aside. Said he had a new product. Gave it to me for free."

He showed them the package. Jerry thought it looked like a package of Pop Rocks or Kool-Aide. Black background with a bad drawing of a camel on the label. *A Trip to Egypt* was the flavor. *Not for human consumption* was printed on the front and back of the package.

"What the hell are you doing, Dennis? You can't be messed up when you're cooking. You need to be straight. Totally straight. Save that shit for later," Jerry told him.

"Screw you, man," Dennis said. He rolled up a dollar bill and snorted a little of the red powder. "Holy shit. Oh my God!" Dennis smiled and slumped down. Crawled into a corner and stayed there all morning, snorting more when his high waned.

The little girl tugged on Jerry's hospital johnny. "What are you guys doing in here?" He wondered why she was all dressed up. Looked like she was on the way to a Jon Benet pageant.

"Get the hell out of here, kid! I haven't seen your puppy. Didn't your mother ever tell you not to talk to strangers?"

She stood there, refusing to budge. What the hell? He moved to usher her out, and deliver a stern threat about what would happen if she told her parents about the trailer. He held her small soft hand and was ready to guide her out when he saw a beetle walk across a fresh tray of meth.

"What the hell is that? Smitty, there's a beetle or something crawling across the product." Jerry yelled.

"It's a scarab," Dennis said from the corner. "A scarab from my trip to Egypt." He laughed and Jerry wanted to beat the shit out of him. *I'll do just that once this kid leaves.* This guy was so high he had no idea where he was or what he was saying. At least with their meth you knew what you were getting. Not even close to pure but you knew. Not like those bath salts his clients were turning to. It was Russian roulette. Maybe a good trip, maybe a bad one. Or you could drop dead.

Jerry didn't do drugs himself. Not anymore. He used to be a heroin addict and had the track marks to remind him, notches on a druggie bedpost. But that was a long time ago. Now he was just a producer and supplier, with scorn and repulsion for his customers. He was a hypocrite but he made a shitload of cash.

The girl wrestled free and hopped to the tray. "It's a dung beetle," she said. "We learned about them in science." She held the wriggling black bug in her fingers.

Shit. She'd seen the meth, touched it.

"Put that down," Jerry said. He moved toward her and tripped.

He wasn't sure what happened after that exactly, except that the whole trailer exploded.

Pain coursed through his arm. He looked down at the bandages. Back in the hospital bed, in a world filtered through gauze.

"Temperature is down, he should be more lucid now," a nurse in white said. *Shining white, like a statue in the sun.*

Half his right hand was missing. He didn't know which fingers were gone but the hand wasn't as big as it should be. With his other hand he felt his face. "What happened to my face? Where's the rest of my face?" He gripped the bed railing and screamed. "Where is the rest of my face?"

"Give him some lorazepam," a doctor said.

"No," the cop said. "He's remembering and we need to take his statement. Please. Just a few minutes."

Jerry looked at the cop with his existing eye. The white crisscross lines made it hard to see. The nurse peeled back the fabric. "You don't need this. It's just an extra piece." She snipped it with scissors and the world came into focus. His past came into focus as well and suddenly the events leading to now were all there right in front of him. Worse than any acid trip.

"Do you remember what you were doing when you had the accident?" the policeman asked again.

Jerry nodded.

TOMB WORLD

JAMES PRATT

The open-topped skimmer bounced across the surface of the dead planet, rising and falling but never quite touching the ground. Courtesy of the planet's inhospitable atmosphere and the vehicle's open canopy, the skimmer's two occupants wore non-matching survival suits that reflected their role in the mission.

"Hell of a planet you picked, ma'am," Templar Swenson said over his H.E.L.L. suit's intercom as he guided the skimmer through the swirling dust. A Class-3, the suit was a few steps below even the lightest of the Hostile Environment Life Link exo-models but still provided a degree of protection via strategically-located plastite armor plates. Even if he had been wearing a bulkier suit, Swenson would have still moved with relative ease thanks to a combination of Tau Ceti-5's low gravity and his bionic enhancements.

"I didn't pick it, the CXA did," xenologist Inez replied as she studied the holographic data scrolling a few inches above her wrist-mounted scanalyzer. The extent of her protection was a standard life-support suit, little more than an insulated jumpsuit with its own oxygen supply.

"The who?"

"The Council of Xenological Affairs."

Swenson nodded. "Oh yeah."

Tau Ceti-5 was a windswept waste incapable of harboring any life beyond the hardiest single-celled microbes. Occasional super storms could send dust particles flying fast enough to penetrate plastite but the *Dunsany* supplied them with a constant stream of data from orbit, sending them real time updates regarding topography and atmospheric phenomena. As long as they kept an eye on the data stream and made it back to the lander before night fell and temperatures dropped below freezing they would be fine.

Swenson made a grunting sound that may have been a laugh. "Hell of a planet the CXA picked, then."

"I told them I didn't need a babysitter."

"Protocol. No civilian goes planet-side on worlds with a D or worse classification unless accompanied by a military escort, not even on a dustbowl like Tau Ceti-5."

"Are they afraid somebody might steal a rock or something?"

Swenson grinned behind his helmet's facemask. People with extensive academic backgrounds secretly intimidated him but Inez's transparent use of sarcasm to conceal her own insecurities put him at ease. Unfortunately those insecurities also drove her to take unnecessary risks. She would bear close watching.

"No ma'am," Swenson replied. "Ever hear of the Yaddith Massacre?"

Inez nodded. "Something killed a bunch of xenologists excavating a hive-city on the dead planet Yaddith. Very tragic."

"That's right. After that, visits to worlds with a D or worse classification have to—"

"Got it. You know, I always wondered what the 'D' stood for."

Swenson shrugged. "Dust. Death. Do Not Touch. Take your pick."

Inez glanced sideways at Swenson. He wasn't handsome by any stretch of the imagination, but he had a surprisingly dry sense of humor and the lean, hard physique of a working man.

"Are we still headed in the right direction?" Swenson asked.

Visibility was limited to a hundred meters or so but, courtesy of the data stream from the *Dunsany,* the skimmer's view-screen showed a three-dimensional representation of the surrounding topology.

"Yep," Inez said, studying the map. "We're still on track."

A quarter hour passed before anyone spoke again.

"So do you like being a soldier?" Inez asked.

"Templar, ma'am," Swenson corrected.

"Do you like being a Templar?"

"It's an honor to do my part for the Terran Assembly."

"But do you enjoy it?"

"It's a privilege to serve the—"

"Do you like it?"

"I was raised on Satcol-12," Swenson replied after a moment.

Inez glanced at him. Of all the satellite colonies orbiting the monster-haunted ruins of Old Earth, Satcol-12 wasn't the most infamous but it came pretty close. One of the oldest satcols still in commission, it was the home of the dregs who had nowhere else to go. "Satcol-12? Seriously?"

"We called it the Big Over because if you lived there, your life was already over," Swenson continued. "You had to learn to fight to survive at an early age. Those are the only things I was ever good at, fighting and surviving. I was recruited for the Legion from a juvie detent center. Command would never admit it but that's where most recruits come from. They gave me a choice; the Legion or hard labor at a deep space mining colony."

"Some choice," Inez said.

Swenson shrugged. "That's okay. I get paid to do the things I'd be doing anyway, plus I get treated like a hero by people who admire what they think I represent."

"What do you represent?"

"Hell if I know, ma'am. Can I ask you something?"

Inez winced. After Swenson's revelation, she was a bit embarrassed to admit that, as the daughter of a high-ranking corporatist, she'd enjoyed a comfortable childhood and a top-tier education. "Sure, if you stop calling me 'ma'am'."

"Why are we here?"

"You weren't briefed on the mission?"

"Just a general overview. Planetary stats, safety protocols, that sort of thing. I'm just the babysitter, remember?"

Inez wasn't sure what to say next. Mission details were classified and she'd simply assumed her military escort would have been informed. But she'd badgered Swenson until he gave an honest answer so now it was her turn.

"How much do you know about the history of Tau Ceti-5?"

"My knowledge of Tau Ceti-5's history stretches back to the exact moment when we landed here."

"Tau Ceti-5 wasn't always a lifeless rock. It has an extensive fossil record that indicates a formerly rich biodiversity."

"Lots of bugs," Swenson said.

"Then they were smart bugs. Artifacts have also been discovered."

"Artifacts. You mean signs of intelligent life."

"Right."

Swenson nodded. "I get it now. The planet was given a D

classification to discourage artifact hunters."

"That's part of it, yes. There are also certain…anomalies here."

Swenson's eyes narrowed. "Such as?"

"When xenologists started excavating this planet and documenting their findings, they soon realized that the artifacts' geological placement didn't make any sense. They were finding artifacts in deeper layers than the oldest fossils."

"Meaning?"

"Meaning that something came to this planet and left its mark long before there was any terrestrial life on Tau Ceti-5."

"Ancient astronauts," Swenson said.

"What?"

"Something I saw on an Old Earth data archive. It was a documentary about how aliens visited Earth in ancient times and left all sorts of evidence." Swenson laughed. "You should have seen the clothes the people in the documentary were wearing. Anyway, what you said made me think of it."

"Ancient astronauts," Inez said thoughtfully. "I guess it's not beyond the realm of possibility. Xenologists have found alien artifacts well over ten million years old."

"But only artifacts, right?" Swenson said. "No culture has ever actually survived that long."

"Not that we've found. The only active cultures we know about for sure are the Shan and the Mi-Go and, well…"

"Being in a perpetual state of war makes them difficult to study."

"That and their alien mindsets make communication almost impossible. As a xenologist I shouldn't be saying this but I'm not sure I mind. Studying fossils and artifacts is one thing but…I was once invited to observe the vivisection of a captive Shan. From a distance it looked sort of like an enormous wasp or mosquito but up close, you could tell it knew exactly what was happening. At one point it looked right at me and…" Inez shivered. "Reading about an intelligent bug is one thing but being scrutinized by one is a different story."

"I've seen Mi-Go up close," Swenson said. "My squad was sent to check on a colony of terraformers that hadn't reported in for weeks. When we got there the place was in ruins. Turned out the Mi-Go had 'harvested' the colonists. Do you know what I mean by 'harvested'?"

Inez nodded. "Mi-Go technology is organic-based. Their

machines are fueled by pure protein. And they advance their technology by evolving it with alien DNA. They even use living brains for data storage."

"And weapons," Swenson added.

"What do you mean?"

"The Mi-Go were still there, setting up one of their mining operations," Swenson explained. "When we attacked, one of them pulled out a severed human head set in a metal harness. I could tell the head had belonged to a member of Psi-Ops because of the omega symbol tattooed on its forehead. Anyway, they'd somehow 'weaponized' it. The Mi-Go holding the head pointed it at my buddy. The head's mouth suddenly opened like it was screaming and its eyes lit up and my buddy's brain exploded. Literally. Then the alien turned towards me—" He motioned toward the ion rifle he had stowed in the back. "So I blasted it in that weird cluster of globules that passes for a Mi-Go's head. Ten megavolts and that was that. Other than the globules and the dragonfly wings, the thing looked so much like a giant lobster I was tempted to cook it."

"But you didn't."

"No. I wasn't that hungry."

"Good thing. They aren't made of the same stuff we are."

"What, blood and guts?"

"At the subatomic level. Some scientists think the Mi-Go come from somewhere a lot farther away than another solar system. You would've been better off eating a Shan."

Swenson thought about that for a moment. "They're probably full of protein."

"Probably. Anyway, as far as we can tell, the Shan and Mi-Go have been around a long time but nowhere near a couple million years. Time has a way of wearing things down, I suppose."

"Or crushing them," Swenson murmured.

"What?"

"Imagine being part of something with a million year history. It would be like a big weight bearing down on you. You'd be crushed by it."

Inez gave Swenson an appraising look. "That's pretty good."

"Thanks. Say, what about Species X?"

"Species X?"

"You know, the floating cancer things."

"Oh, the FPs. That's what xenologists call them. It's short for Flying Polyps. Those things aren't so much a species as overgrown viruses. By comparison, the Mi-Go are about as alien and exotic as an old pair of shoes. I saw a recording of an attempt to capture one. They were only able to keep it trapped in a containment field for about six seconds then it just vanished. Slid through the cracks in the spatial dimensions, as one physicist put it. The way it just hung in the air, dripping and oozing toxic sludge till it disappeared. I used to have nightmares about it."

"Yeah, they're nasty all right. So what's our mission? Recover one of those artifacts you mentioned?"

"No. Before I tell you the mission, there's one more thing you should know. Tau Ceti-5 is covered in lakes of liquid ammonia which sit inside impact craters, all of which seem to have been created within the same short span of time. The event that created those craters is probably what wiped out all life on this planet around 60,000 years ago. At first we thought it was a meteor swarm but now we think it was energy discharges."

"How do you explain that?"

Inez shrugged. "We can't. The general consensus is it wasn't a natural phenomenon."

"So, something entered this planet's orbit and reduced it to cinders with some sort of energy bombardment."

Inez nodded. "Something like that."

"But this planet's been lifeless for…what'd you say? 60,000 years?"

"Correct."

"Other than a full nuclear bombardment, we don't have anything approaching that. So you're saying something was traveling through space around sixty millennia ago, armed with energy-based planet killer weapons and the intent to use them."

"Crazy, but that would be the most logical explanation."

"Why this planet? Is that what we're here to find out?"

"Not quite."

Swenson sighed. "Then why are we here?"

"This planet's under constant surveillance by a network of satellites in geosynchronous orbit. Five weeks ago, one of them detected a localized gravitational anomaly."

"Come again?"

"Something on this planet is creating literal ripples in space/time. Normally you'd only see that sort of distortion in regions of space where…It's not important. Anyway, that's what we're here to investigate."

"Is there a natural explanation for something like that?"

"Only on a much bigger scale."

"Then why didn't they send…I don't know, a physicist or something?" Swenson glanced at Inez. "No offense."

"None taken. And they did."

"I thought you were a xenologist."

"I am. I double majored in xeno-anthropology and theoretical physics." Inez pointed ahead. "We're here."

A range of sheer rocky crags reared up in the distance. The topographical map on the skimmer's view-screen showed that the crags sat in a ring-shape, not unlike the walls of an enormous crater.

Swenson brought the skimmer to a stop within walking distance of the crags. "We'll have to go on foot from here." He touched the view-screen, magnifying their location on the map. "Looks like there's a passage to the interior. Not much more than a crack but we should be able to squeeze through. It'll be quicker than trying to climb that thing."

"How are you doing on oxygen?" Swenson asked minutes later as they made their way through the narrow fissure.

"I still have a couple hours' worth," Inez replied, once more absorbed in the hologram hovering a few inches above her scanalyzer. The scrolling data had been replaced with a holographic map being beamed directly to her scanalyzer by the *Dunsany*. A tiny pair of humanoid icons represented the pair while a shimmering cascade at the heart of the open space beyond represented their goal.

"A couple of hours?" Swenson's index finger nervously tapped his ion rifle's trigger guard. "That's cutting it close."

"I didn't think it would take us this long to get here. Now that we know exactly where we're going, I'll take some quick readings, we'll head back to the lander, then return tomorrow with extra oxygen tanks."

"Yeah, okay." He could have pushed the issue but it was a civilian mission and Inez was technically in charge, plus it was a simple, solid plan. "Does this count as an artifact?" Swenson asked when they finally emerged from the crevice and stood by side by side.

Inez's eyes bulged. "It…it's…"

At the heart of the crater sat a vast, four-sided metal pyramid. Platinum-gold in color, its appearance was a jarring counterpoint to the otherwise bleak landscape.

"It's not showing up on the map," Swenson said. "Something's shielding it from the *Dunsany's* sensors."

Inez tapped her scanalyzer's touchscreen. The topographical map hologram reverted to a virtual data scroll. "The graviton bursts are coming from inside it."

"What a surprise. We should head back to lander and come back tomorrow with hazmat suits."

Without replying, Inez started forward. Swenson sighed and followed. Together they walked the pyramid's perimeter.

"No seams," Swenson observed. "Looks like one solid piece."

"And the surface is pristine. You can even see the dust being deflected by some sort of invisible barrier." Inez reached toward the pyramid.

"Don't!"

"I'm not going to touch the pyramid, just the barrier," Inez said. "Only a little bit of resistance, like a very weak force-field."

"That's fascinating. Now pull your hand back."

Inez activated the scanalyzer's holographic menu. "I'm going to try a manual scan. Maybe its sensors can detect the pyramid at this range."

"Well?" Swenson asked half a minute later.

"It's collecting data now." Inez's eyes widened as she studied the scrolling dataflow being transmitted back to the *Dunsany*. "The barrier is seething with tachyons which might explain the pyramid's invisibility to satellite scans. They could be redirecting the scans to a point in the past or future when the pyramid doesn't exist."

"That…sounds reasonable," Swenson said.

"The technology is incredible but the field itself is relatively weak," Inez continued. "At this range my scanalyzer can identify the barrier and maybe even...Yes! It made it through. It's analyzing the pyramid now. So far it's found eleven…no, make that twelve unknown elements and…wow."

"Wow what?"

"Guess how old this thing is."

"I don't know, 60,000 years?"

"Try sixty *million*. This...this is a major find, the kind that rewrites history."

"Sixty million? That's...wow." Swenson's eyes narrowed. "Hey, if the tachyon thing is keeping the pyramid hidden so well, how did we find it?"

"The graviton pulse led us here, remember? Gravity ignores the dimension of time so the tachyon barrier would have no effect on the pulses."

"I guess that makes sense."

Inez reached toward the pyramid. "I'm going to touch it."

Swenson started to say something but Inez's hand had already broken the plane of the invisible barrier.

"It's warm. I can feel it through my glove. And there's a slight vibration. I wonder if—"

A section of the pyramid's surface rippled around Inez's fingertip like a pebble tossed into a pond. The section faded to transparency and vanished, leaving a rectangular gap in the pyramid's otherwise smooth surface.

"How'd you do that?" Swenson demanded.

"I didn't. At least I don't think I did. "

Inez pointed the scanalyer toward the opening. "Trace amounts of radiation but well within acceptable limits. The temperature's warmer, too. I say we go in."

"I'm not sure that's wise. We have no idea—"

"Just a quick look," Inez insisted.

Swenson started to object but Inez had already switched on her flashlight and stepped through the aperture.

"Wonderful," Swenson muttered, falling in step behind her.

Through the aperture was a long, empty corridor which stretched beyond the farthest reaches of the flashlight beam.

"If you turn off the flashlight, I can switch my helmet to infrared," Swenson said.

"Then I won't be able to see."

"Oh yeah." Swenson activated his helmet lights. "Hey look, there's something on the walls."

The walls were covered with curious images; lacking any hint of linear perspective, each scene was filled with homogenous crowds of alien creatures depicted in a curious angular style. Those creatures which had a discernible front and back were always shown in profile.

Some scenes utilized tiered space, perhaps to imply rank or distance, but nothing to imply depth.

"This…this is…" Inez stammered. "Incredible. And impossible. Incredibly impossible."

"What? What's wrong?"

"The style is incredibly similar to ancient Egyptian art."

"Pardon?"

"An ancient Old Earth culture. The last Egyptian Dynasty ended over 50,000 years ago."

"Egyptian dynasty." Swenson thought for a moment. "That sounds familiar."

"Maybe they mentioned it in the Ancient Astronauts archive."

"Hey, you're right. So how did Egyptian art end up here?"

"This place predates the oldest Egyptian Dynasty by millions of years. The real question is how did these images end up influencing the art of an Old Earth culture?"

"You have a point there." Swenson nodded toward the nearest image. "So what do you make of them?"

Inez directed her flashlight's beam over one image after another. "It's a different species each time but always the same theme—a panicked alien population fleeing one of their own as their cities and habitations burn and fall to ruin around them."

"Do you recognize any of the alien races?"

"Actually…no."

"Do you think they're all real?"

"I don't know. So far we've catalogued forty-two distinct alien cultures, thirty-five of which are confirmed extinct. Hundreds are depicted here, maybe thousands."

Swenson grunted. "That's a lot of aliens."

"And in each scene," Inez continued, leaning in close to one of the images, "something's coming out of the mouth or equivalent orifice of the alien from which the rest are fleeing. It looks like…"

"A big tidal wave of darkness," Swenson finished.

Inez glanced at him then back at the image. "You're right. That's exactly what it looks like."

"So what does it mean?"

"I don't know. Since it's coming from the mouth, maybe the darkness is meant to represent dangerous or hateful speech. Lies, revolutionary talk, words and ideas meant to stir up the masses and ferment unrest. That would explain the cities in ruin."

"I'm no art critic," Swenson said, joining Inez, "but it looks to me like the artist was trying to make the black wave look…not sure what word I want to use. Alive, animated…"

"Anthropomorphic?" Inez suggested, trying to focus on the image rather than Swenson's proximity.

"Yeah, if that means what I think it means. See how the crest of the wave sort of deviates here and here?"

"Like arms?"

"Right. And there's just a hint of two faded spots there, maybe meant to represent eyes. It's as if the wave or shadow or whatever it's supposed to be is a monster set to swoop down on everybody. They're not running from one of their own. They're running from the thing inside him."

"Hmm. Possibly. Maybe the shadow represents something hard to visualize but capable of striking fear into an entire population, like a plague."

"A cosmic plague that jumps from world to world?"

Inez shrugged. "It's just a guess. Let's keep going."

They followed the corridor, which remained covered from floor to ceiling with images of alien carnage, until it terminated at a dead-end.

"Now what?" Swenson asked.

"Look, there's something here." Inez's flashlight revealed a series of characters inscribed in several orderly rows on the wall at the end of the corridor.

"What are they?" Swenson asked.

"I think they're logograms."

"What are—"

"Visual symbols representing words rather than sounds. If I didn't know better I'd swear they were Egyptian hieroglyphics. Then again, I guess we shouldn't be surprised."

Swenson leaned in close, studying them. "Can you translate them?"

"Some look familiar, but if they're really ancient Egyptian or a good facsimile, my scanalyzer should be able to."

Inez activated the holographic menu, selected a menu followed by several submenus, then held the scanalyzer close to the inscriptions.

"*Initiating analysis,*" the scanalyzer informed them in a detached human voice. "*Analysis complete. Match found within current parameter threshold. Commonality rating is seventy-five percent. Projected level of accuracy after contextual extrapolation is eighty-five percent, with a five percent margin of error. Would you like to continue?*"

"Yes," Inez replied.

"*Initiating partial translation.*"

Swenson anxiously watched the scrolling data. "How long do you think?"

"*Partial translation complete. Would you like to continue?*"

"Yes," Inez repeated.

"*Initiating contextual extrapolation.*"

Swenson turned back to the inscriptions. "I'm not even going to..."

"*Extrapolation complete. Would you like to hear the translation?*"

"Yes," Inez said.

"*Translation commencing:*

WE ARE THE MILLION-MANY

FAVORED-TREASURED-HONORED ONES BELOVED

OF HIM-THE ONE—"

"Pause," Inez interrupted. "Restart but only use primary terms from contextual extrapolation. Continue."

"*Translation commencing:*

WE ARE THE MILLION FAVORED ONES

BELOVED OF HIM

OUR NAMES ARE WRIT

IN THE BLACK BOOK

BLESSED CHOSEN OF NYARLAT

VESSELS OF THE CRAWLING CHAOS

OURS ARE THE LIPS WHICH SPEAK THE WORD

AS WE TREAD THE PATH BEYOND

THE GATE OF STARS

FOR IT IS WE WHO OPEN THE WAY

AND ARE THUS MADE WORTHY TO DWELL

IN THE HOUSE OF THE MESSENGER

OF THE ONES WHO LIE DEAD AND DREAMING

FOREVER AND EVER

AMEN."

"What does that mean?" Swenson asked.

"I don't know. It sounds like a prayer."

"To who?"

"Some alien god, maybe? Early humans weren't the only ones who looked up at the sky and wondered if something was looking back." Inez reached toward one of the characters with the tip of her finger. "I wonder if…"

Like the section outside, the panel rippled and vanished.

"Wonderful," Swenson said.

Inez shined her flashlight into the darkness, revealing a bare floor.

"Hello!" Swenson called and several echoes replied. "Sounds like a big, empty space."

"Almost empty," Inez replied. The flashlight's beam reached through the darkness just far enough to hint at a large, smooth-edged something a stone's throw away.

Swenson simply shook his head and followed Inez as she walked through the doorway toward the something, glancing back just in time to see the panel reform behind them.

"We're trapped," Swenson said, turning back to Inez who was removing her helmet. "Are you crazy?"

"What's crazy would be the chamber filling with oxygen, which it is. My scanalyzer says the air's perfectly breathable. Go ahead, give it a try."

"No thanks."

Inez shrugged. "Suit yourself."

Sitting within the chamber was a vast rectangular platform. On the side of the platform facing the direction from which Inez and Swenson had come were more characters which the scanalyzer translated as:

"OH NYARLAT WHO IS HO-TEP
IN DARKNESS YOU REIGN
WEARER OF MASKS
LORD OF SECRETS
HEED THE PRAYERS OF THY SUPPLICANTS
WHO ARE THE MILLION FAVORED ONES
ANNOINT US IN THY SACRED BLOOD
FOR WITHIN THY VEINS THE
CRAWLING CHAOS DWELLS
REVEAL UNTO US THE GATE OF STARS
THAT WE MAY DELIVER THY WORD
THOU ART THE ONE TRUE MESSENGER

OF THOSE WHO WERE AND SHALL BE AGAIN
FOR EVER AND EVER
AMEN."

Inez touched the inscription and the top of the platform burst into light.

"Will you please stop touching things?" Swenson asked, shielding his eyes.

"Look," Inez said, pointing upward.

The light revealed that the platform was actually a pedestal and atop the pedestal sat an enormous statue. Carved from a black, non-reflective material, the statue depicted a strange hybrid creature with a human head mounted atop a crouching leonine form. Where the face should have been was an incredibly realistic depiction of a field of stars. Adjacent to the pedestal and statue was a high set of steps leading up to a platform that stretched toward the starry image.

"What is it?" Swenson asked.

"I think it's supposed to be a sphinx."

"What planet do they come from?"

"Earth. But they aren't real. They're mythological creatures. Back before Tcho-Tcho insurgents destroyed most of the African continent with the tesseract bomb, there was a giant statue of one in the country of Egypt."

"The tesseract bomb." Swenson shook his head. "The beginning of the end of Old Earth. So do sphinxes usually have stars for faces?"

"I don't think so," Inez said, starting up the steps. "Let's take a closer look."

"Hold on!" Swenson called, chasing after her.

An alien form sprawled on the upper platform near the starry field. It had a bloated torso, partially covered in chitin plates and mounted on four spidery appendages. It had two arm-like appendages, one ending in a large set of pincers while the other bore slimmer, more refined digits which might have functioned as two fingers and an opposable thumb. With no discernible neck, the thing's head was set deep between its shoulders. A cluster of emerald orbs assumedly served for its eyes and a beard of fibrous tendrils dangled beneath a puckered orifice the color and consistency of raw beef.

Swenson poked it with his boot. "Looks like it's dead."

Inez started to crouch down beside it. "I'm going to—"

"Don't even think about it. Get some readings then we'll come back better equipped."

Inez pointed her scanalyzer at the statue's featureless head. Even from the nearer proximity of the platform, the field of stars which served as the statue's face looked incredibly realistic. It gave a vertigo-inducing impression of depth rather than volume, as if one could simply step through.

"It's generating a constant stream of gravitons. Most of them are being directed somewhere but enough are leaking out to create a ripple in space/time. That's probably the anomaly we detected. I'm also seeing all sorts of particle decay but something's absorbing the radiation."

"Translation, please."

"I think the statue is generating an Einstein-Rosen bridge."

"Repeat—translation, please."

"A wormhole," Inez explained. "An interdimensional shortcut through space."

"Like the G.A.T.E. network?"

"Technically, yes. But this predates G.A.T.E. technology by at least sixty million years."

"Unbelievable."

"I just wonder where it's a gateway to."

Swenson nodded toward the alien corpse. "Well, if he knows, he's not talking."

"I'm going to touch it," Inez said, starting toward the starry gulf.

Swenson reached for her. "The hell you—"

The entire chamber suddenly blazed with light. Inez stumbled, nearly toppling over the platform's edge before Swenson grabbed her by the arm and pulled her back.

"Now what?" Swenson muttered.

"Incredible," Inez murmured.

The light revealed that the space they took to be a chamber was actually a ledge extending over an enormous circular shaft. The shaft stretched deep into the ground as far as the eye could see. Enormous as it was, the pyramid was only the tip of a far more colossal structure.

Lining the walls of the shaft was level after level of enclosed compartments. Contained in each compartment behind a transparent lid was a body, swathed in foil wrappings and arranged in a state of repose. Like the images outside, each form seemed to represent a different alien species. Some were bipedal, others multi-legged or with no visible limbs at all. Humanoid shapes were vastly outnumbered by multi-segmented and even radial forms with no discernible front or back. Some bulged in ways that implied bulky exoskeletons or odd limbs while others sagged in a boneless fashion. Withered appendages that might have been suckered tentacles, antennae, or feelers poked out through the wrappings of some. Those with anatomies which allowed it bore elaborate headpieces and golden masks, assumedly bearing their wearers' features. Though it would have taken decades to catalog them all, at a glance no two of the alien forms were quite alike.

"What is this place?" Swenson asked.

Wide to the point of bulging, Inez's eyes suddenly narrowed. "The Million Favored Ones."

"What, you mean like in the hieroglyphics?'

Inez nodded. "This place is like a museum, a museum of dead races."

"That would make it a tomb." Swenson nodded toward the sphinx. "Is it my imagination or are the stars moving?"

"The graviton stream's shifting," Inez said, studying the data scrolling across her scanalyzer. "I think the gateway is changing destinations."

"To where?" Swenson demanded. "And who's changing it?"

"I don't know. I…It's stopped." Inez sped through the scanalyzer's virtual menu. "Scanning…There's an atmosphere on the other side."

"Of what? The gateway?"

"Gravity, elemental composition, radiation level…" Inez shook her head. "This can't be right."

"What can't be right?"

"They match Old Earth. I think I understand now. Those images outside, each of them is a world that these Million Favored Ones visited using the gateway. They traveled from world to from world, spreading the…the Word of Nyarlat like—"

"A cosmic plague?"

"I was going to say missionaries but your way might be more accurate. And that's why this world was attacked 60,000 years ago, to put a stop to it. But someone or something survived and used the gateway to escape to Old Earth."

Swenson's eyes widened. "Which would explain how an ancient Earth culture ended up with art and written language from an alien world."

"Exactly. But there's more to it than that. It could account for some of the legends of advanced cultures that supposedly existed in prehistory. Atlantis, Lemuria, Mu…they could have all been based on an actual civilization."

"Wait a minute. Are you saying they're the Ancient Astronauts?"

"At this point, your guess is as good as mine."

"It does make sense," Swenson conceded, "except for one thing. Why didn't they do to Old Earth what they did to those other worlds?"

"I don't know. Maybe they tried and failed. Maybe they thought prehistoric Earth wasn't ready yet."

"Right," Swenson said, heading for the steps. "I think it's time to—"

Inez froze. "Did you see that?"

"What?"

Inez crouched beside the alien corpse. "It moved."

"Not it didn't. That thing's dead. We better—"

"I swear it's breathing," Inez said, leaning closer.

The corpse reached up with its smaller arm, grabbed Inez by the head, and pulled her close. Its mouth unclenched and an oily black liquid sprayed upward, filling her nose and mouth. The thing released Inez who fell back, coughing and choking. Swenson pointed his ion rifle at the no longer moving corpse and squeezed the trigger. A blinding arc of electricity erupted from the barrel, blasting the alien to charred pieces.

"Dammit!" Swenson said, helping Inez to her feet. "I told you to leave your helmet on."

Inez made a gagging sound, hunched over, then after one final shudder stood upright. She turned and looked at Swenson, her eyes now hidden behind a filmy black.

Swenson raised his ion rifle. "Inez?"

She took an awkward step toward him and he retreated a quick two.

"Inez!" Swenson yelled, toggling the charge on his ion rifle down to a single megavolt.

Inez's mouth opened and a liquid black foulness dribbled out, staining the front of her survival suit.

"Sorry," Swenson said, squeezing the trigger.

Electricity arced from the barrel, catching Inez in the chest. She flew backwards, slammed into the sphinx, and tumbled to the platform.

"Dammit," Swenson muttered as he approached the body. The front of her survival suit was burned away, revealing flesh ravaged by the heat of the blast. "It's gonna be okay. I'm gonna get you back to the *Dunsany* and..."

Swenson froze as Inez sat up and clambered to her feet, her jerky movements those of a marionette operated by a drunken puppeteer.

"Inez, please," Swenson begged, raising his rifle once more.

Inez opened her mouth and a fountain sprayed out, blasting him with liquid darkness. Swenson cried out as the black blood of Nyarlat slithered and oozed across him like a living thing, seeking an orifice through which to infiltrate his body and remake him from within. Panicked, he stumbled over the edge of the platform and fell to the ledge below.

Stunned by the bone-shattering impact, Swenson struggled to rise. His titanium-reinforced spine, a surgical souvenir from a hostile encounter with cephalopodan xenos on a giant moon whose name he couldn't remember, safely absorbed most of the impact but when he tried to rise, agonizing pain shot through his right leg. Swenson was trying to pull himself up using his ion rifle as a crutch when he heard a sibilant hiss followed by a heavy impact.

Swenson looked over his shoulder. One of the transparent-lidded chambers had opened and its contents, a gaunt, long-limbed humanoid form, tumbled out. Its golden mask had fallen away, revealing a face solely consisting of a round, toothy maw. The bandaged form drug itself toward Swenson who struggled to position himself for a clear shot. Reaching out with one of its long limbs, it knocked his ion rifle away. The rifle skidded across the floor, tumbled over the edge, and was gone. Swenson rolled over and tried to crawl away but the thing grasped his ankle in an iron grip. He cried out in agony as it pulled him close, flipped him over, and tore off his helmet. The last thing Swenson saw was the needle-toothed maw which drew closer and closer until it swallowed his entire field of vision then darkness.

Faces and forms hidden beneath ragged black robes, the withered priests of Nyarlat, emerged from hidden alcoves. Some hobbled on two legs, some skittered on four or more, and some crawled and slithered and oozed on none at all. Working in silent teams, one group returned the bandaged alien form to its chamber while another gathered up Swenson's remains, which would be stored away for future use. A third group climbed the steps to the platform where they began to reassemble the other alien's charred remains in preparation for the final rites.

Inez impassively watched all that was taking place. The priests who had climbed the platform bowed low before her, showing proper reverence for one who had been anointed in the sacred blood of Nyarlat, which was the Crawling Chaos. Without acknowledging them, Inez turned and, stepping through the Gate of Stars, was gone. On the far side of the galaxy she would soon find a way from Old Earth to the network of satellite colonies where the bulk of humanity now dwelled. Once she had delivered the Word of Nyarlat, she would return and take her place among the Million Favored Ones where they would dwell in the House of the Messenger together.

Forever and ever.

Amen.

UNDER THE PYRAMIDS

H.P. LOVECRAFT

Mystery attracts mystery. Ever since the wide appearance of my name as a performer of unexplained feats, I have encountered strange narratives and events which my calling has led people to link with my interests and activities. Some of these have been trivial and irrelevant, some deeply dramatic and absorbing, some productive of weird and perilous experiences, and some involving me in extensive scientific and historical research. Many of these matters I have told and shall continue to tell freely; but there is one of which I speak with great reluctance, and which I am now relating only after a session of grilling persuasion from the publishers of this magazine, who had heard vague rumours of it from other members of my family.

The hitherto guarded subject pertains to my non-professional visit to Egypt fourteen years ago, and has been avoided by me for several reasons. For one thing, I am averse to exploiting certain unmistakably actual facts and conditions obviously unknown to the myriad tourists who throng about the pyramids and apparently secreted with much diligence by the authorities at Cairo, who cannot be wholly ignorant of them. For another thing, I dislike to recount an incident in which my own fantastic imagination must have played so great a part. What I saw—or thought I saw—certainly did not take place; but is rather to be viewed as a result of my then recent readings in Egyptology, and of the speculations anent this theme which my environment naturally prompted. These imaginative stimuli, magnified by the excitement of an actual event terrible enough in itself, undoubtedly gave rise to the culminating horror of that grotesque night so long past.

In January, 1910, I had finished a professional engagement in England and signed a contract for a tour of Australian theatres. A liberal time being allowed for the trip, I determined to make the most of it in the sort of travel which chiefly interests me; so accompanied by my wife I drifted pleasantly down the Continent and embarked at Marseilles on the P. & O. Steamer *Malwa*, bound for Port Said. From that point I proposed to visit the principal historical localities of lower Egypt before leaving finally for Australia.

The voyage was an agreeable one, and enlivened by many of the amusing incidents which befall a magical performer apart from his work. I had intended, for the sake of quiet travel, to keep my name a secret; but was goaded into betraying myself by a fellow-magician whose anxiety to astound the passengers with ordinary tricks tempted me to duplicate and exceed his feats in a manner quite destructive of my incognito. I mention this because of its ultimate effect—an effect I should have foreseen before unmasking to a shipload of tourists about to scatter throughout the Nile Valley. What it did was to herald my identity wherever I subsequently went, and deprive my wife and me of all the placid inconspicuousness we had sought. Travelling to seek curiosities, I was often forced to stand inspection as a sort of curiosity myself!

We had come to Egypt in search of the picturesque and the mystically impressive, but found little enough when the ship edged up to Port Said and discharged its passengers in small boats. Low dunes of sand, bobbing buoys in shallow water, and a drearily European small town with nothing of interest save the great De Lesseps statue, made us anxious to get on to something more worth our while. After some discussion we decided to proceed at once to Cairo and the Pyramids, later going to Alexandria for the Australian boat and for whatever Greco-Roman sights that ancient metropolis might present.

The railway journey was tolerable enough, and consumed only four hours and a half. We saw much of the Suez Canal, whose route we followed as far as Ismailiya, and later had a taste of Old Egypt in our glimpse of the restored fresh-water canal of the Middle Empire. Then at last we saw Cairo glimmering through the growing dusk; a twinkling constellation which became a blaze as we halted at the great Gare Centrale.

But once more disappointment awaited us, for all that we beheld was European save the costumes and the crowds. A prosaic subway led to a square teeming with carriages, taxicabs, and trolley-cars, and gorgeous with electric lights shining on tall buildings; whilst the very theatre where I was vainly requested to play, and which I later attended as a spectator, had recently been renamed the "American Cosmograph". We stopped at Shepherd's Hotel, reached in a taxi that sped along broad, smartly built-up streets; and amidst the perfect service of its restaurant, elevators, and generally Anglo-American luxuries the mysterious East and immemorial past seemed very far away.

The next day, however, precipitated us delightfully into the heart of the *Arabian Nights* atmosphere; and in the winding ways and exotic skyline of Cairo, the Bagdad of Haroun-al-Raschid seemed to live again. Guided by our Baedeker, we had struck east past the Ezbekiyeh Gardens along the Mouski in quest of the native quarter, and were soon in the hands of a clamorous cicerone who—notwithstanding later developments—was assuredly a master at his trade. Not until afterward did I see that I should have applied at the hotel for a licensed guide. This man, a shaven, peculiarly hollow-voiced, and relatively cleanly fellow who looked like a Pharaoh and called himself "Abdul Reis el Drogman", appeared to have much power over others of his kind; though subsequently the police professed not to know him, and to suggest that *reis* is merely a name for any person in authority, whilst "Drogman" is obviously no more than a clumsy modification of the word for a leader of tourist parties—*dragoman.*

Abdul led us among such wonders as we had before only read and dreamed of. Old Cairo is itself a story-book and a dream—labyrinths of narrow alleys redolent of aromatic secrets; Arabesque balconies and oriels nearly meeting above the cobbled streets; maelstroms of Oriental traffic with strange cries, cracking whips, rattling carts, jingling money, and braying donkeys; kaleidoscopes of polychrome robes, veils, turbans, and tarbushes; water-carriers and dervishes, dogs and cats, soothsayers and barbers; and over all the whining of blind beggars crouched in alcoves, and the sonorous chanting of muezzins from minarets limned delicately against a sky of deep, unchanging blue.

The roofed, quieter bazaars were hardly less alluring. Spice, perfume, incense, beads, rugs, silks, and brass—old Mahmoud Suleiman squats cross-legged amidst his gummy bottles while chattering youths pulverize mustard in the hollowed-out capital of an ancient classic column—a Roman Corinthian, perhaps from neighboring Heliopolis, where Augustus stationed one of his three Egyptian legions. Antiquity begins to mingle with exoticism. And then the mosques and the museum—we saw them all, and tried not to let our Arabian revel succumb to the darker charm of Pharaonic Egypt which the museum's priceless treasures offered. That was to be our climax, and for the present we concentrated on the mediaeval Saracenic glories of the Caliphs whose magnificent tomb-mosques form a glittering faery necropolis on the edge of the Arabian Desert.

At length Abdul took us along the Sharia Mohammed Ali to the ancient mosque of Sultan Hassan, and the tower-flanked Bab-el-Azab, beyond which climbs the steep-walled pass to the mighty citadel that Saladin himself built with the stones of forgotten pyramids. It was sunset when we scaled that cliff, circled the modern mosque of Mohammed Ali, and looked down from the dizzying parapet over mystic Cairo—mystic Cairo all golden with its carven domes, its ethereal minarets, and its flaming gardens. Far over the city towered the great Roman dome of the new museum; and beyond it—across the cryptic yellow Nile that is the mother of aeons and dynasties—lurked the menacing sands of the Libyan Desert, undulant and iridescent and evil with older arcana. The red sun sank low, bringing the relentless chill of Egyptian dusk; and as it stood poised on the world's rim like that ancient god of Heliopolis—Re-Harakhte, the Horizon-Sun—we saw silhouetted against its vermeil holocaust the black outlines of the Pyramids of Gizeh—the palaeogean tombs there were hoary with a thousand years when Tut-Ankh-Amen mounted his golden throne in distant Thebes. Then we knew that we were done with Saracen Cairo, and that we must taste the deeper mysteries of primal Egypt—the black Khem of Re and Amen, Isis and Osiris.

The next morning we visited the pyramids, riding out in a Victoria across the great Nile bridge with its bronze lions, the island of Ghizereh with its massive lebbakh trees, and the smaller English bridge to the western shore. Down the shore road we drove, between great rows of lebbakhs and past the vast Zoölogical Gardens to the suburb of Gizeh, where a new bridge to Cairo proper has since been built. Then, turning inland along the Sharia-el-Haram, we crossed a region of glassy canals and shabby native villages till before us loomed the objects of our quest, cleaving the mists of dawn and forming inverted replicas in the roadside pools. Forty centuries, as

Napoleon had told his campaigners there, indeed looked down upon us.

Thc road now rosc abruptly, till we finally reached our place of transfer between the trolley station and the Mena House Hotel. Abdul Reis, who capably purchased our pyramid tickets, seemed to have an understanding with the crowding, yelling, and offensive Bedouins who inhabited a squalid mud village some distance away and pestiferously assailed every traveler; for he kept them very decently at bay and secured an excellent pair of camels for us, himself mounting a donkey and assigning the leadership of our animals to a group of men and boys more expensive than useful. The area to be traversed was so small that camels were hardly needed, but we did not regret adding to our experience this troublesome form of desert navigation.

The pyramids stand on a high rock plateau, this group forming next to the northernmost of the series of regal and aristocratic cemeteries built in the neighborhood of the extinct capital Memphis, which lay on the same side of the Nile, somewhat south of Gizeh, and which flourished between 3400 and 2000 B. C. The greatest pyramid, which lies nearest the modern road, was built by King Cheops or Khufu about 2800 B. C., and stands more than 450 feet in perpendicular height. In a line southwest from this are successively the Second Pyramid, built a generation later by King Khephren, and though slightly smaller, looking even larger because set on higher ground, and the radically smaller Third Pyramid of King Mycerinus, built about 2700 B. C. Near the edge of the plateau and due east of the Second Pyramid, with a face probably altered to form a colossal portrait of Khephren, its royal restorer, stands the monstrous Sphinx—mute, sardonic, and wise beyond mankind and memory.

Minor pyramids and the traces of ruined minor pyramids are found in several places, and the whole plateau is pitted with the tombs of dignitaries of less than royal rank. These latter were originally marked by *mastabas*, or stone bench-like structures about the deep burial shafts, as found in other Memphian cemeteries and exemplified by Perneb's Tomb in the Metropolitan Museum of New York. At Gizeh, however, all such visible things have been swept away by time and pillage; and only the rock-hewn shafts, either sand-filled or cleared out by archaeologists, remain to attest their former existence. Connected with each tomb was a chapel in which priests and relatives offered food and prayer to the hovering *ka* or vital principle of the deceased. The small tombs have their chapels contained in their stone *mastabas* or superstructures, but the mortuary chapels of the pyramids, where regal Pharaohs lay, were separate temples, each to the east of its corresponding pyramid, and connected by a causeway to a massive gate-chapel or propylon at the edge of the rock plateau.

The gate-chapel leading to the Second Pyramid, nearly buried in the drifting sands, yawns subterraneously southeast of the Sphinx. Persistent tradition dubs it the "Temple of the Sphinx"; and it may perhaps be rightly called such if the Sphinx indeed represents the Second Pyramid's builder Khephren. There are unpleasant tales of the Sphinx before Khephren—but whatever its elder features were, the monarch replaced them with his own that men might look at the colossus without fear. It was in the great gateway-temple that the life-size diorite statue of Khephren now in the Cairo Museum was found; a statue before which I stood in awe when I beheld it. Whether the whole edifice is now excavated I am not certain, but in 1910 most of it was below ground, with the entrance heavily barred at night. Germans were in charge of the work, and the war or other things may have stopped them. I would give much, in view of my experience and of certain Bedouin whisperings discredited or unknown in Cairo, to know what has developed in connection with a certain well in a transverse gallery where statues of the Pharaoh were found in curious juxtaposition to the statues of baboons.

The road, as we traversed it on our camels that morning, curved sharply past the wooden police quarters, post-office, drug-store, and shops on the left, and plunged south and east in a complete bend that scaled the rock plateau and brought us face to face with the desert under the lee of the Great Pyramid. Past Cyclopean masonry we rode, rounding the eastern face and looking down ahead into a valley of minor pyramids beyond which the eternal Nile glistened to the east, and the eternal desert shimmered to the west. Very close loomed the three major pyramids, the greatest devoid of outer casing and showing its bulk of great stones, but the others retaining here and there the neatly fitted covering which had made them smooth and finished in their day.

Presently we descended toward the Sphinx, and sat silent beneath the spell of those terrible unseeing eyes. On the vast stone breast we faintly discerned the emblem of Re-Harakhte, for whose image the Sphinx was mistaken in a late dynasty; and though sand covered the tablet between the great paws, we recalled what Thutmosis IV inscribed thereon, and the dream he had when a prince. It was then that the smile of the Sphinx vaguely displeased us, and made us wonder about the legends of subterranean passages beneath the monstrous creature, leading down, down, to depths none might dare hint at—depths connected with mysteries older than the dynastic Egypt we excavate, and having a sinister relation to the persistence of abnormal, animal-headed gods in the ancient Nilotic pantheon. Then, too, it was I asked myself an idle question whose hideous significance was not to appear for many an hour.

Other tourists now began to overtake us, and we moved on to the sand-choked Temple of the Sphinx, fifty yards to the southeast, which I have previously mentioned as the great gate of the causeway to the Second Pyramid's mortuary chapel on the plateau. Most of it was still underground, and although we dismounted and descended through a modern passageway to its alabaster corridor and pillared hall, I felt that Abdul and the local German attendant had not shown us all there was to see.

After this we made the conventional circuit of the pyramid plateau, examining the Second Pyramid and the peculiar ruins of its mortuary chapel to the east, the Third Pyramid and its miniature southern satellites and ruined eastern chapel, the rock tombs and the honeycombings of the Fourth and Fifth Dynasties, and the famous Campell's Tomb whose shadowy shaft sinks precipitously for 53 feet to a sinister sarcophagus which one of our camel-drivers divested of the cumbering sand after a vertiginous descent by rope.

Cries now assailed us from the Great Pyramid, where Bedouins were besieging a party of tourists with offers of guidance to the top, or of displays of speed in the performance of solitary trips up and down. Seven minutes is said to be the record for such an ascent and descent, but many lusty sheiks and sons of sheiks assured us they could cut it to five if given the requisite impetus of liberal *baksheesh*. They did not get this impetus, though we did let Abdul take us up, thus obtaining a view of unprecedented magnificence which included not only remote and glittering Cairo with its crowned citadel and background of gold-violet hills, but all the pyramids of the Memphian district as well, from Abu Roash on the north to the Dashur on the south. The Sakkara step-pyramid, which marks the evolution of the low *mastaba* into the true pyramid, showed clearly and alluringly in the sandy distance. It is close to this transition-monument that the famed tomb of Perneb was found—more than 400 miles north of the Theban rock valley where Tut-Ankh-Amen sleeps. Again I was forced to silence through sheer awe. The prospect of such antiquity, and the secrets each hoary monument seemed to hold and brood over, filled me with a reverence and sense of immensity nothing else ever gave me.

Fatigued by our climb, and disgusted with the importunate Bedouins whose actions seemed to defy every rule of taste, we omitted the arduous detail of entering the cramped interior passages of any of the pyramids, though we saw several of the hardiest tourists preparing for the suffocating crawl through Cheops' mightiest memorial. As we dismissed and overpaid our local bodyguard and drove back to Cairo with Abdul Reis under the afternoon sun, we half regretted the omission we had made. Such fascinating things were whispered about lower pyramid passages not in the guide-books; passages whose entrances had been hastily blocked up and concealed by certain uncommunicative archaeologists who had found and begun to explore them.

Of course, this whispering was largely baseless on the face of it; but it was curious to reflect how persistently visitors were forbidden to enter the pyramids at night, or to visit the lowest burrows and crypt of the Great Pyramid. Perhaps in the latter case it was the psychological effect which was feared—the effect on the visitor of feeling himself huddled down beneath a gigantic world of solid masonry; joined to the life he has known by the merest tube, in which he may only crawl, and which any accident or evil design might block. The whole subject seemed so weird and alluring that we resolved to pay the pyramid plateau another visit at the earliest possible opportunity. For me this opportunity came much earlier than I expected.

That evening, the members of our party feeling somewhat tired after the strenuous program of the day, I went alone with Abdul Reis for a walk through the picturesque Arab quarter. Though I had seen it by day, I wished to study the alleys and bazaars in the dusk, when rich shadows and mellow gleams of light would add to their glamour and fantastic illusion. The native crowds were thinning, but were still very noisy and numerous when we came upon a knot of reveling Bedouins in the Suken-Nahhasin, or bazaar of the coppersmiths. Their apparent leader, an insolent youth with heavy features and saucily cocked tarbush, took some notice of us; and evidently recognized with no great friendliness my competent but admittedly supercilious and sneeringly disposed guide.

Perhaps, I thought, he resented that odd reproduction of the Sphinx's half-smile which I had often remarked with amused irritation; or perhaps he did not like the hollow and sepulchral resonance of Abdul's voice. At any rate, the exchange of ancestrally opprobrious language became very brisk; and before long Ali Ziz, as I heard the stranger called when called by no worse name, began to pull violently at Abdul's robe, an action quickly reciprocated, and leading to a spirited scuffle in which both combatants lost their sacredly cherished headgear and would have reached an even direr condition had I not intervened and separated them by main force.

My interference, at first seemingly unwelcome on both sides, succeeded at last in effecting a truce. Sullenly each belligerent composed his wrath and his attire; and with an assumption of dignity as profound as it was sudden, the two formed a curious pact of honor which I soon learned is a custom of great antiquity in Cairo—a pact for the settlement of their difference by means of a nocturnal fist fight atop the Great Pyramid, long after the departure of the last moonlight sightseer. Each duelist was to assemble a party of seconds, and the affair was to begin at midnight, proceeding by rounds in the most civilized possible fashion.

In all this planning there was much which excited my interest. The fight itself promised to be unique and spectacular, while the thought of the scene on that hoary pile overlooking the antediluvian plateau of Gizeh under the wan moon of the pallid small hours appealed to every fiber of imagination in me. A request found Abdul exceedingly willing to admit me to his party of seconds; so that all the rest of the early evening I accompanied him to various dens in the most lawless regions of the town—mostly northeast of the Ezbekiyeh—where he gathered one by one a select and formidable band of congenial cutthroats as his pugilistic background.

Shortly after nine our party, mounted on donkeys bearing such royal or tourist-reminiscent names as "Rameses", "Mark Twain", "J. P. Morgan", and "Minnehaha", edged through street labyrinths both

Oriental and Occidental, crossed the muddy and mast-forested Nile by the bridge of the bronze lions, and cantered philosophically between the lebbakhs on the road to Gizeh. Slightly over two hours were consumed by the trip, toward the end of which we passed the last of the returning tourists, saluted the last in-bound trolley-car, and were alone with the night and the past and the spectral moon.

Then we saw the vast pyramids at the end of the avenue, ghoulish with a dim atavistical menace which I had not seemed to notice in the daytime. Even the smallest of them held a hint of the ghastly—for was it not in this that they had buried Queen Nitocris alive in the Sixth Dynasty; subtle Queen Nitocris, who once invited all her enemies to a feast in a temple below the Nile, and drowned them by opening the water-gates? I recalled that the Arabs whisper things about Nitocris, and shun the Third Pyramid at certain phases of the moon. It must have been over her that Thomas Moore was brooding when he wrote a thing muttered about by Memphian boatmen—

> "The subterranean nymph that dwells
> 'Mid sunless gems and glories hid—
> The lady of the Pyramid!

Early as we were, Ali Ziz and his party were ahead of us; for we saw their donkeys outlined against the desert plateau at Kafr-el-Haram; toward which squalid Arab settlement, close to the Sphinx, we had diverged instead of following the regular road to the Mena House, where some of the sleepy, inefficient police might have observed and halted us. Here, where filthy Bedouins stabled camels and donkeys in the rock tombs of Khephren's courtiers, we were led up the rocks and over the sand to the Great Pyramid, up whose time-worn sides the Arabs swarmed eagerly, Abdul Reis offering me the assistance I did not need.

As most travelers know, the actual apex of this structure has long been worn away, leaving a reasonably flat platform twelve yards square. On this eerie pinnacle a squared circle was formed, and in a few moments the sardonic desert moon leered down upon a battle which, but for the quality of the ringside cries, might well have occurred at some minor athletic club in America. As I watched it, I felt that some of our less desirable institutions were not lacking; for every blow, feint, and defense bespoke "stalling" to my not inexperienced eye. It was quickly over, and despite my misgivings as to methods I felt a sort of proprietary pride when Abdul Reis was adjudged the winner.

Reconciliation was phenomenally rapid, and amidst the singing, fraternizing, and drinking which followed, I found it difficult to realize that a quarrel had ever occurred. Oddly enough, I myself seemed to be more of a centre of notice than the antagonists; and from my smattering of Arabic I judged that they were discussing my professional performances and escapes from every sort of manacle and confinement, in a manner which indicated not only a surprising knowledge of me, but a distinct hostility and skepticism concerning my feats of escape. It gradually dawned on me that the elder magic of Egypt did not depart without leaving traces, and that fragments of a strange secret lore and priestly cult-practices have survived surreptitiously amongst the fellaheen to such an extent that the prowess of a strange *hahwi* or magician is resented and disputed. I thought of how much my hollow-voiced guide Abdul Reis looked like an old Egyptian priest or Pharaoh or smiling Sphinx...and wondered.

Suddenly something happened which in a flash proved the correctness of my reflections and made me curse the denseness whereby I had accepted this night's events as other than the empty and malicious "frame up" they now showed themselves to be. Without warning, and doubtless in answer to some subtle sign from Abdul, the entire band of Bedouins precipitated itself upon me; and having produced heavy ropes, soon had me bound as securely as I was ever bound in the course of my life, either on the stage or off. I struggled at first, but soon saw that one man could make no headway against a band of over twenty sinewy barbarians. My hands were tied behind my back, my knees bent to their fullest extent, and my wrists and ankles stoutly linked together with unyielding cords. A stifling gag was forced into my mouth, and a blindfold fastened tightly over my eyes. Then, as the Arabs bore me aloft on their shoulders and began a jouncing descent of the pyramid, I heard the taunts of my late guide Abdul, who mocked and jeered delightedly in his hollow voice, and assured me that I was soon to have my "magic powers" put to a supreme test which would quickly remove any egotism I might have gained through triumphing over all the tests offered by America and Europe. Egypt, he reminded me, is very old; and full of inner mysteries and antique powers not even conceivable to the experts of today, whose devices had so uniformly failed to entrap me.

How far or in what direction I was carried, I cannot tell; for the circumstances were all against the formation of any accurate judgment. I know, however, that it could not have been a great distance; since my bearers at no point hastened beyond a walk, yet kept me aloft a surprisingly short time. It is this perplexing brevity which makes me feel almost like shuddering whenever I think of Gizeh and its plateau—for one is oppressed by hints of the closeness to every-day tourist routes of what existed then and must exist still.

The evil abnormality I speak of did not become manifest at first. Setting me down on a surface which I recognized as sand rather than rock, my captors passed a rope around my chest and dragged me a few feet to a ragged opening in the ground, into which they presently lowered me with much rough handling. For apparent aeons I bumped against the stony irregular sides of a narrow hewn well which I took to be one of the numerous burial shafts of the plateau until the prodigious, almost incredible depth of it robbed me of all bases of conjecture.

The horror of the experience deepened with every dragging second. That any descent through the sheer solid rock could be so vast without reaching the core of the planet itself, or that any rope made by man could be so long as to dangle me in these unholy and seemingly fathomless profundities of nether earth, were beliefs of such grotesqueness that it was easier to doubt my agitated senses than to accept them. Even now I am uncertain, for I know how deceitful the sense of time becomes when one or more of the usual perceptions or conditions of life is removed or distorted. But I am quite sure that I preserved a logical consciousness that far; that at least I did not add any full-grown phantoms of imagination to a picture hideous enough in its reality, and explicable by a type of cerebral illusion vastly short of actual hallucination.

All this was not the cause of my first bit of fainting. The shocking ordeal was cumulative, and the beginning of the later terrors was a very perceptible increase in my rate of descent. They were paying out that infinitely long rope very swiftly now, and I scraped cruelly against the rough and constricted sides of the shaft as I shot madly downward. My clothing was in tatters, and I felt the trickle of blood all over, even above the mounting and excruciating pain. My nostrils, too, were assailed by a scarcely definable menace; a creeping odor of damp and staleness curiously unlike anything I had ever smelt before, and having faint overtones of spice and incense that lent an element of mockery.

Then the mental cataclysm came. It was horrible—hideous beyond all articulate description because it was all of the soul, with nothing of detail to describe. It was the ecstasy of nightmare and the summation of the fiendish. The suddenness of it was apocalyptic and demoniac—one moment I was plunging agonizingly down that narrow well of million-toothed torture, yet the next moment I was soaring on bat-wings in the gulfs of hell; swinging free and swoopingly through illimitable miles of boundless, musty space; rising dizzily to measureless pinnacles of chilling ether, then diving gaspingly to sucking nadirs of ravenous, nauseous lower vacua...Thank God for the mercy that shut out in oblivion those clawing Furies of consciousness which half unhinged my faculties, and tore Harpy-like at my spirit! That one respite, short as it was, gave me the strength and sanity to endure those still greater sublimations of cosmic panic that lurked and gibbered on the road ahead.

II.

It was very gradually that I regained my senses after that eldritch flight through Stygian space. The process was infinitely painful, and colored by fantastic dreams in which my bound and gagged condition found singular embodiment. The precise nature of these dreams was very clear while I was experiencing them, but became blurred in my recollection almost immediately afterward, and was soon reduced to the merest outline by the terrible events—real or imaginary—which followed. I dreamed that I was in the grasp of a great and horrible paw; a yellow, hairy, five-clawed paw which had reached out of the earth to crush and engulf me. And when I stopped to reflect what the paw was, it seemed to me that it was Egypt. In the dream I looked back at the events of the preceding weeks, and saw myself lured and enmeshed little by little, subtly and insidiously, by some hellish ghoul-spirit of the elder Nile sorcery; some spirit that was in Egypt before ever man was, and that will be when man is no more.

I saw the horror and unwholesome antiquity of Egypt, and the grisly alliance it has always had with the tombs and temples of the dead. I saw phantom processions of priests with the heads of bulls, falcons, cats, and ibises; phantom processions marching interminably through subterraneous labyrinths and avenues of titanic propylaea beside which a man is as a fly, and offering unnamable sacrifices to indescribable gods. Stone colossi marched in endless night and drove herds of grinning androsphinxes down to the shores of illimitable stagnant rivers of pitch. And behind it all I saw the ineffable malignity of primordial necromancy, black and amorphous, and fumbling greedily after me in the darkness to choke out the spirit that had dared to mock it by emulation.

In my sleeping brain there took shape a melodrama of sinister hatred and pursuit, and I saw the black soul of Egypt singling me out and calling me in inaudible whispers; calling and luring me, leading me on with the glitter and glamour of a Saracenic surface, but ever pulling me down to the age-mad catacombs and horrors of its dead and abysmal pharaonic heart.

Then the dream-faces took on human resemblances, and I saw my guide Abdul Reis in the robes of a king, with the sneer of the Sphinx on his features. And I knew that those features were the features of Khephren the Great, who raised the Second Pyramid, carved over the Sphinx's face in the likeness of his own, and built that titanic gateway temple whose myriad corridors the archaeologists think they have dug out of the cryptical sand and the uninformative rock. And I looked at the long, lean, rigid hand of Khephren; the long, lean, rigid hand as I had seen it on the diorite statue in the Cairo Museum—the statue they had found in the terrible gateway temple—and wondered that I had not shrieked when I saw it on Abdul Reis...That hand! It was hideously cold, and it was crushing me; it was the cold and cramping of the sarcophagus...the chill and constriction of unrememberable Egypt...It was nighted, necropolitan Egypt itself...that yellow paw... and they whisper such things of Khephren...

But at this juncture I began to awake—or at least, to assume a condition less completely that of sleep than the one just preceding. I recalled the fight atop the pyramid, the treacherous Bedouins and their attack, my frightful descent by rope through endless rock depths, and my mad swinging and plunging in a chill void redolent of aromatic putrescence. I perceived that I now lay on a damp rock floor, and that my bonds were still biting into me with unloosened force. It was very cold, and I seemed to detect a faint current of noisome air sweeping across me. The cuts and bruises I had received from the jagged sides of the rock shaft were paining me woefully, their soreness enhanced to a stinging or burning acuteness by some pungent quality in the faint draught, and the mere act of rolling over was enough to set my whole frame throbbing with untold agony.

As I turned I felt a tug from above, and concluded that the rope whereby I was lowered still reached to the surface. Whether or not the Arabs still held it, I had no idea; nor had I any idea how far within the earth I was. I knew that the darkness around me was wholly or nearly total, since no ray of moonlight penetrated my blindfold; but I did not trust my senses enough to accept as evidence of extreme depth the sensation of vast duration which had characterized my descent.

Knowing at least that I was in a space of considerable extent reached from the surface directly above by an opening in the rock, I doubtfully conjectured that my prison was perhaps the buried gateway chapel of old Khephren—the Temple of the Sphinx—perhaps some inner corridor which the guides had not shown me during my morning visit, and from which I might easily escape if I could find my way to the barred entrance. It would be a labyrinthine wandering, but no worse than others out of which I had in the past found my way.

The first step was to get free of my bonds, gag, and blindfold; and this I knew would be no great task, since subtler experts than these Arabs had tried every known species of fetter upon me during my long and varied career as an exponent of escape, yet had never succeeded in defeating my methods.

Then it occurred to me that the Arabs might be ready to meet and attack me at the entrance upon any evidence of my probable escape from the binding cords, as would be furnished by any decided agitation of the rope which they probably held. This, of course, was taking for granted that my place of confinement was indeed Khephren's Temple of the Sphinx. The direct opening in the roof, wherever it might lurk, could not be beyond easy reach of the ordinary modern entrance near the Sphinx; if in truth it were any great distance at all on the surface, since the total area known to visitors is not at all enormous. I had not noticed any such opening during my daytime pilgrimage, but knew that these things are easily overlooked amidst the drifting sands.

Thinking these matters over as I lay bent and bound on the rock floor, I nearly forgot the horrors of the abysmal descent and cavernous swinging which had so lately reduced me to a coma. My present thought was only to outwit the Arabs, and I accordingly determined to work myself free as quickly as possible, avoiding any tug on the descending line which might betray an effective or even problematical attempt at freedom.

This, however, was more easily determined than effected. A few preliminary trials made it clear that little could be accomplished without considerable motion; and it did not surprise me when, after one especially energetic struggle, I began to feel the coils of falling rope as they piled up about me and upon me. Obviously, I thought, the Bedouins had felt my movements and released their end of the rope; hastening no doubt to the temple's true entrance to lie murderously in wait for me.

The prospect was not pleasing—but I had faced worse in my time without flinching, and would not flinch now. At present I must first of all free myself of bonds, then trust to ingenuity to escape from the temple unharmed. It is curious how implicitly I had come to believe myself in the old temple of Khephren beside the Sphinx, only a short distance below the ground.

That belief was shattered, and every pristine apprehension of preternatural depth and demoniac mystery revived, by a circumstance which grew in horror and significance even as I formulated my philosophical plan. I have said that the falling rope was piling up about and upon me. Now I saw that it was continuing to pile, as no rope of normal length could possibly do. It gained in momentum and became an avalanche of hemp, accumulating mountainously on the floor, and half burying me beneath its swiftly multiplying coils. Soon I was completely engulfed and gasping for breath as the increasing convolutions submerged and stifled me.

My senses tottered again, and I vainly tried to fight off a menace desperate and ineluctable. It was not merely that I was tortured beyond human endurance—not merely that life and breath seemed to be crushed slowly out of me—it was the knowledge of what those unnatural lengths of rope implied, and the consciousness of what unknown and incalculable gulfs of inner earth must at this moment be surrounding me. My endless descent and swinging flight through goblin space, then, must have been real; and even now I must be lying helpless in some nameless cavern world toward the core of the planet. Such a sudden confirmation of ultimate horror was insupportable, and a second time I lapsed into merciful oblivion.

When I say oblivion, I do not imply that I was free from dreams. On the contrary, my absence from the conscious world was marked by visions of the most unutterable hideousness. God!...If only I had not read so much Egyptology before coming to this land which is the fountain of all darkness and terror! This second spell of fainting filled my sleeping mind anew with shivering realization of the country and its archaic secrets, and through some damnable chance my dreams turned to the ancient notions of the dead and their sojournings in soul and body beyond those mysterious tombs which were more houses than graves. I recalled, in dream-shapes which it is well that I do not remember, the peculiar and elaborate construction of Egyptian sepulchres; and the exceedingly singular and terrific doctrines which determined this construction.

All these people thought of was death and the dead. They conceived of a literal resurrection of the body which made them mummify it with desperate care, and preserve all the vital organs in canopic jars near the corpse; whilst besides the body they believed in two other elements, the soul, which after its weighing and approval by Osiris dwelt in the land of the blest, and the obscure and portentous *ka* or life-principle which wandered about the upper and lower worlds in a horrible way, demanding occasional access to the preserved body, consuming the food offerings brought by priests and pious relatives to the mortuary chapel, and sometimes—as men whispered—taking its body or the wooden double always buried beside it and stalking noxiously abroad on errands peculiarly repellent.

For thousands of years those bodies rested gorgeously encased and staring glassily upward when not visited by the *ka*, awaiting the day when Osiris should restore both *ka* and soul, and lead forth the stiff legions of the dead from the sunken houses of sleep. It was to have been a glorious rebirth—but not all souls were approved, nor were all tombs inviolate, so that certain grotesque *mistakes* and fiendish *abnormalities* were to be looked for. Even today the Arabs murmur of unsanctified convocations and unwholesome worship in forgotten nether abysses, which only winged invisible *kas* and soulless mummies may visit and return unscathed.

Perhaps the most leeringly blood-congealing legends are those which relate to certain perverse products of decadent priestcraft—*composite mummies* made by the artificial union of human trunks and limbs with the heads of animals in imitation of the elder gods. At all stages of history the sacred animals were mummified, so that consecrated bulls, cats, ibises, crocodiles, and the like might return some day to greater glory. But only in the decadence did they mix the human and animal in the same mummy—only in the decadence, when they did not understand the rights and prerogatives of the *ka* and the soul.

What happened to those composite mummies is not told of—at least publicly—and it is certain that no Egyptologist ever found one. The whispers of Arabs are very wild, and cannot be relied upon. They even hint that old Khephren—he of the Sphinx, the Second Pyramid, and the yawning gateway temple—lives far underground wedded to the ghoul-queen Nitocris and ruling over the mummies that are neither of man nor of beast.

It was of these—of Khephren and his consort and his strange armies of the hybrid dead—that I dreamed, and that is why I am glad the exact dream-shapes have faded from my memory. My most horrible vision was connected with an idle question I had asked myself the day before when looking at the great carven riddle of the desert and wondering with what unknown depths the temple so close to it might be secretly connected. That question, so innocent and whimsical then, assumed in my dream a meaning of frenetic and hysterical madness...*what huge and loathsome abnormality was the Sphinx originally carven to represent?*

My second awakening—if awakening it was—is a memory of stark hideousness which nothing else in my life—save one thing which came after—can parallel; and that life has been full and adventurous beyond most men's. Remember that I had lost consciousness whilst buried beneath a cascade of falling rope whose immensity revealed the cataclysmic depth of my present position. Now, as perception returned, I felt the entire weight gone; and realized upon rolling over that although I was still tied, gagged, and blindfolded, *some agency had removed completely the suffocating hempen landslide which had overwhelmed me.* The significance of this condition, of course, came to me only gradually; but even so I think it would have brought unconsciousness again had I not by this time reached such a state of emotional exhaustion that no new horror could make much difference. I was alone…with *what?*

Before I could torture myself with any new reflection, or make any fresh effort to escape from my bonds, an additional circumstance became manifest. Pains not formerly felt were racking my arms and legs, and I seemed coated with a profusion of dried blood beyond anything my former cuts and abrasions could furnish. My chest, too, seemed pierced by an hundred wounds, as though some malign, titanic ibis had been pecking at it. Assuredly the agency which had removed the rope was a hostile one, and had begun to wreak terrible injuries upon me when somehow impelled to desist. Yet at the time my sensations were distinctly the reverse of what one might expect. Instead of sinking into a bottomless pit of despair, I was stirred to a new courage and action; for now I felt that the evil forces were physical things which a fearless man might encounter on an even basis.

On the strength of this thought I tugged again at my bonds, and used all the art of a lifetime to free myself as I had so often done amidst the glare of lights and the applause of vast crowds. The familiar details of my escaping process commenced to engross me, and now that the long rope was gone I half regained my belief that the supreme horrors were hallucinations after all, and that there had never been any terrible shaft, measureless abyss, or interminable rope. Was I after all in the gateway temple of Khephren beside the Sphinx, and had the sneaking Arabs stolen in to torture me as I lay helpless there? At any rate, I must be free. Let me stand up unbound, ungagged, and with eyes open to catch any glimmer of light which might come trickling from any source, and I could actually delight in the combat against evil and treacherous foes!

How long I took in shaking off my encumbrances I cannot tell. It must have been longer than in my exhibition performances, because I was wounded, exhausted, and enervated by the experiences I had passed through. When I was finally free, and taking deep breaths of a chill, damp, evilly spiced air all the more horrible when encountered without the screen of gag and blindfold edges, I found that I was too cramped and fatigued to move at once. There I lay, trying to stretch a frame bent and mangled, for an indefinite period, and straining my eyes to catch a glimpse of some ray of light which would give a hint as to my position.

By degrees my strength and flexibility returned, but my eyes beheld nothing. As I staggered to my feet I peered diligently in every direction, yet met only an ebony blackness as great as that I had known when blindfolded. I tried my legs, blood-encrusted beneath my shredded trousers, and found that I could walk; yet could not decide in what direction to go. Obviously I ought not to walk at random, and perhaps retreat directly from the entrance I sought; so I paused to note the direction of the cold, fetid, natron-scented air-current which I had never ceased to feel. Accepting the point of its source as the possible entrance to the abyss, I strove to keep track of this landmark and to walk consistently toward it.

I had had a match-box with me, and even a small electric flashlight; but of course the pockets of my tossed and tattered clothing were long since emptied of all heavy articles. As I walked cautiously in the blackness, the draught grew stronger and more offensive, till at length I could regard it as nothing less than a tangible stream of detestable vapor pouring out of some aperture like the smoke of the genie from the fisherman's jar in the Eastern tale. The East...Egypt...truly, this dark cradle of civilization was ever the well-spring of horrors and marvels unspeakable!

The more I reflected on the nature of this cavern wind, the greater my sense of disquiet became; for although despite its odor I had sought its source as at least an indirect clue to the outer world, I now saw plainly that this foul emanation could have no admixture or connection whatsoever with the clean air of the Libyan Desert, but must be essentially a thing vomited from sinister gulfs still lower down. I had, then, been walking in the wrong direction!

After a moment's reflection I decided not to retrace my steps. Away from the draught I would have no landmarks, for the roughly level rock floor was devoid of distinctive configurations. If, however, I followed up the strange current, I would undoubtedly arrive at an aperture of some sort, from whose gate I could perhaps work round the walls to the opposite side of this Cyclopean and otherwise unnavigable hall. That I might fail, I well realized. I saw that this was no part of Khephren's gateway temple which tourists know, and it struck me that this particular hall might be unknown even to archaeologists, and merely stumbled upon by the inquisitive and malignant Arabs who had imprisoned me. If so, was there any present gate of escape to the known parts or to the outer air?

What evidence, indeed, did I now possess that this was the gateway temple at all? For a moment all my wildest speculations rushed back upon me, and I thought of that vivid mélange of impressions—descent, suspension in space, the rope, my wounds, and the dreams that were frankly dreams. Was this the end of life for me? Or indeed, would it be merciful if this moment *were* the end? I could answer none of my own questions, but merely kept on till Fate for a third time reduced me to oblivion.

This time there were no dreams, for the suddenness of the incident shocked me out of all thought either conscious or subconscious. Tripping on an unexpected descending step at a point where the offensive draught became strong enough to offer an actual physical resistance, I was precipitated headlong down a black flight of huge stone stairs into a gulf of hideousness unrelieved.

That I ever breathed again is a tribute to the inherent vitality of the healthy human organism. Often I look back to that night and feel a touch of actual *humor* in those repeated lapses of consciousness; lapses whose succession reminded me at the time of nothing more than the crude cinema melodramas of that period. Of course, it is possible that the repeated lapses never occurred; and that all the features of that underground nightmare were merely the dreams of one long coma which began with the shock of my descent into that abyss and ended with the healing balm of the outer air and of the rising sun which found me stretched on the sands of Gizeh before the sardonic and dawn-flushed face of the Great Sphinx.

I prefer to believe this latter explanation as much as I can, hence was glad when the police told me that the barrier to Khephren's gateway temple had been found unfastened, and that a sizeable rift to the surface did actually exist in one corner of the still buried part. I was glad, too, when the doctors pronounced my wounds only those to be expected from my seizure, blindfolding, lowering, struggling with bonds, falling some distance—perhaps into a depression in the temple's inner gallery—dragging myself to the outer barrier and escaping from it, and experiences like that…a very soothing diagnosis. And yet I know that there must be more than appears on the surface. That extreme descent is too vivid a memory to be dismissed—and it is odd that no one has ever been able to find a man answering the description of my guide Abdul Reis el Drogman—the tomb-throated guide who looked and smiled like King Khephren.

I have digressed from my connected narrative—perhaps in the vain hope of evading the telling of that final incident; that incident which of all is most certainly an hallucination. But I promised to relate it, and do not break promises. When I recovered—or seemed to recover—my senses after that fall down the black stone stairs, I was quite as alone and in darkness as before. The windy stench, bad enough before, was now fiendish; yet I had acquired enough familiarity by this time to bear it stoically. Dazedly I began to crawl away from the place whence the putrid wind came, and with my bleeding hands felt the colossal blocks of a mighty pavement. Once my head struck against a hard object, and when I felt of it I learned that it was the base of a column—a column of unbelievable immensity—whose surface was covered with gigantic chiseled hieroglyphics very perceptible to my touch.

Crawling on, I encountered other titan columns at incomprehensible distances apart; when suddenly my attention was captured by the realization of something which must have been impinging on my subconscious hearing long before the conscious sense was aware of it.

From some still lower chasm in earth's bowels were proceeding certain *sounds*, measured and definite, and like nothing I had ever heard before. That they were very ancient and distinctly ceremonial, I felt almost intuitively; and much reading in Egyptology led me to associate them with the flute, the sambuke, the sistrum, and the tympanum. In their rhythmic piping, droning, rattling, and beating I felt an element of terror beyond all the known terrors of earth—a terror peculiarly dissociated from personal fear, and taking the form of a sort of objective pity for our planet, that it should hold within its depths such horrors as must lie beyond these aegipanic cacophonies. The sounds increased in volume, and I felt that they were approaching. Then—and may all the gods of all pantheons unite to keep the like from my ears again—I began to hear, faintly and afar off, *the morbid and millennial tramping of the marching things.*

It was hideous that footfalls *so dissimilar* should move in such perfect rhythm. The training of unhallowed thousands of years must lie behind that march of earth's inmost monstrosities...padding, clicking, walking, stalking, rumbling, lumbering, crawling…and all to the abhorrent discords of those mocking instruments. And then…God keep the memory of those Arab legends out of my head! The mummies without souls…the meeting-place of the wandering *kas*…the hordes of the devil-cursed pharaonic dead of forty centuries…the *composite mummies* led through the uttermost onyx voids by King Khephren and his ghoul-queen Nitocris…

The tramping drew nearer—heaven save me from the sound of those feet and paws and hooves and pads and talons as it commenced to acquire detail! Down limitless reaches of sunless pavement a spark of light flickered in the malodorous wind, and I drew behind the enormous circumference of a Cyclopic column that I might escape for a while the horror that was stalking million-footed toward me through gigantic hypostyles of inhuman dread and phobic antiquity. The flickers increased, and the tramping and dissonant rhythm grew sickeningly loud. In the quivering orange light there stood faintly forth a scene of such stony awe that I gasped from a sheer wonder that conquered even fear and repulsion. Bases of columns whose middles were higher than human sight… mere bases of things that must each dwarf the Eiffel Tower to insignificance… hieroglyphics carved by unthinkable hands in caverns where daylight can be only a remote legend…

I *would not* look at the marching things. That I desperately resolved as I heard their creaking joints and nitrous wheezing above the dead music and the dead tramping. It was merciful that they did not speak…but God! *their crazy torches began to cast shadows on the surface of those stupendous columns. Hippopotami should not have human hands and carry torches...men should not have the heads of crocodiles...*

I tried to turn away, but the shadows and the sounds and the stench were everywhere. Then I remembered something I used to do in half-conscious nightmares as a boy, and began to repeat to myself, "This is a dream! This is a dream!" But it was of no use, and I could only shut my eyes and pray…at least, that is what I think I did, for one is never sure in visions—and I know this can have been nothing more. I wondered whether I should ever reach the world again, and at times would furtively open my eyes to see if I could discern any feature of the place other than the wind of spiced putrefaction, the topless columns, and the thaumatropically grotesque shadows of abnormal horror. The sputtering glare of multiplying torches now shone, and unless this hellish place were wholly without walls, I could not fail to see some boundary or fixed landmark soon. But I had to shut my eyes again when I realized *how many* of the things were assembling—and when I glimpsed a certain object walking solemnly and steadily *without any body above the waist.*

A fiendish and ululant corpse-gurgle or death-rattle now split the very atmosphere—the charnel atmosphere poisonous with naphtha and bitumen blasts—in one concerted chorus from the ghoulish legion of hybrid blasphemies. My eyes, perversely shaken open, gazed for an instant upon a sight which no human creature could even imagine without panic fear and physical exhaustion. The things had filed ceremonially in one direction, the direction of the noisome wind, where the light of their torches showed their bended heads—or the bended heads of such as had heads. They were worshipping before a great black fetor-belching aperture which reached up almost out of sight, and which I could see was flanked at right angles by two giant staircases whose ends were far away in shadow. One of these was indubitably the staircase I had fallen down.

The dimensions of the hole were fully in proportion with those of the columns—an ordinary house would have been lost in it, and any average public building could easily have been moved in and out. It was so vast a surface that only by moving the eye could one trace its boundaries...so vast, so hideously black, and so aromatically stinking...Directly in front of this yawning Polyphemus-door the things were throwing objects—evidently sacrifices or religious offerings, to judge by their gestures. Khephren was their leader; sneering King Khephren *or the guide Abdul Reis*, crowned with a golden pshent and intoning endless formulae with the hollow voice of the dead. By his side knelt beautiful Queen Nitocris, whom I saw in profile for a moment, noting that the right half of her face was eaten away by rats or other ghouls. And I shut my eyes again when I saw *what* objects were being thrown as offerings to the fetid aperture or its possible local deity.

It occurred to me that judging from the elaborateness of this worship, the concealed deity must be one of considerable importance. Was it Osiris or Isis, Horus or Anubis, or some vast unknown God of the Dead still more central and supreme? There is a legend that terrible altars and colossi were reared to an Unknown One before ever the known gods were worshipped...

And now, as I steeled myself to watch the rapt and sepulchral adorations of those nameless things, a thought of escape flashed upon me. The hall was dim, and the columns heavy with shadow. With every creature of that nightmare throng absorbed in shocking raptures, it might be barely possible for me to creep past to the faraway end of one of the staircases and ascend unseen; trusting to Fate and skill to deliver me from the upper reaches. Where I was, I neither knew nor seriously reflected upon—and for a moment it struck me as amusing to plan a serious escape from that which I knew to be a dream. Was I in some hidden and unsuspected lower realm of Khephren's gateway temple—that temple which generations have persistently called the Temple of the Sphinx? I could not conjecture, but I resolved to ascend to life and consciousness if wit and muscle could carry me.

Wriggling flat on my stomach, I began the anxious journey toward the foot of the left-hand staircase, which seemed the more accessible of the two. I cannot describe the incidents and sensations of that crawl, but they may be guessed when one reflects on *what I had to watch steadily in that malign, wind-blown torchlight* in order to avoid detection. The bottom of the staircase was, as I have said, far away in shadow; as it had to be to rise without a bend to the dizzy parapeted landing above the titanic aperture. This placed the last stages of my crawl at some distance from the noisome herd, though the spectacle chilled me even when quite remote at my right.

At length I succeeded in reaching the steps and began to climb; keeping close to the wall, on which I observed decorations of the most hideous sort, and relying for safety on the absorbed, ecstatic interest with which the monstrosities watched the foul-breezed aperture and the impious objects of nourishment they had flung on the pavement before it. Though the staircase was huge and steep, fashioned of vast porphyry blocks as if for the feet of a giant, the ascent seemed virtually interminable. Dread of discovery and the pain which renewed exercise had brought to my wounds combined to make that upward crawl a thing of agonizing memory. I had intended, on reaching the landing, to climb immediately onward along whatever upper staircase might mount from there; stopping for no last look at the carrion abominations that pawed and genuflected some seventy or eighty feet below—yet a sudden repetition of that thunderous corpse-gurgle and death-rattle chorus, coming as I had nearly gained the top of the flight and showing by its ceremonial rhythm that it was not an alarm of my discovery, caused me to pause and peer cautiously over the parapet.

The monstrosities were hailing something which had poked itself out of the nauseous aperture to seize the hellish fare proffered it. It was something quite ponderous, even as seen from my height; something yellowish and hairy, and endowed with a sort of nervous motion. It was as large, perhaps, as a good-sized hippopotamus, but very curiously shaped. It seemed to have no neck, but five separate shaggy heads springing in a row from a roughly cylindrical trunk; the first very small, the second good-sized, the third and fourth equal and largest of all, and the fifth rather small, though not so small as the first.

Out of these heads darted curious rigid tentacles which seized ravenously on the *excessively great* quantities of unmentionable food placed before the aperture. Once in a while the thing would leap up, and occasionally it would retreat into its den in a very odd manner. Its locomotion was so inexplicable that I stared in fascination, wishing it would emerge further from the cavernous lair beneath me.

Then it *did* emerge...it *did* emerge, and at the sight I turned and fled into the darkness up the higher staircase that rose behind me; fled unknowingly up incredible steps and ladders and inclined planes to which no human sight or logic guided me, and which I must ever relegate to the world of dreams for want of any confirmation. It must have been dream, or the dawn would never have found me breathing on the sands of Gizeh before the sardonic dawn-flushed face of the Great Sphinx.

The Great Sphinx! God!—that *idle question* I asked myself on that sun-blest morning before...*what huge and loathsome abnormality was the Sphinx originally carven to represent?* Accursed is the sight, be it in dream or not, that revealed to me the supreme horror—the Unknown God of the Dead, which licks its colossal chops in the unsuspected abyss, fed hideous morsels by soulless absurdities that should not exist. The five-headed monster that emerged...that five-headed monster as large as a hippopotamus...the five-headed monster—*and that of which it is the merest forepaw...*

But I survived, and I know it was only a dream.

THE PLAYERS

T.G. Arsenault

Originally from Auburn, Maine, T.G. Arsenault retired from the U. S. Air Force after twenty-two years. His first novel, *Forgotten Souls*, was published in November, 2005 by Five Star Publishing. His short fiction has also appeared in multiple online venues and the anthologies *Octoberland*, *R.A.W. – Random Acts of Weirdness*, *Made You Flinch: Stories to Unnerve, Disturb, and Freak You Out*, *The Gallows*, and the forthcoming anthology, *Anthology Year Two: Inner Demons Out.* His short story "The Eighth Day," also received an honorable mention in the Year's Best Fantasy and Horror, Sixteenth Annual Collection. T.G. Arsenault resides in Western New York. His latest novel, *Bleeding the Vein*, was released in October 2012 from Gallows Press. Visit him online at www.tg-arsenault.com.

Michael Bailey

Michael Bailey is the author of *Palindrome Hannah*, a nonlinear horror novel and finalist for the Independent Publisher Awards. His follow-up novel, *Phoenix Rose*, was listed for the National Best Book Awards for horror fiction, was a finalist for the International Book Awards, and received the Kirkus Star, awarded to books of remarkable merit. *Scales and Petals*, his short story and poetry collection, won the International Book Award for short fiction, as well as the Best Books Award by USA Book News. *Pellucid Lunacy*, an anthology of psychological horror published under his Written Backwards label, won for anthologies for those same two awards. His short fiction and poetry can be found in anthologies and magazines around the world, including the US, UK, Australia, Sweden, and South Africa.

Eric S. Brown

Eric S Brown is the author of numerous books, including the Bigfoot War series, the A Pack of Wolves series, the Jack Bunny Bam Bam series, and the Crypto-Squad series (with Jason Brannon). Some of his stand alone titles include *War of the Worlds Plus Blood Guts and Zombies*, *Last Stand in a Dead Land*, and *Season of Rot*. He has done the novelizations of such films as *Boggy Creek: The Legend is True* and *The Bloody Rage of Bigfoot*. Eric also scripts the *Unstoppable Origins* and *Storm Chasers* comic book series for Unstoppable Comics. In 2014, the first book of the Bigfoot War series will be released as a feature film from Origin Releasing.

Judi Ann Calhoun

Judi Calhoun is a freelance author and artist. At Palomar College, Judi studied under award winning Children's book illustrator, Michael Sternagle. She was on the editorial staff for both *Bravura* Magazine, and photographer for *The Telescope* newspaper and Senior Editor for *The Sword* college yearbook while attending WBC in Escondido California. She was the winner of the Artist Innovation Award for 2009 by Art Works, New Hampshire, and twice commissioned to create a cancelation stamp for the US Postal Service. She is also the author of the YA novels *Sword of Yesher*, and *Ancient Fire, the Chronicles of Shonna Wells.*

Tracy L. Carbone

Tracy L. Carbone is a fiction author from Massachusetts. To date, she has published four novels and one collection of horror short stories. Her short stories have also been published in the U.S. and Canada in various anthologies and magazines. Please visit her Amazon Page or her personal site at www.tracylcarbone.com

Karen Dent

As a member of Essex Writers' and Artists' Guild, Karen's interest in writing fiction grew. She has since sold a number of shorts to various anthologies mostly in the paranormal and horror genre. Her plays (comedy/dramas) were performed in both New York City and Newburyport, Massachusetts. Her film script "The Bloated Beetle" won best screenplay in the Screamfest Horror Film Festival. Currently Karen is working on her first novel, *A Case to KILL For*, a paranormal noir based on the same characters from her short, "A Case To Die For" published in *Damnation and Dames.* Karen is a member of SAG, AFTRA, and the Dramatist Guild. She graduated from The School of Visual Arts in NYC. Visit her online at www.SistersDent.com.

Roxanne Dent

Roxanne Dent has sold eight novels and numerous shorts to horror anthologies. She has also written plays, screenplays, non-fiction articles, and had an astrology column in a magazine. She just completed *The Twelve Days of Christmas*, a Regency novel, and is currently working on a YA paranormal, *The Boy in the Green High Tops.*

Jonathan Dubey

Though born in Saint Johnsbury, Vermont, Jonathan Dubey has lived his entire life (so far) in the greater Berlin, New Hampshire area. He graduated Berlin High School in 1997, and currently works in the Emergency Medical Service as a Paramedic. Jonathan is very involved with local arts scene, most specifically community theater.

Allen Dusk

Allen Dusk is the author of *Shady Palms*, a gritty urban tale splattered with carnage. His short fiction has appeared in Rose Caraway's The Kiss Me Quick's erotica podcast, *Peep Show Volume 2* (SST Publications), *Horror-tica* (Cruentus Libri Press), and *Sirens Call* eZine. Other than writing unique blends of horror and erotica, his favorite pastimes include photography, lusting over old horror movies, and researching supernatural folklore. Ravenous readers can reach him through his website: allendusk.com.

Melissa M. Gates

Melissa Gates splits her time between her family home in Fremont, New Hampshire and her oasis in Rangeley, Maine. Previously unpublished, she draws her writing enthusiasm from her mother, her inspiration from her son, and her skill from the Nashua Writers' Group. Visit her on Facebook.

Marianne Halbert

Marianne Halbert's dark fiction stories have appeared in magazines such as *Midnight Screaming* and *Necrotic Tissue*, as well as anthologies by Evil Jester Press, The Four Horsemen, Grinning Skull Press, Mystery & Horror LLC, Screaming Spires Press (forthcoming), and more. She was a panelist at AnthoCon 2011 and 2012, and her novel, *Honorable Scars*, was a 2012 ABNA Quarter Finalist. Find her at Halbert Fiction on Facebook, or www.halbertfiction.webs.com

David C. Hayes

David C. Hayes is an award-winning author, editor and filmmaker. Most recently, he has written stories for Dark Moon Books, Strangehouse Books, Evil Jester Press, Blood Bound Books and many more. His first collection, *American Guignol,* was released in 2013 and he is the author of *Cannibal Fat Camp, Muddled Mind: The Complete Works of Ed Wood Jr.*, and the *Rottentail* graphic novel as well as many screenplays, stage plays (his Dial P for Peanuts won an Ethingtony in 2011), articles and more. His films, like *The Frankenstein Syndrome*, *Bloody Bloody Bible Camp, A Man Called Nereus*, *Dark Places* and *Back Woods*, are available worldwide. He is the co-owner of Cinema Head Cheese (www.cinemaheadcheese.com), a geek culture website, and you can visit him online at www.davidchayes.com. David is a voting member of the Horror Writers Association and the Dramatists Guild. He likes creepy hugs and all kinds of cheese.

Michael M. Hughes

Michael M. Hughes lives in Baltimore with his wife and two daughters. He writes fiction and nonfiction, and his bestselling debut novel, *Blackwater Lights*, was released by Hydra (Random House) in 2013. He is currently at work on a sequel. When he's not writing, Hughes performs as a mentalist (psychic entertainer) and speaks on Fortean and paranormal topics. He is a Freemason and a member of The Societas Rosicruciana in Civitatibus Foederatis. For a more complete bio and photos, contact him via email at michaelmhughes@gmail.com or at michaelmhughes.com

Joe Knetter

Joe Knetter is a writer from Minnesota. He's a life-long horror fan and spends most of his time writing in that genre. He is the author of three short story collections: *Twisted Loneliness* (intro by Sid Haig), *Vile Beauty* (intro by Bill Moseley) and his most recent collection titled *Room*. His novel *Zombie Bukkake* led to him being interviewed on The History Channel of all places. In addition to fiction he has written over a dozen screenplays that are in various states of production. After spending most of his life as a rum drinker he has now switched over to vodka. www.joeknetter.com.

Esther M. Leiper-Estabrooks

Esther M. Leiper-Estabrooks began writing at age eight and never stopped. She sells fiction, poetry, and columns to magazines all over the U.S. and has won well over 1,000 poetry contests. Her book *WIN!* from Val-Tech Media details how poets can achieve this goal as well. Her first commercial sale—verse novel *Wars of Faery*—appeared in *Amelia* as a twelve-part serial. *Princess Sunrise*, her most recent book which she also illustrated, was published by the Great Northwoods Journal. Currently she illustrates for clients and writes a monthly humor column "For the Love of Words" in the online magazine *Extra Innings*. Esther was poetry editor, columnist, and contest judge for *WRITERS' Journal* Magazine for thirty years. She critiques poems plus book doctors for widespread clients. A show combining her art and poetry starts November 1, 2013 at the Tea Birds Café and Gallery in Berlin, New Hampshire. She's now completing another verse novel, *A Capital Crime* with her pictures. Esther has lectured and given readings as far south as Florida and as far west as Arkansas, plus many states in between. She is active with the Berlin Writers' Group.

H.P. Lovecraft

The late, legendary Howard Phillips Lovecraft (August 20, 1890 – March 15, 1937) is one of history's best-known and beloved authors of speculative fiction. His tales of terror, which include "Dagon," "The Dunwich Horror," "Pickman's Model," "The Call of Cthulhu," and the novel, *At the Mountains of Madness*, endure in the memory and imagination of successive generations of voracious readers, and have served as the inspiration for numerous comic book, television, and film translations. His tale "Under the Pyramids" first appeared in 1924 in *Weird Tales*.

John McIlveen

John McIlveen is the author of *Jerks and Other Tales from a Perfect Man*, and numerous stories, poems, and articles. His first novel *Hannahwhere* is finished and en route to a good home, and he is well into his second and third novels, *Going North* and *Corruption.* He is the father of five lovely daughters and the O&M/MEP Liaison at MIT's Lincoln Laboratory. He lives in Marlborough, MA. www.johnmcilveen.com.

Gregory L. Norris

Gregory L. Norris vividly recalls a night in his youth spent in front of the TV with his Uncle Jimmy and Jimmy's best friend Warren, watching an old black and white mummy creature feature that forever left him terrified—and fascinated—with the iconic horror trope. Norris writes full-time and is the author to the handbook to all-things-Sunnydale, *The Q Guide to Buffy the Vampire Slayer*, *Shrunken Heads: Twenty Tiny Tales of Mystery and Terror*, and *The Fierce and Unforgiving Muse.* Visit him at www.gregorylnorris.blogspot.com.

Philip C. Perron

Philip C. Perron was born in Lowell, Massachusetts. He is the founder, producer, web designer, editor, and co-host of the Dark Discussions Podcast which discusses genre film, novels, and all things fantastic. He lives in Amherst, New Hampshire with his wife, Joanna, and his chiweenie dog, Lilly, where he writes fiction. They soon are expecting their first child. You can find Philip on Facebook and at www.darkdiscussions.com

D.B. Poirier

Love of the Fantasy, Science Fiction, and Horror genres keeps D.B. Poirier up well past the Witching Hour, writing with passion. Terrified of zombies, he was relieved and jumped at the chance to write instead about mummies—until he realized that while zombies only eat the flesh, mummies devour the soul. A New England native, he lives in the Granite State with his beautiful wife and two adorable little girls. He is blessed to have such a loving family and most of the time is happier than any man has the right to be.

Kristi Petersen Schoonover

Myrtle Beach is one of Kristi Petersen Schoonover's favorite vacation spots; she first learned about canopic jars at New York's Metropolitan Museum of Art when she was eight. Her short stories have appeared in countless publications, and her novel *Bad Apple* was nominated for a Pushcart Prize. Meet Kristi and learn more at www.kristipetersenschoonover.com

James Pratt

James Pratt writes depressing stories about gods, monsters, and the end of the world. H.P. Lovecraft is his spiritual advisor, but he also likes strong characterization, two-fisted tales, and maybe even the occasional quasi-happy ending. James has written over seventy short stories, a short Lovecraftian western novel, and an "urban monster" supplement for the RPG Pathfinder system. He has had six short stories accepted for various anthologies, but so far only two, including "Tomb World", have seen print. James has three short story collections available for download on Amazon and Smashwords, all of which will hopefully soon be available in paperback too. James continues to write short stories, is working on a post-apocalyptic novelette that represents his first foray into "furries", and hopes to one day finish a fantasy novel incorporating Lovecraftian gods and races that he started many moons ago. James can be found at: www.jamesdpratt.blogspot.com

M.J. Preston

MJ Preston lives in Canada where he indulges in writing, photography and dark art. Along with his contribution "Run-off 31", he is also the artist responsible for the cover of this anthology. When he is not writing or shooting photography, he can be found North of the 60th parallel running the world's longest ice road as an Ice Road Trucker. He is the Author of the horror novel *The Equinox*, a short called "Counting Paces" (both available on Amazon), and a new novel set for release in late 2013 called *Acadia Event*. Find him online at mjpreston.net and authormjpreston.blogspot.ca

Kyle Rader

Kyle Rader is a writer who doesn't like to color inside the lines. He has written across multiple genres with the expressed goal of doing the unexpected and, most importantly, not boring his readers. His most recent publications have appeared in *Dark Moon Eclipse* magazine, Insomnia Press, and *The Rusty Nail Magazine*. He can be followed on Twitter @youroldpalkile or on his website www.kylerader.wordpress.com He lives in New Hampshire and enjoys playing guitar poorly, yelling at his television, and annoying his long-suffering girlfriend, who is way too awesome to be hanging around with him

Patrick Rea

Patrick Rea is a prolific award-winning independent filmmaker, recognized for his innovative storytelling and creative directing style in horror and suspense. His latest feature film *Nailbiter* won Best Director and/or Best Feature Film awards in several film festivals in 2012, including Shriekfest, Chicago Fear Fest and AMC Theaters KC Film Fest. *Nailbiter* was released on May 28th through Lionsgate Home Entertainment on DVD/VOD and Digital Downloads. It is currently in the Redbox nationwide. Rea is an Emmy award winning writer/director known for his stylized short films, which have screened in over a hundred film festivals around the world. Rea's most recent shorts *Get Off My Porch*, *Hell Week*, *Time's Up, Eve*, and *Next Caller*, have also garnered acclaim and are currently on the festival circuit. In 2009, Rea was co-director on the *Jake Johanssen, I Love You* comedy special, which aired on Showtime throughout 2010.

Suzanne Robb

Suzanne Robb is the author of the novels *Z-Boat* (March 2014 from Permuted Press), *Were-wolves, Apocalypses, and Genetic Mutation, Oh my!*, and *Contaminated*. She is a contributing editor at Hidden Thoughts Press, and co-edited *Read The End First* with Adrian Chamberlin, which made the Stoker Recommended Reading List for 2012. In her free time she reads, watches movies, plays with her dog, and enjoys chocolate and LEGO's. www.suzannerobb.blogspot.com

Gord Rollo

Gord Rollo was born in St. Andrews, Scotland, but now lives in Ontario, Canada. His short stories and novella-length work have appeared in many professional publications throughout the genre and his novels include: *The Jigsaw Man*, *Crimson*, *Strange Magic*, and *Valley of the Scarecrow*. His work has been translated into several languages and his titles are currently being adapted for audiobooks. Besides novels, Gord edited the acclaimed evolutionary horror anthology, *Unnatural Selection: A Collection of Darwinian Nightmares*. He also co-edited *Dreaming of Angels,* a horror/fantasy anthology created to increase awareness of Down's syndrome and raise money for research. He recently completed his newest horror/dark fantasy novel, *The Translators*, and can be reached at his official website or through his agent Lauren Abramo at labramo@dystel.com.

Lawrence Santoro

In 2001, Lawrence Santoro's novella "God Screamed and Screamed, Then I Ate Him" was nominated for a Bram Stoker Award by the Horror Writers Association. In 2002, his adaptation and audio production of Gene Wolfe's "The Tree Is My Hat," was also Stoker nominated. In 2003, his Stoker-recommended "Catching" received an Honorable Mention in Ellen Datlow's 17th Annual "Year's Best Fantasy and Horror" anthology. In 2004, "So Many Tiny Mouths," was cited in that anthology's 18th edition. In the 20th, his novella, "At Angels Sixteen," from the anthology *A Dark and Deadly Valley*, was similarly honored. Larry's first novel, *Just North of Nowhere*, was published in 2007. A collection of his short fiction, *Drinks for the Thirst to Come*, was published in December, 2011. Before that, Larry spent thirty years as a director, producer and actor in theater and television. Since its inaugural show in January of 2012, Larry has hosted the weekly horror podcast, "Tales to Terrify" (http://talestoterrify.com/). He lives in Chicago and is working on a new novel, A Mississippi Traveler, or Sam Clemens Tries the Water. He blogs at blufftoninthedriftless.blogspot.com.

Brett A. Savory

Brett Alexander Savory is the Bram Stoker Award-winning Editor-in-Chief of ChiZine: Treatments of Light and Shade in Words,

Publisher of ChiZine Publications, has had nearly fifty short stories published, and has written two novels. In 2006, Necro Publications released his horror-comedy novel The Distance Travelled. September 2007 saw the release of his dark literary novel In and Down through Brindle & Glass, and November brought his first short story collection, No Further Messages, released through Delirium Books. In the works are three more novels. When he's not writing, reading, or editing, he plays drums for the hard rock band Ol' Time Moonshine. When none of that's happening, he occasionally writes book reviews for The Globe and Mail and The National Post. Savory is represented by Carolyn Forde of Westwood Creative Artists. He lives in Toronto with his wife, writer/editor Sandra Kasturi.

B.E. Scully

B.E. Scully writes tales dark and strange, drinks red wine and murky beer, cooks, reads, studies, and believes in the golden key. Scully lives in a haunted red house that lacks a foundation in the misty woods of Oregon with a variety of human and animal companions. Scully's short story collection *The Knife and the Wound It Deals* is currently available on Amazon and other fine venues along with her critically acclaimed gothic thriller *Verland: the Transformation.* Other published work, interviews, and odd scribblings can be found at www.bescully.com.

Henry Snider

Henry Snider is a founding member of Fiction Foundry and the award-winning Colorado Springs Fiction Writer's Group. During the last two decades he's dedicated his time to helping others tighten their writing through critique groups, classes, lectures, prison prose programs, and high school fiction contests. He retired from the CSFWG presidency in January 2009. After a much needed vacation he returned to writing, this time for publication. While still reserving enough time to pursue his own fiction aspirations, Henry continues to be active in the writing community through classes, editing services and advice. Henry lives with his wife, fellow author and editor Hollie Snider, son (poet Josh Snider) and numerous neurotic animals, including, of course, Fizzgig, the token black cat. For more on Henry visit www.henrysnider.com

Erin Thorne

Erin Thorne is a lifelong resident of Massachusetts, where she lives with her family. She writes primarily paranormal fiction, and is the author of "Diane's Descent", a supernatural novella set in a rural New York town, as well as *Deals Diabolical*, a collection of eight spine-tingling tales. In addition, she's written a book of short stories encompassing science fiction, fantasy, and horror, titled *Behind the Wheel*. Her work has been featured in *Adventures for the Average Woman* (now *IdeaGems Magazine*) and *Reflections of the End (Author's Choice Select Anthologies 1)*. Visit her website at www.erinthorne.org, and her author's pages on Amazon and Facebook.

ABOUT THE PUBLISHER

Great Old Ones Publishing is a press dedicated to genre and dark fiction. We specialize within the horror, science fiction, fantasy, thriller, techno-thriller, mystery, pulp and grindhouse narrative. Our intent is to produce top quality anthologies, collections, novellas, and novels and present our artists, both author and graphic, in the best of light. Our contributors are experienced authors, rising stars, and those that are first time published. You can find us on the web at http://www.greatoldonespublishing.com.